SKANDAL

Also by Lindsay Smith

SEKRET

MY MIND SKANDAL IS MINE ALONE

LINDSAY SMITH

ROARING BROOK PRESS · NEW YORK

Copyright © 2015 by Lindsay Smith
Published by Roaring Brook Press
Roaring Brook Press is a division of Holtzbrinck Publishing Holdings
Limited Partnership
175 Fifth Avenue, New York, New York 10010
macteenbooks.com

Library of Congress Cataloging-in-Publication Data

Smith, Lindsay.
   Skandal / Lindsay Smith.—First edition.
     pages cm
   Sequel to: Sekret.
   Summary: "In the sequel to SEKRET, Yulia and Valentine have escaped
Russia to live in Washington, DC, where they are working with CIA psychics,
including Yulia's increasingly erratic father"—Provided by publisher.
    ISBN 978-1-62672-005-3 (hardback)—ISBN 978-1-250-07369-3 (trade
paperback)—ISBN 978-1-62672-006-0 (e-book)   [1. Spies—Fiction.
2. Psychic ability—Fiction.   3. Adventure and adventurers—Fiction.
4. United States. Central Intelligence Agency—Fiction.   5. Washington
(DC)—History—20th century—Fiction.]   I. Title.
   PZ7.S65435Sk 2015
   [Fic]—dc23

                           2014040757

Roaring Brook Press books may be purchased for business or promotional use. For
information on bulk purchases please contact Macmillan Corporate and Premium Sales
Department at (800) 221-7945 x5442 or by email at specialmarkets@macmillan.com.

First edition 2015
Printed in United States of America

1   3   5   7   9   10   8   6   4   2

For Jason,
who makes everything sharper, brighter, better

CHAPTER 1

"*YULIA ANDREEVNA CHERNINA.*" The general's mouth stretches around the rubbery Russian vowels as he reads from the file before him. "Did I get that right?" He smiles at me like any mistake would be my fault, somehow. "We are here to determine whether someone of your . . . *background* is fit to serve the United States of America in her constant battle against tyranny."

Background. Yes. A tidy little euphemism—I'm finding English has lots of those. What he's asking is whether I'm a communist psychic sleeper agent sent to America to ignite a revolution, but these are ugly words, and America is not a place for ugliness. The America I've lived in for the past three months is impeccably clean. It's shot through with colors and smells and sounds I never could have imagined when I lived in the Soviet Union. And tyranny—tyranny is not encouraged like in the KGB that once controlled me, but something to be stamped out wherever America finds it. By using skills like mine, America can unmask tyranny everywhere. My psychic powers make me a microscope that reveals a festering colony of bacteria on a seemingly clean surface.

The general clears his throat as he flips through my file. Muted sunlight from the oval window behind him casts him in shadow, along with the rest of the panel members seated at his side. "You are a product of the KGB—the Committee for State Security—and its psychic espionage program. Your father, Andrei, testified before this committee that he participated in the genetic research arm of this program during World War II under Stalin's direction, correct?" He doesn't wait for confirmation, from me or the rest of the committee. "And our intelligence indicates that your mother has resumed that research now."

Everything spoken in English sounds muffled by gauze. I can only process it so fast; I can only take in so many words before I have to shake them out to make room for more. But the translation lag softens the blow of what he's actually said: that my mother is the enemy now.

I lean toward the microphone, flinching as it shrieks with feedback. "That is correct, comra—sir."

"Then you understand why you're here today. You realize the grave threat posed by the Soviets and their psychic espionage program. You would agree that General Rostov, head of the KGB First Directorate, must be stopped."

My stomach churns. The soda fountain milkshake I had with lunch feels heavier than polonium in my gut. "Yes," I say, though it sounds too faint. Yes, I want to stop Rostov, the man who used me as a weapon to root out dissidents and spies. But I worry that these Americans will see my mother's fate as tied up in his.

"Glad to hear it." The general's face splits in a smile. "We've already heard the testimony of your father and Valentin Sorokhin, as well as your tutor, Staff Sergeant Davis, who has deemed your language skills sufficient now to join them in their work. But there are a few things I want you to clarify in person."

My eyes dart toward Winnie Davis, my English teacher, on call if the language becomes too dense. She leans casually in the room's corner, brown arms crossed over her crisp Air Force blues. With a smile, she nods at me. She isn't psychic, and I can't read her mind from this distance, but it's the same smile she gives me when I'm practicing English with her. *You've got this. Keep going.*

"I am happy to . . . make . . . assistance." I cringe before I've finished saying it. I'm not cut out for word games, much less spy games.

"You believe that you possess psychic powers," the general says. I think it's a question, but I don't trust my ears. Sometimes I think only thoughts and memories speak the truth to me, and even those can be twisted until I don't know what to trust. He waits a few moments, the air thickening between us. "Well? Go on. Tell everyone what I'm thinking."

I stare back at his shadowed face. "It is easiest for me if I touch you," I say.

Nervous laughter ripples around me until the general shushes it with a wave of his hand. His motions are effortless—downright lazy, compared to the crushing, impatient energy of Rostov, the KGB officer I once worked for. "That's right. 'Reads thoughts and memories through contact,'" he reads from the dossier, then stretches one hand before him toward the edge of the table. "Permission to approach the panel."

I swallow and stand up.

His knuckles are hairy and rough; my fingers hover above them, barely permitting contact. It's been a long time since I've done this. Three months, to be precise; three months ago, I sucked up memories and emotions through my fingertips until I couldn't hold any more, then pushed them all out at once in a torrent of pain. Because I did so, I was able to escape the KGB with Valentin—we fled the Soviet Union to join my father and his new CIA friends—but I've kept my hands to myself since then, or at the very least, refused to look any deeper than the surface, memories collecting on me like a film of nervous sweat.

Perhaps I should be grateful for my gift. But I don't want to be a weapon anymore, capable of causing pain. I don't want to be viewed as an instrument for torture or for condemning average people to death for their thoughts, like I did back in Russia. Rostov used me to hunt dissidents and traitors; he tried to use me to launch a nuclear war, and nearly succeeded. I don't want that kind of power lying in wait just beneath my skin.

But I don't want Rostov to suceed even more.

I let my thoughts sink into the general's skin. A marching band bursts from the contact, coiling through the hearing room, weaving around me and each of the panel members. Trumpets circle the general. Brassy high notes punctuate the drumbeat pounding into my skull. I recognize the melody from one of Winnie's cultural lessons—"Stars and Stripes Forever" by John Phillip Sousa. *Be kind to your web-footed friends, for that duck may be somebody's mother.* I suspect those aren't the real lyrics, but it made for a fun afternoon, belting about ducks at the tops of our lungs while Valentin hammered out the chords on Papa's baby grand.

"You have a musical shield," I say. To protect against enemy psychics, he keeps a song forever stuck in his head, covering up his real thoughts. "I cannot look past that." I lift my hand and the brassy march diminishes.

The general chuckles. "I'm sure you could if you wanted to."

It's not a compliment. I take a step back from the panel, sweat sprouting under my armpits.

"Your father can. Mister Sorokhin can. And your old KGB boss—General Anton Rostov—I understand he's altered *your* thoughts before."

So has my own father, but I'm not interested in discussing that with this stranger. "My power does not work that way," I stammer. "And—and if it did, it would not be my place."

"What if I ordered you to?" the general asks. The woman to his left scribbles furiously. As the general leans forward, the dim sunlight grazes his face—broad, meaty, cut with deep furrows. "Did the KGB ever make you do things that weren't your 'place'?" A dangerous grin unfolds. "Did you obey?"

I remember gunshots, ringing through the haze of Rostov's mind control. I remember my mouth disobeying me, reading out nuclear launch codes as Rostov coiled like barbed wire around my mind.

"That's a rather complicated question." Winnie steps forward from the corner, arms unfurling. "Sir."

"It's still relevant. War often places us in situations with no right choice." His head retreats into his broad oxen shoulders. "In Korea, I had to make plenty of those calls. Who lives and who dies. Trust me, Miss Chernina, we will understand."

My head throbs as a thousand phantom heartbeats push blood through my brain. The young engineer, Natalya, executed for treason after I ran to her for help. My best friend, Larissa, sacrificing herself so Valentin and I could escape to America with my father. Dozens of people whose brains my father scrubbed—warped, altered, or erased—to find me. Cosmonauts incinerated inside the *Veter 1* capsule—I still don't know if Papa and his team member were responsible for the explosion or not, but if he was, and I could have prevented those deaths . . .

"We did what we had to do," I say slowly, neither meeting his gaze, nor Winnie's, "to survive."

Scribble, scribble, scratch.

In Russian, silence is a defensive measure; it's a shovel and a soft patch of earth. But so far, English speakers wield silence like a weapon around me, its threat growing sharper with each word left unsaid. I look down at my bare knees, slow my breathing to match the creeping strings of my mental musical shield, Shostakovich's *Babi Yar* symphony, and wait.

"So, Miss Chernina. Tell us more about your decision to defect to America."

"It was more a decision to leave Russia, at the time." The scratching pencils rise in cadence; my armpits now rival the Vasyugan Swamp. I look to Winnie, but she's turned away from me. Was that the wrong answer? "But—but once Papa told me about his life here, I knew this was where I wanted to be." The words gush out of me with frantic abandon. If I linger on them too long, they'll trip me up. Better to surge forward. "No waiting in lines, no equality through our shared misery. No one is afraid of their own thoughts. I am . . . myself here."

One of the women stops scribbling and snickers, unintentionally letting her thoughts bubble over her musical shield and flow onto the table as I grip its edge. *This kid's accent is straight outta the McCarthy hearings.*

"And why," the general asks, folding his hands before him, "do you now want to work for the United States government?"

I allow myself a slow smile. Now this, I can answer. "I know what General Rostov is capable of." Despite my dense rye-bread accent, I know these words perfectly. "He is not satisfied with the stalemate between East and West, and he will destroy whatever he must to spark a new war. He cannot be allowed to continue. No one deserves his—'flavor,' is that correct?—of pain."

Winnie is nodding at me. I want to smile, but fear has me in its rictus. My jaw aches from clenching it so hard.

"An interesting way of putting it," the general says. "One of our top priorities is dealing with General Rostov and his new allies around the world."

"One of," I echo.

"Let me be clear, Miss Chernina. We welcome the assistance of someone with your skill set." He eases back in his chair and slides a thick folder out of his stack. "But Rostov is not our only concern."

My chest tightens like fingers lacing together. I'm afraid I know what's coming next.

"We cannot ignore your mother's role in Rostov's plans. According to our intelligence, he's tasked her with building a whole new army of mind-reading spies."

My breath rushes out of me like a punch to the sternum. It was a mistake to come here today—I'm not ready after all. "She's cooperating because she must. She is protecting my brother." She was protecting me, too, until I ran away. I push away the constantly hovering question of how they were punished following my escape. She told me to run, after all. She had to have a plan.

The general tilts his head. "Whatever her motivation, she *is* doing this work. And whatever they're working on must be stopped. Do you understand this?"

Shostakovich marches through my thoughts with a slow, sturdy drumbeat. "I understand," I say carefully, "that their work must be stopped."

The general flips through the folder before him, his smile as thin as a knife. "Then we are in agreement." He shoves it across the table toward me; black-and-white photographs flutter free. I bend down, my bad ankle creaking like a rusty hinge, and scoop up the photos. Then nearly drop them.

Crime scene photos. Dead men and women, staring beyond the camera with milky eyes. One victim is sprawled out on the pavement, his hat tilted upward, revealing his stunned face. A woman curls into the corner of a train car. Nothing similar links any of these people that I can tell—race, age, place of death—except they all wear the slippery skin of sudden weight loss and the dark pouches beneath their eyes of too many sleepless nights. And dark trails blaze from their nostrils, their ears.

Something tightens in my gut, clenches hard and ripe and refuses to let go. I'm thankful the images are in black and white, flattening down the gore into less jarring hues.

"What happened to these people?" I ask, hysteria bringing out my guttural Slavic snarl. What I mean to ask is why is he showing me this awfulness—what relevance does it have to our discussion about Mama? But that line of questioning bumps against a bruised and battered patch in my brain. He thinks Mama is behind this somehow.

And I'm scared he might be right.

The general clears his throat. "These bodies have turned up all over North America and Western Europe over the past six weeks. At first, we were afraid we had a biological attack on our hands. Anthrax, smallpox—every couple of years, we get double agents making a bunch of noise about how the Russkies are bringing back the Plague. But we called in the Communicable Disease Center, and their tests for every known disease came back negative. And the geographical distribution—London, New York, West Berlin, Toronto—made no sense for an epidemic."

My ears turn redder and redder with each multisyllabic word. I wish I didn't have to rely on Winnie. I glance toward her, eyebrows raised in surrender, and she translates in flawless Russian.

"They look like they are the victims of a psychic attack. But there are so many of them." I keep shuffling through the photographs—there must be almost twenty people in here.

"That was our thought, too, after we ruled out biological causes. Then we came across another victim while investigating a possible mole in the State Department. The FBI went to the apartment of the mole's handler and found him inside—just barely clinging to life. That one—that's him, right there."

I suck in my breath as I study the last photograph. The man's spider legs curl under his chin; he lies on his side, blood collecting on the rug beneath him. Diamond-cut cheekbones and a pair of scars across one eye.

"I know this man," I say.

The general's eyes tighten like a camera lens focusing. "One of our PsyOps team members was with us when we found him. Said he'd never encountered such a powerful psychic before. I think you've got a name for them—psychics like your father?"

"Scrubbers." Psychics who don't merely read minds—they twist and bend thoughts into whatever arrangement they please. They can conjure entire memories out of nothingness or suppress a thought as if it never occurred. "But—but this man. Pavel. He isn't a scrubber." I tap the photograph. "He was one of our guards back in Moscow, just a low-ranking KGB soldier. He didn't have any psychic abilities himself."

The general squashes his lips together. "Tell that to the poor PsyOps team member. Just being around the guy gave him an awful nosebleed, his thoughts were so strong—said it felt like getting an ice-pick lobotomy."

My hands are quivering like plucked strings as I drop the stack of photos on the table. I know what he's describing all too well. I've been victim to a scrubber's corrosive wave of psychic energy, wrenching my thoughts around, boring through my skull, filling my head with whatever maddening visions he pleases. Scrubbers are impossible to miss. Pavel couldn't have been one—I'm certain of it.

"You said he was still alive when you found him." I meet the general's gaze, avoiding the dead eyes of the photographs as they stare up at me. "Did he tell you anything?"

"The PsyOps member was too busy trying to keep his brain from dribbling out of his nose to read the guy's mind. But the perp said something before he expired." The general peers down at his file. "'Rostov. Chernina. They've gone too far.'"

The pain in my heart, sharp and piercing, dulls the lesser ache of my bad ankle. Chernina. Mama. Pavel didn't have the abilities before, I'm certain of it. Could she really do these things—building a psychic army, amplifying their powers far beyond anything we've ever known? If she were only trying to survive, then she'd do the bare minimum necessary to keep herself and Zhenya safe. This has to be part of a ploy to get her and Zhenya out of Russia. But how?

The general glances to the panel members on either side of him, some sort of wordless, thoughtless language passing between their eyes. "Miss Chernina, we are here because we need your help to stop her. To stop . . . this." He sweeps his hand toward the photographs. "We believe the Soviets may have found a way to activate or enhance psychic abilities, and your mother is the logical choice to head such an endeavor, though we don't know what they intend to accomplish with these psychics just yet. The Psychic Operations team needs your skills and your knowledge to prevent whatever they're working toward. I realize this is a lot to ask of you, but I suspect I don't need to tell you how dangerous an army of these . . . 'scrubbers' . . . could be."

What Rostov's working toward. The last I saw Rostov, his brilliant plan was to force the Soviet leader Nikita Khruschev to start a third world war by launching nuclear missiles at American targets. It may have been a momentary act of desperation, an emotional retaliatory strike for the *Veter 1* rocket explosion. Maybe. But a man like him won't rest until the whole world has bowed to his aggressive version of Soviet supremacy.

"It's only the beginning," the general says. "Rostov has allies around the world, now. Castro, Mao, Kim. Tito and Kadar. Ho Chi Minh." A Who's Who of the Red Menace. Cuba, China,

North Korea, Yugoslavia, Hungary, and North Vietnam. "We've caught their agents here and abroad, all of them carrying out the sort of marching orders we'd expect from a man like Rostov. But they're always a step ahead. We have to learn what they're working toward."

But I'm not listening. I'm padding my way through the dark tunnels of my brain, feeling the edges of bruises that'll never fully fade. Memories my father tried to scrub out; knowledge he and Mama wanted to erase. My parents—both of them—have done awful things before, thinking it was for the greater good. What greater purpose is Mama trying to serve now?

"I'll do whatever I must to stop Rostov and my mother's plan," I say. "But if you mean to hurt my mother, you do it alone."

CHAPTER 2

"LET'S GO TO DINNER TONIGHT." Papa says in Russian, the wind shredding his words. "To celebrate your joining the team." He twists the car's tuner knob from static to static. "That brasserie down on M Street. You love that place."

Neither Valya nor I answer. We've learned, these past few months, that Papa prefers to talk to himself rather than carry on a genuine conversation. We will go to dinner at his French restaurant, and he will drive us home in this ridiculous British convertible, and he will probably be drunk, so we'll park half onto the yard, and then he'll convince Valentin to play piano duets with him, and we'll sing all night long in the conservatory of his townhouse that's so massive it *has* a conservatory. Is this what it was like for my friend Larissa when she peered into the future? Did she see life as this inevitable pantomime, this grim certainty?

"Why is Mama helping Rostov?" I ask, screaming to be heard over the static and the wind.

Papa settles on a fuzzy station playing "Surfin' USA", then

throttles the stick shift to rocket us around an aquamarine Cadillac. The static scrapes at my thoughts, adding to my tension headache, but Papa's head bobs and he whistles along. Right now he looks more like Mick Jagger than my father in his buttery leather jacket and black turtleneck. His face is too stubbly—Mama would have attacked it with a razor days ago. He's wiry as ever, though a teensy belly peeks over his belt buckle from too many nights of rich food and drink and insomnia and cigarettes, but never smoking inside the house, no, because now his English vocabulary includes phrases like "property value" and "mortgage rates." I wonder if Winnie taught him those.

"Papa?" I ask again. "Why didn't you warn me? What's Mama's plan?"

"Do you want to invite Winnie to dinner?" Papa takes his hand off the stick shift just long enough to swat my knee. "I already told her to meet us there. You don't mind, right?"

I turn toward Valentin in the backseat, but the wind throws my dark hair into my face. When I peel it away, he's regarding me with a sad smile on his bow lips and eyes far away behind his thick black-framed glasses. I'm relieved to see him smiling at all. Last night was one of the bad ones. I awoke to find his nightmares twisting into my ribs, driven there by his scrubber ability—he was too distraught to keep it in check. I ran into his bedroom and curled around him, wishing I could somehow cushion him from the splintered edges of his past.

Valentin's always kept some memories anchored firmly in the depths of his mind. I never pressed him on them; we all clung to our secrets like they were the most precious of jewels when we were controlled by the KGB. But as we were escaping East

Berlin, Rostov's scrubbing ability pierced his mind with a serrated blade. Whatever Valentin kept at bay before has washed ashore, bloated and rotten, refusing to stay forgotten. It torments him, I know, though I see him trying to fight it down. Most days, he suppresses it long enough to do his work for the PsyOps Team, and when he comes home with Papa in the evenings, he can smile and talk and cook and live with me. Today is not such a day.

I thread my arm through the gap between Papa's and my seats and rest my palm on Valentin's knee. No sense shouting over the wind. The tempest of the *Babi Yar* symphony calms, and I push my thoughts against Valya's musical barrier so we can speak without words. *Why didn't you warn me they're going after my mother?*

His mouth presses into a thin line. *They keep me in the dark about her, too. But I couldn't tell you anything until they approved you. It's classified.* He manages half a smile. *Believe me, I wanted to, but rules are rules.*

That's what we'd agreed on, when Valya and I first decided to work with Papa and his new American friends. We'd follow the rules this time around; try to trust our teammates and believe in their goals. We want the same things they do, after all—Rostov stopped and the world safe from people like him, people who'd make our very thoughts a crime.

But paranoia is a feeling, and then a habit, and then a part of me, no easier to extract than a vital organ. *Easy for you to say,* I tell Valya. *They let you start working for them immediately.*

Because I already knew English, Valya says. *They wanted to give you time to learn, to feel comfortable here—*

My comfort has nothing to do with this. I clench my teeth. *They trusted you from the start, but not me. Why?*

Papa clicks off the radio and laughs—a sharp, brusque sound. Too sharp. "Because of your mother. My poor little girl. You say you'll help them now, but are you ready to make the hard choices? I don't know if you'll ever be ready."

Oh, so now Papa wants to listen to me, when we're having a psychic discussion that he shouldn't be able to hear without using his scrubber skills. "This is a private conversation, and it doesn't involve you," I snap at him.

Papa shrugs as we clatter off the bridge and onto solid streets. "Guess it does now."

Pearly granite monuments splay before us, rooted in hot green grass. Federal workers cross the street in riots of blue and orange; paisley, lace, and velvet; thick corduroy suits. To our left, cherry trees burst like pink popcorn around the rim of the Tidal Basin. Papa whistles to himself as he waits for the light to change, higher and higher, each note jabbing at my growing headache—

"Pull over!" I shout.

Another shrug from Papa; he swerves the car to the left and parks the wrong way along the curb, whistling while I wrestle out of my seat belt and hop from the convertible without opening the door. Bile burns at the back of my throat.

"Yulia?" Valentin calls as I charge into the snow of shock-pink petals with my uneven gait. I wrap my arms around my chest, the long bell sleeves of my black dress hanging limp like deflated balloons. The wind snakes across my exposed thighs. Why did I let Winnie talk me into this ridiculous mod clothing again? *Bozhe moi.* The heel of one boot snags on a tree root as I bob toward the Tidal Basin's edge.

I wanted this, I tell myself, breathing deep to quiet my roiling stomach. I wanted to run away with Valentin. I wanted America with its nauseating colors and impractical clothes and people who keep one eye trained on me like I'm a communist jack-in-the-box about to spring.

Everything has a price tag in America, and I suppose facing the truth of Mama's work is my cost of admission.

Shostakovich's symphony turns sour as it batters over my thoughts. I do not hate my life here; of course not. I couldn't endure another day enslaved to the KGB, helping General Rostov push the Cold War to its breaking point. I'm no longer his puppet, helping him overthrow Nikita Khruschev and spread his brand of communism around the world. I did not lie when I agreed to stop his newest plan, and it was always my choice to make. My choice, everything is my choice in the land of the free. But I am not gifted with Larissa's future sight to see how unhappy even good choices can make me.

If I'd peered into the future, would I have chosen this version of Papa—jaunty and reckless and unwilling to discuss Mama? Why didn't he warn me they were hunting her? When I first embraced him again, after crossing over to West Berlin, it felt like we'd never been apart. I knew him like I knew the hollow at the base of his ribcage where I used to rest my forehead. But the Papa who told me bedtime stories and used to be inseparable from Mama feels lost to me. He's an unknown Papa-shaped quantity, unbalancing all my equations.

Yulia. Unlike me, Valentin can press a thought into my head without contact. He stands under a blooming cherry tree behind me with a dusting of pink across his shoulders. *I'm sorry. I should have warned you.*

I step back onto the granite edge of the basin. *Please don't keep secrets from me,* I think, concealing the thought in our shared song, but placing it outside of my shield where Valentin, unconstrained by physical touch like I am, can read it. *I want those days to be over.*

The little dimple on Valentin's chin shows as he tilts his head, the one that's a touchstone for my thumb when I stroke his cheeks. *I'm sorry, Yul. I never meant to hurt you. We haven't talked about your mother in so long, and I was afraid of how you'd handle hearing their suspicions . . .*

Poorly, as it turns out. I squeeze my eyes shut. We haven't talked about a lot of things. Whatever haunting thoughts were knocked free in Valya's mind . . .

You think she has a plan, don't you? He takes a tentative step toward me, stopping shy of the basin.

I raise my head and step toward him.

I'm on your side, Yul. Always. If you want my help . . .

Valya . . . I lace my fingers through his hair. Of course I want to believe him; I want to think he'd do whatever it took to keep my mother safe. But he's right: now is the time to play by the rules. We are the guests, the outsiders, the ones with something to prove. Once I understand her plan, then we can find some way to clear her name from these deeds.

Valentin kisses my eyelids where I've clenched them shut. The tension drains out of me, replaced by that dangerous mix of hope and peacefulness. I cup his face in my hands and kiss him back. Of course he'll help me with this, too. His soft lips linger against mine for a moment, the world completely silent around us.

"Okay, kids, you can neck later. I'm starving," Papa calls.

Valya squeezes my hand and steers me back toward the car. *I'll do everything I can to help you make your family whole.*

*   *   *

Winnie is already waiting for us on the sidewalk outside the brasserie. She's a perfectly motionless figure in her pleated monochrome blouse and skirt, silent among the Technicolor waves of Georgetown pedestrians in frothy spring frocks, puckered cardigans, seersucker suits. "Did they not teach you how to tell time in the Soviet Union?" she asks Papa, reining in a smile.

He fires off a sloppy salute. "Sorry, ma'am. It won't happen again." He extends his elbow to Winnie; she rolls her eyes and shoves past him, but her smile's gaining ground.

Valentin takes my arm in his as we duck into the dark wooden brasserie. "You're right, as always," he murmurs, lips right at my ear. His voice thrums in my veins. Particles vibrating, heating up, melting away my earlier heartache. "I should've told you about their suspicions. But no more secrets. Whatever you need to do, I'm here to help you."

I know Valya still has secrets of his own, but I smile and squeeze his hand.

A bell over the door jangles to announce us. "Welcome to Brasserie Bonaparte." The maître d' looks up from his stand with a smile that quickly dissolves. "Ah. Um. I'm sorry, sir." His gaze darts to Winnie before pinging back to Papa. "I'm afraid we can't . . ." His jaw muscles work a nervous jig beneath his jowls. "Our other customers wouldn't like—You see, it's standard for all businesses in Georgetown—" He leans toward Papa. "I'm afraid we don't serve her kind."

Winnie straightens to her full height. "And what kind might that be?" Her voice frays into the upper register. "Servicewomen? Or colored girls?"

The maître d' staggers back as the room shudders and shifts. A jolt of electricity stands my arm hairs on end and turns the screws in my brain. The dark wood paneling warps around me, drinking up my thoughts until I'm left with a dull, fuzzy hunger in my gut. I stumble forward, tethered only by Valentin's grip.

The room settles like a ship righting itself; the lights dim, then return. Winnie blinks, hand raised, index finger extended, then carefully lowers her hand as if she's forgotten whatever she was about to say.

The maître d' stares through me, trying to place my face, then forces a smile to his rubbery lips. "Welcome to the Brasserie Bonaparte! May I offer you a table for four?"

"A private dining room," Papa says, still smiling. "Bring up a bottle of your best cognac—extra old."

The maître d' grabs four menus and leads us through the restaurant. Columns of smoke and the scent of dark wines rise from each table we pass; the diners' heads whip around to chase us as we progress through the honeycomb dining nooks. Specifically, to chase Winnie. But as soon as Papa strides past, a blanket of calm settles over them, and they turn back to their confit and coq au vin, chattering about North Vietnam or the new Elvis film.

The maître d' leads us into a glassed-in dining room, burgundy velvet curtains covering all the windows. "I'll be right back with that cognac." His nose nearly scrapes the floor as he bows.

"Papa?" I narrow my eyes as the door clicks shut. "Was that really necessary?"

"You'd rather Winnie not be able to eat with us? No harm done." He settles onto the low wooden bench.

"You'd rather I what?" Winnie asks, one eyebrow cocked. But the air ripples again and her expression wanes. "I . . . I'm so sorry. I forgot what I was saying."

"You were telling me all about your day, Sergeant." Papa props his chin in his hands.

I glare at him for a few moments longer, but he's forgotten me already. I study him while he listens to Winnie—his stylish jazz club frames and sloppy crew cut and twitchy grin. The Papa I knew in Russia took no risks. He kept his mind empty and his record spotless. I remember walking through Moscow with him once and my hand, clutched in his, slipped from its too-big glove and instantly he was lost to me. I couldn't divine his face from any of the hunkering Russian men around me, their eyes dulled and deferent, their stock boiled-wool coats upturned to guard against wind and wayward stares. He was factory-stamped, assembled on a conveyor belt; only at home with Mama and Zhenya did he expose any personality at all, and even then only after a few drinks. Is this the real Papa exposed before me, or is it another camouflage he wears?

Rostov said Papa was a remote viewer when he was younger— like Sergei, General Rostov's son, he could summon up a place from photographs and then move around it like a ghost. One remote viewer on our old team learned to manipulate objects like a ghastly hand reaching from the other side of the world to shuffle papers, move rocks, close doors. Sergei learned to push his thoughts into others' heads through his viewings. I can force emotions out, now, in addition to drawing them in. And Papa—

What chain of events turned him into a scrubber? Was it always there, and he hid it from the KGB? But Papa doesn't merely change thoughts like other scrubbers; Papa has mastered the art of suppressing memories, and when I was younger, he erased all knowledge of my powers from my mind. Even now, there are soft patches on my brain that mask memories from our old life. Maybe Papa was always the reckless man I found in East Berlin, tossing a Molotov cocktail through a café window.

"A toast," Papa says, smiling at me. "The family that spies together . . ." He trails off and clinks his glass against mine.

Lies together? Dies together? Convenient of him to leave out that we're spying on our *own* family. I gulp down the cognac and let its fiery trail match my mood. I feel Mama's and Zhenya's absence around our table like phantom limbs; how can we celebrate now, when we have so far to go until we're whole once more?

"Cheer up, buttercup." Papa ruffles my hair. "We need you in tip-top shape to stop whatever Rostov's up to now."

And Mama, I think. *Whatever Mama's up to now.* But her name never passes his lips; whether he thinks she's on our side or not, he never seems to think of her at all.

After several rounds of roasted game hens and foie gras and truffled snails, my Soviet ration-sized stomach and bladder have reached their upper limits and I excuse myself to the restroom. Only one room, for men and women both. I jiggle the handle—locked. I slouch against the wall like an American teenager while I wait. Black-and-white photographs line the wall opposite me: Marilyn Monroe and Humphrey Bogart and dozens more faces of politicians, movie stars, artists I recognize from Winnie's tutoring, all posing with the brass Josephine Bonaparte statue at the bar. Immortalized by an impassive camera lens. If only my power were so simple—snapshots frozen in time, nothing more. No messy emotions and secrets and pain piling up without release.

I shove my hands into my armpits and wait.

The door swings open; the bathroom's occupant stops himself just short of crashing into me. He reeks of wine and mothballs. His tweed jacket swallows him like a crumpled wrapper, and his shirt hangs loose from his waistband. He backs up with a grunt, then stares hard right at me.

Sallow skin, the color of bile. Blisters at the corners of his lips and red rimming his eyes. Hair standing up every which way, except for a greasy mustache that droops down. He looks mere hours from ending up in the general's stack of crime scene photos.

A warning shot fires through my mind. I have to touch him—no matter how afraid I am of him, of myself, of whatever I might find. I take a step forward, reaching for the door with one hand but the other grasping for him—

A shockwave rips through me, all my threads of thought fraying apart in the blast. The picture frames rattle against the wall and the door shakes loose from my hand. I double over as steel wool scours through my brain and creamed potatoes attempt to reach back up my throat.

And then it's gone—the sensation, and the man with it. In the distance, the bell over the front door tinkles.

I charge back to our room and throw the door open. "Papa, I think one of the—"

But the maître d' is hovering over the table, smiling vacantly as he collects a folio stuffed with cash. "And a good evening to you as well, mademoiselle," he says to me before backing out of the room.

That burst just now. I close my hand over Valentin's. *Was that Papa? You?*

A muscle twitches along Valentin's jaw. *Your father was adjusting our bill.*

Whatever tension had been inflating in my chest empties. I sink onto the bench beside Valentin. This is my old paranoia, wriggling under my skin like shards from broken glass.

We are not being followed. We are not being targeted.

The most dangerous man in the restaurant is the one who brought me here.

CHAPTER 3

DURING THE DAY, my mind is working in sixth gear: spinning and spinning on thousands of English words and phrases and nuances; soaking up and sorting through countless cultural detrita. Elvis Presley and Pepsodent and *The Sword in the Stone*. Elizabeth Taylor. Things go better with Coke. The genetic research journals Winnie forces me to painstakingly translate. During the day, my brain is cluttered up with so much information that it can't discern what's important; it can't clear out a space to pick at those raw-wound memories Papa tried to suppress, recently torn open, lying in wait beneath it all.

But at night, when sleep clears it away, the four-note symphony Zhenya used to hum threads through my mind and ushers those memories out of the wings.

Mama and Zhenya and I are walking through Gorky Park, a delicate layer of ice crackling under our soles. We take each step with purpose and watch our feet, as if by keeping a close eye on them, we can shame them into not slipping. It is much too cold for this; were it not for Zhenya, we'd be bundled up by the furnace, sipping the ultra-strong *zavarka* tea from the samovar and reading Chukovsky's children's poems. Instead, we are shivering, swaddled up like eggs packed for shipping, all alone in the park.

"Look," Mama says, gesturing to the snow bank on the left of the path. "Look at the beautiful feather!"

It's half-crusted in ice as she pulls it from the snow, and as long as her forearm. Dark gray striations interrupt the drab brown shade. "It's ugly," I say. Zhenya tugs at my hand, momentum pulling him forward along the path. He does not care one bit about the feather, or anything that interrupts him from his walk. He whistles four notes, steel-sharp in the winter air.

Mama kneels down in front of us and watches us with crystalline eyes. Wind rattles through the bare birch trees of the park; in the distance, we hear the low toll of the Novodevichy Monastery bells.

"Do you know the story of the firebird?" Mama asks, her breath white and dazzling as it leaves her mouth.

I burrow my chin into my scarf. "Yes." I'm sure I've heard it before, and I want to finish our walk and go home. I want to throw my arms around Papa's shoulders and warm up in our posh Party home near Rubleyka.

"I don't think I've told it to you before." She holds the feather out in front of me. "Pay attention—this is important."

I groan; Zhenya tugs back toward the sidewalk, but Mama holds firm.

"Once upon a time, a hunter stumbled into the realm of Koschei the Undying while chasing a beautiful bird covered in all the hues of flame. He caught the firebird, but she begged and pleaded for her life. The hunter hated to lose such a prize, but he had a kind heart, so he relented, and the firebird left him a single feather as thanks. 'What use do I have for a single feather?' the hunter grumbled, and tucked it into his belt. But it was too late for the hunter; Koschei the Undying, evil sorcerer that he was, already knew the hunter was on his land."

I am leaning forward now, imagining how it might feel to hold a fiery feather in my hand and watch it shimmer with red and gold.

"The hunter had fallen in love, you see, with one of Koschei's princesses, kept locked up in his realm, and sought to free her from Koschei's grasp. But when he battled Koschei, he found that Koschei could not be killed. The hunter lay wounded and dying, clutching the firebird's feather, heartbroken because he'd never know the princess's love.

"But when he held the feather, it summoned the firebird to him. She told him the secret to defeating Koschei—she told him where he kept his soul, so the hunter could go destroy it. He smashed the egg that held Koschei's soul, and Koschei was Undying no more. The hunter and the princess lived happily ever after."

Mama runs the feather against the side of my face. "Do you understand, then, the firebird's lesson?" she asks.

Zhenya is busy picking his nose, so I answer for both of us. "Sure. You think if we hold on to this feather, someday the bird it fell off of will show up and help us defeat an evil sorcerer."

"No." Mama tosses the feather back into the snow and hoists Zhenya to his feet. "I'm telling you to pay attention. Because no matter how tiny, how weightless, how inconsequential something may seem, you never know when you can use that knowledge or that thing. One day it might just save your life."

CHAPTER 4

THE CENTRAL INTELLIGENCE AGENCY'S headquarters, unlike the very public KGB building looming over the heart of Moscow, is shrouded in trees in northern Virginia and padded with horse stables and palatial French mansions. Papa drives us for what seems like forever along the cliffs overlooking the Potomac to reach it. "Remember," he tells me as we wind through the forest, "this location is secret."

And then we pass the gatehouse swarming with men with machine guns.

The building itself is more Soviet than I'd expected: squat, cobbled from concrete slabs, swerving and contoured in that space-age style. Closed-circuit cameras whine as they twist from the awning to follow our approach. Valentin closes his hand around mine while Papa strides ahead of us, whistling again, his flared trousers skimming the steps.

I swallow my breath as we enter the gleaming main corridor. Marble everywhere—blue, gray, and white. The Agency's seal—an eagle (only one-headed, unlike our mutant double-headed Russian eagles) clutching a shield to its breast—winks at me in silver trim from the center of the floor. To my right, brass stars spangle the marble wall in perfectly even lines.

Papa swings his arm toward the wall of stars. "The Memorial Wall," he says in English. "Each star is for an agent who has died in the line of duty."

The line of duty, I suspect, includes battling Russian spies.

"Well, I'm off. Have fun, you crazy kids." Papa looks at me for a moment. I will his lips to press against my forehead. There was a time in my life when he couldn't stop fawning over me—when he walked me to grade school every morning and scooped me into his arms whenever he came home. I thought it was the real Papa, leaking out of the standard-issue Soviet man for a brief moment before pouring himself back in. But now, with no one to hide himself from, he merely turns and walks down the hall, whistling to himself.

The security guard hands me a badge to dangle around my neck—my photograph, with my full name and nationality typed beneath it. They've added a superfluous *j* to the English spelling of my name. *Yulija*. Now everyone's going to butcher the pronunciation.

Valentin holds up his own badge. "Valentine," he says. Like the American holiday. We laugh nervously, a quick snorting sound. His fingers brush against the nape of my neck as he helps me slide my badge into place, leaving a warm trail of our shared music on my skin. I'm not alone. As disorienting as our new life is, I can survive here.

"Miss Chernina!" A fluted column of a woman, rich olive skin melting into a tweedy Jackie Kennedy–style skirt and blazer, clips toward us on heeled oxfords. "Cindy Conrad. Call me Cindy." She pumps her right hand toward me like a piston. I shake, but her strength far exceeds mine, and my hand flails in hers as her raucous blues music shield spills onto me. "It's not my real name. Come along; I work with the girls separately in the mornings."

I seize Valentin's wrist, leaning back from Cindy. "Wait—why are we separated?" I meet Valentin's eyes. "I'd be more comfortable if Valentin were to—help translate, or explain—"

Cindy smirks. "That's very sweet. But we do things rather differently here than you might be used to, and part of that is keeping the genders separated. For propriety's sake, you know." Another dainty laugh. "What do you think this is—a public high school?"

Valentin squeezes my hand. "I'll be right down the hall if you need anything. *Tebye obyeshayu.*" *I promise.*

Cindy trails a warm perfume from her like a censer as we wind through the CIA's bowels, her caramel-colored bun bobbing high above everyone else. Though I can tell she's slowed her pace to accommodate my limp, we're still moving at a decent clip. I'm amazed how much noise these marble halls contain, circling a lush courtyard where young cardiganed secretaries lounge and smoke and drink from Styrofoam coffee cups. Everyone's talking to someone as they trot from one corridor to the next, sometimes frantic, sometimes giddy. But everyone I brush against—down to the dowdy old woman stocking a breakfast cart—hums with a different melody.

"Everyone has a musical shield?" I ask Cindy, taking care to add an upward inflection to make it a question. Winnie told me my accent makes everything sound like I'm conducting an interrogation.

"We have many psychic safeguards in place—standard training for all CIA employees. He may be a real pistol to work with, but your father has been a godsend for our operational security, let me tell you!" She glances back at me. "You sound like quite the firebrand yourself. I heard about the number you did on Rostov and his 'Hound' back in Berlin. We'll be needing more of that resourcefulness."

There's a current running through the building, a hum just on the horizon of my hearing like an electrified fence. It's similar to the vibration in Papa's townhouse, the by-product of living with two scrubbers. But no one we pass seems to be the source; aside from Cindy, I don't sense that prick and tingle of psychic prowess.

"I don't know how much your father and Valentin have told you about our work here. Hopefully not much, since it's highly classified!" She says it with a smile, but I suspect she's not joking. "Last year, we partnered with the Department of Education to include a psychic battery and examination in their high school testing—that's how we found your teammates. They're all around your age. We do have a few older operatives who volunteered their unique services for America. By and large, though, our program is new, which makes it exciting. We haven't yet gotten regulated to death." Her gaze rakes across me. "I've seen all kinds of psychics, but I've never met anyone with an ability quite like yours."

My touch—she means my touch. I cement my hands to my sides. "Did you also . . . 'volunteer your services'?" I ask, hoping to shift attention away from me. She looks like the 'Ivy League Spooks' Winnie's warned me about. They come from New England money and New England colleges—they have wealth coded into their DNA as surely as psychic powers are coded in mine. They created the Central Intelligence Agency seventeen years ago, after World War II, to put their college educations to good use. I start fabricating a backstory for Cindy. Finishing school and horseback-riding lessons and dinner parties with the Kennedys. College degree, a rare thing for women in America, I hear. Clapboard beach homes on—what did Winnie say again?—Martha's Vineyard. The Hamptons.

Cindy smiles again—it's like a camera flash going off—and herds me into an elevator. "They found me telling fortunes in a New Orleans brothel."

"Brothel," I echo. I'm not sure if Winnie and I went over this word, but I think it has something to do with soup.

"A whorehouse," she says, not missing a beat. "I had the mystical voodoo priestess shtick down pat. Good money, too, until I told the wrong mob boss he was going to die." The elevator doors slide open. "Our office is right this way."

I clamp my dangling jaw shut. So much for Ivy League Spook. I watch Cindy's measured, flawless stride down the corridor, looking for any hint of whatever sort of girl deals with prostitutes and mob bosses, but it's all 18 karat–plated confidence and command. I admire her for the transformation she must have undergone, but her seemingly effortless ability to suppress her past also tightens a fear in me, like a clock's spring winding up.

Our "office" looks more like the Bali beatnik jazz lounge

Valentin and I visited last week than the sober black leather and wood-paneled affair I'd anticipated. Fringed velvet curtains sweep down from the drop ceiling, tucked under the asbestos tiles to anchor them. They turn the large room into a claustrophobic labyrinth. All the fluorescent lighting tracks have been draped with thin sheets of silk in various colors, casting kaleidoscope swirls around the den.

"Ladies! Our new friend is here!" Cindy flutters toward a marble-topped bar and pours herself a glass of something amber and reeking of smoke.

One of the curtains billows as something moves behind it; a hand wraps around it from behind and shoves it back. One girl steps forward, short and lithe, her eyes contracting as she studies me. "I'm Donna. Donna Willoughsby," she says. "Boy, have we been waiting for you."

Donna's glossy blond hair sweeps into a ponytail that forms a perfect inverted question mark. Her skin looks brushed with powdered sunlight; her smile could jam radio frequencies—she looks exactly like I imagine the Beach Boys' "Surfer Girl," though instead of a scandalous bikini, she wears a fluffy turquoise skirt and creamy blouse, with a faint rose cardigan draped demurely over her shoulders.

"It is nice to meet you. I'm Yulia." My right hand twitches at my side. Should I move in to shake? I lurch forward, but then realize I look like a shambling beast from *Invasion of the Body Snatchers* and decide against it.

"*Dobro pozhalovat*," Donna tells me, in a Russian accent that's not flawless, but still cheerful. "I understand you've been working with Sergeant Davis?"

"She's the best," I say. "Anything I . . . misspeak? Is entirely my own fault."

Donna takes my arm in hers, like I'm her oldest, dearest confidant. "She's good. But she isn't one of us. Don't ever forget that."

At first, I think she means because Winnie's colored, and I try to find the right words to protest, but then another possibility strikes me—a divide between psychics and the rest. I don't think of myself as better than non-psychics. I envy them. I lust after their simple, unguarded lives, never stumbling across secrets they wish they could forget, never causing harm with a thought, a touch.

Donna pulls me onto a plush couch, inflated like some space capsule cushion, that threatens to swallow us whole. Another girl swims out of its depths, looking at first like a spider—just arms and legs flailing around. Then a torso emerges, and a mop of black hair that she smoothes into a bouncy, frothy bob. Her features vanish behind rhinestone-flecked catseye glasses.

"I'm, uh, Marylou," she says, the words tiny and fragile when exposed to the air. I reach out to shake with her, but her fingers just crumple against mine for an awkward second before she yanks back and forces a pained smile to her lips.

"Marylou's a remote viewer," Donna says. I look over Marylou again—the fringed bangs and glasses to hide her face, and the shapeless black dress that suppresses her tall, pudgy body. She certainly looks like the kind of girl who prefers to be as far removed from the situation as possible.

"What kind of psychic are you?" I ask Donna.

"Just a mind reader. Nothing special." She smiles with one side of her mouth—like even she doesn't believe this. "But I'm really good at getting people to open up their thoughts to me."

I frown. "Like a scrubber?"

Donna's smile fades; her eyes turn sharp with annoyance. "I don't have to *break into* anyone's head. When I talk to someone, they eagerly offer up the thoughts I need."

"It's basic spycraft," Cindy says, striding toward our enclave. "You make the target more comfortable with you so they'll tell you things they shouldn't. Miss Willoughsby is a psychic extension of that process—making them think about whatever it is they're trying to hide, regardless of what kind of training they've received. They may know not to say it out loud, but they'll sure be thinking about it—and that's all we really need."

Some of her words sail past me, but I get the general idea. If Donna seems overly curious in me, I should probably be concerned.

Cindy clasps her hands together. "Now, then! Let's talk about what I expect from you, Yulia, and introduce you to some of our current projects. First—I expect you to work hard." She raises her index finger in a count. "I want you to push your abilities to their limits. We know so little about our powers and where our boundaries truly lie, and I expect them to be stretched."

I grimace, thinking of the aching emptiness I felt when I forced the Hound's emotions back onto him. The boundaries I've placed on myself—on my powers—are what keep me safe right now. I want to help Mama. I don't want to be a weapon. But I give her a nod.

"Second, you must work *smart*. Don't ever think this is easy work, that you're punching a time clock, reading a few minds, punching out. We need to constantly find new ways to use our powers, as well as creative solutions to problems that our powers *can't* fix.

"Third, this isn't Junior League. I'm not running a charm school. It is my sincere hope that you ladies will get along with one another, but frankly, my dears, I don't give a damn if you hate each other's guts." Cindy smiles; Marylou and Donna giggle, and I suspect this is another cultural reference I've just missed. "However, we're here to work *together*. Russian, American, Martian, I don't care who or what you are. You work for me, and the mission comes first. Understood?"

"Yes, ma'am," I say. I repeat the English phrases to myself: Work hard. Work smart. Work together. I glance at Donna and Marylou out of the corner of my eye; though I'm sure they've heard this speech before, they're leaning forward, eyes fixed on Cindy as they listen. Donna in particular, I notice, strains to mirror Cindy: her smile, her tilted head, her prim smoothing of her skirt.

Cindy drums her nails against the side of her glass tumbler. "Glad to hear it. Now, I understand you've been briefed on the current situation with the deceased, Yulia?"

"The . . . the bodies?" I ask. "I've seen the pictures."

Cindy nods. "Gruesome business. My instinct tells me they must be all working toward a shared goal." She presses two fingers against her lips. "But what are they working toward? Marylou, any thoughts?"

"Um." Marylou looks at her lap. "Well, they aren't working together. It's all spread out."

"Spread out—by time and location, both. Maybe one is intended to pick up where the previous one left off," Cindy says.

"Like a relay race," Donna volunteers.

"Precisely," Cindy says. Donna eases back with a huge grin. "I ran a similar operation in Saigon not so long ago—if one of my operatives realized they were compromised, they left their task unfinished, and the next operative moved in to pick up where they left off."

"But what are they working toward?" I ask.

Cindy takes a slow sip of her drink. "That is the question, isn't it?" She turns to the others. "Ladies? Let's teach Yulia about our 'competing hypotheses' technique, shall we?"

Donna turns toward me with a broad grin slathered on her face. "It's when we explore a variety of possible scenarios, no matter how unlikely they seem."

"Precisely," Cindy says. "Once we've examined each of them, we sometimes find what we thought was a certainty is actually not that likely, and what seemed ridiculous is actually pretty reasonable. So! Let's put ourselves in General Rostov's head. What does he want?"

My chest aches like I'm breathing exhaust fumes. Rostov's spent quite enough time in my head—I don't care to step into his. The other girls' eyes shine with the thrill of a new challenge, however; Donna sits up even straighter as she answers. "He wants the Soviet Union and the forces of communism to win a decisive victory over the West."

"And what are some of the ways he can accomplish it?" Cindy looks at Marylou.

Marylou shrugs. "Open warfare, I guess. But then Russia might look like a bully. So he could goad the US into attacking Russia instead."

"Are there any other possibilities?" Cindy asks.

I feel like I'm watching a hockey match—the three of them taking turns leading the conversation, passing it effortlessly back and forth. We were never asked our opinion in the KGB; Rostov never once regarded us as intellectual equals, or as anything but lackeys to be ordered about.

"What if . . ." Donna fingers her pearl necklace as her eyes dart around in thought. "What if he were being sneakier? Using guerilla tactics—like the Viet Cong. He could be waiting for us to be distracted by something else. Then he'd have the element of surprise on his side. He wouldn't need a large-scale battle."

"That would be classic *maskirovka*—the Soviet art of denial and deception." Cindy tilts her head to one side, like a curious bird. "What sort of distraction?"

"Like these psychics invading different Western cities. Would that be a big enough distraction?" Marylou asks.

"If it . . . takes up our time . . ." I gesture around me to indicate the PsyOps team. "Then we might miss another attack."

Donna and Marylou twist around to look at me, the fake leather couch squealing underneath us. Cindy arches one flawless brow.

"Well, then," Cindy says. "I guess we'd better keep our eyes and ears and sixth senses peeled for something other than a direct attack, shouldn't we?"

She gestures to a tidy stack of folders sitting on the left-hand side of the coffee table, each cover bearing a cheerful barbershop striping on its border and a giant stamp: TOP SECRET. An additional code of jumbled letters beneath restricts distribution to even narrower channels. Winnie explained the main ones to me, though I'm brimming with so much language and culture that I immediately forgot them. I'm sure we had similar data restriction rules in the KGB, but they were a bit plainer in their interpretation: keep this confidential or be executed for treason.

"Each morning, I like for us to keep our minds limber by looking through new intelligence, even if it's not directly related to our current cases. After we're warmed up, then I'll run you through a series of exercises to keep your psychic skills sharp. If we have ongoing missions to work, we'll pursue them at that time, as well. Then, in the afternoons, we work joint operations with the gentlemen." Cindy blinks, once. "Any questions?"

I shake my head. I understood her about as well as I'm going to. The Americans seem to have this down to a science; I worry that I'm too clunky for this well-oiled machine.

"All right, ladies, let's see what the analysts brought us."

Donna and Marylou roll forward to hunch over the coffee table in front of us and start pawing through the folders like they're records in the bargain bin at Woodward & Lothrop's. "North Korea's so boring." "I've already questioned that Cuban defector." "Ooh, can I see the surveillance notes?" They swap the folders back and forth, photographs and typed dossiers spilling from them like entrails, while Cindy retidies their discard heap, her patient smile never wavering.

I reach tentatively toward the pile, half afraid I'll pull my arm back with nothing but a nub. One folder feels fattened in the middle with a stack of photographs—perfect. Not a lot of text for me to struggle through. I flip open the cover, stamped "EYES ONLY: Cindy Conrad," and cycle through the stack of photographs.

They're awful quality. Black and white, with a dearth of gray shades in between, taken through a lens that's distended like a fisheye. Each one is framed in a black ring, like they've been shot through a peephole. The photographs feature the same woman in a variety of settings. Here she's hurrying down a bridge, a fur stole suppressing her face—is that the Lomonosov Bridge in Leningrad? And in the next shot, she's peeling hair from her face in a park. The washed-out colors render her a ghost—only a vague hint of eyes on a vast white visage.

Miss Conrad lurches over the coffee table and yanks the folder from my hands, her blues music blunted and angry as we make contact. The loose pictures spray facedown across the table, but she scoops them up in an instant. "That's not for you. Didn't you see the marking?" She jabs her finger at the stamp on the folder's cover. "EYES ONLY. Unless I give it to you directly, you don't look at it."

"It's okay, Cindy." Donna cups a hand around my shoulder. Her musical shield is soothing, but too sweet, like a thick syrup. It rings a little too false. "She's new. She doesn't understand."

But I barely hear her. The woman hangs in my mind, like a shadow skimmed from the ground and hung out to dry. I know her.

Even under a layer of exhaustion and Party-quality cosmetics caked onto her like a guilty mask I'd know those high cheekbones anywhere.

They're the same ones that stare back at me every morning in the mirror.

CHAPTER 5

I LOCK THE RESTROOM DOOR behind me, not caring who I inconvenience, and park myself before one of the angled mirrors. I study the flash of freckles that marches from one high cheekbone, across my flat nose, to the other cheek. I trace the hollow under my cheeks; it's hardly the cavernous pit it was eight months ago, when Mama and I were in hiding, sharing two food rations with five people. No, I am not the leaf stripped down to its stem that I was then, but I barely resemble the well-fed, doted-upon Party member in those photographs, restored to her former high-ranking glory.

Why are they keeping those pictures from me? I know my mother is part of the enemy's machinery. I have accepted this—am trying to accept it, at least, though I cling to the belief that Mama must have some greater plan at work. If the Americans are going to make me a member of their team, then they must treat me as part of the team. I thought Cindy was showing us trust earlier, asking us our opinions, letting us build our own cases. I thought she was respecting us. While I know they're spying directly on Mama, the fact that they're keeping it from me sets my rusty gears of paranoia churning once more.

Do they have a good reason? Or am I right to be concerned? Competing hypotheses, comparing the possible scenarios—this is a problem my scientist's mind can solve, like sifting through equations and formulae. The Americans know more about Mama's situation right now than I do, I'm sure of that, but I don't know why they're keeping it from me. Do they not trust me, or am I the one who should be on my guard?

Someone pounds on the bathroom door. "One minute, please," I shout.

The obvious hypothesis: Mama is working freely with Rostov. She will do whatever he asks.

"The door's not supposed to be locked." The woman on the other side hesitates. "I'll have to get security."

"Please, I only need a minute."

A counter-hypothesis: Mama is sabotaging Rostov's work from the inside. If this is what she's doing, and the Americans don't realize it, will their meddling ruin her plans? Does she need my help?

The woman rattles the door handle again. I scrunch my eyes shut, struggling to find a quiet space in my mind where these thoughts and emotions can't overwhelm me—

I must help them. I must earn their trust. If I am to keep Mama safe, it will be easiest if I do so from the inside—while following the rules. I am not merely a weapon, after all.

Like an army knife, I have many uses.

I splash cold water on my face. For one moment, I imagine

myself as the ghostly Mama in the pictures, all of the life bleached out of me. For one moment, I am stripped down to the monster inside of me, hungering for a new goal. For one moment, I am not afraid to be me.

I open the door to a security guard, hand raised, trailing a jailer's ring of keys.

"Sorry," I say, eyes cast down sheepishly and cheeks red. "There was a . . ." What was the word Winnie taught me? *Accident, occurrence, disaster*—they are all one euphemistic word in Russian. "Emergency."

My new plan pulses through me like a dangerous bass line under my shield melody as I return to our psychedelic psychic's den. Some trippy record oozes through the room, thickening the air around me. I'm swimming through the watery music—a Hammond organ shimmers against a rollicking drumbeat and sitar chords pierce the air like rays of sunlight. I force my way through the maze of curtains until I finally reach the far corner.

Cindy and Donna huddle together on a pile of pillows, talking in liquid tones. Donna's skirt spreads around her in a perfect circle, knees tucked demurely to one side, while Cindy's wiry knees nestle under her chin. I stare at Cindy through the lens of an operative. I want to know what she knows. I need her trust. I need to be a part of whatever she's involved in.

". . . But surely they asked you to," Donna's saying, her lashes fluttering. "That's what powerful men do."

"That's not for me to tell," Cindy says. But then her thoughts chime against the watery organ chords, completely unshielded, so loud that even I can hear them through the rug we're both touching: *Once or twice. Thibadeaux . . .*

Then her musical shield slams down. They both twist toward me. "Yulia!" Cindy pulls herself to her feet.

"Hi, *Jules*," Donna says. "Mind if I call you that?" But she looks to Cindy while she says it, like her permission would outweigh mine.

"What are you people doing?" I ask. *Guys*, I chide myself. *What are you* guys *doing*.

Donna stares at me, like it's the first time anyone's ever ignored her. "We're practicing my skill. Cindy turns off her musical shield, and I ask her all kinds of uncomfortable questions."

"Not *all* kinds," Cindy says sharply. "There's still plenty you'll never learn, young lady."

"Someday, I'll get your real name out of you." Donna grins.

But Cindy's studying my expression. "Donna, I'm afraid we'll have to continue our exercise later. I'd like to work with Yulia privately for now."

Donna's face twists, but she smooths it out by the time Cindy looks back at her. "Yeah. Of course. I'll just . . . go watch Mary-lou practice, or something."

Cindy beckons me to follow her through the maze of curtains. "Feeling better?" she asks, as we wind through the path.

The room feels pressurized, closing in on me. My breath buzzes in my lungs as I search for the right words. "Um," I say. I have mastered this English stalling technique, at least. "First, I must say something. I know you did not want me to see the photographs in that folder."

"No," Cindy says, voice clipped. "I didn't." Her eyes keep darting back to the shoebox, as if she's eager to end this discussion and resume our work.

"But this is a problem." I swallow through my tightly clenched throat. "In Russia, I could not trust my handlers, you see."

She taps her heel against the linoleum. Her smile is easing away, but she says nothing.

"I do not want that life here. I want to be able to trust you. I want to work *with* you." I look away. "Is this something we can do?"

"I'm not trying to keep secrets from you." Cindy holds her palm up like she's shielding herself. "Our chief doesn't want you to work directly on your mother's case. He thinks it will be . . . easier for you, that way."

"But—but I want to help. Is this because of what I said in my hearing? That I'm not willing to hurt her."

"Honestly?" Cindy smiles. "Yes, that's a part of it. It tells me two things about you. The first is that you have a compass in you still—some dividing line between right and wrong. That the KGB didn't break that part of you." She tilts her head as if she's trying to see me from a better angle. "Though I already knew that about you."

I certainly don't feel like someone with a good sense of right or wrong. From her cool tone, I'm not entirely sure she means it as a compliment, either. "And how do you know that?"

Cindy looks down at her lap; her lips twitch, like she's about to tell me, but then she shakes her head. "Another time." We reach another alcove in the maze, where she plucks a shoebox off of a desk and holds it out to me. "But the second thing it tells me is that there's only so far you're willing to be pushed."

I breathe in slowly, so slow the cold air makes my teeth ache. I know what's coming next.

"I had the field team bring this in for you. We collected these items from the dead spies we're investigating. We need to know who these people were and why they were sent here."

I sink into the nearest couch and balance the shoebox on my knees, trying to touch it as little as possible. "It's been a long time since I've done this."

Cindy settles next to me, barely disturbing the couch. "Take your time."

My hands tingle from disuse. I've learned to keep them to myself in Papa's house, where he and Valentin leave a faint trail of scrubber sound on everything they touch. When Winnie takes me to the Smithsonian museums, I'm too overwhelmed with her translation challenges to focus on the whispered conversations the tourists leave behind. Well, maybe I've read objects at the museum once or twice. A tour group had just gone through, and the guide had read the Old Glory plaque verbatim, so I pressed my fingertip to the plaque and quoted it back to Winnie as if I was reading it.

I learned quite an earful of unpleasant words when Winnie realized I was cheating.

Cindy gestures toward the box. "I understand that you knew one of those men—the one who exuded the extremely strong psychic ability. He had been the contact for a double agent within the State Department."

I study the box's contents: eyeglasses, a pillbox, a tiny notebook, a man's wingtipped shoe. The possessions of the bloody, wide-eyed dead from the photographs.

"I am your teacher and your commander, after all. So when I choose to challenge you, or not challenge you—include

47

you or exclude you—I need you to trust that I have my reasons for it."

I hesitate, palms itching, nervous energy running through me. I don't think I can trust her; not yet. But maybe, by following her orders, she'll reveal more of what she knows about my mother. "Okay." I like this English word: round and flexible and noncommittal. It will satisfy for now.

"Glad to hear it." She pulls her smile back into place. "Now—what can you tell me about these objects?"

I reach for the shoe, but the moment my fingers close around it, blinding white pain fires through me like buckshot. I slam against the back of the couch. Static spirals around me in a whirling storm, blistering with cold. It feels like Papa and Valentin and Rostov all combined, needling through my skin, in and out. My throat is raw—my hand sizzles with electricity.

The office is utterly silent except for the trippy record player; Cindy stares at me with white-rimmed eyes.

"It's been scrubbed of memories. It's completely . . ." I clench and relax my hand in a fist. Is there an English word for this aggressive emptiness, like a void sucking away all thought?

"There isn't anything you can glean from it?"

"I don't think so." I try to envision an edge to the vast nothingness I saw, stretching as far as Siberia in every direction. "Even my father and Valentin aren't strong enough to erase so much. Whose was this?"

Cindy checks the folder in her lap and holds up a photograph. "Your old friend, Pavel. Apparently he was running this man as a Russian agent." She taps the folder. "He worked in the Latin American office of the State Department for five years. The FBI opened an investigation on him a month ago when a co-worker raised concerns he might be committing espionage. Turns out, he was dropping briefcases full of classified documents next to a bench on the National Mall, and Pavel was collecting them."

"And this is Pavel's shoe. After he died." Something rings inside of me, as though I am hollowed out. I didn't truly believe the general when he told me Pavel was a powerful scrubber. But the proof is still crackling through my nerves. Could this really be my mother's doing? Rostov demanded she build an army of psychics, and this man wasn't one before.

Cindy nods. "Originally, we were going to bring you to his apartment so you could search the area, try to find new leads for us, but there was an . . . incident."

I swallow. Incident. Emergency. Disaster.

"Someone burned it down not an hour after we removed his body. We're lucky none of the men guarding it were hurt." Cindy's voice doesn't waver, but her smile does. "The other items are from other locations where we found similar bodies. The pillbox was on a woman who'd last been seen trying to enter the NATO offices in Brussels."

I reach for the pillbox. My pulse ricochets in my ears, anticipating another wave of bleaching noise. As my fingers circle the cold metal, white blossoms suround me. It drinks me in, swallows me into its throat of steel wool and scrapes me all the way down. The bleach rots me away, one layer of skin at a time.

But maybe I can outlast it. If I can skim just one memory—salvage one clue—

The woman curls around a telephone receiver, lying in a fetal position, stiff polyester carpet fibers stamped hard into one cheek.

Her skin is mine, and it is too tight—like a cooked sausage pushing at its casing. The psychic noise pushes back on me from all sides. It's worse now. I gain some sense that this noise has been festering for a while, but now it's consuming me whole. It's invaded my every cell. I am nothing but this painful, piercing noise.

I have a telephone receiver cradled to my ear, propped beside me on the carpet. "Please," I rasp into the perforated holes. "Send someone." My thumb strokes back and forth against the faded rose pattern on the pillbox's lid. "Your cyanide didn't work."

The phone crackles with a voice tinged in frost. "You must finish the mission."

"Please." Speaking is so hard. I can barely feel the word pushing through my vocal cords. I'm strangled by my own psychic noise. "Please kill me."

A labored inhalation, or maybe it's the static in the phone line turning the caller's breath into crackling squares of noise. "You must reach Senator Saxton."

"It doesn't matter." The pillbox slips through my fingers. The carpet fibers pressing into my temple are damp, hot with the smell of copper. "It's too late for me."

I fling myself out of the chattering white void and choke down fresh air. As soon as I've let go of the pillbox, I clamp my hand onto Cindy's wrist and let what I've just seen pour back out of me.

"Yulia!—" she pleads, her tone suddenly sharp and high. The tone of panic and pain. I want her to feel this pain, too. I shouldn't be the only one subjected to such misery. She needs to know what I'm capable of, what these scrubbers are like. I won't suffer alone—

Bozhe moi. My anger is suddenly gone, poured out of me and into Cindy. I pry my hand away.

"Cindy—Miss Conrad—I am so sorry—" I dump the shoe-box onto the ground and curl my arms around my legs, ignoring the twinge from my bad ankle. "I wanted you to see the memory, but I—"

Cindy's breathing heavily; she runs a hand against her taut, silky hair. "No harm done." Her eyelids flutter rapid fire. "Is—is that how you shared your findings with your KGB mentors?"

No. I was only a tarpaulin strung between trees, collecting memories like rainwater, then waiting for Rostov to wring every last drop from me. I shake my head and lower my legs back down, trying to match Cindy as she schools herself to calmness.

"Very well. It was my choice to push you." She raises her chin, regal. "So this woman appears to be a—a scrubber, as well."

I take a slow breath. "I think so. And she was dying. What-ever is causing the bleeding from her ears—the psychic noise—I think she was in great pain, and she tried to end it with a cya-nide pill." I tighten my hands into fists, trying to squeeze down the dark memories lingering against them. "Do you know this Senator Saxton they mentioned?"

"I'm afraid so." Cindy stands, bracelets jangling. "Wait right here."

While Cindy digs around in her desk, I try to keep balance on the couch, as it threatens to reel me in again. Someone laughs from behind me, a snorting sound. I peer over the edge to find Marylou flat on her back on the floor. She's chain-smoking clove cigarettes, and her hair makes her look like she's escaped a volcanic eruption because she keeps undershooting the ashtray by her head. "That was real groovy," she says.

"What? You heard us?"

"Yeah. I liked what you did with your box of stuff." Her pupils are cavernous pits, inviting me in. I can't read the look on her face, both bleary and frighteningly incisive, and I don't like it. "It's like you're reaching through the time-space continuum, you know? And, like, knotting it all together."

I creep back on the couch. "Thanks." The silence between us swells. "I did not . . . know you were down there."

"Always." Another heavy, crushing pause as she takes a slow drag. "Do you think we could swim in it?" she asks. Then, as to clarify, "Time."

Suddenly Cindy is there, peering over Marylou with a click of her tongue. "I didn't realize you were scheduled for an INFRA session today."

Marylou snorts with laughter again. "I'm looking in the Forbidden City—couldn't get past their blockers without one. Following Mao around. I slide in on sunbeams and melt into his shadow, Miss Cindy. It's *poetry*."

"I'm sure you could do it without the 'outside help' if you tried." Cindy turns away from Marylou and settles beside me again. "Project MK INFRA. Our research department had been trying to induce psychic abilities for years through the use of hallucinogens so we didn't have to rely on psychic volunteers, but we had it all wrong—you have to have the genetic predisposition for psychic ability first. Now we're running preliminary trials to see if it can enhance the abilities you all already possess."

"Hallucinogens," I repeat, still trying to process her words.

Cindy smirks. "Don't worry, I'm not keen on letting them run trials on you anytime soon." She opens another folder across our laps. "Senator Arliss Saxton, Congressional representative to the North Atlantic Treaty Organization."

I page through the file. Russian propaganda led me to expect a round, white-suited Southern old boy with sinister facial hair, not unlike the man on the bucket of chicken Papa sometimes brings home for dinner, but Senator Saxton just looks tired. His face is riveted into place with deep pockmarks, and his dark hair has been splashed with white. His stockiness looks like fortification against some unseen threat.

"Congressional representative," I echo. "Is this . . . significant?"

"You have more experience with scrubbers than I do." Cindy thumbs the corner of the file. "You tell me what one could accomplish if they had control of the man who can send every NATO country to war."

CHAPTER 6

CINDY AND I SPEND AN HOUR mapping out every-where they'd found the dead operatives—the possible scrubbers, with blood dribbling from their noses and ears. Sure enough, they show a steady westward progression through the NATO member states of Europe—from West Germany to France to Great Britain—and now to America leaving a trail of security incidents in their wake. An assault on the West German NATO general in the streets of West Berlin. A British aide walks onto the Tube one day and walks off with no knowledge of where or who she is. For almost every seemingly unrelated security incident to befall a government official, a dead scrubber turned up a few days later in the same city, matching the description of whoever had made the attack.

And then there's Senator Saxton, whose dossier I muddle through. Turns out, Saxton had contacted the CIA recently with concerns that someone was leaking NATO documents—files misplaced, reports gone awry. Nothing classified, but he was concerned all the same. Then, last week, he reported an attempted break-in at his Georgetown home, and the Secret Service placed him under protective detail while the FBI and CIA jointly investigated. "Given his position and the other recent episodes," Cindy says, "we can't rule out the possibility that foreign agents are trying to harm him or intimidate him in some way. And if they have one of these powerful psychics on their side . . ."

I can fill in that blank perfectly fine. I've seen what a highly skilled scrubber can do. Force a man to turn a gun on himself. Drive a world leader to input the codes for a nuclear launch. I won't let that happen again. I pore over her reports, letting myself forget, however briefly, that I might be capable of this kind of danger, too.

When we break for lunch my head is laden with so many strange words from the dossier, I can't wait to ask Winnie for help. "There's my little *devochka*!" she calls to me from one of the break room tables. I reel toward her—my anchor, my filter for everything mad in this new world. She hugs me for a moment before I pull away. "How's your first day so far?" she asks me in Russian.

"Rough. But not the worst I've had." I glance over my shoulder, check that Cindy is still chatting in the far corner with Donna, and tell Winnie briefly about the file with my mother. Her lips draw tight as she listens.

"I can't blame you for being upset. But these people are only trying to keep the country safe—you can't blame them for doing their job, for following the rules."

I want to believe her, but her voice is flat, as if she's said these words before. I may still be learning English, but I know the sound of something you have to convince yourself of. "What about Cindy? Do you trust her?"

Winnie's eyebrows lift. "She's tough—just the right kind of ruthless we need. I don't agree with her methods sometimes, but I can't argue with her results."

"But do you trust her?" I ask.

"As much as I trust anyone." She takes a breath like she's about to say more, but the door swings open, and Papa, Valentin, and two others enter the break room. Valentin's stare softens when he sees me. He circles around my chair and rests his palms on my shoulders, murmuring a sweet nickname for me in Russian before planting a kiss on the crown of my head. All the nervousness and fear that's been skittering through me vanishes with that touch. I smile and lean back in the chair.

Is everything okay? he asks, our shared music tangling together like our fingers: the Beatles and Dave Brubeck and *Babi Yar* all at once. *You seem tense.*

I hesitate. Last night was a good night—no nightmares pulsing through the halls. No screaming. No anguish. But I know it's somewhere under the surface, lurking, waiting for its chance. I don't need to burden him with my troubles. I need him strong. *Just a little overwhelmed, is all.* I turn our music bright and summery. *I'll be fine.*

"Have a seat," Winnie tells Valentin, "but we're switching back to English."

We both groan.

Valentin and Winnie banter back and forth about his work with the CIA's new employee class, training them to resist his psychic assault. His English is soft and buttery, a stark reminder to me of his past life as the son of a high-ranking Party official within the Soviet Union—he can cycle through Russian, English, and German like he moves through piano chords. I mostly keep up, but the chattering conversations around us—Cindy and Donna, Papa and his friends—tug my ears in different directions like a cross-breeze whipping me around.

Winnie must notice the fake, baffled smile frozen on my face, because as soon as Valya stops talking, she turns toward me. "All right, Yulia. What do you need help with?"

Everything, I think. "A few words from today's reading. '*Yacht*,'" I say, with my best phlegm-loosening German accent.

"*Yacht*," Winnie corrects me with a laugh. "It's a boat. A rich-guy boat."

I grin back at her. "*Lacrosse*."

"It's a sport, kind of like tennis and football combined. Let me guess, you've been reading dossiers on rich senators."

"Very observant. What else was there . . . '*Adulterer*'. . . '*er*.' Is it someone who is more adult than someone else?"

Winnie stops smiling and glances down at her deli sandwich. "No. It's someone who cheats."

"Cheats?" I ask. "Like at cards?"

"No. Cheats—is unfaithful to their partner. Like their wife."

"Oh," I say, my stomach sinking. "Oh." I can't help but glance in Papa's direction. I've seen him flirt with waitresses and secretaries before, but it's always been harmless banter, as far as I can tell—not seduction, and not warping their thoughts to his will. But Papa naturally radiates a magnetic charm that bends the whole room toward him.

He wouldn't betray his vows to Mama. I'm almost sure of it. But I don't take anything in my new life for granted.

Winnie pries up the soggy top of her bread and studies the mayonnaise intently. "Anything else?"

I shake my head and force myself to smile. "Every third word that Cindy says."

Winnie grins. "Yeah, you and everyone else."

Papa heads toward us with another man around his age who wears a fresh blue suit and a sturdy fedora, which he plucks off as he bows deeply before me.

"Yul," Papa says, "my dear friend, Al Sterling. He helped you in Berlin—you remember?"

The man who may have sabotaged the *Veter 1* space capsule, killing two cosmonauts. I manage a terse smile. "Good to meet you, Mister Sterling." I offer him my hand, and he kisses it— kisses it!—instead of shaking, flooding me with his cheerful Frank Sinatra shield. Valentin shifts beside me.

"You've cleaned up good, kid. Say, your pops and I are gonna catch a Senators game next week—whaddaya say? You too, Val. Get some good ol' American baseball in your blood, huh?" He crunches up one knee and pantomimes what I think is a batter swinging.

"Um. Okay," I say.

"Al and I always have a gas of a time when we watch the Senators. You'll love it." Papa scrubs his hand over my hair. "All the popcorn and Cracker Jacks and wild pitches you can stand."

Al ribs Papa. "And when the Senators flop, at least there's always the cigarette girls to watch!"

They burst into laughter. Papa's laugh, so broad and animal,

58

sounds foreign to me. Have I ever heard him laugh before America? At least the noise fits Al. Al is fresh-faced, with sturdy cheekbones and broad shoulders that I think I've heard Winnie describe as corn-fed. Maybe corn-bred. Cornbread? He smiles like he's never had to frown. "You know, it's just great having you on the team, Yul," Al says. "Brightens your Papa's day, it does. It's really great."

"It's great," I agree, wishing I could melt into my chair. I glance at Papa, wondering if I'll get a chance to ask him about Mama, but he's already bobbing away from our cluster like he's gotten caught in a more interesting current.

"Well, I won't take too much of your time. It's just great to have you here. Oh, Val?" Al points his finger at Valya like he's cocking a pistol. "Get back to work on that thing after lunch, will ya? I gotta head upstairs, talk to the big guy."

I turn to Winnie as Papa and Al leave. " 'The big guy upstairs'— that means God, right?"

She smirks. "In this case, I think he means the Director of Central Intelligence, but they're one and the same around here."

Sterling's jaunty Frank Sinatra shield lingers on my skin, urging us all to fly away on his aggressive cheer. Cindy Conrad appears behind me, Donna in tow, and drums her long nails against the back of my chair. "All right, Yulia, I've arranged a treat for you this afternoon. How'd you like to visit Capitol Hill?"

Without meaning to, my hand closes around Valentin's; the world is only just starting to make sense to me again, with Valya's music bolstering mine in harmony. "Could Valentin come with us?" I ask, though my words sound watery—childish.

Cindy snaps her lips into a thin smile. "I'd prefer if it were just us girls today. Yulia, Donna, me. I think you'll be surprised what doors that'll open for us on the Hill."

"And close," Winnie says under her breath. She tidies her sandwich's remains. "I'd better get back to the translation cave. You'll be all right for the afternoon, Yulia?"

"You can't come with us either?" I ask, though I already know the answer. Capitol Hill is no place for her, and the look that passes between Cindy and Winnie cements it.

Valya lets his music tumble across me and brings my hand to his lips. "You'll do great," he murmurs, then kisses the back of my hand with far more intensity than Al Sterling could have mustered. *Ya tebya lublu.* The words whisper against my skin.

I love you.

I think it back to him, but too soon his hand falls from mine, the cold office air erasing any sign that he'd once been there.

✳ ✳ ✳

I did not think I was afraid of riding in cars—not even the darkened back of a Red Army truck hauling me to points unknown, with rat droppings and a guard with an assault rifle as my only companions. I've ridden in the Austin-Healey while Papa tears across Georgetown with half a bottle of cognac in his belly. But these are amateur fears, warming me up for the sheer terror that grips me in Cindy Conrad's Thunderbird.

She's quiet; sober. But she grips her steering wheel with murderous intent, and every bulbous, pastel-colored car we whiz past ratchets her eyes just a bit wider and makes her smile a little more fierce. I'm not even sure automobiles were designed to go this fast.

The windowpanes rattle and the engine hums like the drone of a distant scrubber.

Donna seems unperturbed by Cindy's maniacal driving. She tilts her face out the window like a dog on a joyride, soaking up every last drop of sunlight she can find. The radio isn't on, but Donna hums her own cheerful bop. Even when we reach a stoplight and Cindy's brake work flings us forward, she keeps humming away.

There you are, Yulia.

I sit up straight as my heart slams into my sternum. I glance around me, hoping I'm imagining things; Donna's still staring out the window at the office workers milling along the sidewalks, and Cindy is steering around the slower cars like she's in Ronnie and the Daytonas' "Little GTO." Neither of them hear this very Russian voice, a voice I haven't heard since it helped me escape East Berlin: Sergei Antonovich Rostov, son of General Rostov, a remote viewer with the ability to push his thoughts into others' heads from afar.

My knuckles blanch white as I curl my hands into fists. Please let me be imagining this. I glance at Cindy in the rearview mirror. If Sergei's in my head, he's either very close by, or he's far, far stronger than before. And if he's much stronger . . . then I don't even want to imagine what else he's capable of. I swallow down the lump of terror in my throat.

Come now, Yulia, I know you can hear me. No need to be shy. What's a little chat between old friends?

I sink into the calfskin seats. Though I can hear him, I don't think he can peer past my musical shield to hear my thoughts. I feel a pressure inside my skull, as if he's pressed up against the bone, waiting for me to push a thought past my shield where he can hear it. *The last time we talked, you said you wouldn't help me again*, I remind him. *So we have nothing to discuss.* I turn up the volume on my shield.

Shostakovich, the Rolling Stones, Tchaikovsky, Stravinsky, it all sloshes around in my head, a catalytic ready to blast this presence from my mind. By fractions, the pressure eases. He's retreating. I indulge myself one long, quiet sigh.

Then he surges back, loud and quick as a gun firing. *You're wrong, though, Yulia. There's so much for us to talk about now. So much that you need to know.*

Desperation bubbles up in me, a consuming hunger for information from the other side of the Iron Curtain. My mother—what if he has a message from her? But I remind myself that this is Sergei. Everything he does is to protect his comfortable, safe future as a celebrated Soviet spy. He won't help me. He can't. I clamp that desperation down. If Sergei's reaching out to me, then it's surely on the order of General Rostov himself.

Panic is tightening inside me like a screw. I may not have a good reason to trust Cindy yet, but I know Sergei far too well. "Cindy?" I sit up straight, trying to force a confidence into my voice that I don't feel. "I think I—"

I lurch forward as Cindy hits the brakes, stopping us just short of hitting a plaid-suited man who unleashes a string of unfamiliar words I know better than to ask Winnie to translate.

Foolish, trusting Yulia. I can almost see Sergei's bitter grin. *I wouldn't do that if I were you.*

"What's the matter?" Cindy looks at me through the rearview mirror.

There's a mole, Sergei says. *We have a mole on your PsyOps team—I don't know who.* He speaks unhurriedly, as if he were telling me about the weather in Moscow. *I'm only trying to help you, Yulia. I don't want to see you get hurt.*

He's lying. I have no good reason to believe him.

But what if he isn't?

I sit back. "It's nothing." Then, ducking my head, "I am sorry."

Now there's the smart Yulia I know.

Prove it to me, Sergei, I tell him. *If you want me to trust you, you'd better do a damned good job of convincing me. Give me some evidence. Tell me—* I hesitate. Dare I let him know how hungry I am for news of Mama? But with the CIA keeping their knowledge of her hidden from me, he might be my only source. *Tell me what my mother's doing.*

Sergei laughs, though the sound is fading away. The pressure in my skull is almost gone now. *Don't you worry. You'll have your proof. And we can discuss it in person very soon.*

CHAPTER 7

SERGEI. I THINK DESPERATELY. *What do you mean? Sergei, how will we meet? What's going to happen?*

But there's no answer. I no longer feel that pressure inside my skull, like the aura of an impending headache. Wherever he's reaching out to me from—the old mansion that was our prison in the southern hills of Moscow, or perhaps the KGB headquarters at Lyubyanka Square, or even just around the corner in Washington, DC—he's gone.

We crest a hilltop, and the Capitol's thick white dome emerges from behind a copse of trees. Cindy jerks the Thunderbird into reverse, throwing Donna and me against the front seats again, then slams us into an empty parking spot along the street. She slings her arm over the seat and looks back at us, her face the picture of composure. "Everything all right, Yulia? You look vexed."

Vexed. If that's anything like conflicted, then yes, that's exactly what I'm feeling. I know I should tell Cindy right away about

Sergei's eerie message, mole or not. But Cindy keeps plenty of secrets of her own. She even hides her own name. And the last thing I want is to appear weak around her—vulnerable to being manipulated by the enemy.

I take a deep breath, rattling loose some phlegm in my throat. "Motion sickness," I say. I smile, though the lie tastes vile in my mouth. *Just for today*, I promise myself. I'll stay on my guard and get through today. Then I can talk to Valentin, and we can figure out just what I should do with Sergei's warning.

Cindy nods, apparently satisfied. "We'll start by interviewing Senator Saxton himself. Donna, he's trained in shielding, but it can't hurt to ask him probing questions nonetheless. Yulia, you can feel out his office space for any signs of foul play—whether by one of these scrubbers or someone else. We're looking for people smuggling documents out, or snooping around when and where they shouldn't. If any of his past visitors happen to be psychics themselves, that'd be a big red flag. If we don't turn up any leads that way, we'll move on to the other NATO representatives." She yanks open her door. "Oh, and if anyone asks, you're students at the Conrad Academy."

"And what is the Conrad Academy?" I ask, peeling myself off the backseat where it's stuck to my thighs.

"My school for promising young secretaries, of course." She perches her pillbox hat into the perfect position atop her head and tugs on wrist-length gloves. "Come on, let's not keep the senator waiting!"

I tug at the hem of my geometric-patterned minidress, willing it to cover more of my thigh. I certainly don't look the part of the demure schoolgirl. Already I feel the prickle of pedestrians' gazes on me: the suited, hatted men and the crisp, Easter egg–colored women.

Donna gives me a quick once-over with one eyebrow raised. "Who dresses you, anyway? Twiggy?"

"Winnie says it's 'the height of fashion,'" I say.

"Well, she's right about the height." Donna thins her lips as she studies the top half of my dark hair piled high atop my head. "I'm sure it's a bit of a culture shock for you, coming here, but you should dress like a proper young lady, like Cindy and me."

Donna loops her arm through mine before I have a chance to protest, like we're the stewardesses on the PanAm posters, and steers us after Cindy. Somehow, Donna's disdain for my mod clothing gives me more confidence in it—maybe I should embrace my odd clothes, my odd words, my odd accent. I smile into the stream of questioning faces we pass as I limp into the Senate Office Building and Cindy flashes her credentials at the guards.

The deeper we wind through the cool marble hallways, the more I sense something opening inside of me—a box I'd locked up months ago. I've used my power so sparingly since that night in the tunnels of East Berlin, but now I'm plunging back into that world without coming up for air. I'm afraid of myself in the same way I used to fear Rostov or Valentin, when I didn't understand their powers—or their weaknesses. This time it's my own mind, my own skin that's turned against me, and I wonder if I can ever be sure which one of us is in control.

I need to limber up if I'm going to take back control of my abilities. I stretch my fingers toward the marble wall and drown in their maddening noise.

Urgency—it shivers like a live wire, powering every memory. Men in suits barking orders back and forth; staccato, frenzied heels clacking on the floor. Perfume and cologne and stale sweat from too-late nights. They scream about Cuba, Korea, poverty, Martin Luther King. They hang on their tentpoles: *If Jack were still in charge* and *we didn't think like that during the war. That goddamned negro and those communist pricks, those pinkos in Hollywood, those bloody Japs, the slants and krauts and Charlies and Chicoms and fairies*, a million phantom enemies guiding their actions with hate and burdening their days.

Everyone's yelling. Is it in the corridor or in my head? I can only hold so many thoughts; it's like someone's held up a camera for a photograph, and hundreds of faces are pressing inward to crowd into the frame. I lurch forward as someone screams right in my face, finger to my sternum like an adrenaline shot, spit spraying against my face—

"Easy, now," Cindy says, snapping me back from the memory. Just a memory. Her hand coils around my wrist to catch me from stumbling. She peels back her lips for a Pantone-white grin. "Having trouble finding your feet?"

"In a figure of speech." No, that's not right. I straighten up and tug my dress back down my thighs. "In a manner of speak."

Heads swivel toward us—toward *me*. I heard in the very walls how little these people think of those different from them—is it written on my face, burned onto my skin, what I am? A psychic, a traitor, a freak?

"It was your accent," Cindy says, slipping the words under her breath. "Also, your shield's weak."

I clench my teeth and let Shostakovich's symphony hammer out the rise and fall of my thoughts as we reach Saxton's corridor.

A pert, mint-clad secretary greets us at his main door. Dark boy-cut hair feathers her tan face, framing her cheekbones. She jabs a hand toward us, fanning out nails that could double as pick-axes. "Anna Montalban," she purrs at Cindy as they shake. "We spoke on the phone."

Cindy's face pulls tight like vinyl. "So we did. My girls and I are thrilled for this opportunity." High shoulders, outsized grin; Cindy plays her role as a polished, well-heeled working woman perfectly. I wonder what else she conceals so effortlessly.

"Please, have a seat." Anna ushers us to a settee pushed against the wall across from her desk. "Senator Saxton is still at lunch, but I expect him back shortly." She settles behind her desk and lets those nails fly across the typewriter keys.

I drum my fingers against the arm of the sofa, determined not to let it overwhelm me like the hallway did. Like I'm relearning to walk, I sink into its memories one fragment at a time. Fortunately, there are no darting shadows or dark, poisonous memories awaiting me. In fact, I don't see suspicious men lurking around the senator, or anyone breaking into his file cabinets—nothing of the sort. Only the rote daily office work I'd expect, of Anna and the senator and his many guests shuffling in and out of the office, digging through file cabinets, typing away at the desk. I glance toward Cindy, wondering if I dare ask her about our mission in front of the secretary, but she's busy melting a hole into the opposite wall with her gaze while she fiddles with something inside her purse.

"Oh! Jules," Donna exclaims to my right. "Let me see your

nails." Before I can give her a weird look, she clasps my hand in her own. *Check out the secretary*, she says, thoughts pressing against my shield while she pretends to study my ragged, unpainted nails. *Doesn't something seem off?*

Aside from her boobs sculpted like torpedoes by those awful "shaping brassieres" under her too-tight sweater, or her grin that tilts too readily into a smirk? The way she's effectively locked us out of any and all chance for conversation with her maniacal typewriter hammering?

I'm reading her thoughts, Donna says. *Do you know how to listen in?*

I nod, though it's been some time since I've done this, too. We peel back our shields just enough that I can peer into a portion of Donna's thoughts, linking into her psychic observations as she focuses on the secretary. I don't like the feeling—my hand in a near-stranger's, our thoughts snarled up together—but I need to reacquaint myself with this sensation, too.

The secretary's thoughts spill across the surface of her brain like an oil slick. She's worried about meeting her girlfriends after work and about impressing Dave, a junior staffer two offices down. Clack-click-clack; her words fall into a practiced tempo with the typewriter keys. She has five dollars budgeted for food and drinks until next paycheck. That leads her to thinking about the money she plans to send to her grandmother in San Juan and her mother in the Bronx. Each thought fits into the next with flawless precision: a tongue and groove custom-made.

But it's not how people think. It's ordered, precise, rehearsed. It's an effect like converting jumbled dictation into seamless sentences on the page.

Even in translation, it sounds completely and utterly false.

I glance up at Donna; she's already watching me expectantly, a single eyebrow arched. I close my mouth and manage a faint nod. My hands scrape back and forth on the couch, scrounging for more clues about Anna like they're loose change, but there's nothing except dim memories of her typing at the desk, or lighting cigarettes for lobbyists while they wait for the senator.

Donna bumps her knee against mine. *Time to show you what I can do.*

The moment Anna stops flogging the typewriter to flip over her page of handwritten notes, Donna leaps up and approaches the desk. "That's such a lovely manicure. Where do you go?"

I stand up, too, and hover behind them, feeling every bit the awkward wallflower I'm portraying as I hover on the edge of their conversation. I run my fingers up the corner of Anna's desk, sinking past the soft wood and into its memories. If Anna's using these flat, eerie thoughts as a shield, then someone must have trained her how to shield her true thoughts from people like us. Trained her to hide—something.

Streams of men, tall and fat and lanky and crusty, skin ranging from ghostly to overbaked but all of it perfectly set against their razor-edge suit collars. Anna flies around the room in her impossible heels. Coffee for this gentleman, sandwiches from the cart for that one, filing this and mailing that and typing yet another letter . . . She does all of it without complaint, without anything short of that smirking smile on her lips.

"Oh, you're from Puerto Rico? I hear it's just lovely this time of year," Donna continues. "How did you wind up in Washington?"

Inside the memories, Anna's thoughts remain a thin

veneer—always on point to whatever she's doing, utterly false, a highly effective shield. What is she trying to hide? I crawl my fingers onto the top of her desk and graze the face of a porcelain figure. It stares at me with gaudy doe eyes that offer up no more memories than what I've already seen. She's not slipping files into her purse when she leaves for the night or breaking into the senator's office. Her behavior is beyond reproach.

None of the men in the memories look dangerous, either—not in the shifty-eyed way we're looking for. There's danger in their words and tone of voice, of course, but it's the dangers of men with more money and power than sense. No foreign agents stealing documents, at least that I can tell—certainly not the kind that could rip someone's thoughts from their mind.

"Oh, that sounds like a gas!" Donna exclaims. "I've been looking for a diner near Dupont Circle . . ."

"Sure, it's good. That or the lunch counter down Pennsylvania," Anna says.

There—a memory frays at the corner of the past. Just one moment in time, but as she touched the desk in the memory, her thoughts looped against themselves, like she tried to patch them up and plaster them over. For just one second, the laugh track of her thought shield hiccupped, exposing itself as a lie.

The office door bursts open and Senator Saxton charges in. "Anna, where's my briefing packet from the Pentagon?"

"The courier won't bring it until you're here," Anna says. She turns to us with a practiced eyeroll. "He keeps forgetting I'm not authorized to handle classified documents."

I tense. If she doesn't have access to classified documents, then maybe I'm mistaken—she's not a valuable asset for a foreign spy to run. But someone's taught her to conceal her thoughts. If she can't steal intelligence for them, then what are they using her for?

"Your one o'clock appointment is here," Anna calls at the senator's back as he retreats into his inner office, then eyes us impatiently.

Senator Saxton backs out of his office. "Of course—I'm so sorry. Miss Conrad?" He steps up to Cindy and cradles her hand like he's afraid a proper handshake might shatter it. "So good to meet you in person. Hello, girls."

This close to Donna, I can feel the moment—feel it in the crackle of psychic power over her skin, hear it in the subtle shift of her shield—when she dons a new mask to contend with someone new. I wonder if her stiff behavior toward me is just another mask. "What an honor it is to meet you, Senator Saxton." She drops into a curtsey.

I nod and mumble a greeting, so he won't hear my Red Scare accent just yet.

"Please, step into my office." He holds open the door for us. "Anna, where are your manners? Go fetch some sandwiches for these ladies."

"Of course, senator," Anna chirps, and trots out of the office.

Once we're inside Saxton's inner office, Cindy locks the door and dumps out four aluminum boxes from her clutch, each of them about half the size of a cigarette box. She holds one finger up to her lips, looking right at me—presumably Donna and Saxton are already familiar with whatever ritual is about to take place. Then she walks the perimeter of the office, clicking a switch on each box and dropping one in each corner.

A hum bubbles up from the carpet. It itches at my arms like a dry patch of skin and fills the gaps of my thoughts like putty in a crack. I try to ease back in my chair, but the sensation prods me into discomfort, distracting like a low-grade fever.

Cindy smiles at me. "My own portable scrubber," she explains. "It deflects every type of psychic we know how to deflect with a series of electrical currents. We have psychic disrupters in the walls at headquarters, and your father's house, as well."

I never noticed, chalking the sensation up to living with two scrubbers, but I'm impressed. We didn't have protection like that in the KGB. "What does it do?"

She gestures to the box in each corner. "By stringing them together, I can make a circuit—like a fence—that keeps psychic powers in or out. Very little can pass through."

The screws inside me loosen by a fraction. I like knowing there are places Sergei can't look—here, at Headquarters, at Papa's home. But whether they'll keep me safe from this mole, if there is one, is another matter.

"So!" Cindy clasps her hands together. "We're still investigating the attempted break-in at your home, senator, as well as the other attacks on NATO delegates. We're going to need more information from you, however. As well as some . . . personal effects." She gives a slight nod toward me.

Saxton leans back in his chair, propping his chin on his fingers. "It's not enough you've got your suited gorillas combing every inch of my townhouse?"

"I guess I'm just confused, senator." Donna twists her ponytail around one finger. Her arm presses against mine and her shield parts, inviting me to link into her thoughts again. "The KGB playbook says that they attempt to recruit someone to spy for them first. Then, only if that doesn't work, that's when they resort to brute force."

I nearly choke on my own tongue—I've never heard about any such "playbook" before, and I was part of the damned KGB. I eye Donna, hoping my face doesn't look too incredulous.

Her expression is the picture of round-eyed innocence as she says, "But . . . you never reported that you'd been approached about spying for the Russians." And I realize that's exactly Donna's point. She knows that he *doesn't* know that. She just wants to get him thinking about any time he might possibly have been approached by someone who could have been an enemy spy—whether he reported it or not.

And it works. Through my link with Donna, we hear it in his wobbling musical shield, laying his thoughts bare for a split second, like a glimpse of a holstered gun under an agent's coat. When he says "Of course not," we know he's telling the truth.

Donna cracks her gum and leans away from me, breaking the link. "Oh, well. The Russkies are always changing up their tactics."

Cold. Ruthless. I thought I knew the meaning of those words when I worked for General Rostov. But I'm finding the translation carries subtle shifts, a cultural nuance that can't be matched up one to one. Perhaps even the same weapon can take a new form.

"Were you at the NATO convention in Brussels when Royal Admiral Jackson was attacked?" Cindy asks.

Saxton nods. "I was. Didn't get a good look at the woman, though." He eyes Donna and me warily. "I understand someone tried to interrupt a London meeting, as well, though I didn't see it for myself."

Cindy thins her lips like she's trying to keep any hint of emotion at bay. "What was being discussed at both of those meetings?"

"Let's see . . . Well, everyone's concerned about these rumors that Khruschev's about to get forced out. Word is, the Communist Party wants to replace him with someone more hardline. Our sources indicate Leonid Brezhnev, the current Chairman of the Supreme Soviet, is being groomed for the position."

I shiver involuntarily. Rostov would certainly approve of someone more willing to face the United States head first.

"Nobody's happy with the civil war in Vietnam, of course—the commie northerners have to be contained. We don't want the Red Tide sweeping even further across Asia, but we're not keen to fight another Korean War anytime soon. That was a waste of time and money and lives, and we ended up back where we started from." He sighs. "What else is there . . . ?"

Saxton drones on, discussing the minutiae of the NATO proceedings. I hear Cindy's and Saxton's banter as though I'm a remote viewer, watching through Yulia's eyes. The strife in Vietnam—Papa made a comment, the other day, that it's just the sort of situation a man like Rostov loves to exploit. The Viet Cong have taken a broken government and tried to piece it back together with blood-soaked red tape. When Rostov sunk his claws into my mind, I saw his lust for strife and for the glory he thought could only come from a world consumed in the Soviet ideals. Wherever revolutionaries seek power, Rostov's shadow is sure to stretch behind them.

"Yulia? Can you read the courier's documents?"

I glance around the table—they've been carrying on and I fell behind. Me—they're talking about me.

"Maybe you can glean something from the documents—see if someone's been pursuing them—"

Her words dissolve into a static buzz like the disrupters she placed. We're grasping for answers, hunting for these scrubbers. They want me to hunt for them by sifting through layers and layers of red tape, one shadow-thin coating of a memory at a time—

"Senator Saxton." I sit upright as all eyes snap to me. Like my improper outfit, there's no use in hiding who I am or what I'm doing. I might as well wear it with pride. "Your secretary—has she been trained in mental shielding?"

"*Yes*," Donna says, as if she was just going to make this point herself. "*We* noticed something odd—"

"Of course we didn't train her." Saxton's gaze fixes on me as he speaks, like now that my accent has revealed me as the outsider, he must keep me in sight at all times or I'll vanish into the night. "She doesn't know enough to warrant it—she doesn't have a clearance or anything. If we train too many folks, they become targets."

I take a deep breath. If I'm wrong, I might undo all my efforts to become a part of this team, but I have to take that risk. I have to stop these scrubbers. I look the senator square in the eye. "Then who did?"

Senator Saxton gapes at me. "Young lady, you're not seriously suggesting I've been harboring a spy in my own office—"

The locked door handle rattles. "It's Anna! I have your sandwiches!"

"Wait," I say, though Cindy's already halfway standing. I need to prove it to him—to everyone. "Please. Let me see if I am right. Donna, can you listen to her thoughts from here?"

Donna throws me the sort of withering look I imagine she's thrown many a would-be suitor. "Of course I can."

"Good. What about you, Cindy?"

She hesitates, mouth open. "My powers don't quite work that way, but—"

"Well, if you can, listen closely." I force a smile to rival Cindy's. "Trust me."

Cindy unlocks the door for Anna. Anna works around the table, depositing wrapped sandwiches, plastic utensils, and uncapped glass bottles of Coca-Cola with vicious precision. When she reaches me, though, I swing my hand wide as I grab my bottle, setting it on a trajectory to spill all over her fuzzy sweater.

Anna shrieks as the brown syrup sloshes onto her stomach—but as my arm swings against her, her circuit loop of thoughts keeps rolling. Not so much as a blip of panic as she rights the bottle before it can spill further. She grabs for the napkins as her thoughts complete the sentence.

Pause.

One, two, three.

And then, her thoughts acknowledge what happened, carefully controlled and fully worded, where any other person's thoughts would be skittering like a seismograph's needle in an earthquake.

Or on a lie detector test.

Donna, Cindy, and I all stare at Anna—I don't know the exact nature of Cindy's powers yet, but there's no way she could have missed that eerie, inhuman wave of thought. Anna slows her frantic dabbing at her sweater until her measured motions match the steady beat of her thoughts. Then she stops altogether.

She looks around the table at us, soaked napkin slipping out of her fingers.

And runs from the room.

CHAPTER 8

BY THE TIME the phone operators connect Senator Saxton with the building security desk, Anna is long gone, and Cindy and Saxton both occupy about three telephones each while they coordinate phone calls with the Capitol Police, the CIA, Saxton's protective detail, the FBI agents combing through his house, and other assorted entities, agencies, and personalities.

Donna and I sit at the conference table, waiting for the adults to finish talking/shouting/screaming into their octopus collection of phone receivers. I'm buzzing with frantic energy. But we can do nothing until orders trickle down from above. Following the rules—like Valentin and I agreed, like Winnie reprimanded. But each time one of the phones lined up on Saxton's desk rings, we both jump, muscles firing like pistons to launch us into action.

"So, Jules." Donna fidgets with her jewelry. "You know, it's okay to, like, talk. You don't have to pretend you're a statue."

I give her a granite stare. She only ever seems at ease when she's filling a perfectly good silence with the sound of her own voice. "What am I meant to discuss?"

"The weather, or what you're thinking about, or—or anything, really, is better than sitting there looking like you think I'm gonna pull a knife on you." She smiles, lopsided. "Are all you Russians so unemotional?"

"Why would we show our emotions?" I ask.

She groans and bonks her head back against the wall. "This is what I mean! Okay, I know how to get you talking." Her grin twists into my ribs. "Tell me all about you and Valentin. How did you two meet?"

And she wonders why we Russians don't share much of ourselves. "When we were both prisoners of the KGB," I say.

"Oh. Right." Donna shuts up for a minute, but then she's at me again, prying me with a new conversational tactic like I'm a lock she's trying to pick. I wonder what she's trying to pry out of my mind. "It must be great being back with your dad again, huh? My *father*—" she draws it out, like she's suddenly affecting a British drawl—"is a movie producer in Hollywood. I hardly ever get to see him now that I'm on the opposite coast."

"What about your mother?" I ask. If she'd rather talk about herself, then I'd rather not field unanswerable questions.

Donna's gaze sinks down to her hand. "Oh, she's around enough. You know—here and there."

Thankfully, Cindy interrupts our conversational stalemate, sinking into the chair across from us with a sigh. She pops open her clutch and pulls a slender deck of cards. They're not playing cards, but have strange illustrations on the faces unlike any playing cards I've seen. "A moment, girls, before we go." After shuffling the cards, she fans them out faceup on the table and drums her nails. I can hear her blues song through the table, though it's nearly swallowed up in the electrical currents' static, like a distant radio station. After a long moment she selects one from the heap.

"Four of wands," she says to no one in particular. She pinches the bridge of her nose, then stuffs the cards back into her clutch and turns to Senator Saxton. "Sorry, senator. It would appear that I'll need a few more favors from you."

He groans. "I have to sleep in a hotel room under armed guard tonight because of your damned meddling as it is. What more could you possibly want from me?"

Cindy's smile doesn't so much as twitch. "Miss Willoughsby here will conduct an interview with each and every member of the American NATO delegation, starting tomorrow morning. Tell them she's your niece and she's writing an article for her school paper. Tell them she's the queen of England, I don't care—just don't tell them she works for us."

Saxton groans. "All right. I'll make it happen."

After he all but shoves out the door, Cindy hisses a few terse words to a burly pair of men stationed farther down the hall, who must be Saxton's armed guards. They had no way of knowing that his secretary had become a wanted spy when she fled past them. Cindy's fingers tremble as she wrestles with her clutch's clasp.

"Are you all right?" I ask her.

"Never better."

She presses her hand to my forearm as she leads us down the

hall. A shudder courses through me as if I've taken a swig of spoiled milk. A skeleton, astride a pale gray horse, trots down the hallway toward us in stuttering steps, a putrid fog following it like a shadow. One moment, it's there, then it winks out, only to return a moment later. A lightning bolt sears through my mind. It strikes a castle, its pearly sides hidden in a dense fog. The images evaporate as Cindy lifts her hand away.

"Is this what you see?" I ask Cindy, keeping my voice low. "Is this your ability?"

"I'm—" Cindy trips over herself. "I think that we . . ." She straightens her hat and strides into the harsh spring afternoon. White burns off the sidewalk and the marble buildings all around us, scorching the shadowy images from my eyes. I yank open the passenger door to Cindy's car and slide onto the sticky seat beside her, leaving Donna alone in the backseat.

"What does it mean?" I ask. "What kind of psychic are you?"

Cindy props her elbows on the steering wheel, cradles her face in those perfect dainty gloves, and lets out a wretched sob, squeaking like a wet sponge on tile. When she sits back up, black mascara and rouge smear her gloves' knuckles. Cindy swallows, then turns to me with sudden exhaustion in her face. Is this her unmasked state? Suddenly, I can see what tremendous work every moment of the day has been for her up to this point, how hard she fights to become flawless, cheerful, precise. Because now every last ounce of it has drained away, leaving a weary woman barely older than Donna and me.

"I'm afraid we may be too late."

"Have you lost your mind?" The voice of Frank Tuttelbaum, the PsyOps team chief, carries straight through the door of his closed office to the break room where Valya and I sit. "We can't launch a manhunt for this secretary on the suspicions of a couple of teenagers and your stupid cards!"

"How can he not think there's a threat?" Valentin asks me in Russian. He slips both of his hands around one of mine and turns it over, tracing my veins with a calm melody.

"Great question. Anna's scrubbed-clean apartment was, what's the phrase?" I switch to English. "The icing on the cake." I wince, remembering our stop at the cramped basement flat on our way back to CIA headquarters. Nothing looked out of place through the windows, but as soon as I touched the door handle, I knew there was no point looking inside—we would find no memories, nothing but abrasive emptiness. A scrubber had already purged it clean. Leave it for the FBI to comb through for physical evidence.

"Did Cindy mention seeing anything? With her powers, I mean," Valya says.

"She showed me something, but I didn't understand it." I rest my head on his shoulder, feeling myself melt into him with sudden-onset exhaustion. "What is she, anyway?"

"I think she's like Larissa—she can see the future, or a probable version of it. But it's not straightforward with all the possibilities laid out, like Larissa's was." His voice hitches on that past tense, that syntactical euphemism, and I find myself flinching, too. We still don't know what happened to her after she stayed behind in East Berlin while Valya and I escaped, but we have to assume the worst. "I think Cindy's vision of the future is symbolic. Murky."

My mother has the same kind of power, though I don't know what form hers takes. If she shrugs it off, like Larissa did, or dives into it with a deep breath, like Cindy.

There's a lot I don't know about my mother. A lot I've forgotten.

Valentin presses his lips to my temple before speaking. "It feels as if hardly any of us have a firm grasp on our gifts. We're always fighting through the murk and grayness."

"And the ones who are confident in it, like Papa, perhaps shouldn't be." What changed in Papa? Has he been stripped down like a clarified solution, burning away everything that hid this part of him? Or has something so potent been added that it overtakes all the rest?

Valentin grimaces. "I don't want to end up like that, Yul."

"Like Papa? No. You treat your power with respect." Rather, he treats it like a massive dog on a too-small leash: with extreme caution. "I've never seen you exploit it without good reason."

He shakes his head, red flashing on his cheeks. "You don't know the temptation to meddle that's always lurking, the power . . . It's always a struggle, Yul. It's exhausting."

"But doesn't it get easier?" I ask. "You're always working at it." I rub my hands together, unthinking; practice, control, yes, these are important, and I've neglected them for too long. But Valya has Papa to instruct him, despite the dubious source. I have no guide, no instruction manual.

"It never feels like enough." Valya shakes his head. "It's always there, pulling at me, coaxing me to twist the world to my favor. I'd rather be without my abilities entirely than surrender myself to them. I don't want to be like—like Rostov."

Or like Papa, I can't help but think, though Valentin would never say it. "I wouldn't let you lose control like that. I'll steady you." I try to smile, but it feels false and creaky. Valya's always serious, but rarely this heavy, this raw. I don't know how to balance him out. I suppose psychic emotions aren't the only kind of emotions I'm clueless about.

"You wouldn't let me?" He buries his nose in my hair; his breathing is slow, but I feel the nervous energy crackling along the surface of his skin, the fear of another sleepless night. "I wish it were that easy. What I worry is that 'letting' me has nothing to do with it."

Mole. Sergei's word rings through me, taunting and blunt. What Rostov did to Valentin—whatever left his mind raw and seeping—what if he found some way to control Valentin, even from here?

No. It's a ridiculous thought, one I don't want to entertain. I should tell Valentin about Sergei's warning. He'll know what to do; he'll know who we can trust; he'll tell me not to fret and that Sergei only wanted to throw me off balance. It's what I need to hear. But the what-if spreads like a rash, demanding to be itched.

"Behave yourselves, my little *hooligani*," Papa says as he struts past us. "English, too, please!" He throws open the door to Frank Tuttelbaum's office with a cheery whistle on his lips. "Still no signs of Anna. She's spooked enough to really run."

Tuttelbaum's and Cindy's chairs screech against the linoleum. "Get inside," Tuttelbaum shouts. "And close the goddamned door."

"I think this concerns the whole team," Papa counters, the cheery melody still laced through his tone.

"Watch it, Andrei, you're still on thin ice with me after that horsecrap you pulled in Moscow and Berlin."

I raise an eyebrow. Did Papa disobey orders by rescuing Valya and me? He'd hinted at it, but I thought surely the value in stealing two more psychics from the KGB was more than enough to outweigh the risk. Is he still being chastised for it?

"Be that as it may," Cindy says, "we'll find her sooner if we involve the whole PsyOps team."

There is a long moment of hesitation, then Cindy and Tuttelbaum emerge with Papa. Frank Tuttelbaum is short and compact, almost like he's the product of a genetic experiment to design the most efficient *homo sapiens*; dark sideburns frame his etched and tanned face. He's not a psychic himself, but powerful enough to be placed in charge of all of us. "All right, everyone, gather around. We've got a situation."

Situation. Some euphemisms transcend language.

Donna stops chatting with the two boys at the corner of the room, one lanky with fiery red hair, the other olive-skinned, tossing his gaze every which way as if looking for unseen assailants. *Judd and Antonio,* Valentin tells me, hand still on mine, *though he prefers Tony.* Marylou was sprawled on the floor, but she squashes her clove cigarette into an ashtray and sits up with a groggy blink. Al Sterling clasps his hands behind his back and stands at attention. The small gesture, so effortlessly echoing a military training, reminds me of Winnie. Winnie. Where is she? My throat tightens up as I scan the room for her and come up empty.

Papa pops his hands into his jacket pockets and leans back against the wall. "Anna Montalban, secretary to Senator Saxton and a recruited spy—"

"*Suspected* spy," Tuttelbaum corrects.

"—has gone on the run after Yulia and Donna determined that someone, probably an enemy agent, had trained her how to shield her thoughts. Given the recent targeting of Senator Saxton and other NATO representatives, it's very likely someone recruited her to provide them with access to Saxton."

"Thank you for that summary, Andrei." Tuttelbaum makes no attempt to turn Papa's name into anything remotely Russian sounding. "Marylou—start projecting to all the known commie beatnik clubs in the District. If she's running in the usual crowds, I wager she'll turn up at one of them."

Cindy bats her eyes to interrupt him, the way some people might raise their hands. "I beg your pardon, chief, but I don't think a trained agent—and Anna *has* been trained—is working with the 'usual crowd' of harmless beatniks you insist on watching like a hawk."

"Harmless? You think Jack Kerouac's harmless, him and all his drug-addled pinko friends? A bunch of agents provocateurs, mark my words."

Cindy's smile pulls tighter. "It's one thing to write poetry griping about capitalism while playing drums and smoking reefer. It's quite another to wage an elaborate plot against the entire North Atlantic Treaty Organization."

Tuttelbaum and Cindy glower back and forth while I sort through the unfamiliar terms. Reefer—some sort of drug, I'm pretty sure; I've seen posters warning against its dangers. Beatniks—those cool cats who dress in black and snap their fingers at the jazz lounges Valya and I frequent. Pinko—pink—a watered-down communist?

"It's still worth checking into," Tuttelbaum says, with a look toward Cindy like a guillotine dropping to cut off any protest.

"I think they're horrible people," Donna pipes up. "I'd be happy to help, too, Mister Tuttelbaum."

Tuttelbaum waves her off with his hand. "Nah, this is a job for the men. A tough job." Donna opens her mouth to protest, but he keeps going. "Tony and Valentine, you'll go with Andrei to check into Anna's circle of friends. We want to know who she went steady with, if any of the guys gave off a creepy foreign vibe, whatever seems relevant. And check out that sob story about the grandma back in San Juan. I'd bet my hat our little secretary is from goddamned Cuba, not Puerto Rico."

"Good luck, *Valentine*," I whisper, nudging him with my shoulder. He rolls his eyes as he climbs to his feet.

"Donna, Judd, Al, you're going to make friends with the commies we've already got locked up. See if they know Anna or who she's working with." Tuttelbaum rubs his hands together, as though he's ready to dive into a feast. "Work fast and we can still be home for dinner."

"What about me?" I ask, glancing around the room. Did I miss my name?

"If they've got a grade-A scrubber working with them, then I don't think you're going to be of much use, tsarina. We'll bring you in once we start pinpointing locations and collecting evidence." He draws his shoulders to his ears—for a moment, the gesture reminds me of Sergei, and his Russian shrug of surrender and acceptance—then he storms back into his office and slams the door.

I stare at the thick whorls of wood on his office door, waiting for my heart to stop knocking against my ribs. Useless. No, I am worse than useless—I have a power, but it's been neutralized, because they scrubbed away any possible memories that I could find. Even the items Cindy showed me this morning took all of my ability to glean anything useful from them.

"Are you all right?" Cindy Conrad sits down beside me, her face a convincing mask of pity: eyebrows drawn down, lips tiny and twisted. Like everything else about her, it feels deliberate. "I promise we'll have work for you soon."

But that scares me even more—objects full of that angry desert of white, stinging sand when I try to look past the scrubbers' noise, eroding my thoughts as I fight to see through the storm. "What about you?" I ask. "Aren't they sending you off somewhere?"

Her expression pinches. "My talents don't always work on command."

I laugh hoarsely. I thought the same about mine, another lifetime ago, when I was a scared little girl trading goods on the black market to feed my fugitive family. Back then, my power was a fluke, just a whisper and a glance of memories. I didn't know about the danger and the power—the pain pushing from my fingertips like an electric shock.

Cindy's gaze darts to Frank's office door. "I'm sorry if the chief upset you. I know he's curt, but he has a lot of experience working the Soviet mission. He was chief of station in Moscow for seven years—quite an honor. He helped bring your father over, too. They were great pals."

I try and fail to imagine any situation in which Papa's personality and the blustery man's I just witnessed might possibly work together. "My father was a different man back then."

"I'll say." Cindy grins wider. "You know, your father's very proud of you."

I tilt my head, catching a thread of her lilac perfume, as flawless as it smelled first thing this morning. I'm sure the day has caked itself onto me with sweat and Marylou's cigarettes, but Cindy's still ever fresh. "What makes you think that?"

"You're all he could talk about when he first came to us. How quick you were in school, how you took care of your brother, your 'science experiments' . . ." She makes little quotation marks in the air with her fingers, and laughs. "He may not show it, but he's thrilled to have you back with him. I don't think we ever would have taken the risk on pursuing the *Veter 1* plans if he hadn't insisted. All for a chance at finding you."

Is she sure we're talking about the same Andrei Chernin? Papa has barely even hugged me in weeks. He calls to me when he comes home from the bars—on the occasions when I'm still awake—like I'm a pet dog, but by the time I creep downstairs he's passed out on the couch.

"He tells me you and Winnie have been translating a number of genetics research papers," she continues. "He actually contacted the Georgetown genetics professor, who agreed to let you work in his lab for the rest of the spring and summer, and then you can enroll as a college freshman in the fall." She tilts her head. "Of course, it's your choice."

I stare at her as if she's just offered me a spot on the next Gemini flight. A deadly, rare, incredible opportunity. I hadn't much considered my future since we made it to America—I was too busy trying to catch up to the present, the language, the culture.

But part of me is desperate to pursue my lifelong dream of mastering genetics, just like my mother.

The other part is terrified of becoming just like my mother.

"I'd love to," I say, wrestling the scared part of me back.

Cindy hops up. "Perfect. I'll let Professor Stokowski know. But I think you've worked hard enough for today. Go dig through my record collection, if you want. Don't worry too much about Anna—I promise, we'll find her soon."

She promises. I watch Cindy sway away on her heels, all confidence and sunlight. I wonder how she can promise a thing like that—how any of us can. Sergei's warning weighs on me, threatening to crack and shatter me. If he's telling the truth, regardless of his motive, then the mole could be any one of my teammates, and trusting the wrong person could mean losing it all.

CHAPTER 9

I AWAKEN WITH A SCREAM, my throat already dry and my nerves leaning eagerly, ready for action, so much so that it's several seconds before I realize the scream is not my own. I'm already standing, bare feet on springy wood floors. Where am I? I blink away the fuzz of sleep from my vision. A hulking piano to my left; a blanket pooling at my feet. I must've fallen asleep in the conservatory. That's right. Valentin was practicing different jazz riffs for open mic night, and I curled up to listen to him while I puzzled through Sergei's warning, safely ensconced in our disruptor-shielded Russian enclave in the heart of Georgetown. I must have fallen asleep, and Valya covered me with the blanket.

Another scream. It's not coming from me. I bolt up the stairs, passing Papa's room on the second floor (door flung open, empty), swinging around to the next flight, cresting it to the third floor, where Valentin's and my bedrooms are. Valentin is wedged into the far corner of his bed, a crust of salt along one cheek and his raw, jagged scream collapsing into a whimper under its own weight. I coil around him like a compression blanket. "*Tikho, tikho*," I urge him in Russian, though I have no idea if he can actually hear me right now. It can take minutes for his nightmares to break and recede.

He curls into my embrace for a moment, then pries back one of my hands, studies it, then drops it. "She's burning up," he tells me. "It's never enough."

I wince. We've lingered at the start of this trail before. None of my usual questions ever succeed in coaxing him down the path, so I stay silent.

"She never meant—" He slurps down air. "She wouldn't want Boris or anyone else to know—"

Boris, yes; Boris Sorokhin. Valentin's father. A Communist Party member who once lived along the gilded Kutuzovsky Prospekt in Moscow's heart, in a sprawling apartment, where he drank high-grade vodka with generals and ministers while little Valya entertained them with his piano wizardry. Past tense, Valya was always very clear on that point, though I don't know what brought an end to it. The usual reasons, I suppose—maybe he fell out of favor with the party. Maybe he was found to be a traitor or a dissident or a miscreant or just plain irritating, and was sent to the Siberian prison camps, or else a tiled basement with a drain in the floor.

Valya shudders, once, sharp, then goes limp in my arms. Now that the adrenaline is working its way out of my bloodstream, I can hear and sense his shield more clearly, and I feel the moment when it changes from noise to signal: from a shotgun torrent of scrubber-flavored pain to a constant hum, his musical shield threaded along its central note. I let those same melodies course along my skin, but I'm careful to hold my fear and concern and, if I'm being completely honest, irritation inside of me like a held breath. I'm a two-way valve of emotion, and I can't risk burdening Valya any further.

"Yulia." He leans back from me, head bumping against the wall. "*Bozhe moi.* I'm so sorry. Again." One hand flops against his nightstand until it lands on his glasses. "Sleeping pills. I'll take them tomorrow night—I promise." He closes his eyes for a moment, but then he opens them again, without meeting mine. "Yulia, I want to ask you something, but I . . . I'm not sure how."

There is a pulse thudding between us, and I'm not sure whether it's his or mine. I miss this—this closeness, this heat between us that evaporates my fear. I catch my lower lip in my teeth and feel my skin melting into his. "You can ask me anything."

He nods, smiling to himself, like he's embarrassed of his own foolishness. "It's about what you did in Berlin." He traces a slow circle on my arm. "Your hands. Pushing out all those emotions . . ."

And like that, our heartbeats fall back out of sync. I back away, suddenly aware of the impropriety of me being here, in this warm and sweat-dampened bed, though I come here more nights than not. *What would Papa think?* asks the voice in the back of my mind. Then I realize the question's absurdity. If Papa were home already, which he clearly is not because he is off somewhere doing whatever maddening things I'm afraid to know about, he wouldn't possibly care.

Valya clears his throat. "I wondered if it could work in reverse. If you could draw away the pain from me."

I stare at my palms, curled around my legs, imagining there is a beast inside them, just waiting to open its jaws. What he says makes sense, but where would I put these things? I'd draw them into me, but would they stay there, lurking under my skin? Pacing like a caged animal?

He bows his head, cheeks darkening. "I'm sorry. It's too much to ask."

"No. It isn't that." I jerk my knee away from him. Suddenly the heat of my own skin is unbearable to me. "But what if I— What if it doesn't work that way—?"

The look he gives me makes me want to melt. Makes me want to give in. But there are holes in my memories that I'll never recover. I can't just fill them with Valya's pain.

His hand hovers near my shoulder, like he's deliberating between clapping my shoulder or pulling me into an embrace. "There's something else troubling you."

I can't suppress the bitter laugh that bubbles out of me. What isn't troubling me? I study Valya through the fog of exhaustion. I can't tell Valya about Sergei's warning, not yet. It's not that I think Valya's the mole—not willingly, anyway. But what if, when Rostov ripped open the wound in Valya's thoughts, he left something else behind?

"Maybe," I say, my mouth thick with sleep. "Maybe it could work. Do you remember what you did for me on the train?"

He nods with a wince. "I helped you recover some of your memories that your father suppressed. I could have permanently damaged your mind. This is different. What if you could just draw out the emotions, not the memories themselves?"

Every now and then, I stumble upon another gap in my brain

where the past ought to be, and I wonder whether it's another memory scratched out by my father, or something I've simply forgotten. "So I wouldn't be trying to recover your memories. Just ease them—remove whatever these strong emotions are you've attached to them."

He watches me for a few moments, expressionless. "Like you did to the Hound. Drawing out his emotions."

"Right. But without the—the using them against you part." I smile weakly, but neither of us finds it funny.

Valentin's hand hovers near my shoulder, wanting to land on me, but he pulls away. "There are things that should have stayed forgotten, Yulia. I'd managed to keep them buried for years. But now they've been dug up and it's unbearable."

"I want to try." My voice wavers as I stare into his glinting glasses lenses. If the resurgence of Valya's memories is part of Rostov's plan—if he's somehow been turned into a mole, I have to try. I won't let Valya be made into Rostov's unwilling tool.

He stretches his fingers wide, sucking in a deep breath. "Just a moment," he says. "Please, only a moment. If it's too much—if it hurts you at any point—"

"I'll stop. I promise." I swallow hard. "I want to help you."

"I know. I trust you. It's myself I can't be sure of."

We lock our fingers together. Our pulses thud against each other, and we breathe at the same pace. At first, all I hear is Valya's shield, dense layers of Dave Brubeck jazz, and our shared Beatles song all marbled together, but note by note, it stretches like a knitted scarf, until I'm able to slip through the gaps.

Waves lap against a distant shore. Breathe in. The waves crash. Breathe out. The waves retreat, foamy fingers clawing uselessly at the sand as they slip away. The sun has already melted into the sea and only its afterimage hangs above the horizon, orange and pink and increasingly navy, salted with bright stars. I breathe in and out, inhabiting Valentin. We dig our bare toes into the sand, letting it slurp around our feet. Our legs are already salt-stained and smeared from a long day of running through the surf.

"The Black Sea is a gift from God, meant just for the Georgian people," a woman's voice says. "Sometimes it is the only way we have to cool down."

I want to smile at her words—I know the wet roast of southern Russian summers all too well—but a different emotion stirs in Valentin. He tenses his stomach like he's bracing for a blow.

"We have to cool down, Valya," the woman continues, from somewhere behind us. "We have to wash this out."

A new smell cuts through the briny air. It smells like burning meat.

Valentin's fear floods through me as an arm wraps around our waist. It's too hot to the touch, like it's been left in the sun far too long. He's a tiny boy still—this woman slings him effortlessly into the air and tucks him under her arm. He's screaming. His skin crackles with terror—my skin. My bones. The terror of eyes squeezed too tight and lungs that won't fill with air. I try to breathe in, but my lungs are on fire and my nose is filled with that awful charred smell—

Valya rips his hand away from me as his musical shield snaps back shut. "Enough." Some of the white-edged fear has left his eyes, but concern twists the corners of his mouth. "That's—that's all I can do for now—"

I gasp for fresh air, but everything tastes stale and moist, and

I can't find a way to *breathe* through it, I can't seem to get the air through my lungs and into my blood. My skull is too tight against my brain. Little Valentin's screams are ringing in my ears. His fear is racing through my veins. Everywhere I look is dark, crushing me with emptiness, a heavy, bloating thing.

"You must learn to let go, little girl. You can't carry all these burdens on your own." Papa is leaning in the doorway to Valya's room. "I'd hate to have to erase you again, just to keep you safe from your own foolishness."

And then he is reaching through the air with his thoughts. His mind pushes into mine like a puppeteer. Air rushes back into my lungs. The terror drains away; the memory turns inchoate, like a faint dream. Whatever I was feeling and thinking before has turned to smoke and drifted away, and I'm left with a clammy sweat, a sense like I've walked into a room and forgotten what I came for.

"Well?" Papa asks me, folding his arms across his chest. His hair is raked back, stiffened with sweat and dried in unnatural whorls. "Are you pleased with yourself?" He tilts his head toward Valentin. "Took away an ounce of his pain to give yourself a pound?"

Valentin and I exchange a look. He looks pretty relaxed for a boy who's been caught in bed with a girl (by her father, no less); some nameless fear lingers over my shoulder, but I can't remember what brought it on. I'm not entirely sure how I came to this moment, in fact—one moment I'm whispering with Valentin, and the next—the next, Papa is looming in the doorway—

I grit my teeth and stare back at Papa. "Pleased with myself about what?" I ask. "I don't even know what I've done! You're always ripping my memories away from me!"

"It's for the best. You could have gotten yourself killed." Papa's face is eased, but there's a tension to his words as he looks at me. I feel emptied out; I can't gauge how serious he is. "You don't understand what you're capable of. You'll never understand."

I clench my hand around a fistful of sheets. "Maybe because you take that understanding from me every time you erase parts of my mind."

"It was for your own good. It took me twenty years to control my power, don't you see? They aren't static. They grow alongside us, and if you push too hard without mastering them, you'll hurt yourself." Again, those icy fingers sink into my brain; against my will, my head twists to face Papa. His face is like marble in the moonlight, hard and only a false attempt at portraying emotion. "You are a child still. You are toying with things you cannot possibly understand, and you would rather kill yourself than show a little common sense!"

If I didn't feel so drained right now, I'd be yelling at him. Pointing out how unfair he's being, what a hypocrite he is when he obviously had to learn to control his powers from somewhere, and how dare he try to make his point by using his powers on *me*. I'd be shaking with the urge to weep that this is what it takes to get my father's attention.

But I am so empty, like the fear I leeched from Valentin has burned clean through me like rubbing alcohol. Papa forced it all away from me.

"Get some sleep," Papa says, leaning back from the door frame. "Both of you. You'll need your rest for tomorrow."

I nod, numbly, and stagger to my feet. Whether it's Papa directing me or my own will, I couldn't say; I feel nothing as I plod down the hall and collapse into bed, too exhausted for words and thought.

But I'm no closer to understanding the nature of Valentin's injury; the answer to the questions humming like a disrupter under the surface of all my thoughts. Is there a mole, and if so, who? Papa, with his hateful threats and casual comfort with taking control? Valentin, and whatever dark secret lies in the waves of his wounded thoughts? Or any of the other PsyOps team members, whose motivations and secrets I can't begin to sift from the foreign, surreal faces they present to me. I'm no closer to grasping the answer, but as I drift off, Anna Montalban's face stares back at me, laughing, victorious. One thing is for certain: our adversary has grown far cleverer than we've ever before seen.

CHAPTER 10

FRANK TUTTELBAUM IS A FORCE of nature in the PsyOps office, and this morning, he's pacing in front of us with all the calm of a hurricane. "Not a single hint?" he roars. "Not one imbecile in the lounge or the jail knows anything about this woman?"

Marylou stubs out her cigarette with a sigh. "She's a ghost, man. She disappeared."

Frank lurches to a stop in front of Marylou. His eyes tighten like a spotlight on her; his face is as red-raged as a Disney cartoon character. I'm waiting for the steam to shoot from his ears. "I was chief of Moscow station for seven years, sweetheart. The Russian target's the toughest nut to crack there is. But nobody, and I mean *no*body, just disappears like that. There has to be some kind of trail you bozos are missing."

Cindy drums her fingers against a pair of cards spread before her. "If I may, sir . . ."

But Frank is on a roll now. I don't catch all his words, but I get the general idea: incompetent, fools, should have never let women like Cindy and Donna and me work in the field. I glance at Valya, but he's stone-faced, as if this outburst is no surprise. Another day on the PsyOps team.

"Six of Pentacles, inverted." Cindy cuts into Frank's rant. "Anna is probably confused, lost, running out of options. We just have to keep digging until we can find where she'll be vulnerable."

"She mentioned a diner in Dupont Circle that she goes to a lot." Donna smoothes her glare into a cloying smile for Frank. "We could ask around there."

Judd shakes his head. "But what about Senator Saxton? Shouldn't we be worried about him?"

I squeeze my hands together, one palm warring against the other, tension rolling back and forth. Someone here could be actively trying to sabotage us, if Sergei's to be believed, though we certainly seem to be doing a good job of sabotaging ourselves, whether intentional or not.

"Or maybe there's, like, a secret underground lair where all the commies hang out," Marylou says. "Like in the James Bond movies."

We have less than nothing, because we once had a trail and we lost it. I try to quiet the pounding in my head as they bicker back and forth, tossing out more and more ludicrous conspiracies. My mind is scraped raw with half-remembered fragments of last night—trying to help Valentin with his pain. Fearing Rostov had made a mole out of him. Papa, forcing me to stop. He took something from me—yet again, he found it easier to erase the past than dredge it up, examine it, accept the results, no matter how cruel. Whatever insight I'd glimpsed at in Valentin's mind is lost, and Papa's keeping the peace once more in his own selfish way.

Frank's shouting, pointing—he's giving out more assignments. Valya, Cindy, and Judd are to retrace Saxton's steps and question his neighbors about the recent break-ins; Al, Donna, and Tony will interview the other NATO delegates. "Marylou and Yulia." Frank scratches at the steel-wool stubble on his chin. "Get some practice in. Lord knows you two numbskulls need it."

Unless Papa's not doing it for himself at all, but for Rostov, the longest spy game imaginable to infiltrate the Americans—no. *Bozhe moi*, Yulia. You can't let Sergei knot up your thoughts like this. Either there is a mole or there isn't, but I can't be distracted. I have to stop Rostov. I have to save Mama—

"Yul. Hey." Frank snaps his fingers in front of my face. "Speaking to you here. Do I need to get Sergeant Davis?"

I wrestle back my first acrid response and force a smile to my face. "No, sir. I understand you."

"You know how to work with remote viewers? Linking into their thoughts?" he asks.

"Yes."

Frank snorts. "Well, time for you to learn the next step. Marylou?"

Smoke weaves out of Marylou's nostrils and mouth. "Yeah, yeah, don't be a cube. I'll show her how it works." She stubs out her cigarette and beckons me back toward the girls' room. "Exciting first week, huh, Jules?"

"Maybe too exciting." I settle into a nest of pillows while

Marylou finds a new record to play. Harmonicas breeze along as a man and woman sing about deep purple fogs. "What is this next step?"

Marylou flops onto the pillows beside me. "Ready for me to knock your socks off?" She grins. "Are we close enough for you to read me?"

I fold my arms across my chest so they aren't against hers. It's faint, but I can hear her thoughts humming, lazy and unselfconscious. I scoot back across the floor until the sound retreats. "Now I can't."

"Good. You've let a remote viewer in your head before, right?"

I nod carefully, trying not to let myself think about the alleged mole. I have to clear my mind if I'm going to let Marylou in. Then, in a flash, Marylou's thoughts knock up against mine. I pry back my shield enough to share thoughts with her.

Good job. Now for the fun part. Try looking back through my mind—like we're linking our powers.

I don't like this—I much prefer keeping our powers separated by barriers as thick as aquarium glass. This is how a scrubber takes control of someone even if they're trained to repel them; peeling back some of my shield is how a mole might gain the upper hand. Sergei and I did something similar, back in Moscow. I learned then that distance wasn't always enough to protect me from Rostov's hate. I close my eyes and press back, tentative, waiting for Marylou's syrupy shield to soak me up.

I slip into her mind. Now it's as if I'm hovering just above her, seeing the room from where she lies. "So this is how you view."

She giggles. *Pretty much. It gets trippier, though. Get up and walk to the other side of the room.*

I stagger to my own feet, fighting to bring my vision back into where I'm standing instead of where Marylou is, but it takes some effort to swap between Marylou's sight and my own. With Sergei, once I'd linked into his sight, I generally stayed in his viewing until our mission was finished. From Marylou's sight, I see myself wobble and nearly trip over a box of files.

Watch it, cat, you are slated for crashville. Not as easy as it looks, huh? I catch sight of her grinning. *Switch to your sight when you're moving around until you get the hang of it.*

All right. I align my sight, keeping her thoughts back in reserve in my mind. *So this is it? I can see through your viewing, and you can use me to scout ahead?*

It gets even better. Through Marylou's sight, I catch a flicker of movement. *I've got something in my hands. Go around the corner, then reach back through my mind to where I am and see if you can read the memories off of it.*

Ah, yes—I've done something similar with Sergei, before, when Rostov forced me to help him examine memories beyond a locked door. But I'd done it while physically touching Sergei. This makes sense to me as the next step, but the nerves inside me frazzle all the same. I weave through the curtained maze, keeping Marylou's viewing in the back of my head.

What're you waitin' for? Marylou asks. *Go on. Show me what you got. We need you to be able to cycle easily between my viewing and your own sight.*

I plunge back into Marylou's vantage point—the sensation's

dizzying, spinning my mind unsteadily like a top about to fall over. The record music slinks into the vision; the floor feels solid like linoleum beneath me again instead of the carpet I'm standing on at the opposite side of the room.

Marylou's pointing toward an old dimestore paperback, near her but not touching her—Nancy Drew, by the looks of it. *Come tell me what you see.*

Like a ghost of myself, I imagine slipping closer and closer to Marylou. My body is like a strange cloud of energy—I can feel where it exists in the remote viewing, but cannot see it. I brush my arm against Marylou's as I reach out like a phantom to touch the book to see if she reacts.

She twitches. *Yes, I can feel you bumblin' around.* She smiles, lopsided. *Go on, try the book.*

I brush against the book in the viewing. But there's nothing. I don't fall into any memories or glean any emotions. The viewing wavers. My corner of the room, wood-paneled and dark, bleeds through Marylou's sunny corner.

Oh, come on, Jules. Hold tight for a minute more. Pretend you're, I dunno, trying to hold your breath that extra second before you have to come up for air.

As easy as that. Right. I hold my breath and push past the waver; try to claw my way back into the viewing. Once more, I reach for the book and trace one finger along its cover—

—a sunny spring day, the shadow of the Washington Monument spilling across us as we reach up to flip the page—

—and as I lose my grip, I'm torn out of the memory, out of Marylou's viewing, slamming back into my own skull with a head-spinning slap.

Careful, Jules, don't give yourself a condition! I can hear Mary-lou's laugh from across the room. *Don't worry, you'll get there. Soon, you'll be able to share images with the whole team and see what everyone else sees through me—trust me, it makes our work much easier. You just need practice.*

And practice we do—all morning long, until the rest of the team returns, without a single sign of Anna Montalban.

☆　☆　☆

"What a waste of time," Donna grumbles as Al threads through the afternoon traffic. "Every single one of the NATO delegates I interviewed lied to me about *something*, but not about anything useful for our case."

"If they're willing to lie about one thing, are they more likely to lie about something else?" I ask.

Donna nods. "Sure, but now I know how they act when they're lying. When it came to hunting down Anna Montalban, I'm pretty sure they're telling the truth. At least we still have this lead."

Yes, it took quite the battle between Cindy and Frank to follow up on Donna's suggestion to investigate the diner that Anna had mentioned the day before. I couldn't resist but try to frame them each in the context of a mole—Frank's blustery, red-blooded hatred could conceal his true loyalties. Cindy, on the other hand—I've only started to glimpse at the deep currents beneath her frosty veneer, and I wonder what more they might contain. I wish I could forget Sergei's warning and concentrate on the task at hand—wish I could brush it aside as carelessly as Papa brushes away anything that interferes with his carefree life.

Al Sterling turns Donna, Judd, and me loose on Connecticut Avenue, just north of Dupont Circle, a wide boulevard that reminds me of the older parts of Moscow with its thick, overdressed buildings, all of them four or five stories in height, and splashed with imperial shades of blue and gold. Streetcar cables spin a web across the sky, though the cars stopped running a few years ago. I catch an overpowering whiff of flowers—a plump woman sells them from a bucket on the street corner, a quarter for a whole bouquet. The smells of coffee brewing and bread baking and lunch frying and even leather ripening at the shoe store all mingle into a dizzying potpourri.

And lording over the whole tableau, at the top of the hill, sits the Soviet embassy. Its design reminds me a little too much of the mansion where Valentin and I were effectively prisoners of the KGB, let out of our pens under armed guard for the sole purpose of hunting down traitors. Even at this distance, I can spot the slow stride of a soldier, marking off the embassy's boundary as he makes his patrol rounds.

A tiny, wicked voice at the back of my mind asks me why my life is any better now, marching to America's drum. I am still hunting people for their thoughts. I can imagine Sergei taunting me, telling me I am still trying to remake the world in someone else's vision. The doubt, however, is strictly mine.

But when I look past the rainbow landscape, the shops with overflowing shelves, the rattle and hiss of daily life that spills from every mouth and machine, I can see the difference. It's an absence—an absence of guards, of bindings, of a rabid fear to comply. And in that absence, human will and creativity and resourcefulness have grown, unchecked, filling every possible crevice like some tenacious, lovely weed. These people refuse to be stopped. There is nothing to stop me here.

"I'm gonna park the car," Al calls out his rolled-down window. "You kids have fun. If you get into any trouble, just give me a shout—I'll be right around the corner." He taps his temple.

No guards with machine guns monitoring our every step when we're permitted out into the world, no threat of violence against my family if I make an unapproved move. Yes, I can live like this.

"I'm so excited to see what you can do," Donna says as we wait at the crosswalk. Judd hovers behind us, arms crossed. "It's nice to have another girl on the team."

"What about Marylou?" I ask.

Donna sighs, ponytail swinging. "She doesn't *count*. She almost never talks, and when she does, you wish she'd stop. She's more of a clueless beatnik than that guy on *Dobbie Gillis*." She peers at me from the corner of her eye, like she's challenging me: *Don't be like Marylou. Talk, but only in a way that amuses me.*

Donna pauses in front of the big window of a men's suit shop, watching a young man having his measurements taken, the tailor straining to wrap the tape around his sculpted chest. Donna traces her index finger along the windowpane, one curving line, then another to mirror it—the shape of a heart. But she's gone from the window and swaying down the street in seconds, the boy already forgotten.

"I guess I don't blame you for being shy," she says. "I mean, Russia must be *so* different from life here. Gosh, I'm from California, and even I don't understand Washington yet." She smiles so perfectly that I can't imagine that's true. "In Los Angeles, everyone is so gorgeous, and they just want to share and share when you talk to them. I had no trouble learning anything I could possibly want to know from someone. I barely had to use my ability at all. But everyone's *so* suspicious here."

Maybe Washington isn't so different from Russia in that sense.

"How about you, Judd?" Donna looks over her shoulder at the lumbering hulk. Shoulders not built for a standard-width door frame, and arms aching to escape the sleeves of his too-tight plaid shirt. In silhouette, he looks like Sergei, which sends a nervous current running down my spine. But he's got sun-blasted freckles all over his face and arms, and his wispy hair dances like a flame in the wind.

"What?" Judd grunts. He looks down at Donna, who barely reaches his ribcage.

But she smiles, and twists the already-curled tip of her ponytail around one finger. "I imagine city life is totally different from Kansas or wherever it is you're from."

"Indiana." Judd shrugs—even a simple movement from him is an earthquake. "Doesn't matter to me where I am. I do what I was made to do."

I don't see that straining concentration that I usually see in dedicated mindreaders—always filtering the air around them, scooping up the thoughts of passersby and pitching whatever they don't need. "And what is it you were made to do?" I ask.

He snorts, like a laugh with his mouth closed, and a big grin pushes up his cheeks. "You'll see."

Again, I'm reminded of Sergei—the hulking gait that makes me feel so fragile and tiny in comparison. Sergei could be watching me right now, a thought that chills me even further. I'm not safely behind an electrical shield.

Donna stops us at the edge of the block and checks the address of the shop front against something scrawled in loopy handwriting on her left palm. "Here we go," she says, drawing back her shoulders. Donna, nervous? I tamp out my own spark of nerves and follow her inside the diner.

A waitress nearly runs us down, both of her arms spread wide with dishes scaling them like plated armor. "Comin' through!" she shouts. Donna leaps back with a squeak. Another waitress glances our way from behind the low breakfast counter situated down an aisle of bright turquoise booths.

"Grab a seat wherever," she shouts to us, gesturing with a giant glass pot of coffee.

Donna hesitates a moment, gaze sweeping across the diner, then she eases into a smile and sidles up to the counter. "Actually, I'm supposed to meet one of my big sister's friends here."

The waitress's eyes flick to us from under her blue eyelids, and then turn back to the mug she's refilling. I look over the man at the counter. He's thin, and his suit doesn't fit right, but he smiles just as much as he should on his lunch break, and there's a half-finished crossword puzzle folded beside his plate. I let my shoulder rub against his as we crowd around the gap in the counter. Though I can't make out all the thick English phrases, his thoughts flicker and swirl like any other person's, without any sign of panic, paranoia, or deceit.

"Well, who's your sister's friend? I know most the regulars." She tops off the man's mug, and turns back to us. Her name badge reads "Peggy," which is short for something, but I can't remember what.

"Um, Anna, I think . . . ?" Donna tugs at her ponytail. "She's supposed to talk to me about typing school?"

Peggy's smile is gone. Her mouth compresses until all that shows is her off-color lip liner. "Yeah, I know who you mean. She ain't around right now."

Donna throws her hands up. "Gee, that's just swell. Can you believe my sister? Probably told her the wrong time." Her stance shifts suddenly, like a mirror image of Peggy's—tight mouth, curved spine, playful tilt to her head.

"You're welcome to wait." Peggy slaps three laminated menus onto the counter. "Herb, settle up, I got payin' customers who need a chair."

The man at the counter—Herb—looks up from his crossword puzzle. "C'mon, Pegs, I don't get paid 'til Friday. Can't you put it on my tab?"

Peggy rolls her eyes, spins to the cash register, and pulls out a coffee-stained ledger. Something passes between Judd and Donna that I'm not privy to: a thought bundled up in a shared code, maybe, or a familiar language built from running multiple missions together. I wonder if I'll ever find that level of comfort working with them. I settle onto the sticky vinyl stool and bat away the bland memories that reach for me from its surface.

Herb shuffles off, and Judd claims his stool, pinning me between him and Donna. Donna keeps chatting with Peggy, asking her inane, pointed questions—about Anna, about other customers, about the food—everything. I can't believe Donna doesn't see Peggy's irritation in the hard line of her lips and the puckered skin around her eyes. Finally, Judd orders an enormous platter of pancakes and sausage, and Peggy stalks off.

"What are you doing?" I hiss at Donna. "You're making her hate you. She isn't going to tell you anything."

Donna narrows her eyes at me. "Are you gonna tell me how to do my job? You can't even hear what she's thinking, can you?"

I shake my head. "Not without touching her—"

"Then don't tell me it isn't working." Donna bows her head toward mine. "Sure, it's easier when I can butter someone up and get them to spill everything to me on their own. I barely even have to look at their thoughts when they do. But sometimes, I just know someone's gonna hate me from the start." I can smell her acrid bubblegum as she cracks it. "So why fight it? If I can push all their buttons, they won't tell me what I want to know, but they'll gosh-darned sure be *thinking* about all the things they don't wanna tell me."

"You make them dislike you on purpose?"

"Why not? *I* know I'm a likable gal. Who cares what they think?" She winks at me, then straightens back onto her stool, attention roaming across the smoky diner. "Judd? Are you ready?"

"You got it." He swallows a mouthful of pancakes, then hangs his head in his hands. I frown. Is he praying? Most Americans I've seen do that *before* they eat.

Someone yelps in the kitchen, at the far end of the diner. I turn toward the window in the wall that opens to the fry cooks. A huge tuft of smoke billows out of the hole, black and woolly, then retreats. A few seconds later, a wave of heat hits my face with so much force I can feel my eyelashes curl.

Peggy shrieks at the other end of the counter, then grabs a

plastic pitcher of water and runs for the kitchen. Other wait-resses are doing the same, joining the stuffy chaos, shouting back and forth. Customers stand up, at the lunch counter or in their booths, craning their necks, commotion rippling across the diner as a smell like burnt meat wafts our way.

Donna swings herself over the counter and swipes the ledger from next to the cash register. "M . . . Montalban." She runs one finger down the gridded paper. "Last entry is from two nights ago. She sits in the corner booth at the front—by the windows. Come on, Jules, it's your turn at bat!"

I glance nervously toward the shouting mass at the kitchen's entrance as I stand. Another fire, though one far more severe, looms before me when I blink: flames bursting from the *Veter 1* space capsule.

"Corner booth," Donna repeats, flicking her fingers toward the diner's front.

I shake the memory away and push upstream through the crowd of patrons. The corner booth is abandoned; one red vinyl cushion is split open like a wound, its yellow foam innards bared. I slide onto the booth and run my hands over the table, sinking deep into the stuffing and the memories accumulated on it.

At first, the memories fight me; they form a dense net of fog that pushes against me—the telltale aftermath of a scrubber's presence. But I press on. The white fog scrapes against my arms and face like brambles and I keep pushing, straining even though I'm surely snared in place. I have to see the memories at the other end of the fog. I have to know our enemy.

Anna Montalban coalesces around me in the booth. Her coffee mug rattles as she sets it back down. I feel a dry, sucking desperation in my throat; it tastes both like cigarette smoke and like the painful absence of cigarette smoke. Anna reaches into her purse and brush her fingers against crinkled cellophane, but jerks her hand back out when someone slides into the booth across from her.

"*Se hace tarde,*" she says. The words are just shapes to me, but I try to paint them onto my mind. With a roll of her shoulders, Anna looks up and into a face like death. A dark-skinned man sits in the booth, but sickness has washed his skin in vulgar yellow hues; his thick black mustache looks stiff with filth. I can't hear his thoughts, or rather his shield, but something bitter and rank radiates from him.

"*Los Rusos malditos,*" the man says with a voice like a bus engine idling. *Rusos.* I understand that much. Russians.

The man reaches into his breast pocket and offers Anna a cigarette. As she slips one out, I catch a glimpse of something wrapped around the cigarette—black, shiny like microfiche—but she slips it off the cigarette and pockets it before I can look closer.

White creeps into the seams of the memory, radiating from the man—the scrubber; the hot, tangy stink of grease from the present-tense diner follows. I grit my teeth and tighten my grasp on the seat cushion. I have to stay in this past. Just a little longer.

The man watches Anna for a minute, eyes bulging out of sunken sockets. I've seen that look before—this man, or at least, the man this shadow used to be. Who is he? But as I lose focus on the scene, the empty white vastness cinches around me, those brambles digging into my skin. Later. I'll have to place him later. He reaches into his breast pocket.

"No." Anna tenses. "I'll place the film, but I never agreed to this."

"It is the most important part. You know what will happen if you don't." He brings out a silver cigarette case, letting it flash in the harsh diner lighting. "You or Saxton, Anna. It has to be one of you."

Her thought-shield unravels for a moment as she struggles to keep calm, but I can feel her hands still twitching in her lap long after she schools her face into calm. "Fine. Give it to me."

He hands the case to her; she clicks the button on the case's front just long enough to glimpse inside. The contents are definitely *not* cigarettes, I can tell that much, but what they are, I can't say for sure. Long cylinders, with a flash of glass and steel. I think I hear liquid sloshing as she drops the case in her purse.

"Now, remember," the man says. "I won't be around by the time you're finished, but if you don't use it, they *will* know—"

The memory shudders. Sirens alternate red and blue through the diner's glass front, out of sync with the neon blinking OPEN sign. I claw at the white fog, but it's too thick—it shoves me back into the present. How are these scrubbers so powerful? I'm exhausted from pushing through their barriers; I'm no match for them. I squeeze my eyes shut to clear the afterburn of the overhead lights and stumble toward the counter, an unfamiliar dizziness turning the room into a shifting funhouse around me.

"I saw all I could. We must go." My words slosh together. I'm rocking from side to side. Dimly, I hear the swell of chatter all around us, screams and stomps and people in thick coats pushing past us—firemen? They are ushering us toward the front door. We must go now, I am sure of this, as sure as I can be of anything with this foggy soup in my head. But Judd is calmly peeling a one-dollar bill out of his wallet and laying it on the counter.

"Oh, don't get your hammer and sickle in a twist. I dunno how you Russkies do it, but we actually pay for our food here." He grins, lopsided, and tucks his wallet back into his pocket.

The world shudders around me, and I find myself on the sidewalk, struggling to stay standing upright. I feel glass—cool glass under my palm. We're outside the diner. I lean against the glass, gasping for breath. The scrubber may be gone, but his grating, agonizing power is still scouring through my system like a disease.

Judd and Donna loom before me. "Well?" Donna asks, keeping her voice under the rapidly multiplying shouts of diners and spectators and firemen. "Anything useful?"

"We'll see." I try to read Donna's expression but she's swimming before me. "How did you know there would be a fire in the kitchen?"

Donna snorts. "You're joking, right? The fire *is* Judd's power."

His face burns bright red. "Well, I learn from the best. Mister Sterling can do way bigger blazes than I can."

I stare at Judd. "You caused that? On purpose?"

"You wanna make somethin' of it?" He leans forward, teeth bared, freckles swallowed up in his suddenly flushed face.

I don't like his tone, and I'm not sure what the something is he's asking me to make, so I ignore the question. "Someone could have gotten hurt!"

"Don't be such a Pollyanna." Donna rolls her eyes. "He has better control than that."

Judd nods. "It's really easy. I tell the fire where to go, and where *not* to go. The fire won't hurt anyone without me telling it to."

"How can you be sure?" I ask. My palms itch, prickly with sweat; my head spins as I try to stand up from the glass. "Do any of us really know our limits?" *You'll never understand what you're capable of,* Papa's voice echoes in my head.

"*Some* of us aren't afraid to use our powers," Donna says.

"Well, maybe you should be."

Donna and Judd exchange another look. I'm tired of their looks, and understanding only half of what they say and do. I'm already sick of running around without any guidance, grasping at straws, at conversations in noisy diners. My mother and these murderous scrubbers and General Rostov are out there somewhere, and I'm too lost to stop them. Another fire truck howls in the distance, cutting through the brain fog that is partly from the scrubber's memory and partly from the haze that shrouds my every moment in this country, trying to make sense of these people, their words, their intricate spy games . . .

"There you kids are." Al Sterling strides toward us, his fedora askew from pushing through the crowd. "Judd? Is this commotion your doing?"

"Yes, sir!" Judd beams at him, red touching his cheeks again.

Al laughs and claps him on the shoulder. "Nice job, kiddo! Really—stellar work. You're gonna put me out of a job one day." He turns to me. "Manage to get anything useful for us?"

The man, the scrubber. I know I've seen him before. Where does he fit in? He must not have been as sickly looking as he is now, though he's still fixed in my mind with those hollowed-out eyes, that wilted mustache.

Bozhe moi. It hits me. The restaurant in Georgetown we went to with Papa. I break through the static whiteness and see him now, crashing into me in the hallway of Brasserie Bonaparte. He's the same man, I'm sure of it. My thoughts buzz. I'm suffocating under all this panic, this pain from pushing too hard past the scrubber's haze, this inescapable terror that has chased me across the globe. Fear claws at my lungs, pushes at my skin. I can't hold this all inside.

"Come on, Jules. You must have seen something." Donna rests her hand on my forearm. "What did you—?"

All my frustration and paranoia bubbles up, surging into her arm where she touches me. It's a slippery thing, my terror, and this noise, this relentless noise in my head has worn away my strength. I can't rein it in. In one sharp moment, my emotions turn into an arc of electricity, leaping from my skin to Donna's.

She howls and leaps back. "What the hell?!" she shrieks, cradling her arm against her chest. "You crazy commie bitch! I'm gonna tell Frank what you did!"

But I am empty now, too empty to find sympathy for her fears. "I didn't mean to . . ." I begin, but I trail off. What do I care?

"What did you . . . ?" Donna interrupts herself with a sharp gulp. Her stance transforms from shock to terror—she looks around, frantic with energy, whipping her head every which way. "Oh, God, everyone's after us. Why can't we stop them?"

Tears quiver in the corners of her eyes. I see my reflection in them, my emotion: the same fear and frustration I'd felt moments before. Only now, I feel nothing. It's drained from me and into her. I look straight through her. The thick air of the street retreats from me and I'm left with nothing but a woolly buzz in my head.

"What did you do to her?" Judd asks, his boyish face turning sharp with suspicion. "You just did something with your mind, didn't you?"

I shrug. I'm drained. I can't muster up anything like sympathy or regret. I reach for those emotions, but I have no reserves. "It's my touch," I say, but I'm already too bored with this conversation to explain. I just want to sink into the fuzzy white warmth that's calling my name, promising to strip these petty problems away from me.

"Hey, kiddo?" Al's rounded eyes peer through the blurred haze of memory. "Did you know your nose is bleeding?"

I almost remember seeing the glistening blood on my fingertip—almost remember shaking with a dry laugh—before I collapse right there on the sidewalk into a milky, vast embrace.

CHAPTER 11

I'M PROPPED UP IN BED, padded on three sides by a thick shell of down pillows. Valentin sits in a chair beside me, his fingers knotted together, his dark hair plastered against his forehead with sweat. I groan, shrugging off the dregs of sleep, and readjust myself so I can see him better. His eyes flick up toward mine; he smiles, fleeting, before his lips soften into their usual murky expression.

"You're awake." He says it like he's convincing himself. I stretch my fingers toward him on the comforter and he closes his hand around mine like a shield.

"One of the scrubbers is working with Anna." A vein in my head contracts with each beat of my heart, painful and crisp. "I saw him at Brasserie Bonaparte. He gave Anna something at the diner—"

Valentin runs his thumb along the ridge of my knuckles with a whisper of our song, "I Wanna Hold Your Hand." The Beatles ease away the panic in my pulse, letting me leech some of his calm and draw it into me. My muscles unclench.

"When you . . . well, did whatever you did to Donna, she caught a glimpse of him. What you'd seen in the memories." Valentin keeps stroking my skin, channeling calm toward me, but I can feel him tensing. "They've dispatched a whole squadron of FBI agents to hunt for him. You don't need to worry about anything."

My hand clenches under his. How I wish that were true. We still don't know what Anna and this scrubber want with Senator Saxton—what the strange case was he passed to her, the one she initially refused. And if they're a part of Rostov's attempts to build a "psychic army," then how are they realizing his goal of destroying the United States? Catching Anna or this man is only the beginning; they are the loose thread we need to pull on to find out where it leads.

But I can't do anything about it now. I need to clear my head; I need to think of something good. "Valentin." I turn toward him. "Come here." My voice sounds thick to my ears. I feel heavy with a sudden need for comfort. I want this boy beside me; I need him in my arms, softening my own sharp edges. The boy who ran away from home with me so we could clear our minds. They hurt him; they filed off whatever lock kept his demons at bay, but he's still my Valentin, despite his pain. He's the steady ostinato bass line beneath all my songs.

His curved lips twitch, smiling, as he lowers his eyes from mine. "I'd love to, but I think . . ."

Cindy Conrad's head pops into my room. She's a dazzle of pink and blonde and caramel against the dark taupe walls of my bedroom. "Are we awake?" she asks, in a voice that channels a grade school teacher.

"Did you find Anna? The scrubber?" I ask. Valentin starts to disengage his hand from mine, but I tighten my grip. *Stay*, I beg him, in Russian as well as through our own silent code of shared songs. *I need you.*

Cindy stands at the foot of the bed. Her pressed silk overcoat hangs at perfect angles as she clasps her hands in front of her. "We're doing our best to search for them, based on the details you . . . transferred to Miss Willoughsby." A frown creases her smooth features. "I'm assuming that was the same . . . technique that you used on me yesterday, as well. What precisely is it?"

My head sinks through the stack of pillows, and I wish it'd keep on sinking right through all three floors and the finished basement of Papa's townhouse. That "technique" is the thing I fear doing every time I use my power; the thing I did to the Hound when he tried to stop Valentin and me from escaping Berlin. Emotions and memories and bitterness building up on my palms like a crust, then shooting off of it all at once, punching through another person's skin, as if I'd shot them with adrenaline, only instead of that jolt, it's sadness. It's regret. It's whatever emotion is overwhelming me at the time, spilling over, too much for me to contain.

"I'm not sure I have the words for it," I tell her.

"I'll get Winnie, if you like."

I shake my head. "In any language, Miss Conrad."

She taps something against her lips; it looks like one of the brightly colored cards she'd had with her at the senator's office. She looks me over, expression shielded by the card, then steps forward. "Perhaps I can be of assistance."

She lays the card down in front of me, faceup. It depicts a naked woman kneeling before a pond, stars streaming through the sky and her hair as she pours water into the pond and the earth both. Or is the water flowing up into her hands? I can't tell for sure.

"The Star," Cindy says. "I always visualize it when I think of you. The water is meant to show emotions and memories—you pull them into you and push them onto the world and minds around you."

I nod, but something tugs in me. I'm never as calm and confident as this woman. Her cheeks are flushed with happiness and health, whereas when I tried healing Valentin last night, I thought I was going to drown. She looks like a vessel, immutable, as the currents flow into and out of her with frightening ease. I don't think I could ever harness such peace.

I glance at Valentin and listen to the quiet melody flowing between us through our joined hands. Back and forth—I couldn't say which one of us is the music's source. When I breathe, it's Valya's calm trickling into me. When he shudders and jolts at night, it's my arms that shield him from his tormenting thoughts.

"But I don't have that kind of control over it."

Cindy's smile at that moment looks the closest to genuine that I've ever seen from her. "You'll get there, through practice and failure," she says. "Tell me more about what you saw at the diner."

I sink back into the pillows. "Anna met with this man two nights ago. He's one of the powerful scrubbers you've been finding—his thoughts were eating away at hers."

"And you have a clear image of what he looks like?"

His dried-up face looms before my eyes, splotchy and out of focus like I've stared at the sun for too long. But it'll have to be enough. "If you have a . . ." I grope for the English phrase. "A person who draws faces, like for the police—"

"A sketch artist?" Cindy asks. "We have something much better. But what else happened in the memory?"

"They were speaking Spanish at first, but switched to English so they wouldn't get strange looks. He was arguing with her—he was trying to convince her to do something. Because something bad would happen if she didn't."

"Blackmail, extortion—common spy tactics."

I commit those ugly words to memory. "Extortion. Yes, that's the word. Then he gave her some things. When she took a cigarette from him, there was something black and shiny wrapped around it."

Cindy presses her lips together. "Microfiche, maybe. It's used for photographing documents." Her eyes flick upward. "Wait, you said he gave it to Anna? She didn't give it to him?"

"Yes. What does that mean?"

Valentin leans forward; Cindy jumps as though she'd forgotten he was there. "Usually," he says carefully, "the spy is the one stealing information."

"Right. If she's a spy, we'd expect her to be stealing secrets from the senator's office, not bringing them in." Cindy sighs. "It doesn't make sense."

I crick my neck, trying to work out the needling stiffness in it. "Well, there must be a reason for her to take it from him. What if she's changing the senator's files? Giving him false information?"

Cindy nods rhythmically, like she's clicking off each piece of information as it snaps together in her mind. "Yes. Yes, could be."

She stands up. "Frank isn't going to like this," she says under her breath. I'm not inclined to care what Frank thinks, but I say nothing. "Anything else you remember?"

"After he gave her the film, he gave her a cigarette case, but I don't think there were cigarettes inside. He wanted her to use what was inside, but I don't know how, or why." The words still ring in my ears in the scrubber's caustic voice. No one says anything for a few seconds.

"And you didn't get a look at it." Cindy grimaces as I shake my head. "Not even a guess?"

"There was a liquid of some sort. Like vials, something like that."

Cindy's warm skin turns a shade lighter, but she says nothing. "All right. Okay. Get your rest. First thing tomorrow, you're going to work with Tony to look for any other records of this—this scrubber. Valentin?" Cindy peers down her nose at him. "Do let the poor girl get some *actual* rest, won't you?"

"Of course, Miss Conrad." Heat flushes his cheeks.

After the heavy report of her heels vanishes down the staircase, Valya tucks my hair behind my ear. "You're certain you're all right?"

I want to talk about this monstrous weapon my powers have become. I want to tell him about Sergei's warning. I want to take away Valya's suffering . . . I twist toward him and lose myself in the comforting depths of our songs. How can I tell him these things? How can I add to his barely contained pain for my own needs? I can't do it—not now. Maybe later, when we aren't so desperate in our hunt.

A grin plays on my lips—we could both stand to smile more.

Just this once, I want to push these problems from my mind, these equations to which I can't find solutions, and focus on the good in my life. On my Valentin, and his warm heart and warm skin. Sergei and the mole and our secret pains can wait a few hours more. "I'll be all right."

His slow smile makes it so easy to forget.

"So," I say, "are you going to let me get some *actual* rest?"

"I had no such intentions," he replies, resting his cool forehead against mine.

"Hooligan." I sketch his jawline with my index finger, heat and hunger lurking just below the surface of my skin.

"Red Menace," he says, and buries his lips in mine, all the music between us crashing and intersecting in one heavy, glorious symphony.

✮　✮　✮

I wake up on the edge of my mattress, pinned in only by my sheets, Valya anchoring them on top of me. His glasses are off, and white cotton socks peek from the frayed hems of his slacks. He looks so much younger when he's asleep. When he isn't thrashing and screaming with nightmares, at least. I work my way out of the sheets and fold them over to cover him up.

Every segment of Papa's townhouse is painted in a different rich hue, all the shades you'd find in a Dutch oil painting, but when the house is still and unlit, the colors retreat to a murky gray. My windowpanes are washed in the deep indigo of sunset; it'll be another stormy spring night. I'm not used to all this wetness, all this air that's merely cool instead of cold. I miss the sight of my own breath hanging before me, reminding me that I'm alive. I haven't seen snow since we left Berlin, though everyone bundles up at the first hint of clouds like they might have to dig themselves out of a blizzard at a moment's notice.

I peek into Papa's bedroom, thinking for a moment that I'd heard a voice in there. The room is dark, but his closet is lit, the doorway ajar. As I draw closer, I realize it's only a radio I'm hearing, though I don't understand what strange sort of broadcast he has it tuned to. A woman's voice recites a string of numbers in Russian, while a magnetic tape reel set up next to Papa's radio records the transmission.

The woman's calm voice belies the hairs she's raising on the back of my neck. I don't know what the numbers mean, and a question lodges in my throat as I stare at the recording equipment and its slow methodical spin. One word stands out in my mind, offering me an unsettling possibility:

Mole. Mole. Mole.

No. Papa couldn't be a mole. Everything he's done already, everything he's working for still—it's all been to set us free. The Papa who worked so hard to rescue me from the KGB couldn't possibly do such a thing.

But I'm not sure I know Papa anymore.

I back out of his room and tread through the gray house. "Papa?" I whisper. Surely he has an explanation for it. Tree branches whip past the front windows as I head to the main level, leaves scattering. My pulse canters, trying to reconcile the storm outside with the silence in here.

I lean against the door frame that separates the kitchen from the parlor. Or am I trapped in here with a traitor, and the answers I need are outside?

"Yulia?"

I leap half out of my skin, bashing my temple on the door frame. "*Bozhe moi!*"

Winnie rushes toward me from the breakfast table, "Oh, lordy, I am so sorry! I didn't mean to scare you!"

I hold out my hand to fend her off. "Don't touch me, don't touch me," I plead, afraid for what emotions might be crackling with the adrenaline under my skin.

"It's okay." Winnie tilts her head. "It's just me."

"I know—I just didn't want to—" I suck down fresh air. I'm in control; I'm not going to hurt her like I did Donna and Cindy. "Why are you sitting in our kitchen? In the dark?"

Winnie settles back into her chair and cups her hands around a mug of coffee, though no steam rises from it. "Good to see you up and about," she says, tentatively, like this is only one of a dozen phrases she was preparing. She wears her standard blue uniform under a navy rain slicker, but her heels peeking around the kitchen table legs look taller than usual.

"Why are you here?" I ask again.

Her lips round on an answer but then Papa clambers in from the conservatory, all brassy music and dark leather jacket and permanent grin. My stomach sinks to look at him. After his outburst last night, he drove us to Langley in the morning, filling Valya's and my silence with inane chatter about the weather, as if the weight of enough noise could crush whatever ill feelings remained. "There's my little girl!" He waves his lips over my scalp, dangerously close to actually dropping a kiss there, before swooping away with an arm extended toward the kitchen door. "Are we all ready?"

"Sure." Winnie stands and dumps her coffee in the sink, then turns on the faucet to wash it down. Her eyes dart toward me for a brief second. "Sorry, Yul, but I've got to borrow your father for the evening. Emergency meeting."

I glance at my bare toes. "Should I get ready?"

Winnie stammers for a second before Papa steps in. "You're not doing any work until tomorrow. At the earliest! Now, while I'm gone . . ." His voice is so bright that it takes me a moment to realize I'm being lectured. "I know you were both clothed, but I don't want you kids in the same bed together anymore. Valya's a good kid, but neither of you want any . . . complications, now, do you? Good." He pats my arm. "Here's some cash if you kids want to grab a late dinner at Clyde's."

I barely feel myself taking the stiff, glossy twenty-dollar bill from him (enough for three dinners, even on Georgetown's main drag). Sure, Papa. Whatever you say, Papa. We wouldn't want any "complications."

Does he sees Zhenya and Mama and I as complications, imposing on the charmed bachelor's life he's made for himself stateside? Are we the gnawed-off foot left behind in the trap when he made his escape?

The convertible's tires wail down the twilit street as I shuffle through the kitchen and unlock the back door. Wind tears through the trees overhead as I step onto the patio, outside the circuit of the psychic disturbers. The usual sounds of laughter and animated chatter that reach us from Georgetown are silent to-night. The coming rain presses heavy against my skin.

"Sergei?" I whisper. I feel like an idiot. Like I'm calling for a dead cat, or praying to a god I don't believe in. "Sergei? Are you here?"

The insects flatline around me, ready for the impending rain.

I glance up at the green, heavy sky. I have to know who Sergei claims is the mole—I have to stop jumping at shadows and strange radios. Even if he's lying to me—I have to slow this frantic whirring in my head. And if the CIA won't share information about my mother with me, then maybe, just maybe, Sergei can.

"Sergei, whenever you're ready to talk . . . I'll be here."

CHAPTER 12

I DREAM OF MAMA again that night—the Mama who bound our family together, sturdy as glue. She is lying in bed, in our house in the wealthy Party neighborhood of Rublovka, a quilt tucked tight around her. Zhenya lies beside her, humming to himself, while I button up my lightweight autumn coat. "I'm sorry, Andrei," she says, holding out a thermometer. "You'll have to take Yulia to the park by yourself today. I've got a fever."

But I'd just seen her holding the thermometer to her bedside lamp. I open my mouth to say as much, but there's permafrost in her eyes when she looks my way, and I clamp my jaw back shut.

Papa sinks to his knees at her side. "No, Nina, don't be silly. If you're ill, then I must stay with you. I'll make you soup—do you want some tea? Maybe I can fix a nice roast for you. I'll send Yulia to the Party grocer to pick us out a nice cut of beef."

"For heaven's sake, I already have a blanket if I want to smother myself. Take care of our daughter." She nods at me. " I just need some peace and quiet, and *you* need to get out more. Besides—" She coughs into her hand. "I think I'm contagious."

After a few more rounds of protests, Papa grudgingly leaves her side, though back then—seven years ago, it must have been—he always wandered about, slightly dazed, when he did so, like an amputee being forced to adjust. He saunters through the soggy leaf-strewn street with me, puffing at his Pyotr I unfiltered cigarette, his eyes as dark gray as the sky. "Do you think your mother's all right?" He's speaking more to himself, I assume, because I don't answer, and the green-uniformed lady who usually follows our every move is missing today. "I hope she didn't catch anything at work."

When we reach the playground at the end of the block, he doesn't offer to push me on the swings or play any of the games we usually play when Mama is with us. I swing back and forth, alone, watching the few other kids that chase each other in the field. Stupid Papa. I scissor my legs, aimless. Why must he be so blinded by Mama that he doesn't even notice me?

Then I spot the man smoking next to Papa—short, with stocky features and an oddly cut coat unlike all the Russian fashions. A foreigner. I narrow my eyes, and strain to hear them—but they're only making small talk, griping about the impending weather. The swing's chains creak as I glide along, listening in. Somehow, the conversation turns scientific, onto Papa's favorite topic—psychology. They talk the whole afternoon. I keep waiting for our usual green-coated shadow to interrupt them and tell the foreigner to move along, but she's nowhere to be found.

"Well, nice to meet you, Andrei. I'd better get my little one back home." The man squashes his cigarette on the ground when I hop off the swing and stroll over. "We should get together for drinks sometime. Let the kids play together."

I can't believe the smile on Papa's face as he puts his arm around my shoulders. "A pleasure to meet you, Frank."

When we return home, Mama's up and about, humming to herself as she cooks supper. I catch Zhenya in one of his warmer moods. "What was that all about?" I ask Zhenya.

He shrugs. "As soon as you left, Mama went outside to chat with that lady in the green uniform." He's absorbed in his music sheet, not looking up at me. "The lady kept trying to follow you to the park, but Mama wouldn't shut up. What a weird illness, huh?"

What a strange illness, indeed.

CHAPTER 13

TONY PEERS AT ME from under a greasy lock of hair. He's too scrawny for his oversized frame; his joints look incapable of supporting his lanky limbs, and his Adam's apple bobs freely on a toothpick neck as he fidgets in the break room chair. His pimples stand out like indignant punctuation marks on his tan skin. "Hey," he says, looking the complete opposite direction from me when I take the chair beside him.

"Hello." I glance over at Cindy and Al Sterling, heads bowed together in urgent whispers in front of Frank Tuttelbaum's office door. "Cindy said you can find the scrubber."

"That's right." Bob, bob.

"Are you a remote viewer? Like Marylou?" *Like Sergei*, I think.

He snorts. "I'm way better than that."

I'm not sure what the correct English response is to such a declaration, so I say nothing.

"You work through touch, right?" He rubs his palms back and

forth against his jeans. "Give me your hand and think about the guy. Let me in to the image."

I clench my teeth and slowly place my right hand in his. His skin is clammy, much colder than I'd expected; some unidentifiable grit rubs between our palms. How easily I've forgotten the feel of other people, those whose shape and texture and emotion I don't know like I know Valentin's. I peel back the frantic strings of Shostakovich's symphony, then dribble out the percussion, then the marching bass—only when I'm sure my emotions are firmly reined in do I let it all fade away. The sallow-skinned man with a grungy mustache, white static eating away his features. Scouring blasts of thought. I see his sunken eyes and his jagged eyebrows and the sweat running down his cheek—

"Okay, I think I got it." Tony lets go of my hand and takes a deep breath. "Carlos Fonseca, born in Havana, Cuba, in 1928, but later became a citizen of Mexico. Last known whereabouts: the border crossing in El Paso, Texas, in July of 1961. No further information."

I raise one eyebrow. "How do you know all that?"

He punches those knobby shoulders up into the air in a shrug. "Please. The border crossing records are way too easy. I memorize them in, like, seconds. Photos take a little longer, but not much. Wanna check the photo bank with me?"

I glance over at Cindy; she's pounding one fist into her open hand while Al makes "mmhmm" noises. I turn back to Tony. "Do they need to come with us?"

"Oh, we don't have to go anywhere. It's all right up here." He raps his fingertip against his temple.

I place my hand in his again, nervous energy running through me. I try to draw on a reserve of calm like Cindy admonished me to yesterday. Control these emotions instead of merely being a conduit for them. I want to be like the Star Cindy showed me; if any emotions spill out of me, they should be safe ones. I try to think calming, watery thoughts, like the images in the card. Waves lapping rhythmically against a shoreline. The sun melting into the horizon, red spilling against the waves. Valentin's screams ripping through the salty air and his mother's fiery embrace searing into my waist—

I jerk back from Tony with a yelp. The terror drips out of me slowly. But Tony just watches me, head cocked to one side like a curious sparrow. I clench my hand into a fist, waiting for my heart rate to return to normal.

"That's the western shore of the Black Sea," he says, though it sounds like there's a question behind it. "By the town of Sukhumi. I can give you the coordinates for it, if you want."

"Is it?" I'd guessed as much, since it was from Valentin's memories as a boy. Before his father was promoted to a senior Party official. He rarely speaks of those days, not that he talks about his past much anyway. Walks on the beach. Violin and piano duets with his mother, late into the night.

"What happened to you there?" Tony winces. "It looked . . . awful."

I shake my head. "It's—it's not my story to share."

"Okay." He looks at his knee, bobbing up and down with nervous energy, then takes a deep breath. His knee goes still. "Okay. If you can keep your, uh, your thoughts to yourself . . ."

"I'll be fine," I snap.

"—Then let's look through the photo bank."

He takes my hand again. I'm rattled from letting Valentin's

nightmare seep out. I can feel new fears buzzing beneath the surface of my thoughts like a shorting circuit, but I try to make my mind empty. After a few seconds, black-and-white photographs start to flicker across it, as if projected onto a screen. Faster and faster—hundreds of photographs whiz past, of all different faces and buildings and objects. It's dizzying. They turn into a blur of grainy surveillance photos. I only just manage to get a grip on one image before it's torn away, that split-second shot of trees dissolving into a woman's laughing face, which tears into a smoky nightclub—

"Got it." The images halt. "That's him, right?"

My head is still spinning from the parade of pictures, but as the image before me takes shape, the unmistakable profile of the scrubber manifests, glancing over his shoulder as he ducks into a doorway. The awning over the door reads 1301. "That's him."

"1301," Tony says. "I know I've seen that somewhere before." Tony taps his temple. "Ever heard of a photographic memory? Well, mine's like that, cranked to supersonic. Hmm, 1301, must be something the FBI has under surveillance. Where are you, 1301 . . ."

Another dizzying zoetrope of images marches past, all of building façades now—I'm pretty sure they're all in DC, though it's too fast for me to be certain—and slowly, the array converges on a single building. An apartment complex. It must have been gorgeous once, but the carved stone accents are weathered and cracked, and the air-conditioning units in the windows sag like tired babushkas. The awning out front reads 1301.

"There we go. Now, why did the FBI have surveillance on it?" Tony's voice has taken on a smug lilt as he asks these rhetorical questions—I can only gather it's because the answer is already awaiting him inside his head, or wherever he's drawing all these pictures and records from. Sure enough, the pictures in his thoughts have now been replaced by typed documents, all of them formatted similarly, with a big seal stamped across the top.

"Bingo." Tony lets go of my hand, and the images shimmer and vanish. "Mister Sterling? Can you pull a file for us?"

Al looks up from his conversation with Cindy. "Sure thing, kiddo. What's the serial?"

Within minutes, a busty file clerk arrives with a folder for us. "Just like you requested, Mister Sterling!" Her voice sounds squeaky, like it's been squeezed through a tube. "You need anything else, just ring on down the records office. Of course, you can ring us even if you don't need anything."

Al winks at her before turning back to Cindy, who groans and yanks the file from his hands. "FBI surveillance request, approved by a federal judge." She slaps it down in front of us. Tony flips through the typed pages and we read it together, though I'm not understanding nearly as much as I'd like.

"The Stratford Apartments in Shaw." Cindy scans the folder. "Looks like this old widow in the building complained to police about the constant noise from one of her neighbors—said people were coming and going at all hours, I quote, 'speaking Spanish and Russian and all manner of heathen, godless communist tongues.'" Cindy grins at that. "After the Bureau's counterintelligence grunts did an initial stakeout, they saw a few 'persons of interest' acting suspicious around the building—making chalk marks on the sidewalk in front of it, standard tradecraft—so it's been under infrequent surveillance ever since."

Tony nods. "I recognize some of the other individuals photographed outside the building. Chin Xu, a Chinese embassy employee with an unspecified position. Borsca Szabo, a Hungarian national who's turned up in surveillance photos of other suspected foreign agents—"

"Thank you, Encyclopedia Brown, we'll pull those files later. For now . . ." Cindy props one hand on her hip, looking me over like she's assessing fruit at the market. "Yulia? Feel like a drive through Rock Creek Park?"

I take a deep breath—what feels like the first I've taken in days. It feels like we're finally surfacing for air, finally untangling the first knots on this case.

"What's at Rock Creek Park?" Papa calls, as he storms into the room, Valentin and Judd trailing behind him. "The Stratford Apartments?"

Cindy lowers the file folder. "How did you know about that?"

"FBI called, alerting us to an interesting complaint they'd received," Papa says.

"Is it about 'heathen, godless communists'?" I ask with a smile.

But Papa doesn't smile. I don't know if he's capable of being rattled, but he's as close to it as I've seen him. No whistle on his lips; his hands are jammed awkwardly in his pockets like he's trying to contain them. "Same old woman as that complaint, yes," he says carefully. "But she has a new problem this time. An awful smell coming from next door, like when a rat's died in the walls."

Dread sinks in my stomach like a weight.

"Should we let Frank know?" Cindy asks.

"No time. He's in a meeting all day, anyway. We've got a full squadron of DC's finest guarding the entrance, so let's hurry. No way the bastards can scrub the place before we search it, this time." Papa holds out his hand for me. "Yulia. It's your show now."

"I told you," the old woman says, peering out of her cracked door. Her hair is set in pink rollers; she's sipping Ovaltine from a glass. "I told you them atheists were up to no good. It's not right, that they should be peddlin' their un-American lies right here in this great nation's heart."

"Don't worry, ma'am. They won't be troubling you any longer." Even Cindy's smile looks ragged. "Now, if you'll just answer a few questions for us, I promise we'll be out of your hair in no time."

The woman's rheumy gaze drifts from Cindy to me. "My, what's this world coming to? We've got lady cops now? Little girl cops?"

"Something like that," Cindy says through clenched teeth.

"Is that Ovaltine you're drinking?" Donna asks. "Gosh, my grandma used to drink that all the time." Her voice starts to quaver. "Oh, I miss her so . . ."

The woman winces, then slowly pulls the chain out of her door. "Why don't you come inside? I'd be happy to make you a glass."

"Gee, would you really? That'd be just swell! And then we can have a nice little chat . . ." Donna twists around to throw us a thumbs-up—and the door clicks shut behind them.

"Yes, better lock your doors. This isn't going to be pretty," Cindy mutters under her breath.

Papa props one arm on the door frame. "Would've been cleaner if Valya or me just took care of the old lady."

Valya's face goes white, but Cindy claps her hands, too loudly, before Valya or I can protest. "Well, then! Donna should be able to gather whatever the old lady knows about the goings-on here." Her smile strains at the seams. "Now let's see what *you* can find out for us, Yulia."

Yulia. Quickly! There you are!

I stagger back, my pulse so loud in my ears I can barely hear anything else over it—Papa and Valentin talking, the security guards, the creaking floors—my pulse and Sergei's voice swallow them all up. I try to fight down the rising tide of panic before I answer.

Who's the mole, Sergei? I hesitate. *Please—either help me, or don't. Stop leading me on.*

I don't have long. They'll know I'm—

Silence. The pressure in my head starts to fade. *Sergei?*

Then he weighs in again, slipping one last message against my shield before vanishing again. *Check the stovetop.*

Please, Sergei, wait. I need to know— My shield softens. *I need to know if my mother's all right.*

But he's gone. Cindy watches me, arms crossed, one eyebrow creeping up as she waits.

The stovetop. Check the stovetop. And don't tip anyone off about Sergei's help. What is it they say at the jazz clubs when Valya and I catch a show? Stay cool. I take a deep breath and reach for the door.

As soon as I put my hand on the doorknob, the vibrations reach for me from the walls, shuddering and shaking my molecules apart. White sparks dance across my eyes as the door falls open. My ears fill with needling noises, like a too-silent night.

I step inside. I see the room, I hear the room, but I am not part of the room. I am walking on a tightrope. If I were to fall off on one side: the reality of this dead body, stretched across the rug, thick red liquid dried in a trail from its ears to the floor. The reality of that smell, pressing into my chest cavity with its rotten stench. But if I were to fall the other way: a vast white plain, stretching as cold and heartless as Siberia.

"There's definitely been a scrubber here. Probably the man who lived here." I walk in a wide arc around the body, breathing through my mouth. "And he is definitely the man I saw with Anna Montalban. He warned her, though. That if she didn't do what she was supposed to, the next one would come after her."

Cindy hovers beside me. "The next what?"

Papa scratches his chin, his stubble sounding like sandpaper. "The next. The next scrubber? The next body? How far apart have these deaths been occurring?"

Cindy checks the stack of papers in her hand. "Between six and nine days apart. It's fairly consistent."

"Like it's a chain," I say.

"Or like a relay race," Cindy offers.

I nod, reaching my hand out for the black telephone sitting on the floor. Only then do I notice how empty this apartment is. The Murphy bed pulled down from the wall, a telephone, an ugly rug, a radio—nothing else. I sink down next to the telephone and brush my fingertips across the receiver.

White static ricochets through me—the scrubber's lingering aftereffects and the crackle of a bad connection, all tangled up together like a ball of barbed wire. If this man is part of a chain, a relay, a ring of spies, carrying out orders in succession, working for Rostov's unknown plan, I have to fight past this residual noise. The hot smell of copper tickles my nose. I have to uncover the memories. I have to push past this hungering white and reach beyond—

"C-21." The slimy voice, interwoven with fuzz, must be Carlos Fonseca's. Slowly, he coalesces around me, though he's blurred, too much for me to see clearly.

"We are growing impatient, C-21."

Carlos tugs at his too-tight shirt collar; a sheen of sweat runs down his jaw, though it's still cool for April. "Relax. I'll make the drop with H-22, in case Montalban fails us. But it won't be necessary. I'll get to him, I promise."

"You do not have long," the voice says. I strain to hear it closer, but the static is too strong; all I can tell is that it's a man, speaking too slowly and precisely to betray an accent. "We need you to make the drop now. It must happen before Saxton departs."

"Two more days. I still have two more days. I'll reach him, I swear."

The voice on the other line cuts through the static like a whip-crack. "We will call again in one."

I jolt back from the telephone as the room swims back into view. "He told them yesterday he had two more days. But they're going to check on him again soon. We have to work quickly." I swallow. "He talked about reaching Saxton before he departs."

Cindy grimaces. "All right. Let's keep looking. Quickly."

There aren't many other places to look. I let my fingers hover over the walls, the stained and twisted bed sheets, but the static crackling off of them warns me away like an electrified fence. This place is too empty to offer us much in the way of memories. Whatever Fonseca was up to, he must have conducted it outside of this apartment.

I glance toward Valya, who's standing closest to the kitchenette in the far corner. I start toward him, but guilt and fear over turning to Sergei for help have cemented me to the spot. "Check the stovetop."

He pokes around the range top. "Yes—looks like he tried to burn something. *Molodtsa,*" he praises me. Using the tip of a pen, he lifts charred bits of paper out of the crevices of the gas range top. One looks like the corner of a photograph, by the way it's melted from the glossy paper backing; another bears the spiderweb markings of a map. Just scraps, but scraps, I can work with. Even a scrap can hold the memory of the whole.

"Bag it. We can look at them more closely back at the offices." Cindy's speaking through a silk scarf she's wadded up over her mouth and nose. I squeeze my eyes shut. What's Sergei playing at? Why on earth is he helping us now?

Papa touches my arm gently, but his scrubber noise is like a spark jumping from him to me. "Yulia. We've got to know who this next scrubber is. What they want with Saxton. You're sure there isn't anything else you can glean?"

I look away from his narrowed stare, like a spotlight sweeping across me during a midnight escape. "Not with a scrubber of this power. It's so empty here—I can't imagine there is much more—"

"I'm not talking about reading the objects, *devochka.*"

A fly buzzes past us to fling itself against the grimy window. The overripe smell of fermented meat thickens in the space between Papa and me. Yes, I know exactly what he means. My stomach whines in protest.

"Andrei." Cindy folds her arms, bangles clacking together. "We do *not* need to subject the poor girl to that." The Metro police officers at the doorway step back, as if they're afraid Cindy might volunteer them instead.

"And why not? Why, she was just demonstrating to Valentin and me the other night how very confident she is in her abilities." Papa shoots me a glare. "Apparently she's all grown up now, and perfectly capable of handling whatever we ask of her."

Damn it, Papa. Heat surges up from within me, pressurized. This is the same father who took the blame for me when we were playing hide and seek, and I knocked Mama's figurine off the bookshelf?

Valentin steps between Papa and me. "Andrei Dmitrievich," he pleads. "Please don't make her do this."

Papa's face is perfectly, irritatingly blank. "She thinks she's mastered her powers. So let her," he says.

Cindy and Valentin both look to me for a response. But I shove past all of them and step right up to the body, the toes of my boots pressing into the too-pliant flesh. I bend down into a squat, keeping the weight off my bad ankle, and study Carlos's face. The darker skin along the cheek that rests on the ground, where his blood has pooled. The splotches of rot.

"Yulia," Valya says. "Don't listen to him. You don't have to do this."

But if I want to follow the trail back to Rostov—and therefore Mama—then I have no choice.

I spread my fingers wide and press my palm against the corpse's shoulder.

Carlos's skin gives way under his shirt with a sickening, sloshing sensation. For once, I'm grateful when the chattering white fog envelops me. Somewhere, on the other side of the mist, a man is screaming. I walk toward the noise, ignoring the way the mist stings at my bared arms. An invisible wall presses back at me; trying to force my way through is like trying to strain myself through a sieve. But I have to see what's on the other side. I have to know what these scrubbers want.

Carlos Fonseca thrashes around his bare apartment, clutching at his throat as blood pours from his ears and eyes. The screams are his—his agonized howls. He didn't take the cyanide pill. He's fighting whatever's killing him to the very last, and it's making his power go haywire, filling the air with its deadly isotopes—

I do not need to see this man die. I need to see what happened before.

The mist weighs against me as I push backward in time. I can only see fragments, tenuous and watery. Carlos entering the Stratford building. Carlos riding a bus through downtown Washington. Carlos at the market, his shoulder pressing too hard against a man's as their hands meet, just for one second—

There. Something passes between their hands. I need to see the other man—is this the H-22 he said he made the drop with? Passing information or an object along. Like a relay race. Who is he passing it to? What's being passed?

The man's face is turned away from Carlos. Tan skin, short-cropped blond hair, a few inches taller than Carlos. I cling to the memory, trying to stay locked inside it, but I can feel hot blood tickling at my nostrils again. The whiteness seeps into the image, the scrubber's static trying to force me away, but I have to resist. I have to see H-22.

The telephone's shrill ring pierces the air. I'm thrown out of the memories, my hand uncurling from the corpse's shoulder, and I sprawl backward on the rug. There's blood running down my nose again. Valentin rushes to me and cradles my head, but Papa lays his hand on the telephone receiver and looks at me, expectant. For a moment, I can almost imagine he's putting his trust in me. The phone rings again.

"How did he identify himself on the phone call?" Papa asks.

"C-21."

Cindy's face looks stricken. "Andrei, you can't—"

Papa offers me a brief smile, quick as a camera flash, and picks up the phone in the middle of the third ring. "C-21."

Neither Valentin nor I move; the only thing I feel is blood curling its way around my upper lip. Papa holds the earpiece away from his head. In the held-breath silence of the apartment, the voice on the other end of the line is painfully loud.

"You are still alive." There is a pause, though it doesn't sound like hesitation. "What about H-22? Will he make the trip?"

Papa glances toward me. I manage a weak nod. "Say that you made the drop," I whisper.

"H-22 has the materials he needs for the trip." Papa's stance is too relaxed for this terrifying game he's playing. His free hand hangs motionless at his side.

"Why are the police at your building?"

"The old lady next door," Papa says, without a moment's pause. "She's complaining about us again."

The silence grows and grows, like a rubber band stretching too tight. Pressure builds up inside of me as I force myself to sit up. I wish I knew something else to tell Papa to say. There has to be something we can fill the silence with. Valentin's hand tightens around mine, and Cindy leans forward, head drawing down to her chest. But Papa remains stony, unmoved by their stalling tactic. Is he doing this for the same reason I touched the dead man? Is desperation to find Mama fueling his courage and bluster, or is this just another of his careless games?

"You told us you would kill the old woman," the voice finally says. It's burnt around the edges now, hot and angry. "Who is this?" Then, lowering almost into a growl, "You cannot stop us."

The dial tone pierces the oppressive quiet. Papa slams the phone back onto the cradle.

"*K chortu*," Valentin says, snarling.

I drop his hand and scrub at my nose with my sleeve. "We have to find more information." My fingers hover over the rotting man before me, this bag of flesh and bones that should hold all the answers we need. "The man he passed something to. Details about the trip. If we can find this H-22—Or if we can find Anna Montalban—"

Cindy shakes her head. "There's nothing more we can do here. Yulia, I won't have you endanger yourself any further. If you can't salvage any more memories from him . . ."

I look to her, pleading, but I know she's right. Another drop of blood splashes onto my knee. "We can't lose the trail."

Valentin catches my gaze, his dark eyes hooded. Cindy may not realize what this means to me, but in an instant, I see in his stare and in the wave of his music pouring over me that he understands my need to hunt Mama.

"Don't worry," Cindy says. "I have a feeling I know exactly where they may be headed."

CHAPTER 14

"I UNDERSTAND—now listen to me, I under*stand*, Winnifred, why you're doing this."

I pause midway to the restroom and lower my foot to the ground, silently. My head swivels toward the circle of harsh lemon light radiating from Cindy's desk lamp, spilling into the darkened hallway ahead of me. I can see Cindy and Winnie more easily than they can see me. I breathe slowly and keep Shostakovich in my head at a dull thrum. Cindy had left me alone this morning to read the items we recovered from the stove in the apartment while the rest of the team hunts for Carlos's new contacts. It's nice to know I can melt into the shadows as easily I once did on the streets of Moscow, forgotten. It makes mole hunting easier, whether I'd planned to or not.

"If you really understood, you'd be out there with me." Winnie's voice is harsher than I've ever heard it. It brings out her Southern drawl. "This is your fight, too. Just because you snuck by with your daddy's lighter skin—"

"What I *understand*," Cindy hisses through her teeth, "is that it's goddamned hard enough for us to prove our worth as it is—be that as a woman, as a member of any given blend of races—that there's no sense complicating it with rebellion."

Winnie snorts. "Is that how you see it? Asking for some basic human decency is an act of rebellion?"

"The way I see it . . ." Cindy's voice lowers. "The McCarthy days aren't so very far behind us. There are men who will use any excuse they can to claim you're threatening the nation's security."

"So what? I'm good at my job—the best. I'd have to be, to get my foot in the door here."

Cindy clicks one heel against the linoleum. "They overlook it for now *because* you follow orders and do your job well. If you value that uniform you wear, you'd be wise not to risk that."

"Is that a threat?" Winnie asks. "Are you threatening to tell Frank about my Urban League friends?"

"Sooner or later, you're going to have to choose between the military and your ragtag band of overly optimistic dreamers. You may be able to reconcile the two, but people like Frank Tuttelbaum don't understand the subtleties . . ."

Cindy closes the door, muffling their voices into English-shaped thuds I can't understand. I hurry to the restroom and splash cool water on my face, washing away the grime of secrets and betrayals that I don't fully understand.

* * *

When I head to the break room for lunch, Winnie is watching a rebroadcast of last night's news with Walter Cronkite. "The communist forces of North Vietnam's Viet Cong are nearly fifty thousand strong," he intones, eyebrows bristling as he stares at us through the screen. "The South Vietnamese are not likely to last long against their guerilla warfare tactics."

Winnie drums her nails against the wood-paneled television set that's as wide as a Cadillac. I settle onto the couch in front of the set and prop my chin in my hands. "Are we going to go to war?" The *we* slips out before I can catch it, but I let it go. This team, this agency, this city, this country are a part of me now, no matter what that brings.

Winnie's mouth is curled down like a comma. "Depends who you ask, I suppose. Some people think war is never the answer; others think it always is. Senator Goldwater thinks we're letting the dark forces of communism run roughshod over a free and peaceful democracy."

"But what do you think?" I ask.

"I think if we try to help, we're just going to send a bunch of poor and probably colored boys to die in the jungle." She shrugs. "But it's not my job to think. Come on, let's work on your medical journal translations. You were having trouble with the article on viral genetics?"

"Yes. I did not understand 'tautomeric forms' . . ."

I dig the well-worn journal out of my bag and we work through the article for a few more minutes. I want to soak up every scrap of knowledge I can so I can contribute to the lab at Georgetown, but something Winnie said nags at me. Guerilla warfare. Cindy had been teaching me basic tradecraft earlier in the week, but she hadn't mentioned any such thing. After Winnie helps me stumble through a dense paragraph on viral phenotypes, I lean back in the chair and pinch the bridge of my nose. "What does it mean, the . . . 'guerilla warfare tactics?' Is this something—" *That we did.* "That the Soviets do?"

"Well, we haven't fought the Soviets in direct combat, but I can imagine they would. Guerilla tactics are sneaky—lots of sub-terfuge and disguise, with small forces picking off large ones," Winnie says. "It's not like World War II—the enemy doesn't paint a bullseye on themselves with a swastika."

The enemy could be anyone. I certainly know the feeling.

We've wrung out a few leads, at least—the fragments of paper we fished out of Carlos's stovetop match an area in northwestern Paris, though I wasn't able to dig any further memories out of them. Still, we are no closer to finding our scrubbers, or their access agent, Anna Montalban. I know I should be thanking Sergei for the tip—if he'd reach out to me again. Instead, I feel a tension in my gut like a loaded mousetrap. I keep thinking of Cindy and her competing hypotheses, comparing scenarios both likely and unlikely against the known facts. What if this, too, is just a distraction?

It's Saturday morning, and Papa is nowhere to be found around the townhouse. I check the street; no sign of the Austin Healey. Stomach rumbling, I throw open the door to the baby blue re-frigerator and paw around the mess of produce and brown paper–wrapped meats in search of something to fix for break-fast. Wilted lettuce, three bottles of milk in various states of emptiness, a massive jug of orange juice that looks best suited to performing dialysis . . . It's more food than the three of us could eat in a month, and yet most if it has gone bad; we're hardly ever home to cook. Papa is always dragging us to greasy burger joints and swanky steakhouses and everything in between.

Finally I unearth a carton of eggs and pre-sliced bacon. While they fry on the range, I fiddle with Papa's electric coffee percolator, the coffee jingle from the radio springing into my mind, uninvited. Good to the last drop.

Valentin stumbles into the kitchen, hair sticking every which way, and slips his arms around my shoulders from behind. "Mm! Smells like capitalism. Delicious!"

"Might as well use it up before it goes bad." I turn in his arms and kiss him. "Go ahead, don't let me interrupt your morning etudes. I'll bring you breakfast in the conservatory."

"How dreadfully *bourgeois*." He grins. I swat him with my dishtowel until he runs off to practice his piano scales. Open mic night at Bohemian Caverns is fast approaching, and he thinks it's his best chance to catch the ear of a record label scout. I flip the eggs, my smile growing with every hiss of the stove and every perfect glissande of his chords. We make quite the pair, the musician and the scientist.

If only our lives were so easy—science labs and jazz halls. A drop of bacon grease leaps up to sear my arm, and I mutter a curse under my breath. We're still miles from reaching Anna Montalban and the next scrubber in the relay. From understanding how this relates to Rostov, and what he means to do. From saving Mama. From uncovering the mole, if there is one.

I can't find the mole on my own, and I don't trust anyone else to help. I twist the dishtowel around in my hands, frustration seeping out of me in fits and starts. When I peered into Valya's memories that night, I didn't see those signs of Rostov, his scrubbing powers frizzly and sharp and impossible to miss. Valentin can't be an unwitting mole. Paranoia binds me like a rusty chain, but I will not let it claim this victory over me. If I can't trust Valentin to help me, what more do I have left?

Sunlight gilds the conservatory, pouring in the high windows and spilling across the plush chairs, the wooden floor, the sleek piano. After playing his newest experimental theme for me—jazzy and punchy and full of fire—Valentin and I nestle on the couch and stuff ourselves with as much bacon and eggs as we can bear. I flop back into his arms, belly up, and bask for a few moments before taking a deep breath.

"There's something I need to tell you about," I say. His arms tense around me and I hear him swallow. "Something I need your help with."

He nuzzles his nose into the back of my head. "Anything you need to say. Don't be afraid of me."

I laugh, bitter. Back in Russia, the mere sight of Valentin was enough to send tremors of panic through me. The sound of his power set my teeth on edge. But now I fear myself far more than I ever feared Valentin. "It's Sergei." I cringe, closing my eyes for a moment to avoid Valya's reaction. "He's been talking to me in my head."

Valentin jerks forward. "How? Is he here right now?"

"No—no, Papa has those . . . current-boxes in the walls. The psychic disruptors. When we were escaping Berlin, Sergei—he was able to project himself into my head, like Marylou does.

I hadn't heard from him since then, but then he did it again the other day. He says there's something important he needs to tell us."

Valentin pinches the bridge of his nose with a sharp exhale. "All right. Something important. About Rostov or your mother? Do you think he's warning us, or is he trying to manipulate us?"

Fear spreads its wings inside my chest, filling up all my empty space. "He said there's a traitor on our team."

Valya is silent for a long time. Though he's not sharing his thoughts with me, I know exactly what must be running through his mind; it's running through mine, too. The question of who to tell and how to tell them, if anyone at all. Of the futility of our efforts to stop Rostov—whether they will be our undoing.

"It could be a lie, like you said." I glance away. "He might want us paranoid. He could be trying to make us feel vulnerable. I can't imagine Sergei has come around to our way of thinking, but I suppose it's possible. He's the one who told me to check the stove at Carlos Fonseca's apartment."

I feel the moment it hits him when he slumps back into the couch. "How long ago did Sergei contact you?" He asks it slowly. Too steadily.

"A few days ago." I'm motionless. For all that I'd dreaded sharing this knowledge, I feel hollowed out, lightened. It's a relief not to bottle it up any longer. "I had to be sure that Rostov—I was afraid that the troubles you've had—"

His laugh scrapes like sandpaper. "My troubles are purely my own, Yul. Can you trust me on that?"

I bite my lower lip. "Of course I trust you. But you've had so much else on your mind, and I didn't want to be—"

"A burden? A nuisance? Don't you understand, Yulia? You're my reason to fight." His limbs are stiff. "And we said—no more secrets."

Shame flushes through me. Of course he's right. A thousand protests rush to my lips, all my half-baked fears, but I squash them down. "I'm sorry, Valentin."

"I'm sorry you had to carry this weight." Valya's arms are still around me; he rocks back and forth, considering. "It could be a lie, you're right. But that's a costly risk to take. If there were a mole, it might explain why we're always a few steps behind. Why we can't find Anna Montalban, or why everywhere we look is scrubbed clean of memories." He tilts his head. Under my cheek, I feel the hitch in his breath. "But it doesn't answer our questions about your mother? What's her plan?"

The tremor starts in my toes, a live wire coming loose from its moorings, working its way up my legs and through my spine into my brain. I'm shaking, the seed of fear growing into an entire forest within me, my emotional attunement acting like a positive feedback loop.

Hypothesis A: Mama has surrendered to Rostov's plan fully and will do whatever he asks of her. She will push them onward toward whatever devious end he demands. She is no longer the mother who took Zhenya and me into hiding just to keep her integrity.

Hypothesis B: Mama is conducting a psychological warfare campaign of her own. She appears to be cooperating with Rostov, but is really working toward a different goal. But what? Does she need my help? Does she need us to protect her from our own teammates?

"I'm scared, Valya. Even if Sergei is lying, I have to listen to him—he's the only person who can tell me what's happened to my mother. I don't know if she needs our help. I don't want to hurt her."

I'm trembling still, the fear rolling over itself inside me like a rising ocean tide. I can't control my terror of failing Mama, of failing my family. And I'm petrified that I've become what Papa accused me of—a victim of my own ignorance, a monster with no idea of the power she wields.

"Yulia." His shield melody swells. "We can do this, together. Until we know what your mother wants from us, I think it's best for us to focus on whether our team is really safe—whether Sergei's telling the truth."

"You're right. It's a start."

He kisses the crown of my head. "Let's focus on finding this traitor, then, if there really is one to be found. When I joined the PsyOps team, Cindy taught me that people who betray their countries are motivated by a few common factors: money, ideology, compromise, ego, revenge." He ticks the factors off on his fingers. "We can look at each of our teammates for these things."

He's appealing to the scientist in me—seeking order from chaos. But experimentation and observation are only two types of approaches; other things can be learned from blunt interference. "Of course," I say, "you could always push past their shields."

He shifts on the couch. I've caught him off guard. "N-not against these people. They're supposed to be our teammates. I can't just—I mean, unless I'm really, really certain . . ." He squeezes his eyes shut. "Yulia, it isn't right to use my scrubber ability that way. I can't ever do that again."

I shake my head back and forth. "I understand you're afraid of your ability, but everything has its uses."

He shifts and sits up, pulling away from me, but says nothing. Instead there's just a roaring noise in my ears, like an incoming wave. Waves. Valentin's past. I can smell the tangy sea breeze, feel the sand squishing between my toes—the echo of memories I'd gleaned and just as quickly lost. Valentin hasn't woken up screaming since the other night, but I can see the strain in the dark grooves under his eyes.

It stings, this hollowness in me of not knowing what troubles him so. "This isn't about our team. You helped me remember my past. Why won't you let me try again to help you move on from yours?"

His arms go slack. "Your father might be cruel about it, but he has a point. You shouldn't have to handle that much emotion. I refuse to hurt you with it."

I stare him down as if I don't even recognize him. "Hurt me? I'm trying to help *you*!"

"Well, maybe I don't need to be helped," he snaps. "Maybe I'm just fine as I am."

I scoot to the far end of the couch. Maybe I am too eager to try to fix others' problems; I've certainly tried to save those who didn't want saving before. Zhenya, Sergei, Larissa . . . Perhaps even Mama, now. But Valya? He's been suffering ever since our confrontation with Rostov—nursing a wound that won't heal. "You're a wreck. You scream in the middle of the night. You'll barely use your ability. You call that being just fine?"

"I call that keeping you safe," he says, eyes narrowed.

"Don't bother. You or Papa, either one." I shove off of the couch and gather our plates. "I'll be as dangerous as I want to be."

"Like your father?" Valya asks. I cringe. He isn't fighting fair. "I see how well that works out for him."

"What works out for who?" Papa flings open the back door of the conservatory. We didn't see him approaching through the side garden. Now I hear the Austin Healey's motor growling along the street. "Yulia, did you forget your appointment?"

"What appointment?" I ask.

"With Winnie? She's waiting in the car. You're supposed to meet your new professor at Georgetown, clean his lab, learn about some of his research projects. Glad it's you and not us, huh?" He elbows Valentin as he slides past us. "What say we hit the movies, Valya? They're playing a new Annette Funnicello film at Georgetown Theater, and with that broad on screen, who cares if it's Disney?"

I turn to Valya, but he just twists his lips sadly and lowers his gaze. "Sure, Andrei. Sounds like a riot."

☆   ☆   ☆

Winnie's walking so fast I can barely keep up, eyes darting along the neighborhood streets like she's searching for assailants. I lumber after her in my uneven gait along the cobblestone road. "It was very kind of Cindy to arrange this for you," Winnie says, in a tone that could harden lava. "Georgetown is *very* exclusive. They don't let just anyone in, you know."

Ah, so there's the issue. When she first started tutoring me, Winnie and I always shared the common bond of

160

outsiders—strangers in a strange, light-skinned, English-speaking land. It was the least common denominator of our daily lives, though at least I had some buffer—I had to open my mouth before I was completely dismissed, whereas her very presence was enough.

"I'm sorry, Winnie. I know it is—" I grit my teeth, trying to land on the word with the proper connotation. "It is *difficult* for you—"

She snorts. "Difficult? Please. I've got a skill so good people *have* to ignore my skin. Don't feel bad for me. It's everyone else I worry about."

A skill so good they can't ignore it. She'd said as much to Cindy, too, but Cindy implied there were limits to their willingness to overlook their prejudices.

I wonder if my spot on the PsyOps team is similar—if I'm an asset whose ego needs stroking, whose delicate temperament means she must be handled like raw plutonium: rubber gloves, hazmat suit, two-foot concrete barrier, and on a remote Pacific island if at all possible. I thought they'd been warming to me, but maybe I'm one more piece of weaponry to maneuver into place, and to hope I don't jam at a crucial moment.

We're almost onto the Georgetown campus now; a couple saunters toward us, hands linked between them, taking up the whole sidewalk. Winnie plows straight for them like it's a game of chicken (I know this because Papa plays it with drunk college boys sometimes) and at the last second, they let go of each other's hands, each squeezing against their respective side of the sidewalk. I slink after Winnie with my head bowed.

"Are you afraid of me?" I ask Winnie, scampering to catch up with her. "I thought Cindy was starting to trust me, but now . . ."

"But now, what?" Winnie arches one brow.

I'd forgotten Winnie's rule. Finish your sentences. Trailing off is cheating. "I think she is trying to . . . placate me. Because of my mother."

Winnie's mouth flickers with the briefest smile at my vocabulary usage, but it's gone as fast as it came. "Who knows with Cindy? For someone who's always watching out for herself, she doesn't always watch out for herself, if you know what I mean."

I don't even begin to know what Winnie means.

Winnie presses her hand between my shoulder blades to steer me down a colonnaded path. "Given a choice between the chance for a small victory now and a bigger one later, she'll take the one now, every time."

"But she can see the future," I say.

Winnie grimaces. "Maybe that's the problem." She shakes her head. "Some people forget where they came from. They're always looking for the next rung on the ladder. Never forget where you came from, all right?"

A thick oak door flings open before us; a fuzzy white-haired man stares at us with eyes that look ready to leap out of his skull. "Winnifred? Yulia?" he asks. He actually pronounces my name right. "Please, come in! Oh, here." He looks down at the mold-encrusted glass vial and pipe cleaner in his hands. "I suppose you should be doing this."

He thrusts them toward my stomach and I cradle them against me. "Doing what?"

"Well, giving them a good scrub! Sink's over there." He ushers us into the laboratory, which looks more like a minor chapel with its ragged stone walls and soaring ceilings. As he shuts the heavy door behind him, I could almost imagine we've stumbled back into the Middle Ages if not for the gleaming white electron microscope I spy in one corner of the room. Everything smells like dish soap and dust. "When you're done with that one, there're nineteen more just like it."

I find the giant ceramic basin and turn on the hot water spout. After a glance at the stack of vials on the counter, each of them crusted with the same slimy mold, I hunt down a pair of latex gloves and pull them on with a satisfying snap.

The professor hops up onto the soapstone counter next to the stack of dirty vials, Winnie close behind. "So! I'm Fred Stokowski. I'm from Europe myself, you know."

I peer at him out of the corner of my eye. "Europe" is hardly equivalent with Russia these days.

"Polish by birth, but I managed to escape during the fall of the Third Reich." He rubs his hands together and tilts his head back, as if it's weighed down by a rush of memories. "So, what got you interested in genetics?"

It's like asking me why my hair is black. How could I avoid the subject? My parents devoted much of their lives to researching genetics, and their own genetic markers, most of all. The markers they passed along to me. Coiled up tight like a fist in each of my chromosomes is a mystery sequence of proteins that has made me this way, given me this extra sense, this otherness that lets me prowl in the memories of others. And in my brother is a completely different, but equally mysterious code that keeps him locked deep inside his own head instead.

"Lots of reasons." My cheeks heat up as I scrub the tubes. "I love the idea of a . . . a blueprint that we all carry. That there are so many locks just waiting for us to make the right key for them."

As Winnie translates the patches I missed, Professor Stokowski nods for a bit, hand curled around his chin, like my response is taking him some time to unpack. "I like that. Yes. I understand you've read some of my research already? So you know I'm very interested in unlocking the genetic code. Have you worked on any research teams before?"

Unless by "worked on," he means that my entire existence is part of a massive Stalinist experiment in human enhancement, managed by my own parents. The selective breeding of psychics, more or less, to produce stronger psychics still. "No, Professor."

"No problem. I'll have you stay late today to work through some introductory labs." He waits for Winnie to help me along, then hops off the counter as I set the glassware out to dry. "I'm happy to let you tinker around with any of the samples we have in cold storage, as long as you submit a written proposal of your intended usage for them in advance. Other than that, I'll be expecting you to help out with my afternoon practicums, and you're welcome to join any additional research projects that need an extra brain. Fair enough?"

"You are very kind." I tilt my head in respect. "Thank you, Professor."

"Of course." He gestures toward the electron microscope in the corner. "Once you're done cleaning those, we can talk research."

As I'm tidying up the lab, I keep pausing to gawk at the carefully illustrated charts he has taped along the walls—chromosome pairs marking out the known genetic diseases, heredity tables, and a portrait of Gregor Mendel, the father of genetics, a monk who loved to breed his bean plants. A corkboard near the microscope catches my eye, as well; research topics printed on watery purple mimeograph pages are pinned to it. "What are these?" I ask Winnie. She leans in close to translate the topics for me. *Recessive traits of* Apis mellifera. *Choroidal hypoplasia heredity in rough collies. Provirus from* Bornaviridae *altering genetic sequence in* Apis mellifera.

"Afraid I can't help you much with the Latin," Winnie says. But "altering genetic sequence"—even I can grasp the gist of that.

"Professor Stokowski?" I glance over toward his desk, where he's grading a stack of papers. "What is this research project?"

He hops up and joins me at the corkboard. "Ahh! That's a fun project. I do love my honeybees." He taps his finger against the abstract. "Basically, I found a virus that alters the genetic code of its honeybee host. We're still trying to nail down how it chooses what chunks of code to remove, though, and whether we can alter its choices. Very preliminary work, yes."

Winnie lifts one eyebrow; I quickly turn away from her. "I would like to work on this project," I say.

"Sure thing, kid! I'd love to have some help. Say, have you ever worked one of these things before?" He pats the gleaming barrel of the electron microscope. "Here, swab your mouth; I'll do one, too. You, too, Sergeant."

We all scrape the insides of our cheeks with a long swab and smear the saliva onto a petri dish. My hand trembles as I slide my dish onto the microscope tray. The code is right before me. Professor Stokowski's genes and mine, side by side, like a "Spot the Differences" pair of drawings in the *Highlights* magazine

Winnie made me read. Professor Stokowski points out some of the obvious differences in their structure, but he can't point to what I really want to know: the exact nature of the power coursing through me. I keep the sample locked up in the research cabinets, though, for another day. Maybe if I can break my own code, I can finally understand the true nature of my power, and be the one in control.

CHAPTER 15

TONY'S ANALYSIS of the burned Paris maps and a murky premonition from Cindy lead us to the next NATO convention on the situation in Vietnam, chaired by none other than Senator Saxton. We'll be observing the proceedings and hunting for the next scrubber in the chain. Cindy's forecast was none too helpful—the Page of Wands, which she claimed meant we shouldn't squander an opportunity we've been given (much to Frank's chagrin)—but it's better than nothing. According to the countless maps and grainy satellite images Cindy has brought with her on the flight to Paris, the NATO Headquarters are housed in a odd, ragged chevron-shaped building called the Palais de l'OTAN, because the French prefer their acronyms to run backward, Winnie tells me under her breath. "It's really a lovely view from the palais," Cindy chirps, pacing the aisle of the Starlifter military plane. "If you look straight down the avenue, you can see the Arc de Triomphe."

Which is funny, because I doubt she's going to let us see so much as a glimpse of the Parisian skyline.

Marylou demonstrates a new technique for us, as well—if we all chain into her remote viewing, we can communicate with each other. "Like a Handie-Talkie," she says. Useful when we're covering a large building, like the palais, but I don't like the idea of exposing my thoughts to the whole team—for my sake, if there's a mole, or for theirs. I try not to imagine what could happen if I hurt all my teammates the way I hurt Donna that day.

We pore over building plans on the flight until we're all exhausted, blueprint edges curling under our fingers with each jolt and shudder of the plane. The recycled air tastes like metal and smells like antifreeze; I can't fall asleep while I breathe it in, imagining it spreading its chemical tendrils like roots into my lungs. Valya tosses and turns in his seat beside me, crackling with a nightmare from his past, questions pressing against his teeth but never quite escaping.

I glance toward Papa's chair; he's snoring loudly, and his arms and legs are flung so wide that even merry Al Sterling looks pained, huddled against the far side of his seat. Marylou's head keeps lolling against me on my other side, until she wakes herself up with a snort. Donna is sleeping with perfect posture, of course, and not a sound or a single glimmer of drool on her chin. Only Cindy is as sleepless as me. Our eyes meet for a fleeting second, then she turns back to her deck of cards.

As soon as we touch down, we cross the tarmac for one blindingly sunny second before cramming into the back of a windowless bullet-proof van for an hour-long, halting and stuttering journey through the streets of Paris, which are lovely, we're told.

"Let's run through our assignments one more time." Cindy rubs her hands together, surveying our assembled crew inside the van, as we all groan. "Andrei and Al?"

"Smoking outside near the van. We'll make sure we're in range for me to start a blaze and for Andrei to push back against intruders' thoughts, if they make it to the front door," Al says in a sing-song voice.

"Judd? Valentin?"

"Patrolling all the entrances to the assembly hall," they say in unison. "And starting a fire if I need to," Judd adds. "Which should be always."

"But it isn't. Donna?" Cindy asks.

She puffs up her chest. "Working the crowd before the first session. Talking to everyone, seeing who's nervous, what's on their minds." She glances at me. "Though I don't need any more of *your* thoughts."

"You'll be just fine, won't you, Yulia?" Cindy asks, in the bladed tone of a weary mother willing it to be true. "What else will you be working on?"

"You and I will be patrolling the perimeter. Looking for clues in the past and the future," I say.

Winnie jumps in before Cindy can talk again. "And I'll be right here with Tony, monitoring the shortwave for suspicious chatter."

"You speak French, too?" Papa asks. She nods, cheeks darkening. "Goodness! The sergeant's talents know no bounds!"

Cindy clears her throat. "Excellent work, all of you. Now, we absolutely must protect our NATO delegates. These scrubbers have been targeting them steadily over the past few months, and it's a safe bet that's their goal here, too. But our primary

objective is to capture one of these scrubbers—*alive*, please—"
She narrows her eyes in Papa's and Al's direction. "For questioning."

"But if you've got to kill them," Winnie counters, "I wouldn't feel too bad about it."

Cindy's fingers flutter against her pearl necklace. Somehow, she looks as fresh and polished as when we took off, while I'm feeling overripe. Even Donna's ponytail is frayed around the edges. We look less like a team and more like a line-up.

For Valya and me, that's exactly what the rest of our teammates are.

What about Cindy? he'd asked the other night, when we had the house to ourselves to speak freely. *The "ego" factor makes sense. She's always trying to prove herself.*

You could say the same about Donna, though. I'd frowned. *What about Tony, for revenge? Frank's always passing him up for missions, since he's more of a behind-the-scenes guy.*

Valya's nose twitched as he considered. *Possible. But he seems so unconcerned about everything. Politics, certainly.*

So does Al, but he has the ego and money motives in spades.

He sighed. *I suppose everyone has their vulnerabilities. We'll keep watching.*

Paris doesn't look or smell at all like I'd expected. When we were in East Berlin in January, the devastation of World War II was visible everywhere, leering down on us like gargoyles from their perches: a whole block of demolished buildings here, pockmarks from shrapnel spray there, and symbols of the Third Reich hastily painted over or chiseled away. But Paris has already been reborn—eager, I suppose, to seal off its memories of the occupation as quickly as possible. As I glance south of the NATO headquarters, toward the Seine River, I see nothing but the uniform slate rooftops sloping down and away from our hill, and the merry bob of construction cranes.

Cindy watches as I drift down the sidewalk, fingers caressing the streetlamps, fluttering through the bushes, tracing the grooves of the stone building façade. The NATO building is a new construction, made to house the headquarters when the Alliance was formed after the war, but I see the old city block hovering like a ghost over its shoulder. As I press into the memories, I feel the earth rumble under the churn of tank treads and the distant thudding of bombs. I smell blood in the air, and musket powder, from wars and battles even older.

"Anything?" Cindy asks. I shake my head. "Me either." She rolls her shoulders, once more appearing, for a fleeting moment, like her real age, and not the worldly businesswoman she strives for. "I must commend you, Yulia, on your efforts to adjust to life beyond the Iron Curtain. Frank didn't think you were worth the effort, but I'm thrilled your father defied his orders, just this once."

"Did he really disobey Frank by rescuing us?"

"Of course he did. I've noticed he has a bad habit of doing that." She peers over her shoulder with an accusatory smile. "I know you and Valentin are used to working on your own, but I would encourage you to try harder to integrate with your teammates. There's a lot more you can accomplish from inside the system than on the periphery."

Cindy stops abruptly, her upturned chin lowering, then strips off one glove. I brush my fingers against the nearby wall, but catch nothing out of the ordinary in the memories. "What is it?" I ask.

With her bare hand, she seizes my wrist, nails clawing into my skin. I'm about to yelp, but then a strange vision washes over me, flickering around us like underdeveloped Polaroids as she shares her power with me. Skeletons—dozens of them, swirling around us, grinning as they climb from rickety coffins and snag their fingerbones in my hair.

"Judgment," Cindy whispers.

The skeletons form an arc around us. Cindy squeezes tighter; the vision heightens, swallowing us up like a too-real dream. I can see the stringy ligaments and clumps of tissue clinging to the hollows of their bones, a patch of hair here, some rotting flesh there. The stench of death, cloying and sweet like burnt sugar and spoiled meat, seeps into my skin and clothes.

I didn't see it at first—not without eyeballs nor facial expressions nor even thoughts to read. But as they press closer to me, stale air pushing from dried-out lungs, I sense their purpose. They're waiting for me. They want something from me. Their bony hands reach for me—

Cindy lets go of my arm, and the vision dissipates. Cindy's glimpses of the future—they're much more allegorical than Larissa's, but they unnerve me all the same.

"What do they want?" I ask, some unnamed emotion tight as a collar around my throat. Repulsed, honored, frightened, relieved—I have no idea what this feeling is, much less how to release its choke hold on me.

Cindy's shoulders slope down. "The Judgment card can mean a decision; salvation from a leader . . . But it can also mean forgiveness and renewal. Redemption, sometimes."

"How specific," I mutter. "Why are your visions so . . ."

"Allegorical?" Cindy asks. "It's just how I make sense of the world. I grew up with the tarot. I suppose my thoughts have always been organized around the archetypes it presents."

I'm about to tell her about Larissa and how her premonitions work—when I feel a jolt of static like an electrical shock on the street post as I brush past.

Cindy and I look at each other instantaneously, as if our magnetic poles, aligned toward past and future, have suddenly snapped together. "What was that?" I ask, at the same time as Cindy whispers, "I saw something more."

She clasps her trembling hands before her. Five of Wands. A struggle—a battle for control. And—and I see labyrinths, winding paths blocking the way to victory."

My breath feels heavy as granite in my lungs. "I heard the scrubber."

Marylou's voice slices into my thoughts as she projects herself into our heads. *Miss Conrad! Yul! Andrei and Al need you out front!*

Cindy races ahead of me with the ping of heels on concrete as I limp along beside her. I tap each post in succession, just quick enough to follow the trail without the static consuming me, unfolding a gap in the past on each from when the scrubber passed by. He—or she—is like a bleach spill, eating away a swathe of history; I can't see the details of what happened but the spill itself is proof enough.

I round the corner to find myself in the middle of a standoff.

Near the building entrance, three NATO military guards stand with their guns drawn, moving as if they are wrestling for control of the weapons against some invisible attacker. Al Sterling has sunk to his knees on the concrete sidewalk; the sleeves of his smart linen jacket only reach past his elbows now, their edges singed black, and his exposed forearms are red and blistered. Papa stands beside him, leaning forward as if into a gale-force wind, his face wrenched in deep concentration as a trickle of red drips from his nose.

As I turn to look at the assailant, however, the whole world flashes into whiteness. I am floating; I am a dandelion seed, drifting in the breeze. I have no desire to be a part of whatever is happening around me. The cool air curls and buoys me, cleansing me, stripping away any cares, any concerns . . .

A snapshot of Cindy running past me burns into my eyes. Cindy pulls something from her purse, but white presses in, snaring me in place. I fight to see past it as hot metal sears my nostrils. Where'd Cindy go? There—Cindy presses the item—a small rectangular box—to the neck of—well, of someone. She and the person she's attacking are a shifting blend of bodies to me, even as the image hangs, stagnant, in my mind—

I drop to the pavement with a gasp. A chill courses through me; red splotches the stones beneath me. When I look up again, Cindy is wrestling with a husky man as the guards close in, screaming at her in French. I pull myself onto shaky legs; the old wound in my ankle throbs in protest.

Valentin, Donna, Judd—protect the delegates. Keep them in the building. Find a room you can secure with the disruptor devices, Cindy orders through Marylou, though the words are garbled and chewed around the edges.

I can't view the delegates, Miss Conrad, Marylou screams back, as if from the far end of a tunnel. *There's something—blocking their location—*

The scrubber rips the box from Cindy's grasp, and the white haze returns. This time, though, it's much weaker; with an effort, I can force my way through the haze, though it feels like someone's coiling barbed wire around my brain.

Rage. It's boiling under my skin, straining, begging for me to let it off its chain. I want this scrubber to suffer. I limp past Papa, hunched on the ground, his face purple from exertion. I want the scrubber to pay for what he's trying to do.

Our eyes meet. The scrubber stops flickering, and for just a few seconds, rage fuels me as I fight the fog, and I glimpse the man beneath the psychic disguises: cracked, bleeding lips; jaundiced eyes; pouches at his jowls from sudden weight loss; the tight, quivering, captive stare of extreme sleep deprivation. But I also see the tan-skinned, blond-haired, narrow-jawed man beneath.

"You can't stop us, Chernina," the scrubber wheezes, blood-flecked eyes locking on mine. "We are endless. We will always make more."

CHAPTER 16

THE SCRUBBER BREAKS eye contact with me; with one deft yank, he pulls Cindy forward and past him, taking advantage of her imbalance. She topples to the sidewalk with a crack. I leap forward, but the noise is back, thick as beet soup.

I can only make out snatches of the world around me, but it doesn't matter. I've already seen the scrubber's face. I call up my memory of him.

Marylou? Tony? I ask. *Can you match this man's face?*

Perfectly, comes Marylou's reply. *Tony's checking it out now.*

The scrubber is charging into the street. A car is stopping; its driver appearing to willingly surrender the vehicle, though I know better. Tires screeching against the cobblestones. As the scrubber escapes, the haze fades.

Papa seizes me by the shoulder. "Come on, let's stop him."

He commandeers a car for us—a sleek, sharklike black Citroën. Papa piles into the driver's seat, Al into the passenger side, and me in the back. Our surveillance van roars to life behind us as

Cindy climbs in with Winnie, Tony, and Marylou. We peel away from the curb and head down the pastoral shrub-lined avenue, right toward a roundabout with Cindy's beloved towering Arc de Triomphe.

Tony's got a name for us, Marylou announces. *Heinrich Muellen, a Czech national. Was in Washington on a work visa, but it would appear his only "work" is with the KGB. His face matches a false passport for a passenger jet that flew out of Dulles yesterday.*

The "us" he mentioned. Any leads on that? I ask.

There's a pause before Marylou answers. *We have a few leads. Hang tight.*

We swing toward the Arc and take the spoke for the Champs-Élysées. Stodgy stone buildings sprout around us on both side of Paris's chicest thoroughfare. Row after row of ornate storefronts fly past us. The wheaty scent of fresh-baked bread from the boulangeries reaches into the car, but it turns my stomach. I'm too electrified to enjoy the scenery. Too determined to catch the scrubber while he's still breathing.

Papa swerves into oncoming traffic to cut ahead of a taxi. Horns blare around us; Al Sterling screams at Papa, jabbing his finger to the right. *I'm trying to find Heinrich,* Marylou tells us, *but I can't stay focused on him. He keeps deflecting me.*

Al Sterling crushes his hat in his fist. *Give me a clear view as soon as you lock on, and I'll blow the bastard's gas tank.*

The grill of a massive truck suddenly blocks my view of the boulevard as it roars from an alleyway. "Papa!" I scream.

He swerves back into oncoming traffic, but the truck clips our rear, shearing off our bumper with a metallic screech. We fishtail for a few agonizing, eternal seconds before Papa rights us.

"Is the truck part of his team?" I peer out the back window. The truck has stopped now, blocking traffic in both directions behind us.

"No," Papa says through clenched teeth. "He's controlling other drivers."

Tony's voice cuts into my thoughts. *Got a few snapshots of Heinrich for you, but I'm afraid you aren't gonna like this.*

Why not? I ask.

Tony doesn't answer for several seconds. Finally, Marylou pipes up. *It's a photo of him in Russia, leaving a research lab with General Rostov. And . . .* Marylou's trippy musical shield buckles with a surge of nerves. *And your mom.*

Before I have a chance to reply, we're tossed back over to the right as another truck skips the median, heading for us straight on. Papa's face turns purple and a vein twists against his temple as the truck slowly changes course back to its side, truck bed swinging frenetically. Al drums his fingers against the car windowsill. "C'mon, Andrei, if you can get me a little closer . . ."

We suspected Mama's involvement—Rostov demanded a psychic army, and the leading psychic geneticist seems poised to give him one. But maybe I'd been hoping against hope that these scrubbers were an anomaly. I could believe in Mama complying with Rostov in the short term for a longer goal, but now, having my nose rubbed in the gruesome details—

Revulsion tastes a lot like fear, which tastes a lot like anger when it's chewing a hole in your gut. The feelings are scrabbling for escape, but I have no way to release them.

Papa parts the cars around us, clearing a straight shot for us to the minty Renault we're pursuing. I can tell we're gaining on

Heinrich by the static fuzz creeping into my thoughts, though Papa's efforts at controlling traffic tamps it down. He jerks the steering wheel from side to side, wrestling with Heinrich for control of himself, while Heinrich's car ahead of us bobs and weaves similarly.

I hold my breath as the green lawn of the Tuileries drops away around us and we clatter onto a bridge across the Seine. The nearby cars rattle erratically, pawns in the psychic battle. "Almost there," Al chants. "Just a little closer—"

Papa slams on the brakes with a yelp. Too close—Heinrich is fending us off, white noise screeching in my head like sparks from flint. We skid perpendicular to the bridge. My heart is buzzing against my ribs like a trapped fly as the hood of the Citroën grates against the stone railing. Pedestrians scream and scramble away—no, some of them are charging for our car, a look of rage on their faces as unseen powers drive them—

"Hold tight," Papa says, and throttles the car into reverse with the grinding of gears.

We lurch backward just as another sedan dives for us, trying to knock us off the bridge. It clips us, propelling us forward, then it ramps up and over the stones.

"Shit!" Al hisses. "Shit."

"We'll catch him." Papa sets his jaw and weaves around the wreckage toward the end of the bridge.

We clatter off the bridge, into the southern side of Paris, and within a few blocks, we're on the green Renault's tail. I squeeze the door handle so hard my nails puncture the vinyl covering as the white static storm envelops us.

"Here goes nothing," Al says, voice strained. "When he gets

out of the car, Yulia, how about you do him like you did Donna and the Hound while I make him nice and toasty?"

Flood him with these negative emotions. This man tried to hurt us; he's working for Rostov. Certainly he deserves it. But as I try to imagine myself doing so, all I feel are the puppet strings lashing around my wrists once more.

Al clenches his fists and leans forward, eager; Heinrich's car jumps up onto the curb as thick black smoke spews from his muffler. He rolls the windows down, more smoke pouring from inside. Papa slows down just a hair as we gain on him. Flames leap from the open edges of the scrubber's car. He throws open the driver's door and staggers away from the car as a massive fireball billows out and up—

The blast knocks the scrubber to the ground as the smell of hot metal floods our car. Is he down? Please let him be down. Please don't make me have to—

Papa cries out; our car lurches across traffic and swipes against a street pole, our hood crumpling into a round poster board. "Papa?" I force myself off the back of Al's seat. My shoulder throbs, but if I have any other injuries, they're buried under a flood of adrenaline. "Papa, are you okay?"

"I'm fine. My door's wedged shut." He tugs at the door handle, but the outside of the door clangs against a lamppost. "Go! Don't worry about me. Get him!"

I scramble out of the back on the passenger's side. Al is stalking toward Heinrich, who's sprawled across the pavement among a crowd of spectators. Al guides the roaring flames down the sidewalk, straining to reach Heinrich, but Heinrich's face—ever-shifting faces, really—is contorted with focus; Al's steps slow as static crackles around us. We stop. Why are we here again? My gaze drifts over the burning car, the gawking Parisians, the man struggling to his feet. I recognize that these things are before me, but there is no purpose to them; they are not relevant. If I could just remember my purpose here—

The crackling tapers off, replaced by a dull pounding in my skull.

The scrubber's gone—fleeing around the corner. I try to shake off the lingering film of his control and take off running after him. His noise trails behind him like the stink of ripe garbage, leading me down a narrow alley. If I stay just far enough back, I can follow his static noise on the cold stone walls without getting close enough for him to distort my thoughts . . .

Chains rattle somewhere around the bend, like someone's climbing up a fence. I flatten against the wall, then once the static recedes, peek slowly around the corner. Heinrich's loafers disappear over a metal gate that's been chained and padlocked shut. Though it's in the middle of a grungy alley, the stone opening reminds me of the entrance to a mausoleum.

"The Catacombs," Al Sterling says, jogging up behind me. "Come on." He launches himself at the gate and scrambles to the top, then reaches down an arm to help hoist me up. I kick and scrabble against the links, unable to gain purchase until I'm halfway over.

"What did they feed you back in Moscow, anyway?" Al asks. "Feathers?"

We shuffle into the heavy darkness of the gated-off stone antechamber. The floor slopes down sharply, leading into further depths that I can't see; I reach for the wall to brace myself, but quickly wish I hadn't. The cold stones are slimy with runoff, and immediately a sharp memory—a glint of steel, a stinging lash across my neck—makes me pull away.

But the deeper we descend, the quicker the light dies out, smothered in the oppressive, stifling air. Al pulls a lighter from his pocket and ignites it with a click. In his hands, it glows ten times brighter than a regular lighter would.

Human bones line the walls around us—femurs stacked lengthwise, their knobby ends worn smooth as polished wood. The archway before us is crowned with grinning, yellowed skulls. Bile burns at my throat. Now I recognize the thickness in the air, denser than mere humidity; it's the muffled memories of the hundreds of thousands of dead it must have taken to build this lewd labyrinth.

I wrap my arms tight around my chest and turn sideways to squeeze through the narrow arch. I will not touch these walls. I cannot carry the weight of so many memories. As Al's light glides over each row of bones along our path, though, I feel as if those empty eye sockets are watching us, as if their memories are just waiting to envelop me like a plague the moment I get too close.

Is this what Cindy's vision of Judgment meant for me?

What's the matter, Yulia? Sergei's voice slinks around my thoughts like an overly friendly cat. *Afraid of what you might find?*

I nearly slam into Al. My heart pounds like a dirge. *Sergei. Where are you? Why is Rostov sending these scrubbers after us?*

Come, now, you're a clever girl. Why do you think?

Because he doesn't want NATO meddling in the civil war in Vietnam. Or maybe he wants us to go to war in Vietnam. And he's trying to use his scrubbers to control the delegates. But—I clench my hands into tight fists. *But why is my mother helping him? Is she really creating these scrubbers? They weren't psychics before. And why are they dying?*

His laughter pings against my musical shield, like a kid throwing rocks. *Of course they're her work. I suppose not everyone's afraid to make the most of their gifts.*

I am an ungrounded wire, crackling with anger and frustration. He can't be right. She wouldn't tell Sergei, of all people, if she had another plan. There has to be something more.

I stagger forward on the uneven ground and reach out to catch myself on the wall of bones. Sergei laughs, the sound ringing through my skull. *You didn't mind touching dead bodies the other day.*

My head whips upward. *You saw that?*

I'm always watching out for you, Yulia. Someone has to. He laughs again. *Someday, you'll thank me for it. Maybe someday very soon.*

What do you mean? I ask. *Sergei?* I peel back a fraction of my shield. *Who is the mole?* But there's nothing but the ringing silence of Al's and my shoes on the grimy catacomb floor.

"Keep going, Yul, keep going." Al tugs at his charred, ragged shirtsleeves. "We'll find the bastard."

But even as he says it, we reach a split in the tunnel.

Al's grip tightens on his lighter; the shadows on the bones quiver in reply. "Okay. Let's go left. Each time we come to a fork, keep taking the leftmost turn, got it? Try leaving a trail of memories for us to follow." He smiles weakly. "Your pops'll kill me if I get you lost, you know."

I relish the idea slightly less than I'd relish the chance to toss the radio in the bathtub with me, but I nod. "Thank you for not making me go by myself."

We move slowly into the next chamber after scanning ahead of us. Its walls hum with a psychic resonance I'm afraid to identify. But I must. With Al's eyes on me, I curl two fingers around the ball grip of a femur.

The memories hit me like an electric current. The scrubber is close—very close, possibly the next chamber over. But as I open my mouth to warn Al, the skeletal memories flood through me. Gravediggers, piles of bones—no, that skull is looking at me, I'm sure of it—a lightning storm tearing through my head. Yes, the bones are coming alive. They are crawling toward me, bringing with them a white, soothing breeze, promising to carry me away. Whispers thread around me like spider silk. Chanting. Begging me to stay with them, to sink into the cool, wet earth. Bony fingers reach for me, buzzing with faint static—

No, Yulia! Marylou cries. *It's the scrubber. You have to fight him off!* A dark image pushes against the haze, against the roaring of voices. The scrubber and his unsteady appearance emerge through an archway. His static rolls forward, threatening to crush me like an avalance. But I have my own weapon: a tide of emotions, sweeping me along, hungry and eager for a target. Yes. I can stop him, just like I stopped the Hound. If I can keep control of myself just a moment longer—

The static engulfs me, like I'm at the base of a waterfall and the voices are pouring onto me. I shove off of the femur and reach forward. I have to unleash these feelings. Just a few more steps and I can reach him—

Click. I see the world in snapshots through the haze of

scrubbing white. Al Sterling lunges forward with a scream, an order that's buried under the words of the tortured, clambering, skeletal dead.

Click. The skeletons surge forward, all around me, crushing me in their brittle bones; they urge me to sleep, to forget my fears and concerns. *Do not fight*, they beg me. Their memories press into my skin. *Stay and listen to our tales.*

Click. Al's lighter clatters to the stone. The shadows of Al and another man, his psychic noise blazing like a nuclear blast, form one monstrous mass across the skeletal chamber wall, then merge into total darkness as the light extinguishes.

My emotions surge back into me, suffocating, scouring. I fall into the scrubber's haze, riding on a tide of empty white.

CHAPTER 17

I DREAM OF RUSSIA: of Mama tucking me into bed at our dacha while a fierce blizzard fills our windows with white. "Hush now," she tells me. "Sleep. When you wake up, the worst will have passed."

But I do not sleep well. In my mind, I am trapped inside a maze of bones, and I can feel the thudding steps of a Minotaur drawing nearer from all sides. Rostov and the Hound and his fleet of altered scrubbers. Mama, wielding a gleaming syringe. I scream at her in Russian, but she shifts into the scrubber, and Al Sterling wrestles with her. He staggers back, rubbing the vein in his forearm and begging me not to tell.

Someone steps in front of me—Cindy? Donna? I scream at them, trying to make them understand, but I can't put the words in the right order. *He is poisoned. I am poisoned. The mole is poisoning us. I will poison you all.*

Dimly, I am aware of an engine drone. I breathe in stale, stratosphere-cooled air and slowly open my eyes. We're back on the Starlift, and everyone else is either asleep in their chairs, cross-armed and pouting (Donna), or sprawled on a makeshift cot (Al Sterling and, apparently, me).

The damned scrubber again. I touch my upper lip, but find no blood. I twist around to study Al on the cot next to mine; he's slumped against the bent metal wall of the plane, staring straight ahead. If he sees me, he doesn't acknowledge it. I suppress a shudder. That haunted look aligns too closely to what I saw in my fevered dreams.

Were they dreams? My gaze travels down his tattered, burned sleeves. I'm looking for something—a snake bite? Something in the soft inside of his elbow. But the puckered, seared skin of his forearms makes for great camouflage; I try to remember what I'm searching for, but the tighter I try to grasp the thought, the quicker it slips from my mind.

"Yulia." It's Valentin—I hadn't even noticed him curled up beside my cot. "How are you feeling?"

"Tired of letting these scrubbers get the better of me." I slump into his outstretched arm; he pulls me into a warm embrace. "I'm feeling . . . tired. What happened?"

Valya grimaces. "We lost the scrubber. When we caught up with you in the Catacombs, he was long gone."

I sink further against him. I'm too tired to muster up anger. At Rostov and Mama and their army, at Sergei, at my own weakness. If I could have just fought past his noise, embraced my powers . . .

"We got Senator Saxton and the rest of the NATO delegates out of there safely and they're all under their respective country's protection, but the trail is cold again."

I frown. "There was only Heinrich? He didn't have any backup?"

"No one we could find, no."

"But he seemed to know exactly who I was. If they knew we were coming—" I do not say what I am thinking, *If the mole told them we were coming*, but Valentin must be thinking it too—"why wouldn't they bring reinforcements?" I groan and slump back on the cot. "I'm sorry. I'm sorry I couldn't stop Heinrich. We can't seem to catch a break."

Valya traces a slow, soothing circle on my shoulder. "If your theory on this . . . relay . . . is correct, then Heinrich's time is almost up. Maybe we'll have better luck stopping whoever comes next."

"But we have no idea who they are. And no idea about what Rostov's directing them toward," I say. My eyelids sag, the weight of exhaustion and my own futility too much to bear.

"I'm afraid not." He presses his lips to my forehead. "But there's nothing we can do about it until we're back at Headquarters. Get your rest, Yul."

I lean against him, savoring his warmth, his scent, his music humming on his skin. But the last thing I see before I sleep is Al Sterling's intense stare, drilling right through me from the other side of the plane.

☆   ☆   ☆

Cindy sits me down at Langley the next day, towering over me in heels while the couch endeavors to slurp me up. She purses her lips and looks me over like I'm an "interesting" piece of art.

"Would you like to talk about what happened in Paris?" she asks.

I flinch and stare down at my fingers, spreading them out before me. The catacombs, drenched with so much pain and suffering . . . And then the scrubber's noise like a toxic spray. "I'm sorry I let the scrubber get away, Miss Conrad. It was just too much."

She tilts her head, a smile softening her expression. "Of course the scrubber was too much for you. He was too much for any of us—even your father. I'm more concerned about the effect the environment had on you."

My cheeks burn with shame. "I'm sorry, Miss Conrad."

"Sorry?" Cindy tilts her head. "We learn through failure. I certainly have. What are you sorry for?"

I tuck my hands in my lap. "I just don't know what to do with those strong emotions. They overwhelm me."

"That's why I'm going to have you work on your emotional control this morning." She smiles again. "I don't want you to feel like you have to be a sponge. You should be in control, Yulia, deciding for yourself what affects you and what doesn't. Like the card I showed you—the Star."

For the rest of the morning, Cindy, Donna, and Marylou take turns summoning up memories—good, bad, anything tied to strong emotion, as long as they don't tell me the emotion in advance—and I must draw it away from them, name the feeling, and release it without experiencing the strong emotion myself.

After Marylou's memory of getting locked in a closet by bullies at her elementary school left me sobbing in a corner of the room, however, Cindy conceded that I might require more assistance than she previously anticipated.

"I want you to read this." She hands me a strange book titled *The Science of Being and Art of Living*. "It's by Maharishi Maharesh Yogi."

I flip open to the first pages and stare at the words. "'Transcendental meditation,'" I read very slowly, drawing out each syllable without understanding a letter of it. "'Inducing a wakeful . . . hypometabolic . . . physiologic state.'"

Cindy purses her lips together, then takes the book back from me. "On second thought, maybe I'll just teach you myself." She slips out of her heels—sugary pink today—and daintily sets them aside before settling onto a pile of pillows. "Sit cross-legged. One leg on top of the other."

I follow her lead, legs crossed, back straight, wrists resting on my knees.

"Now. Think of a phrase—a *mantra*, it's called—that empowers you."

Papa's old adage drifts through my thoughts, as carefree as his whistling. *An empty mind is a safe mind.* But I've seen what his idea of an empty mind entails—scrubbing away memories of my power, trying to make me forget what I am. He desired to protect me, to be sure, but the truth always finds its way back in the end; forgetting has harmed me more than it's helped.

I scrunch up my nose in thought for a few moments, but nothing else comes to mind. "Can you give me some ideas?"

Cindy wiggles her toes. Without her heels and her looming

posture, she looks much more vulnerable. "Do you want to know my mantra?" she asks, head lowered.

I nod.

"*My past cannot hurt me now. My future cannot stop me now. All I have is now.*" She keeps her gaze lowered while she says it, lashes shrouding her eyes, but I feel I have a glimpse into her hard, fearful life in New Orleans that put a tremble in her hands. Her voice, however, doesn't waver, but the way she guards the words reminds me of the old babushkas in Moscow, standing at the site of the demolished Church of Christ the Savior (now a swimming pool, courtesy of Uncle Stalin) and whispering prayers they hope only God will hear.

"I like that." I smile. "Really—there's a . . . a balanced quality to it. Philosophical."

"It's very zen," Cindy agrees. "It focuses on being in the moment. You need something that grounds you in the moment, too. Something to let you know that the emotions inside of you don't control you. They don't have to affect you."

I grimace. "None of us really knows our limits," I mutter to myself. Papa doesn't have to scrub me to infect my thoughts, it would seem.

Cindy raps her tongue against the roof of her mouth. "What about . . . I am as solid as an oak tree?"

I shrug, feeling unmoved. My leg is starting to fall asleep in the awkward pose. "No. I want to be like—like that card you showed me. The Star."

"Others' thoughts and memories can pass through your mind," Cindy says, "but your mind must remain your own."

I sit up straighter. "*My mind is mine alone.*"

Cindy nods, leaning toward me. "Let's work with that." She sucks in air. "Take a deep breath, slowly, then let it out very gradually. On each exhale, think your mantra to yourself. Push away any other thoughts that try to creep into your head." Her shoulders slump as the usual starch in her posture eases away. "Your music shield should be far in the background, like gentle waves lapping at the shore . . ."

I tremble, thinking of Valentin's awful ocean memory. "Or— or like the breeze through the birch trees."

"Yes, like that, too. Breathe in . . . *My mind is mine alone.* Breathe out . . . *My mind is mine alone.*"

The words ring through me, clear and calming like a distant carillon. Shostakovich recedes to the background; the psychedelic record on the record player melts around us into cool liquid sound. It does not touch me. My fears for Mama and Zhenya cannot reach me. *My mind is mine alone.* The scrubbers cannot scratch at me here. *My mind is mine alone.*

After a few minutes, I open my eyes, feeling calm, yet somehow awake, like I'm humming with psychic energy ready to be put to use. Cindy hops to her feet and slips back into her heels, transforming once again into the glossy professional. "Donna? Are you ready to share a memory with us?"

Marylou sits up, eyes wide and bleary. "Donna's talking to the boss-man . . . man." She snorts. "It's funny, because you're not a man."

"Yes. Hilarious." Cindy leans over Marylou and snatches up a scrap of paper. "Who told you to take three of these?"

Marylou stares at her for a long, uncomfortable moment, almost as if Cindy is some strange new species she's never encountered before. "Tuttelbaum," she says finally, one eye squinting as she takes a step backward.

Cindy harrumphs. "No more MK INFRA experiments for you. They make you too dependent on outside factors to perform well, when you should be developing your innate ability."

"Oh, don't be such a square." Marylou draws a box in the air. "I'm, like, this close to bustin' through Castro's defenses, man, all thanks to those pills. If I can get, like, five more . . ."

"You could do it just fine on your own if you tried." Cindy crushes the paper in her fist. "If Frank thinks he can turn us all into his perfect psychic drones—"

"If Frank thinks what?"

Frank Tuttelbaum stands behind Cindy, a lacy drift of curtain coiled in his thick fist. Almost vanishing into his broad side is Donna, a smug smile smeared on her glossy bubblegum lips, and her hands tucked demurely in front of her. There's nothing smiling about Frank's expression, however.

Cindy's face blanches. "I believe further discussion of the MK INFRA program is warranted before we allow our operatives to—"

"Yeah, well, you've got bigger problems than our scientists, Conrad." Frank yanks the curtain from the ceiling and pitches it aside. "My office. *Now!*"

As Cindy scampers off with Frank, Donna sashays into our den, pats the still-skittish Marylou on the head, then drifts down onto the couch and spreads her skirt out in a perfect arc around herself.

"What's happening?" I ask Donna, glancing between her eerie smirk and the doorway where Frank and Cindy left.

Donna fixes her grin on me and narrows her eyes. "Now we're even."

I cross my arms, suddenly cold. "Even with what?"

"You hurt me with your stupid little emotions trick the other day," she says, "so I told Frank all about your secret plot. The one you were rambling about on the flight home—how you're a mole and you're going to poison us all? Foil our plans to capture your evil scientist mom? What are you, some kind of sleeper agent the KGB sent over here to infiltrate us?"

Anger weighs down on me like a slab of stone. I can't breathe through my rage. I try to work through Cindy's transcendental meditation routine, but I can't remember all the steps.

"Oh, well. Doesn't matter now. No way Frank will let you do anything for us again, so you'll have to find someone else to poison."

Anger draws tight around my lungs, fighting against me as I try to breathe deeply. I'm not the poison. I'm not the mole. For a moment, I can almost taste how good it would feel to let my fist crash into her nose; I can smell how she would cry and scream. The anger rises like a tide. How delicious it would be to let these emotions take control.

My mind is mine alone. I chisel the words into my skull. *My mind is mine alone.*

Donna's not the real threat right now. *My mind is mine alone.* I can't be a weapon for any faceless emotion. *My mind is mine alone.* Or any person.

If only I could be sure that were true.

Al Sterling pokes his head into our den and slaps his hand against the wall. "Frank wants everyone in the break room."

I follow Donna and Marylou with leaden feet. This time, the whispers swirling around me are no hallucination. The entire PsyOps team—my team, I think feebly—is gathered around the cigarette machine, the coffeepot, the curved Frigidaire. And at their heart looms Frank Tuttelbaum, his bloodshot eyes fixed right on me.

"It has come to my attention," Frank says, his gruff tone quelling the whispers, "that the powers that be did not vet our Russian 'friends' here as thoroughly as they should have."

I glance at Papa, but he's engrossed in chewing on a hangnail, not even glancing Frank's way. Valentin's gaze is fixed firmly on his shoes.

"I've had concerns for a while now that someone within the PsyOps team was passing information to the Reds, but after your spectacular bungling of the Paris operation, there's little room for doubt. Thank God we've got a diligent, *competent* psychic on this team, who overheard the thoughts of one of you traitors."

My jaw hangs as I look toward Donna, whose cheeks burn red over a nervous smile. I was barely conscious when she overheard me, and certainly not capable of rational thought. "Sir, if I might explain . . ." I glance around for Winnie, but she's nowhere to be found. My throat spasms shut. I need Winnie to explain for me. How can I make him understand?

"Explain?" Frank wheezes with laughter. "What's there to explain? Do you deny your willingness to see your mother rescued?"

"But what if she's on our side?" I ask, but the words have all the weight of smoke.

Frank's smile swells like a tumor. "I'm sure. And that's why she's creating this army of scrubbers, right at General Rostov's disposal."

What can I say? I look to Papa, not really expecting him to speak in Mama's defense—not anymore—but hoping he might look at least somewhat incensed. But he's nothing. He's as still and emotionless as the formaldehyde-soaked Lenin in his tomb.

"Now, Andrei, you and I go way back, and I'd like to think we understand each other. But we're on the brink of war with North Vietnam, and we don't need meddling from more Commies at home."

Cindy clears her throat. "We're still a long way off from declaring war on the Viet Cong, sir. In fact, they just announced a new round of eight-party talks next week. The Pathway for Peace summit—"

"Are you looking to get reassigned, too, Conrad?" Frank asks. His upper lip curls back. "I hear the boys in the bayou have been missing you something fierce."

Cindy's face blanches and her eyes bulge as she seizes her pearls as though they were trying to strangle her.

"As much as my gut tells me to throw the three of you Russkies in jail, the man upstairs would rather investigate such charges fully before we act, which would only bog down our urgent work needlessly with all that gobbledygook. So I'm pulling you three off the case until we can spare the time for a formal investigation."

Off the case.

Off the trail that leads straight back to Mama.

Off the task of hunting for a mole.

Frank bares his teeth in a rough grin. "I'm sure you will cooperate fully, and allow us to do what needs to be done."

I look back to Papa. If there was ever a time for him to use his powers, it would be now. I think I could forgive him for that. But he turns without a word and leaves the break room.

"This has to be some misunderstanding, right?" Judd asks. "I mean, me and Val were making great progress tracking down potential targets, and we—"

"Put a sock in it, Opie, before I slap you back to Mayberry." Frank wags a thick finger at Judd. "That's the thing about these Reds—they'll win you over, but they've always got a trick up their sleeve."

"Mister Tuttelbaum," Valya says. "Frank. I assure you, our desire to stop Rostov is just as strong as yours. Perhaps more so."

"Then you'll have nothing to fear from the investigators. Until then, you're benched, got it? You report directly to me and no one else. And I do not want to hear any complaints unless you want a free ride on the next U2 to cross Soviet airspace. Do we understand each other?"

"Perfectly," I say through clenched teeth, and follow Valya from the room.

CHAPTER 18

IN MY DREAMS, Mama is walking me to school one morning; at age nine, I am still wearing the blue jumper and white blouse that all schoolgirls wear, and my hair has been braided and topped with a white puffy barrette. As we shuffle down the sidewalk, my new loafers scratch and *schick* against the concrete covered in salt poured out in anticipation of the winter's first snow.

Mama's hand is tight around mine; I can feel her agitation building without even looking at her. It itches against my skin like a spreading rash.

"Why do you keep staring at the sidewalk?" She yanks my hand, sending my head snapping up. "Do you think it's going to bite you if you don't keep your eye on it?"

I bend my head down with force now and scrunch my face into a scowl. "Everyone else walks like that."

"Do you know why they do that?" She tilts my chin up, forcing me to see all the other pedestrians: bent-over babushkas with faded scarves tied tight around their hair, factory men with their coat collars turned up, women in padded parkas and ill-fitting slacks.

"Sure," I say. "Because it's cold."

"The cold doesn't matter. It could be the middle of July, and they'd be walking the same way. It's because they're scared."

I crinkle my nose. "When I'm scared, I pull the covers up over my head."

"What, when you're in bed? What are you afraid of then?" Mama asks.

"Monsters," I say. I think back to the scary movie we'd watched at the Party kino, *Aelita, Queen of Mars*, where a Soviet cosmonaut had to free oppressed Martians from the bourgeois Martian elite. "Aliens. Capitalists."

"And have you ever met an alien or a capitalist?" Mama asks.

I think for a minute before shaking my head vigorously, as if I'm trying to shake off even the idea of encountering such a ludicrous, mythical beast.

"That's what I thought. So what is there to be afraid of? Eh?" She tweaks my nose. "Nothing. It's the things you miss when you are too busy being scared that should have you worried."

"Like what?" I ask.

"Good question. You'll never know the answer unless you start paying attention. Do like I do, little *devochka*." She glances skyward, and my gaze follows, as the early morning sun dances across the golden cupolas of a shuttered church. "Don't forget to look up."

CHAPTER 19

ON OUR FIRST DAY barred from the Rostov case, Valya and I draw up a chart of every one of the team members and write up arguments for and against each of them being the mole. *Revenge* tops my list for Donna, in thick, steady letters, but she's already exacted that; Winnie's list grows lengthy, with *Ideology* claiming the lead. I already know she volunteers her time with civil rights groups because I overheard her and Cindy arguing about it. Everyone glances over the shoulder for the ghosts of the McCarthy hearings, when any deviation from the norm got you labeled a communist, an agitator, a threat, Winnie once explained to me. But is dissatisfaction with the current situation enough to drive her to spy for the Russians?

Once we exhaust all possibilities with no clear leader for the mole, Valya goes to practice for the open mic contest while I read through Professor Stokowski's research notes. I felt like we were on the verge of a breakthrough before the Paris trip, identifying the mechanisms in which viruses target specific genes. The dense mathematics of nucleotide pairing and biological reactions distracts me, at least for a while.

"Why don't you kids play outside?" Papa suggests, when he comes down for lunch. "I bet some sunshine will do you good."

But it's not sunshine I need—it's answers. I need to find out what Rostov is trying to accomplish with his scrubbers and who he's sending them after next. How does attacking NATO delegates bring him closer to war? If it's assassination he's after, there has to be a simpler way—one that doesn't involve designing his own army of scrubbers. Why the extra effort? I puzzle over it, each permutation in my mind tracking Valya's musical shift in scales, in key, in mood. Heinrich knew exactly who I was. Did Rostov want Heinrich to draw us away? If so, to what end? What if we'd managed to catch Heinrich? Who's coming for Senator Saxton next?

Al Sterling drops by to argue with Papa in hushed, bristly tones for a few minutes, then offers to drives me back to Doctor Stokowski's lab for the afternoon. He must have just cleaned his car upholstery, because the whole car ride, my brain feels foggy as if from chemical fumes and I'm on the verge of nausea. Al's usual stream of chatter is absent; I hope he hasn't bought into Frank's nonsense about us being the moles. He pulls up in front of the biology complex and wipes a thick sheen of sweat from his forehead.

"Well," he says.

I wait a few moments for him to continue, but he says nothing, so I let myself out of the car and watch him tear away.

As soon as I'm inside the lab, I fire up the electron microscope and pull my samples from storage. C T G A A T T G C. Strings of proteins march across my vision as I whittle down the genetic markers on my samples, hunting for the snippet of code that makes us what we are. Peptides and nucleotides. A simple string of code, coiled up tight. Add some carbon and some endless patience, and you'll have yourself a living, breathing watery meat-bag that likes to think it's intelligent. Tweak it a bit more and it can read your mind, as well. But what happens if you tweak those tweaks? How far can you push it before it's too unstable, and its own mind devours itself, blood leaking out of its ears and nose?

Now that I have a better grasp of what markers I'm looking for, I can easily pick out the psychic samples from the rest. Donna's compared to Frank's, mine compared to Winnie's . . . One set baffles me for a moment, though—the psychic markers start out suppressed and stretched, but as I tinker around with some other projects, they slowly reconstitute themselves. I check the sample label. Marylou.

So rather than amplify her psychic abilities, the LSD and whatever other drugs comprise the MK INFRA cocktail actually impede her psychic ability, loosening the genes themselves. She's just so high she thinks it's making her work better. I try drops of the acid on a few other samples, with the same result.

"Ready to get to work on our research?" Doctor Stokowski joins me, as soon as he's done grading papers. I nod and tidy up my workspace, but my eyes keep tracking to the measurements I recorded. How could the CIA's scientists not realize the INFRA project was making them weaker instead of stronger?

"Look, Yul, I found a fun new virus for us to toy with!" Professor Stokowski deposits a tray of vials in front of me.

I lose myself in splicing code for a few hours, but the nagging questions over the ineffective drug never fully melt away.

✶ ✶ ✶

We've been back from Paris from almost a week and I'm suffocating in my own skin. The silence from Langley across the Potomac River aches like a tooth. After almost a week of research with Doctor Stokowski and overanalysis with Valentin and a number of sleepless nights as Valya's nightmares persist, I'm starving for hints of how Mama's doing, what horrible developments Rostov has made now. How can I stare up at the same sky as them and not hear the clang of battle? How can I not feel the seismic shift of Rostov's schemes?

Finally, one afternoon, Winnie shows up at Papa's townhouse. "I'm sick of work," she tells me. "Let's take a trip."

Winnie is to the movie theater what an inquisitor is to a dungeon full of torture devices. My job is to translate the entire movie to Winnie, from English to Russian. Word for word. "You'll like this one," she says, as we flip down the sticky seats. "Some of it's already in Russian. So you can translate that to English for me, instead."

I curse in Russian, an elaborate and obscure enough curse that hopefully even she can't decipher it.

The next ninety minutes feature some of the most jaw-droppingly bewildering cinema I've ever seen. The weird little man from *The Pink Panther*, which Valentin and I saw on our own recently, is playing almost half the roles in the film—shapeshifting seamlessly from a meek American president to a diabolical war room adviser with a fascistic salute and deranged grin. Doctor Strangelove, they call him.

I am not entirely sure what the purpose of the film is, aside from showing men drinking, smoking, flirting with women, and dropping absurdly huge bombs from airplanes. The Americans and Soviets both are shown as clueless political leaders far more interested in watching things explode than brokering any sort of peace.

"It's satire," Winnie says, after I stumble through one of the translations with an incredulous look on my face. "They're making fun of our leaders for being hungry for war."

"You understand why this is a strange concept to me. This 'making fun of our leaders' business." I grin.

As the chubby cowboy rides his colossal bomb onto the Siberian plains, something needles at the back of my brain. I twist in my seat, scanning the rows behind us, but we're the only people in the theater that I can see. The projector dances across my hand as I shield my eyes for a better look. It felt like a scrubber, slipping past us, like a phantom cobweb clinging to my skin. I look back at Winnie, but she was laughing at the cowboy. Well, she couldn't have felt it, anyway. People like her can't feel a scrubber until it's far too late.

"I'm sorry. I need to visit the restroom," I tell her, and slip out of the row.

The movie theater, tucked away in a lower level of Georgetown down by the canals, is dark and grimy on the brightest of days. I sniff out the scrubber's trail, fainter than a fine perfume.

My heart thuds rapid fire high in my throat. Could this be the next scrubber in the chain?

I round the corner and plow into Papa's chest.

"Yulia! There you are. Al and I wanted to join you and Winnie for the show."

"Don't bother. The movie makes no sense."

"You see? Waste of time." Al punches Papa in the arm. "I shouldn't be here anyway. Frank'll have my hide if he knows I'm talking to you."

"Now, now, don't run away just yet. We can catch Doris Day next door."

I start to catch my breath as they stroll past. The strange sensation I felt wasn't the new scrubber. It must have been Papa, conning his friend into talking to him. Or conning whoever Papa felt like conning at the moment.

But the itch at the back of my mind doesn't abate when I head back into the theater.

CHAPTER 20

THE NIGHT AIR on U Street quivers like an autumn leaf, eager to take that leap from its tree. U Street is the leftover stone from carving out Georgetown: it is dark skin and harsh neon and thick metal bars on the windows, it is cinder-block churches and hookah dens and sunken eyes that follow you as you pass their stoops. Jazz music and Motown tunes pour from every doorway like spilled beer. Papa's house is in DC, but this, *this*, Winnie tells us, is the true city of Washington. Chocolate City, they call it. The workhorse heart pumping behind the fancy filigree veins of the National Mall and all the other tourist traps.

I can't pretend to know what Winnie feels, but I imagine this might be a small taste. To be the odd one out, the skin tone that people point at as you pass and grab their children by the collars to keep them from running into you. I may be an exotic species, *Homo sovieticus*, around other whites, but among them I can blend into the background, as long as I don't make a noise. Winnie with her education and military training has more in common with

Frank Tuttelbaum than I do, but she's the one left curling her fingers around the chain link fence as she watches us from outside.

Tonight, though, Winnie is lit from inside by a three-wick candle. She's torn free of her Air Force uniform shell and has emerged in a polka-dotted dress that swirls around her curved slender calves. The whole cab ride here, she and Valentin batted around various jazz composer names and terminology like kittens playing with yarn.

"Miles Davis—" Winnie started, then choked on a grin that seemed to bloom out of her like a flower.

Valentin leaned in closer. " 'Kind of Blue'—"

"—Those two *notes*!"

He and Papa are both in what Winnie called their beatnik camouflage: black turtlenecks and tight brown corduroy slacks. Winnie dolled me up in a silky, slinky green dress and twisted my dark hair high atop my head in something called a "beehive" before painting my lips ruby red. "That Val of yours is going to catch the eye of every woman in the place," she told me as she spritzed us both with perfume. "Might as well show 'em up front that they don't stand a chance."

But I'm not worried about beatnik girls with their clove cigarettes and their Liz Taylor Egyptian eyes stalking Valentin. I'm worried about the trail to Mama that grows colder every day, the information Valentin and I are working from growing older and less useful. Even though we aren't on the case, I keep imagining her scrubbers' psychic noise creeping up on me like an itch at the back of my throat. It's nothing, it's nothing. *My mind is mine alone.* Yet every twitch of my psychic antenna sets my head swiveling.

But tonight, I want to relax. Tonight is for my Valya, and our new, exciting life in America, the good shaken and served over ice with the bad.

We reach the end of the block, and Winnie uses nothing but a stern glare to push past a cluster of fedoraed men blocking the sidewalk. Our destination rises from the concrete like a brick and neon reliquary. "Bohemian Caverns" reads the looping neon sign, meandering around the building's sides beneath a ribbon of signage painted to look like piano keys. A golden saxophone sign hangs off the building's corner like a beacon.

We have reached Valentin's temple of jazz.

His hand closes around mine for a brisk squeeze as he gawks at the building, the lights dancing across his glasses. Every single one of his heroes—if they've played in DC, they've played in the Caverns. And the labels' talent scouts are sure to be in the crowd, prowling, marking down the names of who's hip and who's square.

"You're gonna kill 'em, tiger." Winnie jabs him in the ribs and leads us through the black door, carved with the strange symbols of a sacred ancient temple.

The staircase appears chiseled out of fake rock, as if we're spelunking into the bowels of the Earth on a journey to the Inferno. The sounds of conversation and warming-up musicians reach us scattershot, skittering across the strange acoustics. It smells cool and smoky and damp, like instead of subterranean pools there's alcohol seeping up out of the depths.

A trumpet twitters maniacally as we descend into the cavern, where fake stalagmites form archways between several chambers that cluster around the central stage. A leggy brunette, her Audrey

Hepburn cigarette pants making her look svelte instead of starved, pads past us as she eyes us each in turn. "I'll take the whole package," she purrs, before blowing a cloud of too-sweet smoke in my face. This must be the reefer the news keeps warning me about. I fan the cloud away, but my eyes are already watering.

We find the signup sheet near the platform, guarded jealously by a pompadoured greaser whose black leather jacket and wallet chain jangle like a trip to the Laundromat, and by a colored boy around our age in the finest three-piece suit I've ever seen in my life. The latter tips his hat toward Valentin. "'Bout time we got to hear you cook, Val."

"Mister Tibs." Valentin shakes his hand. "Can I get you on my dance card?"

"That'll be up to the Big Daddy." Mister Tibs jabs his thumb at the greaser, who's looking me over like he's trying to sear my image into his retinas. I cross my arms and shrink back.

"That depends, cats. You gonna mesh me that doll of yours, Val?" the greaser asks.

The English words are spreading out in my head like a strange buffet—each word on its own, I grasp, but I can't make sense of their composition. I look at each of the men in turn, trying to read them. Mister Tibs has stopped drumming on the podium; the greaser's smile turns a little darker with every second that passes, like he's savoring our unease. Valentin's hand curls into a fist around mine.

"What's your name, babydoll?" the greaser asks me. When he leans in toward us, he stinks of cigarettes and minty Brylcreem hair gel—a little dab'll do ya, the ad says, but he used the whole tin, just to be safe. "I'm a lot more fun than Red Square here."

My eyes start to water—maybe it's the reefer and clove smoke—but then I feel that familiar scrubbing itch, skittering like a bug across my skin. "Valentin," I say, dropping his hand. "Don't."

The sensation fades. But the greaser is watching us like the last minute has eluded him. "Oh . . . Oh. Hey, look, cats, it's Red Square. The coldest Cold War cat I know." He flicks the pencil to Valentin. "You and Mister Tibs gonna finally cook it together?"

Now it's Mister Tibs's turn to eye us—all of us—like he's not sure what alien spacecraft we just stumbled off of. "Uh . . . yeah. That'd . . . that'd be a blast." He cocks one eyebrow at the greaser behind his back.

"Looking forward to it," Valya says, and shoves the sign-up sheet back at them.

"What did you scrub him for?" I hiss at Valya as he drags me away from the platform, weaving us through the thickening swarm and billowing smoke.

He clenches his jaw, expression darkening. "*I* didn't."

I glance over my shoulder at Papa—he's been so uncharacteristically quiet, I'd almost forgotten he was here. He gives me a wink and turns back to the cluster of beatniks who have enveloped him like old friends.

Valya and I reach the bar, which looks like it was carved out of the caverns, though all the hollows have been lined with mirrors and turned into shelves brimming with liquor bottles. The bartender slides Val two drinks without even asking him what he wants.

"You don't usually drink," I say.

Valya grips his glass so tight I can hear the ice rattling. "I don't usually improvise in front of a hundred jazz aficionados," he replies.

We both take an oversized swig from our drinks.

"I know we have a lot going on, but I've been thinking," he says slowly. "A few weeks ago, you'd offered to help me . . . And I wondered if you'd be willing to try again."

Helping him heal from his past. I lean in closer. The dark smudges under his eyes have only gotten darker. "I can try. But you heard what my father said . . ."

"I have endless faith in you, Yulia. You're my guiding star. I know you wouldn't hurt me. I worry more about my own power."

I run my thumb over the ridge of his knuckles. "You're not like my father, or Rostov. You don't go out of your way to hurt people with it, or use it to your advantage."

"But I could, don't you see?" He uses his hand to draw a circle around the club. "I don't have to give a great performance tonight. I don't have to perform at all. I could make every single person in this room believe I've just given a show better than Duke Ellington. Why would I bother with the hard work of trying to win the normal way, when I already have the keys to the kingdom?" He shakes his head. "For as long as I've been aware of my curse, that temptation has always been there, digging its claws into my shoulder."

His curse. My powers have been many things to me—a danger, a burden—but I don't know if I'd ever deem them an evil spell I had to break. I squeeze his thigh, wishing I could take away that pain with just a touch. "It's admirable that you don't use it that way. It's one of the reasons I love you."

Valya laughs dryly. "Your father thinks it's foolish. Anyway, that's not my point. What I'm trying to tell you is—this memory. The one that wakes me up at night. If I could be rid of my power, if there was any way for me to shed it . . . I would."

His eyes are wide and pleading behind his glasses. I don't doubt him for a minute. But if I can learn to manage my own powers, then surely he can make peace with his own. I just need to show him that he can.

"*So*, Yulia," Winnie says, as she sidles up to us. "Enjoying yourself? Feeling lost yet?"

I clink my glass against hers. "Doing well so far."

"Yeah, that's because you've been talking to Valya all night." She crosses her arms. "I think it's time to play your favorite game."

"*All* your games are my favorite," I say with my best attempt at caustic American sarcasm. Valya grins behind his glass as he takes another drink.

"Tonight you're going to talk to at least five different strangers here—*in English*—and I want to hear about five new slang terms you learn." Winnie narrows her eyes. "Val's group goes on stage second, so you'd better get a head start if you don't want to be working during his set."

Five new slang words? Not my favorite task, but it's better than translating an entire movie for Winnie, especially weird political ones. "What will I win?"

"The satisfaction of a job well done. Oh, and let me know if you find any cute men my age." She rolls her eyes. "I need a nice, uncomplicated man in my life."

I raise one eyebrow, wondering who has her so disgusted. "I'll do my best."

I start with Mister Tibs, since he already knows Valya and I like his easy smile, and there's a sharp, percussive, rhythmic patter to his speech that hints at his drummer's blood. "'Jive,'" I shout at Winnie as I pass her and a gaggle of what must be some of her off-duty friends—Motown-coiffed colored girls in pastel gowns who smell like roses. She gives me the A-OK sign with a wink and a rounded finger and thumb. Maybe I can get Valya to introduce the two of them later.

The greaser rounds up the first set for open-mic night, cobbling a quartet out of the random entrants—saxophone, trumpet, bass, and drums. Their first number starts shaky, but turns into a real "barn burner"—another new term I have learned from Chin Soo, a Korean man in a golden tux with a round face and a martini in each hand who lords over a cluster of scrawny white beatnik girls who laugh like howler monkeys at everything he says. Valentin relaxes when the group's next number fails to incite revolution and thunderous applause, and in exchange for teaching me more phrases, Chin Soo bolsters his girls' waning interest in the mediocre music by goading me into saying various phrases in my thick accent:

"We have ways of making you talk."

"Workers of the world, unite!"

"Your papers, please."

"Lenin lived, Lenin lives, Lenin will live again!"

As Valentin and I start to wander away, one of the girls splays her clawed fingers across my arms and looks into my eyes, her gaze glassy with earnestness. "I just wanted y'all to know," she drawls, "I don't think y'all Russians are as evil as they say. And even if you are, *I forgive you.*"

I thank her for her generosity and follow Valentin to the platform.

He's so nervous, he's buzzing like a live wire. You wouldn't know it to look at him, but I can hear it on his skin. Taste it in the air. The air in the cavern—did I think it smelled too sweet, too stale before? It's just right, shimmering with green and purple lights and the clouds of smoke, like the jazz music itself has congealed around us. Valentin beside me and Papa at the far end of the room—two magnetic poles of scrubbery noise, tearing my molecules in different directions. I should be used to this noise. I shouldn't feel it prying me apart like the claw-end of a hammer is easing out the nail that holds me in together.

The greaser announces the next improv set. Valya on piano. Mister Tibs on drums. A big, burly man on clarinet, and Chin Soo on upright bass.

Papa and Winnie join me and in solidarity, we stake a seat right at the edge of the stage. Valentin draws his other three musicians around the bend in the piano for a solemn conference, his face long and his tone as urgent as when we plan spy operations. They have three songs in which to win over the reeferheads and beatniks and greasers and rowdy boys and mod girls, all of whom grow more drunk, more stoned, more horny, and more impatient as the evening progresses. Three songs, and they can be invited back to the Caverns to play closed events, get signed by one of the label suits, or sink into the oblivion of unknown artists at large. Valentin wants this, more than almost anything he has ever wanted in his life.

At least, more than he has ever wanted anything in America, now that we are free of Rostov's grasp.

Their conference concludes. The crowd quiets, but the noise of a scrubber's brain flip flops inside my head; it rings like too-abrupt silence. I glance toward Papa, but his eyes are on the stage.

Valentin plays the four notes of a major chord, softly, helping the other musicians find the key. The clarinetist counts to four with a swing of his arm.

Three syncopated chords. Then three more. They're thick, they punch me in the sternum. Maybe I'm a little high because I can see the chords' colors shifting with the music's mood, following the bright, ostentatious spins of the melody. People are cheering and rocking back and forth and snapping their fingers to the beat. Winnie leans forward, hands clasped together, already prepped to burst into wild applause. Even Papa, draped like a wet noodle in his chair, has a blissful grin on his face.

This is my family now, I realize. Me and Papa and Winnie and my Valentin. This is home, right inside these syncopated, jewel-colored chords, and that thought plucks me like a piano's string. For one moment, I cannot imagine bringing Mama into this life of jazz clubs and Paris missions and greasy diners on the avenues. Where would she fit around the table? How would she react to such a crowd?

Then I hate myself for the thought; the emotion rises up in me on a tide of alcohol and whatever other substances I'm soaking up tonight. How could I think such a thing? How could I let myself even entertain the thought of leaving things the way they are, when there is so much more they could be?

Mama should be there—and there, and there. I feel all the places in my head and my heart that Mama should fill. All the negative space, in the eaves of one of the false stalagmites or in the gap left on a bench that must have been left for Mama and Zhenya.

I watch Papa as his fluid arm scoops up his drink and he sips it with a carelessness I could never achieve. How could a man react so strongly when he thought I would hurt myself the other night, trying to help Valentin, but feel nothing at all when it comes to the painful emptiness that Mama has left?

The clarinetist finishes his solo and fades out to triumphant applause—now it's Valentin's turn to shine. I shove thoughts of Mama deep down, back into their box, and let my emotions ride on the clattering, shimmying piano chords. Valentin's fingers roam up and down the keys, they hush, they shout, they turn bitter and hateful as he bashes the keyboard, they sing with praise. Mister Tibs is watching Valentin play with a rounded O for a mouth, keeping up only the barest of rhythmic clicks and cymbal snaps. Chin Soo seems to have forgotten how to play as he watches, eyes wide. The whole cavern holds its breath like one great bellow deep in the earth.

Finally Valya's solo ends and he slumps toward the piano, crushed under an avalanche of claps and snaps and cheers. My palms burn as I applaud like a maniac for him. Papa puts two fingers into his mouth and whistles with delight. Chin Soo and Mister Tibs take their turns at solos, and they perform wonderfully, but I'm still drunk on Valya's sounds and the crowd and this whole wide wonderful world into which we've been set free.

Finally, all four musicians recombine for the last frantic iteration of the main melody, and when they finish, the cavern is nothing but noise, frantic noise. Slapping on tables and popping bottles of champagne. Noise scratching at my thoughts with its sharp claws. For a moment I think it's a scrubber again, but I must be losing myself on the wave of chaos. How could this moment be anything but perfection?

Valentin and the others take a nervous bow. They confer on song number two; I hear Valentin whistle something under his breath, though it's too rowdy around us for me to make it out. He settles back down on the piano bench, then turns to the audience, face carved from granite.

"This next song is called 'Yulia Takes Flight.'"

Winnie giggles and kicks her legs, then jabs her finger toward me from above, as if to announce to everyone, *This is Yulia, here she is, watch her fly!* I stare, stunned, as the first delicate piano notes threaten to swallow me whole. They feel like sticky quicksand slurping me down. He said I take flight, but there's no mention of what I'm flying to or from.

To Papa. Away from Mama and Zhenya.

To freedom. Away from fear.

To a perpetual state of confusion, of unknowing, of helplessness. From routine, from mastery of all the Soviet system's games and all their thousand rules.

To our future. Away from our past.

But if that's true, then why is our past still carved, unhealing, into our brains?

Valya's song for me is as delicate as lace, neither happy nor sad, but instead full of sly, creeping jazz chords from the clarinet and bass and filigree trills from the piano. It flies, but it sinks as well. There's no solo rotation this time; it ends with a watery, eager spread of piano chords as the drums dissolve into juicy cymbal rolls.

Everyone around me is screaming and hollering and pumping their fists, but I am pinned in place, cemented to my chair. My cheeks are wet; I swipe at them, leaving a trail of mascara along my arm. Valentin stares at the keys as if he means to burn a hole through them with his mind. Finally, slowly, as if forcing himself to, he looks up to meet my eyes.

Spasibo, I mouth to him. *Ya tebya lyublu.*

He lets out his breath like it weighs a hundred pounds and spreads a broad grin across his face.

"Yul-i-ya! Yul-i-ya!" Winnie starts the chant, but it spreads hungrily to Papa, to all the tables around us, sweeping across the cave. Valentin stands and approaches the edge of the stage, hand held out to me. We grab each other by the wrists; he hoists me onto the stage and pulls me into a victorious embrace.

Everyone is cheering, everyone is screaming our names. Even Mister Tibs and Chin Soo and the clarinetist are cheering for *us*.

"Yul-i-ya! Yul-i-ya!"

Yulia.

It's in my head, scratching from the inside like a rodent trying to escape. I freeze. Is it Sergei's voice? The reefer and booze? Scritch-scritch-scratch, the sound of scrubbers swirling all around, but they must be Papa and Valentin. Everyone's screaming my name, everyone's buzzing with scrubbery pain. A man in the corner stares through me, not cheering, not smiling, dripping with sweat. No, wait. It's just Al Sterling. I almost didn't recognize him. Of course it's just him; he decided to show up after all, Frank's rules be damned. I am hallucinating the noise in my head. I am out of my mind; there is no one inside of it.

"For our last song," Valentin asks, "will you sing along, Yulia?"

More wild screaming. I stare at him, confused, like maybe he was speaking Dutch or ancient Sumerian or some other language I can't comprehend.

"Don't worry. You'll know the song when you hear it." He readies himself before the keyboard and nods out the four-count to the others.

The tail end of a phantom Russian melody pours out. "Moscow Nights"—one of my favorites. I curl my fingers around the microphone and start the first verse. My voice is thin, though I'm hitting the right notes; like my power, I can't just open up my throat and let every ounce of hurt and nostalgia and longing and joy escape.

Then Winnie leans forward, bolstering my voice with hers. With an elbow to his ribs, she gets Papa to join in too, brassy and bold. Winnie smiles at him, though she's quick to qualify it with a roll of her eyes. Moscow Nights. Those lovely, snow-flecked Moscow nights. I am not at home unless I'm snug in Moscow's arms.

Moscow nights, snow twinkling around Mama and Papa and Zhenya and me like falling stars. The Kremlin is a beautiful red against the inky sky; everything looks gilded with gold as the snow hides all of the dirt, all of the suffering. I sing and stomp my foot with the rhythm like the old folk singer groups.

I do not miss the Moscow nights, but I miss what came with them—the love of my family, all of us happy and joined, and my childish certainty that nothing could ever tear us apart.

Al Sterling stares at us from the corner. His stare itches up my arms like scratchy wool. Everyone's leaning forward like they want to bathe in our voices, but it's so thin, raspy and shredded though they are from the smoke and the noise growing and swelling in my head.

Somehow we make it to the final verse. Everyone's clapping in rhythm to the song (more or less) and the clarinetist is warbling all over the place like a drunken starling. I am lost somewhere between the lyrics and the truth of the Moscow nights they try to romanticize: bitter cold, blistering psychic noises chasing you down, bits of razor wire embedded in your palms, the very people you're trying to help betraying you.

We reach the end of the song with absurd vibrato, and everything seems to happen at once.

Al Sterling stands up, nearly tumbling over, sweat running down his gaunt cheeks.

Valentin bounces a single chord back and forth between his two hands like a tennis ball, deep low octaves and high sparkling ones.

Papa's smile starts to slip as he notices his friend, his bleary, drunken gaze sobering in an instant as the static sparks and snaps.

Mister Tibs's drumstick snaps in two as he bashes it against the rim.

The clarinet squawks.

My knees buckle underneath me.

Papa shoves through the mindless, screaming crowd toward the exit just as Al Sterling charges for him.

Valentin stands up from the piano.

Papa cups a hand around his mouth and beckons us toward the exit. "Yulia, run!"

CHAPTER 21

THE COOL, SLIMY WALLS of the staircase (Is this really a cave? Are we lost, like Marylou, in the stream of time and space?) make for bad handholds as we clamber upward, Papa close behind us, and Al behind him. The cool April night air douses me, washing away the smoke and haze; it's too clean and empty. Breathe in, out. Like Cindy taught me. But I can't hold onto my breath from the smoke and the singing and the panic that's pulling like a garrote at my throat.

We are running. Well, Papa and Valentin are running; Winnie is clip-clopping behind them in her heels, and I am bobbing up and down like a pogo stick on my good ankle and my bad. Three scrubbers in a row ahead of me, blazing down U Street like a satellite's contrail, all their signals and noise crackling behind them.

Al Sterling. The memory floods back to me, torn at the edges but enough for me to piece together: the scrubber in the catacombs of Paris, looming over Al with a syringe. Al Sterling, getting injected with the super scrubber serum. The current scrubber in Rostov's chain.

The men vanish into the alley next to Ben's Chili Bowl, all lit up like a carnival in yellow and red. There is a scuffle—a thudding sound. Someone yelps like a beaten dog. I round the corner of the alley just as Al breaks out of Papa's tackle. Valentin is clutching his hand and hissing through his teeth.

"What happened?" I shriek, though my feet are still carrying me toward the end of the alleyway. Toward Al—but, he is no longer Al; he is one of Rostov's scrubbers now.

"He tried to jab me—with that—"

Something metal glints on the ground, but my attention's jerked away. Papa grabs for Al, but Al effortlessly flings him backward. Papa's arms flop uselessly against the shattered glass paving the alleyway, as if he's warring with himself. I lurch forward. Did I take that step? My head is spinning, buzzing like a swarm of wasps gathering to strike.

"It's not too late to surrender," Al says, but the words are forced through his vocal cords like it's a sausage grinder. His voice sounds so harsh, so foreign. "We can bring you back into the Party, Andrei. Antonina would be very proud of you."

But the voice isn't Al's chipper, carefree tone. It's General Anton Rostov's voice.

Papa stands up and forces one foot in front of the other. Al is cornered. I can barely make out his face; it's just a mess of confusion and sweat and a sinister grin. I crouch. No. I am not choosing this action. This fog in my head, raw as asbestos, is shredding away my control. My hand closes around the metal on the alley pavement? A syringe. Just the right size to hide in a cigarette case.

Like the one Anna Montalban had.

As soon as I have that thought, though, it's swallowed up in confusion. The only clear thought I have is of Rostov, his desperation to make the world dance on his red strings. The scene before me is only a series of surveillance photos:

Papa lumbering for his best friend as if his feet are made of uranium.

Winnie staring at us from the alleyway, blood running down her nose.

Al Sterling's hand closing around a bottle of liquor someone left in the alley.

My thumb finding the plunger.

Valya's eyes gleaming white in the neon night.

I am the wasp. I sting.

"Forgive me," Al's voice pleads. "I can't let him—I never meant to—" But it's squeezed away by Rostov's mad laughter. Al pours the bottle's contents over himself and pulls his beloved Zippo lighter from his pocket.

I collapse at Valya's feet, wondering why he sounds like an air raid siren.

As everything goes dark, the smell of burning meat wafts around me, sweet and smoky, making my mouth water for a half-smoke from Ben's Chili Bowl.

★　★　★

I blink, clearing away the empty world I'd been drifting in. I am lying on my side, broken glass under me. The noise is gone. The toxins in my veins and my brain have burned themselves out, self-immolated. Valentin is slumped beside me while Papa is tamping down a fire at the dead end of the alleyway. Why did he start a fire? Why am I crying?

Bozhe moi.

It comes back to me in fits and starts: Rostov taking over Al through the serum, and Al setting himself on fire to stop Rostov.

Papa stands over his friend's incinerated corpse. For the first time since we've been reunited, his face has lost its creamy smoothness; his forehead bunches up and his eyes squeeze shut like clenched fists. *This is it*, I think. He may not feel anything for Mama anymore, but this is the moment that will break him.

I turn to Valentin, but he's sprawled beside me, gasping for breath. At the sight of him, my mind clears. Rostov took control of me, too—the syringe—

It's jutting from Valentin's forearm. Right where I plunged it.

I scamper backward, horror wriggling out of me in sharp bursts, like explosions under my skin. "No—No—No—" Over and over. What else is there to say? What else is there to do? This moment in time is a well of gravity, infinitely heavy, and the rest of my life is collapsing on this point from both sides of the continuum.

"You didn't mean to," Valya is saying, but his teeth are chattering together, biting off bits and pieces of his words. "You couldn't help it."

Winnie staggers toward us, her eyes red and swollen. "Andrei? Yul? What's happening?"

I can't bear it as she notices the needle in Valya's arm, as she looks between him and me. I back away, hard, cold brick pressing into my spine. My hand is over my mouth; dimly I sense my teeth digging into my fingers. No. No. Valya. No.

But then the air around us crackles, and Papa's face is as cool as ever as he reaches over and rips the syringe from Valya's arm.

"We must go." He holds out a hand for me, and one for Valya. "Now. If it's not already too late."

✱   ✱   ✱

"I feel fine," Valya insists, jaw tight, Adam's apple bobbing in a nervous gavotte. "I'm fine. Nothing is wrong."

Papa slings his arm over the back of my seat as he maneuvers the Austin Healey into the street parking spot. "Get your rest, all the same." Something flickers across his face—like a split-second image looming through the static of a badly tuned TV set. It's a look of compassion, concern. The look he got whenever Mama had a bad headache, or Zhenya retreated into himself. A look that told me he cared.

That look is like a crack spreading in the dam that keeps my emotions at bay, and I'm not sure if I can hold this all in anymore. Papa, showing emotions. Is that how dire the situation is?

Valya crawls out of the backseat and opens my door for me. I reach for his hand. I need to squeeze it, reassure myself he is still here, but he jerks his hand away. He looks at me, guilty, some half-apology stuttering on his lips, but I turn away, burning with embarrassment and shame.

"I—I'm sorry, Yulia." He hangs back as we climb from the car. "Until we know what this is, it's better if—I mean, if it's contagious—"

Of course we cannot touch. "I understand." But it stings worse than a slap, all the same.

"Stay near the phone," Papa says. "Rostov's too vindictive to stop with Al. This won't be the end." He throws the Austin Healey back into gear and tears away.

Valya and I bob up the sidewalk, one foot of air separating us, one whole cubic foot of atmospheric pressure keeping whatever is inside of him at bay. We fumble at the door—he tries to hold it open for me just as I try to let him go inside first, then we're both pushing in, shoulders nearly crashing together, then finally I duck under his arm. Inside Papa's house, I can smell the sweat and smoke and alcohol and fear that clings to me. I check the phone in the conservatory, make sure it's in its cradle, then stretch the cord out so I can reach it from the chaise lounge where I intend to collapse for the night, though I know my nerves will be standing at attention throughout my dead sleep, ready to answer Papa's phone call if and when it comes. I settle onto the chaise and tug a fluffy chenille blanket over me. I kick my boots off only as an afterthought.

The piano bench groans as Valya settles onto it.

"Thank you for my song." I'm too embarrassed to meet his eyes. "Every note was perfect."

He slides on the bench so he's angled toward me. Just a few feet away. I stretch out my arm. I can almost, almost, reach his knee . . .

I drop my hand. My fingers trail along the cold wood floor. There is a great depressurized zone in my chest where there should be a solid mass: a Valentin wrapped up in my arms. The emptiness there makes me float, untethered. I need his anchor.

"I don't care about the dangers right now. Please let me touch you," I say.

His head is lowered; he glances at me through his lashes, through the shield of his glasses lenses.

I fight to keep my hands from fluttering. "If these are . . ." *Our last moments together.* "If there's any chance . . ." *That I'll never be able to touch you again.*

He hears the unspoken words, the unformed thoughts, that fill the pauses in our shared music, flowing back and forth between our heads like a wave. It's more than a psychic ability, the way we know each other's contours in the dark and know each other's thoughts. He stands, slowly; pulls toward me as if caught in my gravity. He sits on the edge of the chaise and I curl around him, arms around his waist, my nerve ends sighing with relief the moment his warmth meets mine.

And he is warm. Has he always been this warm? Is this the onset of a fever, some disease that will burn him up from inside? A symptom of something worse? No, I have to quiet my mind—smooth out these panicked thoughts like wrinkles in a sheet. Savor this moment. Sear it onto me so it can never be taken from me.

"Your offer to take my bad memories," he says, fingers stroking my cheek like it's the warmup for a concerto. "The ones that hurt . . . that I can't clear away. Does your offer still stand?"

I sit up. My pulse is cantering as I lean toward him, syncopating with our psychic wavelengths. "I'm here for you." My fingers stitch around his, custom-fit. "I'll always be here."

He clenches my hand in his. "I know. I've never doubted you, Yul—even when you doubt yourself."

Once again, emotion bubbles up in me, threatening to boil over, but I cannot waste the space for it. I repeat my mantra, over and over, until it hums in my veins: *My mind is mine alone.* "I'm ready," I say.

Valentin's eyelids sink shut as he grips my hand tighter. As his music unravels, I fall deeper into it, the conservatory melting into his swirling thoughts. Melodies snake past, and fragments of ideas, half-formed and then discarded, until all of his armor falls away, and I am enveloped in his memory.

Sand, still warm from the height of the day, scratches between my toes—Valentin's toes. In his memories, his skin—my skin, now—has that clammy just-drying feel as a breeze carries away some of the heat from my bare legs. There is a symphony in my head—no, not a symphony. This is scaled-down music, intimate, but no less powerful. A violin and a piano, the theme charging forward and retreating, like waves against the shore. Dark without being sad, stormy without being a downpour, and peppered with warm, bright rays.

"Schumann," I say as my fingers patter the theme along my slender thighs. "Sonata No. 1."

I turn to look at my mother, expecting to see her smiling, pleased that even as I play on the shore my heart is still back on the piano bench. Her dark curls pool like oil around her head as she leans back in her chair; her skin, tanned and hardened from decades of seaside life, is crusted with salt and sand. But she is not smiling. Something snaps tight inside me; I stand up straighter. A shadow stretches over our shoulder as a cloud crosses the sinking sun.

"You heard what those boys were saying about you, Valya." She does not move a single feline muscle, she does not open her eyes, but I hear the transformation. She has slipped out of the wonderful, loving mother who plays violin with me and fallen into that dark and roaring abyss. This other side of my mother is the only monster I fear in the dark.

I glance down the shore, at the older boys—twelve, thirteen—shoving and kicking sand at each other. When they passed, they looked at each other; I heard what they thought of me, a wimpy little kid, a scrawny no one, not fit for the Georgian life. *A spoiled Party brat*, one thought. The others used darker words.

I dig one toe into the sand. "I don't care what they think."

"But you know what they think." Her golden skin has taken on an amber tint. Radioactive. I step back, instinctively, hearing the flames crackle in her thoughts.

"It doesn't matter." I swallow. "I'm not gonna change their thoughts." Schumann's tempest of violin and piano swells in my chest like a hurricane pressure.

"It always matters. It will matter one day, when you take the wrong thought from someone's head." She climbs up from her chair, sinuous, slithering. "When you set your father's bed on fire. When you feel the flames eating you alive."

"Just because *you* can't control it—"

I stop short, but it's too late. The unspeakable words have been spoken.

"Control? Do you think I wish to control it, like it's some pet I can tie up in the yard?" Juicy drops of sweat wreathe her face as she stalks toward me; her skin is now the brilliant red of too many hours in the noonday sun. The air around her shimmers, smelling spicy and sweet, like grilling meat. "I would be rid of it. In an instant. Rid of it for both of us."

It is far too late. She has fully transmuted into her other self, the one who knows no reason. Like a wildfire, this rage must consume everything before it burns itself out.

"Every morning and every night, I pray. To those gods they tell us no longer exist—to gods that could not exist, for how could they curse us so? I pray they will strip us of this plague. Sear it out of us, bleed it out, whatever they wish. But they don't answer me. Look at me, Valentin Borisovich! Look at me!" Her short curls stand out, wild; sand melts in the wake of her footsteps, glimmering like a path of glass. "They won't answer me!"

"We can control it, Mama. I promise, I'll keep it under control." But my voice is so tiny; the air, thick now with salt and smoke, smothers it.

"No. We must answer the prayers for ourselves."

Before I can move, her arm is around my waist, searing into my flesh until we have melted together. Flames jump from her fingertips as she charges into the surf. I am screaming; I am trying, vainly, to drill into her mind—to find purchase in that cauldron of frenzied thoughts—but I am flailing.

She runs deeper. Water surges up my nose, the salt water stinging as it pours down my throat. Mama is on fire, and even as the cool water fills me, it is a relief. It embraces me and tugs me under. The undertow of the waves are like an exhale, pushing me further down still.

I am weightless, frozen in flight. The heat from her diminishes. Finally, she has cooled her fire off without igniting the world around her.

But I am sinking.

I thrash but she is motionless, eyes open, smile easing across her face. The Schumann concerto thrums darkly under my skin.

My lungs grate as I suck down nothing but sea. I struggle to pull free from her grasp, but she has hardened like steel around me—as if she was a molten rod, and the sea was the cooling trough to temper herself in. Vomit builds at the back of my throat, demands to escape. Black spots crowd around my vision.

Air. I need air.

I push into her mind. *Please, Mama, please—you want to swim back to shore.* Her eyes fly open; they stare through me, into the murky depths. But she doesn't obey. Her choice to die is too heavy for us to budge. I can't get a handle on it; I can't knock it loose.

Mama, please—

I am sinking—

Let me go.

Mama is still, so very, very still and cold and heavy, trying to weigh me down like cement. Her thoughts are sluggish and syrupy. All I can do, all I have the strength for—is to force her to release me.

One finger, then the next. Her arms slacken as I make her pry them away. This is my curse: to command others' minds, even if I can only manage as small an act as this. My vision falters—air, our brain is screaming, I need air—but I have to catch one more glimpse of her as I break free, and she sinks into the darkness below. I shove up, sky breaking around me as I surface, as I wheeze in one watery gasp of air—

And the world goes black around me.

The images of the memory fade, but I am ringing with its emotions, crusted onto me like the ocean salt. My arms sag, leaden, with the sadness and despair; my chest tightens with fear and the convulsions that follow a brush with death. Guilt fills my gut like molten iron. My eyes well up and spill over and drip into my mouth, strong and brackish.

Valya's stare is a thousand miles away, but a smile tugs at his lips. Though the memory remains, it's been stripped of its toxic emotions. "Thank you," he murmurs, and slumps back against the chaise lounge.

The panic inside me builds. I claw at my throat, desperate to get fresh air. I'm drowning. Valya's mother is drowning me, drowning both of us in her desperation to rid herself of her curse and Valentin's—

But it isn't a curse. *My mind is mine alone.* This is my gift. *My mind is mine alone.* I take emotions in, I draw memories in, and I push them away just as easily. I am the vessel. The Star. The emotions need not stay with me.

My breathing slows; fresh air fills my lungs, pushing out the memory of water and fire and pain. With each passing moment, I'm able to part through the emotions, and they fall away from me and evaporate. The tears dry on my cheek, a salty trail the only evidence they existed. My chest rises and falls like the endless waves of the sea.

Valentin smiles at me through his exhaustion; his gaze meets mine through half-closed eyes. "You did it," he mumbles.

"We did it." I curl around him. Panic ripples through me again as I think of the unknown sickness inside of him, but I needn't become the panic—I let it ebb away. I want to be calm. I want to enjoy this moment, this warm Valentin in my arms.

"I'd forgotten just how cruel she could be." He strokes his thumb along the point of my shoulder. "Sweet and brilliant and intensely loving one moment, and then—like a conflagration.

Papa learned to leave the house when she got that way; he had the burn marks to remind him of what could happen when he stayed. But I didn't have a choice."

I nestle my head deeper into his chest. "She blamed herself, didn't she? For passing the 'curse' on to you."

Valya nods. "She never did find balance with her own ability, so she was sure I couldn't, either. She wanted to spare me that pain by—by killing us both. And I couldn't save her. I had to force her to let me go, even though it meant . . ."

There's a heavy pause; I hold my breath, waiting for him to start crying, but instead he barks with a dry laugh.

"I—I'm sorry. I've never been able to admit it before. I feel—I feel so light, now." He kisses the top of my head. "Thank you."

"I'm sorry you've had to carry it around for so long."

"I'd kept it hidden for a long time, same as Andrei hid your memories." Valentin winces. "Everyone must do that to some extent, but for people with powers like mine, we can bury them even deeper. Suppress the bad memories, or even the good ones, if that's what we need to do to carry on. Wouldn't you forget the most painful or embarrassing moments of your life, if you could? It's hard to resist."

My arms tighten around him. "I can see the appeal." But I don't want to forget. I want to keep every last memory for myself—of Valya, of Mama, of everyone I love, to warm me during the darkest nights.

He tucks one finger under my chin and tilts my head toward his. His breath gusts, slow and warm, over my lips. His pulse thuds against mine. "I love you, Yulia."

Calming warmth spreads over me like a blanket, replacing the empty void of emotion inside me. I am of this moment, but I want to feel this moment fully. "I love you, Valentin."

He kisses me slowly. We kiss like we're memorizing every contour and plane of each other's lips, faces. The curve of him here and the swoop there, a topographical map that I can cling to, no matter what happens.

☆　☆　☆

The front door slams shut, followed by the clatter of several pairs of shoes—Papa's easy, casual gait and a frenetic ping of high heels. Valentin and I sit up from the chaise lounge, where we've fallen asleep. Suddenly, Valya jerks with a piercing yelp—a burst of static. It's gone as quick as it came, but his eyes lock with mine. My heart leaps into my throat. This was not his nightmares; his memories don't torment him anymore. This is something new. The serum is starting to take hold.

Papa flicks on the overhead lamp. The conservatory at night adopts an eerie aquarium quality; heavily shadowed tree leaves press against the windows, watching us in our little bubble of light.

"I thought you were going to call." I expect Papa to scold us for touching, for doing whatever things he suspects us of doing in his absence, but he just jams his hands into his pockets and looks to Cindy for guidance.

Cindy studies both of us, shaking as if she's about to unravel, like she's a spool of thread and her spindle has been pulled out. "We captured Anna Montalban in Miami," she says.

CHAPTER 22

I DON'T THINK I can sleep through the long, interminable wait for Anna's plane to arrive in Washington. I don't think I can sleep, knowing what Valya's suffered through, and not knowing what poison is pumping into him with each beat of his heart. But sometime in the deepest hours before morning, sleep comes to collect its due.

I dream, again, of Mama. We'd found the bird on our afternoon walk, one wing stretched out, rubbery, and dragging on the ground as it hopped in circles. Zhenya laughed and snatched a stick from the ground to poke at it, but I pried it out of his fingers. "It's hurt," I scolded him, in as stern and motherly a voice as a ten-year-old could manage. "We have to help it."

It was September, and still warm enough that I could make it home without my hat and scarf, so I scooped the bird into the knitted cap and wrapped the scarf around it like padding, thinking, foolishly perhaps, that it might feel comforting, like a nest. The bird glared at me with black, glossy eyes, the feathers around them damp and crusted. Each jostle along our path home brought a fresh squawk of indignation, a small protest in the larger indignity of its abduction.

Mama clucked her tongue as we came in the door; she pulled on rubber gloves and eased the wing out straight, not flinching when the bird shrieked and pecked at her. "It's broken badly," she said. "Looks like he was attacked by a bird of prey. He has wounds on his stomach, too."

Somehow the word *attacked* pushed tears to my eyes, as if it had ripped away a scab. Mama peeled off her gloves and pulled me into her arms with a sigh, pressing my face against the warmth of her jagged collarbone as she awkwardly patted my head. "It's the way of things. It's not your fault. It's just how the world works."

Even so, she helped me mix together a paste of cherries and water, and we fed it to the bird with an eyedropper, his beak opening and closing in a silent question when he wanted more. Mama helped me tape a tongue depressor to his wing with medical tape, and we used hydrogen peroxide to try to clean the wounds on his stomach.

He should have healed up. Zhenya kept his promise to leave him alone; we made the bird comfortable in a cardboard box on the windowsill so he could bask in sunlight and see the sky that we wanted him to return to soon. But within a few days, his will to live must have dried out, for I woke to find him stiff and cold, already smelling musty.

"Why did he have to die?" I screamed at Mama, as she dug a hole in the backyard of our dacha. "It's all so senseless. There's no point in it."

The shovel fell from Mama's hands, clattering against the

freezing earth. She seized me by the shoulders with startling swiftness. Her nails dug into my arms through her wool gloves; her eyes tightened to two blazing points as she knelt before me, urgency rippling through her. I felt bolted into place by that intense gaze. I didn't dare so much as breathe, lest I disrupt the moment with a tuft of frozen breath.

"There is always a purpose." Cold spit flecked across my face as she hissed out the words. "The more senseless a death seems, the greater a purpose it can serve. The less sense it makes, the more we must honor it. Remember it. Vow to never let it happen again. Do you understand me?" She shook my shoulders; my brain rattled in my skull. "Do you understand?"

"Yes," I muttered, though of course I did not.

How could I? I had no real perspective on death. The most senseless, most tragic deaths, like those of millions of Russians in the Great Patriotic War or in Stalin's purges, are like a great weight on a cosmic scale, and the only way to balance them is to heap justice on the other side of the scale—through honoring, through remembrance.

And maybe, just maybe, through revenge.

CHAPTER 23

THE THUDDING SOUND that's swallowing up all other noise in the safe house room cannot possibly be coming from me. But I feel it like a drumbeat under my sternum. *Ba-bump. Ba-bump.* I cannot sit still. I cannot watch Cindy and Papa do their crazed multiple-telephone square dance, their words just phantoms under the furious beat of my heart.

My mouth tastes dry and swampy, like I haven't brushed my teeth in weeks. I look down at my fingernails. I need to trim them. But how can I bring myself to take part in this mundane act, to do this routine thing, when it will forever lock me on the side of After? Enough time cannot have passed since Valentin was attacked (*since you let yourself be forced to attack him* ba-bump), so therefore I can take no further action until it undoes itself.

This is the logic of denial, blundering its way around my head, blind and banging into every raw memory in my perforated brain.

Ba-bump.

"Let's go." Cindy's arm is through mine, though we might as

well be swaddled up for a Russian winter for all that I can feel her. No memories, no musical shield, no nothing passing between our skin. "I need your help with her, Yulia. I can give you at least half an hour before Frank Tuttelbaum arrives, but then you'll have to leave. Come on. It's time."

We are going. We are chasing another wild goose. Anna Montalban, who has been sitting in a cell in the safe house for several hours now, a bulky camera lens watching her every move as we wait, on the other side of the camera, for any signs that she is wearing down. Twenty hours. Twenty hours since the man who used to be Al Sterling set himself on fire after Rostov forced me to inject Valentin with whatever poison ravaged him. In twenty hours, I have tried to sleep; I have tried to lodge Valya permanently in my mind, so I might never forget his face, but each time I glance away from him, I find some other crucial detail missing from my mental picture. Already I am forgetting.

No. I have to harness the anger that pulled me from my dreams. I have to unravel whatever's been done to him, and Anna might be our only way of finding out what it is and how to undo it.

Donna cracks her gum and bows her head toward mine. "Look . . . I'm sorry about Valentin, okay?" She sighs. "I don't know if Frank's right about you, but hopefully you understand that if you want to save Valentin, questioning Anna together is our best shot."

I think I'm supposed to tell Donna I forgive her or that I understand or that we can put it behind us, but I don't have the energy for such words. Even if I wanted to forgive her, though, I cannot go into that room to question Anna. I can't be that near to her, this traitor, this attacker, this woman who has somehow hovered near the poison inside Carlos and Heinrich and Al Sterling and now Valentin and come out unscathed. I'm watching her through the black-and-white closed-circuit television as she smokes in the concrete questioning room; water stains along the wall behind her stand out in crackling relief on the screen, which skews everything into harsh lightness and dark. Her eyes and hair—hollow, dead black; her skin and dress—blinding white. When she opens her mouth it becomes a gaping pit of deep black.

"Fine," Donna says, when I don't answer. "Suit yourself. I'll crack Anna Montalban without you."

Cindy shakes her head. "We could really use your help questioning Anna, Yul. Let me handle Frank—you let me know if you're ready."

Winnie settles into the chair beside me as Cindy and Donna leave, and fixes her gaze on the screen. "I'm so sorry, Yulia. I wish there was more I could do."

I stare at the angry slash of Anna Montalban's mouth on the distorted TV screen.

Papa offers me a hasty, too-broad grin, though his teeth clench hard on his cigarette. After he puffs the cherry to life, he leans back in the seat and pats me chastely on the shoulder. "Why the horse face, kiddo? You tryin' out for *Mister Ed*? We'll get whatever we need from her. Don't you worry your pretty little head." He sends a thin ribbon of smoke spiraling skyward, then stubs out his cigarette and heads down the hall after Donna and Cindy.

Winnie smiles sadly. "See? Your pops'll take care of it."

I twist around in a flash. "My father doesn't take care of anyone but himself."

Winnie leans toward me, matching my stance, but her voice stays eerily cold. "And what makes you think that?"

"He barely acts like he knows me. I'm his roommate, not his daughter. And what has he done to help Mama? To save her before she goes too far? Why is he off drinking and flirting every goddamned night instead of trying to bring Mama here safely?" Rage swells on my fingertips like blisters, like it's scalding me from within. I should call upon my mantra, but deep down, I want to feel this rage.

Winnie's face softens; she puts her hand on my knee. "You mean he hasn't told you."

I'm boiling over. Everything is steam, and I'm ready to unleash a teakettle scream. Bad enough that Papa should keep secrets at all, but that he should tell them to someone besides me? It takes every ounce of self-control I've ever had, every trick in Cindy's meditative bag, to keep from screaming. When I do manage to speak, my voice is a sharpened blade. "Hasn't told me what?"

Winnie's no-nonsense varnish is peeling. Is it sympathy that's pushing her toward telling me the truth? I can almost smell it on her, like fresh-baked sugared apples. I can hear it in her rippling Ella Fitzgerald shield. "Well," she says slowly, "I suppose that's for him to say."

My pulse quickens as a dark thought takes hold of me. I clench my hand around Winnie's. It's too much effort to fear my power;

why shouldn't I embrace it, like Papa so cheerfully does? If I can ply Winnie's sympathy, pour it into her like I did to Donna that day, give her that little push toward telling me the truth—

No. I can't be like Papa, manipulating others on a whim. The rage dulls; the boil slows. My mind is mine alone.

My hands sink into my lap as Donna appears on the television screen.

The dark wells of Anna's eyes lighten a degree as her lashes raise, her eyes tracking Donna's movement around the table. Anna isn't restrained, but she leans forward, like a leering fighter; she's primed for a bout.

"Really? They're giving me to you, stupid little girl?" Anna snorts, loud and grating, in Donna's face. "You don't know shit. You don't understand *anything*!"

We can only see a sliver of Donna's face in the screen, but her shoulders are trembling. Donna grips her own ponytail and twists it around one finger, again and again. "Then I guess you'd better explain it to me."

Anna leans back into the chair. Her eyes are lidded again—dark horizontal bars as she squints at Donna. She sucks at her cigarette, dark gray patches appearing in her sucked-in cheeks, then exhales right into Donna's face. "You are toast, little girl. Your whole little world is toast. This . . . system of yours? Your little happy capitalist smiley bubblegum face?" Anna draws a circle in the air with the cigarette. "Toast."

"You weren't so sure about that two weeks ago, when you met with your handler. Carlos Fonseca." Donna opens the folder in front of her, but her bravado is fading, making her hands shake as she shoves a photograph at Anna. "You told him you never agreed to go as far with the plot as he wanted you to go."

Anna's smirk slackens. She uncrosses her arms and legs, slumping forward now without the rigidity to her spine. "How do you know I said that?"

Donna smiles, sitting up straighter. "We have our ways."

"How the *hell* did you know I said that? Don't play games with me, little girl!"

Anna lunges forward. Donna leaps back with a yelp, chair squealing against the concrete floor. I jump to my feet, forgetting I'm in a separate room from them.

"She'll be fine," Winnie says, though I notice she's already lit a fresh cigarette from the dying old one. "Your father'll help her out if he has to."

Though Donna hasn't said anything, Anna looks like she's realized this, too. She sits back down, though she's at the edge of her chair now, like she can't get comfortable. "Careful," Donna says. "I'd hate for them to take your cigarettes away."

"I'd like to see you try," Anna purrs.

Donna squares her shoulders. "Fonseca gave you two things at the diner. A roll of microfiche, and a bunch of vials. You're going to tell me why."

I exchange a glance with Winnie. "She's not going to tell her anything."

"Donna doesn't need her to say anything—just think it."

I shake my head. "I doubt she knows enough to help us."

Anna is silent, waiting Donna out. Donna tries a few other approaches—the grandmother she'd overheard Anna mention when we first met her, her friends here in America—but nothing sticks. *Ba-bump.* Valentin needs answers. *I* need answers— whatever else the team wants out of Anna, I need some hint as to what's happening to Valya, and if there's any way to stop it.

I shove out of my chair and storm from the monitoring room and into the hallway of the nondescript suburban house. "Yulia?" Winnie shouts, chasing after me. "Yulia, are you okay?"

Cindy catches me by the shoulders just outside the interrogation room, where she and Papa watch Anna through a smoky two-way mirror. "Yulia." She tilts her head at me. "I thought you didn't want to take part in this."

"Well, Donna's not making any progress."

"Then let the grown-ups handle this," she says. "I wanted to give Donna a chance to soften her up, but we can send in your father—"

The grown-ups. I snort, whirling on Cindy, tearing my arm from her grip. "You think my father's a grown-up? That hateful old fish Tuttelbaum? Phony fortune-tellers like you?"

"Phonies?" Cindy snaps.

"I've seen quite enough of how our missions play out when we let you 'grown-ups' call the shots. I'm not letting you ruin our only chance at saving Valentin."

"There's nothing to ruin. She's an errand girl at best—I doubt they let her in on anything."

"Which makes any attempt from me useless." Papa mashes his fingers into the corners of his eyes, like he's trying to squash out a headache. "I know you want to cure Valya, but I don't think this bird has any song to sing, even if she wanted to."

"We'll see about that." I yank open the door to the interrogation room.

Donna and Anna look up at me as one, both a little frightened, both a little angry at my intrusion. Donna recovers first, eyelashes flashing like a quick shutter speed. "Why, Yulia!" She grips her ponytail like it's a ripcord. "So good of you to join us."

"The hell you want." Anna spits onto the floor. "The *hell* you want."

"Don't pay me any attention at all." Breathe in. My mind is mine alone. "I'm not even here."

I position myself behind Anna, palm pressing down into her shoulder. She twists around to look at me with a scowl, but then slumps back down. She's wearing a sleeveless top; there's plenty of space for our skin to connect. Perfect. Slowly, she turns back to Donna. I nod at Donna, who's considering me with a raised eyebrow. "Please. Continue."

Donna nods slowly. "Right. Where were we—yes. The microfiche. The vials. What were they for, Anna?" Donna asks, her voice gaining an edge.

I close my eyes. On the inhale, I summon up my memory of what I'd uncovered in the diner, the way Anna's fear and apprehension felt when I viewed it then. She felt—*wrong*, then, about what she was doing. The guilt weighed on her. Hadn't Carlos scolded her then, hadn't he had to threaten her? How had she felt, that moment right before Carlos called her bluff? What was pushing her away from Carlos's goals?

On the exhale. Weariness—the mental toll of keeping a secret like hers, of working against her boss, Senator Saxton. The warm promise of absolution. If she can spill what she knows, she can be unburdened. She can be free of all this weight and fear.

Anna's thoughts flicker; exhaustion eats at her stony façade. Donna's eyes meet mine with the faintest smile tweaking her lips.

"It's a . . . serum. Some kind of crazy medical experiment they're doing." Anna shudders. "I wasn't trying to hurt anyone, okay? They threatened me. I had to either inject Saxton, or—or myself."

Fear. Breathe in. Find Anna's fears—getting caught, having Carlos make good on his blackmail threats. Hurting her grandmother in the Bronx. Deporting her back to Havana. *Compromise is another important tool in espionage,* Cindy told me. *It's like blackmail, but . . . grayer.* Breathe out. The fear bubbles like soap, enveloping Anna in its oily skin.

Donna's smile broadens as Anna's shield crumbles further. "But you didn't. You didn't inject him, or yourself—you ran from us and the KGB both, didn't you? Why?"

"It needed time to take control, all right?" She tries to wriggle out of my grasp, but I tighten my hold. "They wanted me to inject it five days before the NATO convention was set to vote on North Vietnam. I figured I'd wait until five days before, then I could run. They wouldn't know I hadn't done it until it was too late. But *you* idiots ruined that for me, didn't you?"

Donna's eyes narrow. "Why does the KGB care what we do in North Vietnam?"

North Vietnam. I breathe in. *Ideology can often prompt espionage—a communist sympathizer can be persuaded that their acts will serve the cause.* She wants to help Carlos and Rostov and all the other members of his faction. I let the emotion fill me up:

a conviction that telling us will not prevent her goals from being reached. Breathe out.

Anna studies her nails—her once-flawless manicure now chipped and ragged. "Silly girl. They're going to push you warmongers into a war you can't win."

The folder slips out of Donna's hands. "It's true, then? Rostov *wants* America to attack one of Russia's allies?"

"Yes. He wants you pigs nice and distracted with the Viet Cong, huh? Throw some slop in the trough, *oink oink*, piggy doesn't even see farmer coming up with the ax." She cackles. "Then we come in, and—*crunch*."

Donna and I flinch as one. We look at each other, and in a wordless, soundless, thoughtless agreement, we push onward.

Ego. Anna's got it in spades. I fill her up with confidence, and she brags about how she never had to break into Saxton's classified files; she just added her own false documents to them, like the microfiche Carlos had given her. She doesn't say the details out loud, but Donna's sparkling eyes say it all—what Anna isn't saying, she's reading from her mind.

Revenge. For Senator Saxton's complete lack of respect for her—though she admits other secretaries in the Senate Office building have it far worse. For the treatment her mother received when she first brought them to New York from Cuba, and how they had to hide their true identity after Castro's coup.

"Really," Anna admits, once Donna and I are sagging a bit in our seats and Anna's voice is turning dry, "I had plenty of reasons to go along. I just—I didn't agree with them about everything. There were things they wanted me to do that I just couldn't agree with."

"Like what?" Donna asks, chewing on her pen's nib.

"Well, once your teacher or whoever she is made the appointment with Senator Saxton, they told me I should try to inject one of you kids instead."

My stomach fills with chill dread.

"And I just didn't think that was right. I mean, I'd seen what the serum was doing to Carlos, after all. I didn't think it was fair to do that to a *kid*. And I sure as hell wasn't gonna use it on myself."

I slump back against the wall. Breathe in. Breathe out. The wall's chill seeps into my back, freezing the terror that wants to run rampant in me. I can't afford to let it. Not right now.

"So it's the exact same thing," Donna says. "The serum isn't just the power. It's what kills them, too."

I don't meet Donna's eyes. I don't need to. She knows without looking at the expression on my face. The poison spreading like fire in my thoughts. That the exhaustion in Carlos's bones, the sickness on his face, must be what's coursing through Valentin right now.

That the serum is whatever killed Carlos in his apartment, blood gushing from his ears.

"What's the serum supposed to do?" My voice is shredded and raw. I don't have to work to summon up the requisite amount of fear and rage to push onto Anna Montalban. It comes all too readily.

Anna drops her cigarette onto her lap, and brushes it out with a yelp. "It's—it's supposed to be some sort of mind control serum, okay? I thought they were pullin' my leg, really I did, but after seeing how Carlos acted, I wasn't so sure. They've got some guy—this Rostov guy you mentioned, I think that's him—and he's supposed to be able to, I don't know, use the person you inject like some kinda marionette." She coughs. "Sounds like horseshit, right? If I hadn't seen it for myself, I wouldn't believe it a bit."

Dimly, I can hear Donna asking follow-up questions. But my mind is elsewhere, spinning a web, drawing lines from point to point. Mama's army of scrubbers for General Rostov. Their hasty deaths. Al Sterling's abrupt change. They're being used as beacons for Rostov to reach across vast distances and manipulate others' minds.

Valentin. He's turned Valentin into his puppet.

Frank Tuttelbaum's voice roars from outside the door. We've just run out of time. But revenge is a filament burning hot and bright inside me. I need vengeance. To make sense of the deaths of countless people killed in Rostov's quest for power. To give purpose to the purposelessness of this shadowy war. But most of all, I need the sweet revenge of hot blood on my hands and devastating emotions freshly ripped from my veins. I need revenge for whatever toxins are running through my Valentin.

"How is Rostov going to accomplish this?" My grip on Anna's shoulder tightens. "What is he pushing the scrubbers toward?"

"He's trying to get the American decision makers under his thumb. It's why he wanted Saxton—wanted to make him his little puppet to get NATO into the war. Now I think it's the convention," Anna continues. "This Pathway for Peace summit. They want to push America into war with Vietnam at it. Make a big scene, cause a scandal. Start an—an *international incident*." She snorts with laughter. "Crazy, right?"

I think of Nikita Khruschev reciting nuclear launch codes into the telephone, dancing like a puppet on Rostov's strings. A war—a hot war, not our current feints and back-alley feuds—is just the thing Rostov craves to assert Russia's supremacy once and for all. "Not to a man like Rostov."

The door flies open, revealing Frank Tuttelbaum's scarlet face. "Donna. Yulia. Out. *Now.*"

Donna's face is shining brighter than her California tan, and she can barely keep from squealing until we're out of the room. "That was awesome, Yulia! You and me—it was like we were dancing, we played her so well together!"

But there is a thick wall of insulation padding me from her and all the rest. Everyone is muffled; the only clear sound I have is my own breath, drawing in, spilling out. I no longer need this rage, this fear. They dissipate around me; they crackle and fade. My mind is mine alone. I am just a vessel for these feelings. Nothing good nor bad can cling to me.

Cindy Conrad says, "Well done," but looks away quickly, like she's ashamed by our success. Or ashamed of what she knows will come next.

"I don't suppose I need to tell you how much trouble you're in. All of you." Frank's voice is as thin as razor wire. "And you understand, Yul, what this means for Valentin."

"Yes," I hear myself say.

"We're gonna have to quarantine him. Lock him up somewhere safe." He grinds his teeth. "Don't give me a reason to lock you up, too."

My eyes are scanning the safe house. My feet carry me away from the prisoner's quarters into the front part of the house, the part that still looks like a proper house if you're peeking in the windows. I search Valentin's face. Dark circles under his eyes— but why shouldn't there be? It's been a long day. Days. Something in between. Time, washing away from us, eroding what time we have left. It's all too soon.

"Yulia." He stands and wraps me up in his arms, his heavy eyes pleading with mine. "I love you. Please don't forget that."

"Valya—"

But Frank's guards are prying him out of my arms. I think I am scratching at someone as I try to hold him close; though I am empty of all emotion, my body is still reacting off instinct, a fierce determination to protect my own.

I think I might be screaming. My throat burns and burns. They are dragging him down the hall; he's leaning away from them, trying to hold onto my gaze until the very last second.

"I love you, Yulia!" he screams.

And then they are gone.

And I am sinking to the bottom of the Black Sea, blissful emptiness taking over me despite the fire I feel inside.

CHAPTER 24

WINNIE IS DRIVING ME HOME in the Austin Healey. I wish she'd keep her eyes on the road, but they keep sliding over toward me, gleaming in the moonlight, like she's expecting me to disappear if she doesn't keep a constant vigil. As we cross the Potomac River, she clears her throat. Nothing good ever comes from someone clearing their throat. It's always bad news, a lecture, an unpleasant truth. I gird myself with emptiness.

"You got through that whole interrogation without having to rely on me a single time," she says.

I uncross my arms. At least she's not going to give me some half-baked platitude about loving and losing. "Donna did most of the talking."

"Still. It makes it easier." She drums her fingers against the steering wheel. "I'm not going to be around anymore."

I momentarily lose my hold on the void, and panic starts to seep in. The spring air turns muggy and heavy, pressing me down against the seat. "What? Why not?" I clench one hand into a fist. "You can't just—leave me."

"Trust me, Yul. You'll be just fine without me. I have faith in you."

"But why are you leaving?" I ask.

She presses her lips into a thin line. "Lots of reasons. I used to think the Air Force was the way for me, but I've got to accept—a colored girl isn't going to make Master Chief anytime soon, no matter how many waves Doctor King makes. I'm taking a job with the Urban League."

"But our work is important," I say, fully aware of the absurdity of the statement. For all our effort, we haven't prevented anything. We're always a step—or more—behind.

Winnie pats me on the knee. "Let me tell you a little secret, Yulia. My leaving has nothing to do with you. You've been a pleasure to work with."

I lower my eyes. "But it has something to do with someone else."

She nods. "That's a part of it, yeah. Your father is . . ." She whistles out her breath. "He's a challenging man. A great man, but . . ."

"I know he goes out on the town with you sometimes." I stare into the dark fingerling trees as they crowd along the riverbank. Winnie drives much slower than Papa; I can see each branch as it flies past. "Is that the thing you were surprised he hadn't told me?"

"Look, Yul, we go out on the town together, but that's all we do—Scout's honor." She holds up three fingers with a sad grin.

"He and your mama . . . It's just too complicated. It's not right. Something needs to be resolved there, and I'm not wading into any of that." She swallows again. "Is that honest enough for you?"

I shake my head, too numb to know whether I'd be laughing or crying right now if I allowed myself to feel—so many emotions ready and eager to fill me up. Much better not to let a single one inside. "At least I'm not the only one who doesn't understand what's happened between them."

"If there's a single soul in this world your papa ought to trust," Winnie says, "it's you."

★   ★   ★

Papa meets us on the front lawn. "Excellent! Fancy a nightcap, Sergeant Davis?" He extends his hand to collect the keys from Winnie, and he leans in to peck her on the cheek, but she ducks away.

"No, I think you two need some father-daughter time." She spins on her heel. "G'night, Yul. Andrei."

"Sure," he says, eyes fluttering. He whistles as he follows me up the walk, but the notes are tighter, shorter now. "I think I'll have a drink. How about you, buttercup?"

"I'm good." I round on him as soon as he shuts the front door and slip into Russian—cruel, guttural, harsh. "Mama created whatever's inside Valentin right now, and it'll kill him. If he doesn't kill himself first, like Al did."

He scratches the stubble along his jaw. "It would appear that way."

"When we find Mama—the CIA is going to hurt her. They're going to want her to pay for creating all these monsters. They're going to say she's partly responsible for all the attacks. It won't be like the way they treated you or me, Papa." I lean in close. "I need to know what's going on. Does Mama have a plan? Because I want to think she wouldn't go along with Rostov, but I'm having a hard time believing it right now."

I watch his eyes, but they're staring past me. He could be absorbing everything I'm saying, or he could be measuring out a new cocktail recipe in his head. Nothing on his face gives me the slightest clue which it might be.

"Don't you feel anything?" I cry. Frustration creeps into me on Shostakovich's sliding strings; anger pounds like a drum. I trick myself into thinking that letting myself feel a little more can't hurt. "Aren't you scared for Mama? Are you *glad* they're going to hurt her? Damn it, Papa, just tell me you feel *some*thing!"

Papa's gaze drops to meet mine. He studies me for a moment like he's just now cluing into the conversation—like he's replaying the past few seconds in his head, trying to remember what I've said. Then he slumps back against the door and sinks down onto his heels.

"An empty mind is a safe mind," he tells me, in the miserable voice of a scolded boy.

I bash my fist against the door. This rage filling me feels so *good*. I want to let it burn and burn. I don't need to disconnect from this because it can't hurt me. It can only make me stronger. I am my own weapon, and I will turn my rage against Rostov. Against anyone and everyone responsible for this mess. Except for Mama—I'll save her for the very last. I'll give her one chance to undo this hell she's wrought.

And if she won't clean up her own mess, I'll turn it on her, too.

"I've forgotten," Papa says. His voice bobs like a toy boat in the ocean. As much as I don't want it to, it erases some of the rage from me. "I've forgotten what she looks like."

I stagger back from him. The blind anger crashes in on itself like a wave; I'm dragged under by its weight. Breathe in, breathe out. My vision softens. I glance down at Papa, at his hands tucked between his knees; a single bulging tear runs down one cheek. "Mama?" I ask him. "How could you forget?"

"Easy." He laughs; more tears start to flow. "I erased every memory of her."

"What? Why?" I manage to say.

"It was the only way to do what needed to be done." He tilts his head back, looking up at the grand chandelier dangling down into the foyer.

I drop to the floor in front of him. I'm empty now. No match for gravity. I open my mouth, but it's too dry to speak; the rage has burned through me and left nothing but ash. I shake my head. "No. There had to be some other way."

"You know what torture it was for me to be away from her— even for the day. When she was at work and I wasn't, then that door opened, I would—" He works his jaw, searching. "I would—"

"The look on your face," I say. "Like you were seeing a sunrise for the very first time."

"Yes. Yes, that's it." He stares at me. "And she made me stronger—I remember that much, because I know how powerful

I could be with her around, and how weak I feel right now. She was my scaffolding. There's nothing to support me now."

I squeeze my eyes shut. "You couldn't stop touching her. Your hand was always at her elbow, her waist, her shoulder. Tucking her hair back from her face." I choke back a sob. "She was your life outside the lab. You loved Zhenya and me, but I thought it was because of what we meant—because we were something you'd made with her."

Papa's hand shields his face. "She insisted. *Insisted.* That I had to do whatever was necessary to rescue our children from the Party—and if this was necessary, to allow me to leave Russia, to rescue you—" He gulps for air. "I couldn't bear to leave her behind, otherwise. The fear of not seeing her, not knowing if she was okay—it would've killed me. I couldn't do what needed to be done, over years and years away from her, to save her. I had to cut it out of me. And if I were caught—if they had tried to find out if she was involved—then she'd be safe."

I remember the last moment I saw Papa. At the time, I thought he was leaving to visit friends; he'd tucked a cigarette into his lips and threw his scarf over his shoulder. His glasses fogged as he stepped out into the frosty evening, the air blue from a hidden sunset. He didn't give Mama a kiss, didn't give me a second glance. He was simply gone.

That night, Mama woke us up, and we went on the run.

"I did what she asked. I brought you here, safe and sound. I've done what was necessary to protect you. To carry out her plan, whatever it might be. Don't you see?" He bashes a fist against his thigh. For a moment, I imagine I can see him as Cindy might, with her strange visions—I imagine him clutching his own bloody heart, torn from his chest, throbbing with erased memories. "There is nothing left. Nothing but this emptiness, and I can't seem to fill it up."

I'm crawling on my hands and knees toward him, my head heavy with warring emotions. He took my memories of my power from me; he didn't give me a choice. But he chose to do this to himself. For us. I tuck myself under his outstretched arm. He is not the man who balanced Mama like a scale, who only ever showed his true face once safely locked in our home. But he is still my papa. He wraps his arm around my shoulder, hot tears spilling into my hair. I breathe in and out with him, our chests rising and falling together. His sorrow seeps into my skin, but I am the Star. I let it evaporate, leaving us both in peace.

"What can we do?" I ask after a long minute. "What's next in her plan?"

"The last stage for my part of the plan was rescuing you. She said she . . ." He squeezes his eyes shut, straining for the right memory. "She said the next part was hers to handle. That when she was ready for our help, she'd let us know."

"But there has to be something we can do! What if she does end up needing us?"

Papa shakes his head, slow and weary. "I don't know if I can. I'm afraid that for all I've done to myself, it won't be enough. For all the memories I've erased, I'll take one look at her, and it will all come back. I won't be able to do what I must."

"How could it?" I ask. But he hadn't had the nerve to erase my memories fully; there was still a shape of them pressed into my brain, like comics picked up on Silly Putty. With Valentin's help, I'd recovered most of them. Did he really have the power to erase his fully when he couldn't even do it to me?

"All these jagged lines where she's been severed away. My brain won't listen to me. It knows the pathway to her, but when it goes down that pathway and finds nothing, it gets angry. It gets hungry for something." He pads his breast pocket, searching for a cigarette. "So I give it what I can."

All the food and alcohol. Cigarettes and fast cars, and his flirtatious, carefree attitude. I look at him sideways.

"You have to be strong, my Yulia," he says. His arm falls away from me; his eyelids sink shut as if swollen. "We have to help her."

I stand up slowly and smooth out my dress. Whatever panic and fear and love and hate I've felt in the past few minutes, I'm leaving it there, on that floor. I don't have time for those things.

"I will, Papa. I promise."

Papa lifts his head and wipes his eyes on the sleeve of his stiff leather jacket; the sleeve pulls back to reveal an impossibly ornate wristwatch. "Shit," Papa says. "It's time."

"For what?"

Papa unfolds from the floor. His usual carefree expression has returned, but he takes my hand and squeezes it like he did when I was a little girl and he was afraid I might slip from his glove, even for just a moment. "When we were working together in Berlin, at the end of World War II, we received all our orders on an encrypted radio frequency." He guides me to the staircase with a wince. "You see—I still remember the codes, but I can't see her face hunched over the radio with me. But she's there, lurking at the edges, like a cobweb that won't clear away."

"I'm sorry," I tell him. For the first time since I came to America with him, I think I truly do feel sorry for him. The hurt and betrayal and confusion are still there, but now, at least, I can sympathize as well.

He leads me into the master bedroom suite on the second floor and clicks on the light in the auxiliary closet. I freeze in place as amber light washes over the array of equipment inside—the hulking recorder, its reels already spinning; the radio set that looks like it belongs inside a space capsule.

Papa yanks the headphone cord out of the radio and an eerie melody floods the room, tinkling as innocently as an ice cream truck rolling down the street. But something about the static woven into it freezes my blood; it sets off a painful tugging in my chest, like it means to reel me toward it.

Papa's eyes are slits and he's smiling with the same yearning I feel, but then he shakes it off and spins another dial, introducing a blast of static. I shake my head, clearing away the emotion. "What is this?" I ask.

"They call it a numbers station. As long as we had a short-wave radio, we could always get encrypted messages in the field." He flips through a pad of graph paper; it's bloated with page after page of numbers scrawled in evenly spaced sets of five, with Cyrillic letters written underneath. "The station identifies itself with the song, then a coded message follows that spies deep in the field can easily decode, as long as they know the key."

The song fades out; Papa shuts off the static blast.

"Rostov embedded the music with some sort of . . . wavelength," Papa explains. "A curious element of our powers I figured out during the Great Patriotic War. Music affects our brain waves, you see, and while we can shield our thoughts with some songs, others can be used to synchronize our thought patterns—it turns them into a homing beacon. When someone's thoughts are synchronized to a known pattern, they're easy to trace, even at great distances."

"You used that on me before," I say. "When we crossed paths in Moscow. I remember the melody—one of Zhenya's little tunes—"

Papa whistles those notes, sending a piercing pain straight through my heart. "It made you into a beacon, so I could always find you." He swallows hard. "A shining light to lead me to shore. My darling Yulia."

I turn my head away. I hadn't realized how resigned I'd become to the Papa I've known the past few months; these reminders of his sweetness and adoration for me are a little embarrassing and a little heartbreaking all at once. "So it's easier for his agents to track us down, making us a beacon in the same way?"

"Precisely. I haven't shared this station's existence with our PsyOps friends just yet. If they heard it, it could cause serious harm—the potential to turn us all into beacons if they listened to it directly. That's why I play the static—so I can still listen in without my brainwaves getting synchronized. Rostov still uses this station to communicate internationally; he probably uses the same wavelength to control his scrubbers, too."

Like Valentin's about to be. I swallow hard.

A woman's voice chimes in, scratchy like Valentin's jazz records, reciting strings of numbers in a choppy succession. Papa scribbles the sets of numbers down, face scrunched up in deep concentration.

He drops the pencil halfway through and twists around to stare at me with a hollow gaze. I frown at him. "What? What does the message say?"

He stares at me with red-rimmed eyes. "They're coming to the States."

CHAPTER 25

I'M ALREADY WAITING at the doors to Doctor Stokowski's research lab when he arrives at six the next morning. "Miss Chernina." He removes his hat and fishes for his chunky key ring. "You're awfully early for today's sessions."

"I have some ideas for the virus research." I follow him into the room and start pulling covers off of the electron microscopes, then I open up the storage refrigerator that contains the samples I swabbed from Valentin, Papa, and myself. In my bag is the sample Valentin swiped for me yesterday, before we went to the safe house; I'm crossing my fingers it's still active. "We can already train them to recognize certain sequences, yes? Now I want to encode the virus to attack a specific code sequence."

Doctor Stokowski's hand rests on the spin dial where the inert viral strains are locked up. "Let me guess. That added sequence on the samples you've been bringing me?"

"Yes, exactly that." *Our* chromosome samples—mine and Papa's. Showing where a congenital virus, the source of our psychic powers, had twisted itself into those taut little springs of genetic code. It's a part of us from birth, nearly impossible to rip free.

I need to rip it free.

One sharp breath, in and out, and my mantra crowding out my protestations. A steady stream of images thread through my mind: Papa, broken and sobbing on the foyer floor. Valentin's mind frizzing with the first onset of the serum. The faces of all the dead scrubbers, staring ahead with milky eyes. My plan will take Valya's psychic ability from him, but it's the price he'll have to pay.

I shove my lab notebook at Doctor Stokowski and wait for him to read through my experiment proposal.

Doctor Stokowski hands the notebook back to me and peels off his glasses. "Well, you certainly have a firm grasp of the material." He wipes the lenses on his sweater. "I understand that you won't be able to give me much information in the way of context for this experiment, but your methodology looks sound. I have just one condition."

"Of course," I say.

"Make good on your intentions to enroll in the biology department this fall." He pushes his glasses back up his nose.

I smile through my frazzled nerves. "You have my word."

We unleash all his favorite research viruses on segments of the samples I brought to see how the different kinds react to it. It's like watching an alien army invade, like *Invasion of the Body Snatchers*: the virus injects its DNA-altering sequences into my helpless saliva cells, and Papa's, and Valya's. In each case, we've altered the virus to erase a certain chunk of code, feasting on it for nutrients, and it's doing just that—but it's damaging everything around them, as well.

Doctor Stokowski helps me tweak and refine, changing the virus's potency, its payload, its propagation speed. But whenever it's strong enough to rip out the altered psychic genetic markers, then it shreds the surrounding code, as well.

"There isn't any way you can bring me a sample of whatever infected this sample?" he asks, gesturing to the tray of Valya's DNA, after our latest effort turns my genetic material into Swiss cheese. "I think we're on the right path, but it's causing too much damage to the cells around it. I'd have to study the source virus to understand how to minimize the damage."

He means the serum, but I only have its aftereffects, how it looks now that it's snared itself on Valya's genes. My chest is caving in. I can't hold onto my breath. But I cannot let this panic crush me. I push it away from me, let it crumble and erode. If the Russians are coming, more of Rostov's pawns, then surely they have more of the serum with them. If we can disrupt their goals, if we can analyze the serum more closely . . .

Far too many ifs for me to pin Valya's life on, but I have nowhere else to turn.

"I'll see what I can do."

"Absolutely not," Frank Tuttelbaum howls, perfectly audible from the other side of his office door. "If we start tailing every van of Russians to pass through this city, Secretary Khruschev will pitch an even bigger fit than he usually does! We can't afford to draw that kind of attention to the CIA."

Cindy murmurs something to Frank that I can't hear as Papa gives me a look. He's been handling our idleness, officially restricted from team duties, about as well as I am. "I take it he's not impressed with Anna Montalban's information on the peace summit."

"If we can interrupt the Soviets' Pathway for Peace delegation when they arrive, who knows what we could learn from them?" I lean forward. "Think, Papa. The delegates themselves could be the scrubbers who are supposed to disrupt the summit. If we can capture them before they reach the embassy, and if they have the serum on them . . ."

"You'd have to block traffic all along Dupont Circle. Good luck with that. Last time that happened was during Doctor King's march last summer. Where are you going to find the resources for that? Especially with Frank barring us from active operations."

"Then I guess we'll have to do it on our own." My gaze drifts toward the translators' office. Winnie's in there right now, packing up her belongings now that she's retiring from the Air Force. I remember her argument with Cindy over her work with the Urban League. I suppose Winnie did have to choose, in the end, between the safe but short military track and—how did Cindy put it?—overly optimistic dreamers armed with nothing but picket signs.

I poke my head into the office and catch Winnie's eye. She groans and sets down her banker's box of files. "You look like you're up to no good," she says.

I smile. "Only with your help."

I almost feel sorry for the Pathway for Peace Soviet delegation when we reach Dupont Circle that afternoon. Or rather, when we park several blocks from Dupont Circle, which is the closest we can get, as the whole neighborhood has turned into one massive, gyrating, chanting sea of color and noise. Some people carry placards—"I TOO HAVE A DREAM," "I SIT WITH ROSA," "SAY NO TO WAR," "HUGS NOT BOMBS." Others sing back and forth: calls and responses ranging from protests to Motown songs.

Donna and Judd stare as a juggling competition breaks out around us. "What in the . . ." She squeaks and dodges a beanbag as it swishes straight through her ponytail.

Winnie's barely able to contain her smile as a man holding an Urban League sandwich board gives her a sly wink. It's not only Winnie's League members out in full force, though they launched the event at her urging; they called on their friends, who called on theirs, and a full-blown protest/street festival/rally has broken out, to send a message to the summit and the rest of the world when they catch it on the nightly news. Skinny white girls in flowing dresses weave through the crowd, passing out carnations; everywhere I look, the races and sexes and subcultures and classes have swirled together into a street carnival that celebrates as much as it scolds.

"Is this what you had in mind?" Winnie asks me in Russian, as Cindy's momentarily distracted by her heel catching in a sidewalk crack.

I smile back at her. "It's perfect."

"No," Winnie says, "not perfect just yet. Let's catch these assholes first."

I've got eyes on the Soviet delegation. Spotted them getting out of their van, and they are furious, Marylou announces in our heads, the message tangled up in the agreed-upon musical number that our entire team can hear for this operation—"Moscow Nights." *Five delegates with three plainclothes guards. Guards are around them in a tight triangle—might be tricky to split one or two of them off.*

I'm sure we can manage something, Papa replies.

Marylou pushes the image of the group toward us. *Head toward P Street. You've almost reached them.* I can only make out some of their faces, but none of them look like any of the guards or team members from my days with the KGB. I relax a little at that, glad I won't have to encounter a familiar face, though I had been hoping against hope that Mama might be among them.

Tony's identified the first delegation member, Marylou updates us. *Anatoliy Totchkov. He taught at the Red Army Military Academy before joining a Special Projects research team. An interesting choice for a peace delegation. What do you wanna bet he's part of the team that designed the serum?*

Let's grab him, I say. One of Mama's scientists—he could fix my attempts at curing Valentin in no time.

Patience, Cindy answers. *We'll delay whichever members of the delegation we can while putting our people in the least amount of danger.*

We prowl the crowd for a few minutes more, shadows on the periphery of the delegates' path. Finally, an opportunity presents itself: I can almost hear the smile in Marylou's voice when she shows us a pair of fire-eaters performing close to the delegation. *Judd, want to have some fun?*

Papa shoves ahead of us. *Let me get in place and we'll be ready to go. On your count, Judd . . .*

Three.

Within the hour, we'll have captured Rostov's operatives, sent to disrupt the peace talks. I can find out the key to curing Valya. And maybe, just maybe, we can learn the next steps in Mama's plan.

Two.

I enjoy the joyful chaos all around me, for just this moment. I savor the sun heating my face and the sweat trickling down my back.

. . . One, Judd says.

The fire-eater had been in a safe circle with his fellow performers, but he spins wildly and leans toward the delegation members as they pass. His expression is empty as he takes a deep breath and spews a gout of flame right into the group. Someone screams. The air warps around us, a strange mix of extreme heat and a crackle like impending lightning. The crowd shifts, compacting under Papa's thrall, elbows and eyeballs and someone's spiky Jackie Kennedy brooch all colliding for a moment—and then the world sets itself right once more.

"Hello, comrades," I say, sidling up to the two delegates we've culled from the herd.

Papa is standing tall over the delegates, his hatless hair gleaming deep chestnut in the sun. "Looking for us, comrades?" he asks, flicking his Zippo open. "Judd. Help me out here, son."

The tallest man in the delegation—Anatoliy, I'm

guessing—tries to juke around Papa, but the air warps again as Papa seizes control of him, and he falls back into line.

"No, you don't." Papa puffs his cigarette to life.

"Well, well. If it isn't a whole family of rats." That smug, nasal voice chills me straight to my marrow. My heart leaps into my throat. Misha, or Mikhail—one of my fellow teammates back at the KGB—stares at me from where he's pinned between two of Papa's pawns. "Well . . . only half the family, I suppose." He assesses me with sparkling blue eyes and a smirk twisting his lips. His parents had fought in the Great Patriotic War with Mama and Papa; now he and his twin sister, Masha, aspire to be KGB officers themselves. If he's been sent on the delegation, then he must be well on his way.

And if he's here, what if the rest of the team—what if Mama—isn't too far behind?

I charge toward him, anger powering me like a locomotive. "Where are they?" My hand closes around his throat. "Masha?" I shout, calling for his sister, a remote viewer like Sergei and Marylou. "I know you're watching. Get a good look at your brother, because he's about to tell us everything—"

Misha whimpers as rage pours off of my skin, scalding him as surely as a spray of steam. "You stupid brat!" he whines. "You're too late!"

I squeeze harder. "What are you planning for the Peace Summit?" I can feel the rage pouring off me like lava. Misha's eyes are wide as he squirms, trying to escape my grip, but he still manages a harsh laugh.

"There's no use trying to stop us. You might as well spend time with your idiot boyfriend while you still can." Misha's blinding smile cuts through his face as he glances skyward. "Masha? If you would, please?"

Metal screeches against metal. The people around us gasp; as Papa's concentration flickers and his spell over the crowd breaks, they shove and throb with panic. I glance up to find the streetlamp above us teetering precariously, bowing toward me—

Papa snatches me in his arms and tackles me to the ground as the streetlamp crashes down. Glass sprays away from the spot where I'd just stood. Misha grins down at us from the other side of the post's arm, then vanishes into the sea of gaping tourists.

Their remote viewers can do that? Marylou asks. *Not fair!*

I shove against Papa's arms and slip free of his grasp. "Stop him!" I scream at the chattering onlookers. I stumble over the post, bad ankle twinging, and shove against the thick wall of people, all of them gaping, pointing, questioning, only just now reacting to the strange events unfolding. Papa chases them alongside me, though Misha's already slipped beyond Papa's range. Papa shoves people aside in front of our path, and none too gently—rather than a soft mental suggestion that they step this way or that, they go crashing and stumbling, flung forward, arms bent, a violent scattering of birds.

But it isn't enough. My mind is working in overdrive; the rest of the world feels stuck in slow motion, like a bad fight scene in a Western. There's too much emotion, noise, panic, thickened by the fog of countless humans, breathing and sweating and shouting and twisting through the streets.

I breathe in. *My mind is mine alone.* I breathe out. I can do this.

I force my way through the crowd, one layer of humanity at

a time, swiping my hands against people's sleeves, snatching up fleeting memories of Misha's movements to guide my way.

I tried to warn you, Yulia. Sergei's voice rings through my head. His sad tone, like he's a puppy I've just kicked, has ossified into something sharp and dangerous. *But as usual, you don't listen to me.*

I jump over a bicycle as it falls—seemingly under its own power, though I know better—into my path. *Where are you, Sergei? Why did they bring Misha to the Pathway for Peace summit? Are the others with him?* I swallow hard. *Is my mother?*

Ahead, through the gap between two old ladies' oversized sun hats, I glimpse Misha's light brown hair, his pearly white skin untouched by the sweltering spring sun here in the swamplands of the District. I squeeze past the women with a hasty, heavily accented apology, but my bad ankle is already shooting currents of pain up my leg, slowing me down to a crawl. I grip the corner of a building and suck down fresh air. My mind is mine alone. Pain is nothing to me.

But when I round the corner, the alley is empty.

Yulia? Is everything okay? Marylou asks, like a mosquito buzzing in my ear.

My hand contracts into a fist—a hot white ball of anger. I will release my anger right here. I will not let it control me.

Did you see where they went? I ask.

Negative. As soon as you rounded the corner, everything went white, like this big flash of light—

Like an atom bomb going off, I reply. *Like a burst of static tearing through your brain.*

She hesitates for a long moment before replying, —*Yeah, kind of like that.*

Scrubbers, I say. I peer through Marylou's vision at the rest of our crew; Papa's shoving his way through the crowd in one direction while the others push onward in another. The delegation seems to have split apart in every which way, and we're each chasing a different lead.

I slump against the brick wall. I'm fighting hard to shove my despair away from me. It drips from my fingertips like an electrostatic charge. But it keeps building right back up. I'm sorry, Mama. When you told me the story of the firebird, you told me to pay attention. But I must not have paid it closely enough.

I blink, clearing the swelling tears away. Wait. What else did Mama leave for me to remember? What other memories have been surfacing lately, like corpses that won't stay drowned, just waiting for me to clear the dust away?

And then I see it wavering, ever so gently: the fire escape ladder, pulled down for easy access from the alleyway. My firebird feather. Just waiting for me to notice it.

Because Mama didn't just tell me to pay attention.

She told me to look up.

CHAPTER 26

AS I CLIMB UP the fire escape, it's quickly apparent which window I'm looking for: the one with heavy blackout curtains, still swaying from the last person to crawl through them. I fall into the bland white room, expecting to be overwhelmed with psychic noise, but it's curiously still; the entire room is the plainest, least memorable office I've ever seen. If I didn't know what I was looking for, I'd think I'd made a mistake.

But despite the lack of psychic residue, I can't mistake the heavy spin-dial file cabinets or recording equipment tucked demurely under a desk; the ashtray filled with ash from long hours of operators hunched over a table, transcribing conversations they've snatched from the airwaves. This may not be a psychic operation, but it's an operation, nonetheless. A nest of Soviet vipers, coiled up in listening range of countless government buildings.

I twist one finger around the cord of a pair of headphones, connected to a giant reel of magnetic tape. The image of a pucker-faced Soviet woman leaps out at me, scribbling notes in Russian shorthand. She uses no psychic countermeasures; her thoughts are right out in the open for me to read, though she tries to keep them focused on the task at hand. Do these agents have any idea of Rostov's plans? How complicit are they in his mad desire to seize control?

None of this is helping me find Misha or Sergei or the rest. Misha *had* to have come through here. I trace my fingers on the window frame, the doorknob. Why aren't I seeing him in the past few minutes' memories?

Marylou's voice interrupts my thoughts. *There's a doorway down the hall that I can't see past. They might have some sort of psychic countermeasure in place there.*

Thanks. I'll check it out. I close my eyes and let the room envelop me. There the disruptors are, that dull hum juddering into the gaps between my thoughts. *Any further signs of the delegation?*

No, but we're doing our best. Tony's pulling records on all the delegation members he laid eyes on, and your pops is chasing down some of the other delegates, though they seem to have melted into the crowd.

Thanks. I'll let you know if I find anything more.

Be careful, Marylou says.

I find the hallway she mentioned, musty and water-stained, with a single crackling lightbulb overhead. I rest my hand tentatively on the doorknob. Silence. Cool, empty silence. No past, no future, no nothing. I can barely even hear the current of the suppressing devices.

I open the door with my breath held. But it's only a staircase, leading deep into darkness.

The staircase switches back and forth as it descends. I climb down three flights, if I were to guess, before it levels out into an underground tunnel. The deeper I sink into the tunnel, the more I feel its subterranean rumble in my bones. I have been this way before. Not here, not these tunnels, but one thousands of miles away, under Moscow. I'd tried to escape our KGB facility once, through the secret Metro tunnels, with only a desperate plan to sustain me. Now I'm not running away from my fate, but toward it, begging it to round the corner with that eager gust of wind that presages an approaching Metro train—

Come now, Yulia. Sergei's voice is all around me. I can feel him in the porous concrete walls of the tunnels, tugging me toward an opening. *Did you really miss me that much?*

"Where are you, Sergei?" I step into the open chamber carefully, keeping my back angled toward the wall. The room is much bigger, and the dark concrete walls eagerly swallow up the light from the industrial sconces.

I'm right here.

A halo of sodium light spills around his golden hair as he steps into the room from the far end. His face is shrouded in shadow, but I'd know that hulking outline anywhere.

"Sergei." I take a step toward him. Fear and relief and anger are roiling through me, but I breathe in, I breathe out.

No, that's not right . . . Sergei says. "Maybe I'm right here."

A metal door clangs shut from inside some hidden recess; another Sergei looms out of the frame. I can barely make out the hint of a half smile carving across his face.

"This isn't funny, Sergei." I back against the doorway. Sweat lacquers my polyester dress against my skin; my bad ankle is throbbing, begging me to sit down and give up this foolish chase.

Or maybe I'm here?

Sergei swings through the doorway right next to me. For a brief moment, his face is right before mine, cool air swooshing across my cheeks as I catch a glimpse of his maniacal grin. I jump back with a yelp.

"What do you want?" I cry. "What have you done to yourself?"

The Sergei in front of me reaches toward me. I hear the static crackling across his skin before I feel it, hungrily jumping back and forth between the diminishing distance between his hand and my cheek. His caress on my face is like the scrape of a dull razor blade.

I want to make you understand, Yulia. This is the only way.

White smears the edges of my vision. It corrodes the harsh corners of my emotions and my thoughts; it begs me to surrender to that empty calm at the eye of the storm.

Yes. Surrender. Don't you see? The other two Sergeis slink toward us, both smiling, striding at the same confident clip. *Life is better when we don't fight against what we've been given. Look at how my powers have grown and changed, the more I work with them instead of fighting them. You never would listen to me, but I always knew what was best. Rostov has given us a good life. He'll make the world safe for us.*

"How can you give up so easily? What happens to you the day your dreams don't align with Rostov's?"

But how could that ever happen? Why would I ever want anything other than this?

The scrubbing white has ensnared me, as sure as any vine. I'm rooted in place. I can feel my voice weakening, the words drying up and falling away like dead leaves. I will be reborn again with the coming spring. But first, I must shed these silly thoughts. I must clear out the weeds so the truth can grow.

As the other Sergeis surround me, touching my shoulder reassuringly, cupping my head like a comforting brother, I can see the logic in his argument. I see him smiling and laughing with Larissa, running through Gorky Park as the snow thaws and fresh green shoots emerge from the filthy ice. The Moskva River flows again through the heart of the city, rumbling with the lifeblood of the Soviet Union as it carries ships, as they in turn carry food, medicine, clothing, machinery to all the workers of the world.

It is the Moscow I left behind; without me and my poisonous, traitorous thoughts, it has thrived. Larissa has thrived, no longer subjected to Valentin and me with our devious, ungrateful schemes. Sergei has thrived—he scored the winning hockey goal for Spartak in their most recent game. I can hear the ice swishing beneath his skates.

There are conflicts, still. Secretary Khruschev is too weak to do what is necessary to safeguard such a life, but there are courageous men—General Rostov, Chairman Brezhnev, and Rostov's good friend in the KGB, a man named Andropov—who will do what is necessary to correct the Soviet Union's course. They pity the capitalist workers beyond their borders, who labor with no guarantees, who must scrounge for change to buy homes, cars, food. But the Soviet leaders will uphold the promise of Marx and Engels. They will bring revolution to these downtrodden souls.

They will force it upon them, if they must.

"No."

I shove my palm into one of the Sergeis' faces. That memory of him and Larissa, his fingers gingerly tucking back her hair—what darkness waits in the shadows of that gentle sunlight? There it is—he watches Larissa in a tiled interrogation room, strapped into a chair as a record player drills the guiding tenets of Rostov's philosophy into her brain. Bright bursts of static disrupt her thoughts and keep her focused on absorbing the lesson. Sergei hunches over a radio transmitter as it broadcasts the twinkling, brainwave-syncing music from Papa's radio station. Rostov and the Hound stand in the doorway, reshaping Larissa's thought waves as they fall into frequency. She must pay for her disobedience in Berlin. She must be shown the error of her ways. And if we cannot teach her, Rostov says, we must remake her mind.

You're lying, Sergei cries. *We didn't really hurt her. It was for her own good—*

What other memories can I find? Here we are, a much older one—younger Sergei, maybe eleven or twelve, weeping hysterically as his father—Rostov—brandishes a folded-up belt. "You must not be my real son," Rostov snarls, as Sergei tries to curl up in his mother's arms—Lyubov Kruzenko, another KGB officer—but she shoves him away. "A real son of mine would have a better grasp on his powers by now," Rostov says.

Everyone loses their temper, Yulia, and he was right. We must perform our very best to make his vision real.

His thoughts push back, the static shattering like ice, splintering and shredding at my concentration. But I am the Star. The pain needn't stay with me. I fight through the static haze and search for more.

The locker room at Luzhniki Stadium, after Sergei's goal-winning hockey game. Sergei slams his locker shut and looks up into the leering face of his team captain. "Maybe if you didn't waste all your time with those Party sycophants," the captain growls, "you could play like that every game, instead of muddling around half asleep."

The memories build and build. Sergei and his brother as little children, the Hound already showing signs of his genetic disease, and Rostov exploiting it to the fullest. Larissa sobbing hysterically in Sergei's arms with a fear, an echoing memory, that she can't put into words. The faces of hundreds of Soviet citizens whom Sergei has exposed for their treasonous thoughts; they were packed up and shipped into the far reaches of Siberia for reeducation, hard labor, and death.

This anger, confusion, pain—they are not my emotions to cling to. But they are Sergei's, still raw and open.

And so I take hold of them. And make them burn.

The Sergeis fall back from me with a howl. *Dammit, Yulia!* The voice comes from all around me. *What have you done?*

Tears stream down their faces. Unlike me, they have no other release for the pain. Unfortunately, they have something stronger—a scrubber's pulse, throbbing through me. I back into a wall, searching for an exit, but I can barely see through the white haze that's enveloped me like a shroud. It's drawing tight around me; it's laced through my blood and filling my lungs. It would feel so good right now to be empty, to let it consume me. The memories hold no power over me, but the scrubbing, churning white is too much for me to fight.

I'm sorry, Yulia, Sergei whispers through the fog. *I'm sorry it has to end this way.*

Just before I collapse into oblivion, the shadow of a fourth figure stretches across the chamber. Then everything is blissful, empty white, encasing me in its permafrost, its silence, its calm.

CHAPTER 27

"YULIA." A GIRL'S VOICE cracks through the frosty layer that's encasing my thoughts. "Yulia. You have to wake up."

My arms and legs are filled with shards of ice that scrape and snap as I try to move. Slowly, a blond girl emerges from the blizzard—hair draped around her pale face, blue eyes rounded with fright. "Larissa?" I ask, almost certain she's another memory shaken loose, come to taunt me for my failure.

"Yulia. Yulia, it's me." She squeezes my hand in hers. Solid. Warm. Her Russian is soft and fluid.

The white haze evaporates; I'm starting to see the contours of the concrete chamber. I'd been chasing Misha, hunting for the Russian delegation—and found Sergei. There had been three Sergeis pressing in, trying to persuade me to let Rostov's plan continue. And now Larissa is here—

"Where are they?" I force myself to my feet, but my skin still feels crunchy from disuse; my bad ankle has swollen up and presses fiercely against my boot.

I scan the ground. Three bodies are crumpled in a ring around me. Larissa stands up and moves over to one of them, then snaps a metal circlet into place around its throat. The body wavers, like a television channel going out of focus, then transforms—instead of muscular, Slavic Sergei, it's a frail, elderly Asian woman, hands clenched into tight fists as the rest of her body goes limp.

I check the other two bodies—eyes staring dead ahead, breaths shallow and labored. Neither of them wear Sergei's face, though they both have the same metal rings around their throats. "Where's Sergei?"

"It wasn't really him," Larissa says. "It's Rostov's new army. They're designed so that Rostov can take control of them any time he likes. Sergei can access them, as well."

"So they were puppets on Sergei's string." I grimace.

Larissa tucks a strand of hair behind her ear. "Sergei is . . . not the same as he once was. The old Sergei is still there, but he's wrapping himself up more and more in the Party teachings. I'm trying, Yul, but every day, I have a harder time foreseeing a future where he rejects his father's path for him."

Bozhe moi, have I missed Larissa. Always finding the good in everyone—always dedicating herself to helping people find their most optimal path. She gave up her own freedom to give me mine. But what about her? "Are you all right? The image I saw—Did they really—"

"Lefortovo Prison." The KGB prison in the heart of Moscow. Larissa smiles somehow; that brave smile pains me more than a frown could. "They sent me there after you escaped. I . . . survived. It wasn't Siberia, yeah? I could see my future, the light at the end of the tunnel—I could see what choices would allow me to leave with my mind more or less intact. Your mother showed me a few tricks to keep my sanity."

I force myself to sit up. "You've been working with my mother?"

"Of course. Our powers are—are similar." But Larissa's voice softens, like she's covering up a secret. "We figured it out, together. What needs to happen."

"Yes!" I could cry. I'm so relieved. "I knew she had a plan!" I look up at Larissa and take a deep, steadying breath. "Tell me what we need to do."

"How about I show you?"

I trail behind Larissa through the twisting tunnels. In between empty chambers, they narrow so much that we have to turn sideways to squeeze through, but then it widens into halls with three or four metal doors branching away from them.

"The KGB has been building these tunnels for years," Larissa explains as we walk. "They branch away from the Soviet embassy at the top of Connecticut Avenue and stretch all over northwest DC—perfect for shuttling spies into or out of the embassy and evading your friends up top."

The walls hum with electricity, but I can't find any signs of the scratchy psychic radiation I felt coming off the scrubbers that Sergei had controlled. "You don't have to help me, you know. I saw what it cost you, the last time you did." I hesitate. I can force emotions onto people, but I'm no good at expressing them in words. "I can't bear to see you get hurt again. Not on my account."

Larissa smiles sadly, her gaze looking toward a future I can't see. "You're not making me do anything. This is what I need, too."

"What about Sergei, Misha, everyone else? Aren't they

watching us right now?" I glance upward. "You stopped the scrubbers with that—that metal thing, but—"

"I'm sure you're familiar with 'that metal thing,' seeing as how we stole the tech for it from your team. Those little current boxes you place in a room to block our remote viewers?" Larissa nods. "Same principle."

"So it keeps them from being taken over by Rostov or Sergei or—or whoever. Protects the target from any psychic interference. Then, you just have an angry controller to deal with. Does Sergei know it was you who blocked him?"

"Yes, but we used some slightly more primitive espionage techniques to settle him down." Her grin broadens. "Amazing what a little chloroform and a kerchief can do."

I could hug her right now. "How the hell did Rostov let you get ahold of chloroform?"

"Oh, *Rostov* didn't." Larissa slows and turns to face me, expression suddenly solemn. "Your mother gave it to me."

Bozhe moi. Mama. "She's here?"

Larissa grips my arm to steady me. "She needs you, Yulia. We both do. She's taught me so much about making sense of the future, but there's only so much we can do together."

"But it's simple. Surely Mama and I can figure out a way to reverse the effects of the serum, right? We can take away Rostov's army of scrubbers and cure Valentin. And free you and Mama."

"Yulia . . ." Larissa stops in front of a metal blast door. The corners of her dainty mouth twitch downward; I remember that look in her eyes, the one she gets when she's seen a possibility in the future looming large, and is weighing how divulging her knowledge will affect its course. She did this to me when we were planning our escape from East Berlin. Did she see, back then, that she wouldn't be able to escape with Valya and me? Or was it something worse she saw then, but was able to deter it by staying back? It makes my head hurt to imagine it.

I meet her stare, impassive, accepting of whatever she needs to say.

". . . I just want you to be prepared," she finally says. "It won't be as easy as all that. Rostov brought us here to oversee his 'operation,' after all, and he has some safeguards in place to force us to carry it out. But we will do our best to help."

"Of course," I say. But I'm already charting escape routes and calculating formulas that Mama and I can test for the cure.

The door groans on rusty hinges, and Larissa ushers me inside.

While it's the same concrete as the rest of the vast tunnel network, this chamber is massive. Rows and rows of fluorescent lights buzz overhead like a swarm of wasps, bathing the gleaming metal scientific tables and racks in a bleached-out glow. Tubes and wiring and petri dishes cover every square inch of surface area; in stark contrast to Doctor Stokowski's tidy, by-the-book lab protocols, this looks like Doctor Frankenstein's madness made manifest.

A woman in a white lab coat—stained here and there with splotches of blood and blue pigmentation—turns to face me.

Mama. Under all the extra wrinkles, the exhaustion, I see straight through her, right down to her genetic code. I see the wistful smile she plasters to her face whenever Zhenya has a fit;

I see the spark in her eyes, faint but visible nonetheless, that reminds me why she persists against all odds.

"Yulia." Her arms open wide. Like slipping into an old habit, I'm stumbling into them, I'm folded into her embrace, her softness, her sweetened chemical smell. "It's time for us to get to work."

✦　✦　✦

Mama pulls out a metal stool for me as she settles onto one of her own. She motions toward Larissa; without a word, Larissa scampers off to a far corner, where Zhenya is hunched over a notebook of music paper. Zhenya. My brother. He looks up at Larissa as she sits next to him, breaking out of his private fugue, and listens as she speaks to him in low, familiar tones. Envy sears through me. Though Larissa's suffered greatly, she has my mother and brother; this is what I've traded for Papa and Valentin and our comfortable American life. Is this what it's like for her to always see the branching paths of choice? To always know what doors she's closed to herself by walking through another one?

My hand closes around Mama's. "I ran like you told me. I found Papa and escaped. But—but you didn't tell us what to do next."

Mama's hand is stiff; she won't meet my eyes. "I didn't want to—to worry you. It's never a guarantee, the futures that I see. I knew there would be challenges. I had to keep you in the dark."

All the doubt and anger comes surging back. It's as if Mama's nearness makes everything brighter, sharper, crueler; I'm fighting harder to dispel this resentment. "What, you don't think I'm strong enough to do what needs to be done? Maybe if you let me in on your plans, I could decide that for myself!"

Mama's head lowers; she glances over at Larissa. "I told you she wouldn't understand."

"Understand what?" My throat closes up as I stare at her. "Something that you can see in the future?"

"Yes." Her voice wavers. "I created the serum; I gave Rostov this tool. But I'm not doing this for Rostov. I'm doing it for you."

I know she has to have some good reason for doing what she's done—for spreading a psychic plague. But she can't have meant for this to happen. For Valentin—"Mama. Mama, how is this supposed to help me? If it was all to bring you here, I understand, but this seems like so much."

She shakes her head frantically, squeezing tears through her lashes. "I know what you're thinking. But there's a greater purpose." She forces her lips into a smile, but it looks false. "You'll understand one day. I can't explain it to you now, but I promise, you'll understand."

"Well, what can you explain? I'm very close to undoing the serum—I understand the basics." I pick up her lab notebook and start sketching on the graph paper. "The psychic genetic code rests here, right? On the twentieth and twenty-second chromosomes. And your virus attacks that code—amplifies it until it's too big and the whole thing collapses under its own weight."

Mama nods. "That's the gist of it. I took cultures from the Hound. The way he can amplify other psychics' powers, you know, and how easily he becomes a vessel for Rostov to control. I knew there had to be a key to it there. Of course, it's highly unstable in anyone else's genes. It keeps growing and growing, which is why they don't survive for long . . ."

"All right. So how can we safely reverse it?"

Mama twirls a pencil back and forth between her fingers. "Yulia . . . I didn't design it to be reversed."

I stare down at my sketches. The answer is here, I'm sure of it. "It doesn't matter. There has to be a way. Right? There's always a way." I box off a portion of the code. "When it amplifies this bit of code, it makes it too difficult to extract without damaging everything else. So maybe if we—if we reverse the amplification effects . . ."

Mama leans back from the table, chewing at her lip. I know this look. The look she used to give me when I asked when my little brother would be normal—the look when she's tossed between a harsh truth and a gentle lie. "I just don't know, Yulia. I can't—I can't see the outcome. I can't see anything past . . ."

Larissa stands back up. "Antonina. We don't have much time."

Mama nods, shaking off whatever frightful things she saw in our future. "Yes. If you want to stop Rostov, you'll need to take control of his scrubbers. He controls them through the Hound. The Hound is an amplifier—I'm sure you remember how Rostov would use him to make himself even more powerful. So with the scrubbers, the Hound both amplifies Rostov's ability and links them all together so he can control them at once."

"Sergei can do it, too," Larissa explains. "Any sufficiently strong psychic can, as long as they have access to whoever is the amplifier, which in this case, would be the Hound."

"So if we can gain control of the Hound, we can stop Rostov's scrubbers," I say.

"Right." She sketches a quick map of the compound. "They're keeping him here. We can help part of your team get back to disrupt Rostov, but you'll have to have someone ready to stop the scrubbers, too. Disable them, so they can't continue with whatever orders Rostov has passed along for them to carry out at the summit."

"One moment. Let me show this diagram to my teammates." *Marylou*, I say, leaving the thought outside my shield like a beacon in case she can hear me. But she must be blocked by the devices that encase us like a Faraday cage.

Larissa stands up. "The circuits—they run throughout the tunnels. We need to switch them off. I'll only be able to do it for a few minutes, though, or it'll trigger an alarm."

"We only need a few. Sergei and Misha won't be out for much longer," Mama says. She grabs a thick file from across the table and pulls it toward us as Larissa heads for a control panel. "Then I'll need you to memorize these faces. These are the men and women Rostov has recruited from the KGB's ranks who will be infiltrating the Pathway for Peace summit—they've all been injected with the serum at the same time so they'll be at the peak of their power. You have to memorize their faces, Yulia. All of them. Can you do this?"

There you are! Marylou exclaims. *Lord almighty, Jules, I've been looking all over for you.*

Is Tony with you? I ask.

Tony's voice comes across loud and clear. *Right here.*

"I can do even better," I tell Mama.

After Tony's absorbed the minions' faces—Russian delegates, compromised convention workers, and more—and Larissa reactivates the shield, Mama moves on to the next stage. "If the peace summit fails to produce Rostov's . . . desired effect . . ." Mama uses the clipped, euphemistic Russian that I remember so well. Every word layered with meaning, laden with a graveness and significance that can't be found in a dictionary. "Well, we'll have to ensure it doesn't come to that."

I glance back over at Larissa and Zhenya. "What about the three of you? We can escape right now, while Sergei and Misha are out. We—we can synthesize the cure at Professor Stokowski's lab. I'm already so close—I'm sure with your help, we'll finish in no time."

Mama and Larissa exchange a look—another hasty wordless agreement, one I'm not privy to. "We have to stay here, for now," Mama finally says.

I look from Mama's tense expression to Larissa's widened eyes. What has them so frightened? "Has Rostov done something to you?"

Zhenya cries out in the corner; Larissa squeezes his hand and makes shushing noises. "It's almost time, Antonina," she says.

"Time for what?" I slide off the stool and walk toward the corner to join her and Zhenya. "What's the matter with him?"

Zhenya's eyes lock on to mine. He sees me. He's here, really here, engaging with me. "Took you long enough," he says.

I smile, though I'm aching to throw my arms around him. "I missed you, too." I turn to Mama. "Come on. Let's leave now, before Sergei's awake."

"It's Rostov. If we stray too far from him, this—this control he has over us—" Mama flinches and seizes my wrist, giving me a fleeting glimpse of the sharp agony that scraped through her at the mere thought of trying to escape. "We can't leave here without his direct order. Otherwise, my—" She dabs her nose with a kerchief; though she hastily stuffs the kerchief back in her pocket, I can't miss that flash of red. "I'm sorry, Yulia. You'll have to do this on your own."

"What?" I cry. "Mama, no! Don't be ridiculous. I'm not leaving without you. We'll—we'll figure out a way to break you free."

Larissa looks away, a curtain of golden hair shielding her face from me. "We're working on it."

"Trust me, Yulia. Trust us a little bit longer. The best you can do right now is stop Rostov's attack on the summit. Can you do that for me?"

"All right, we'll stop them! But Mama, I have to come back for you—"

She seizes me by the shoulders. Once more, I feel ten years old, being scolded by my mother who knows and foresees so much more than I can ever dream to comprehend. Her eyes bore straight into mine. "Stop Rostov's scrubbers at the symposium. It's the best solution that I can see."

"But, Mama, what about the serum?" My throat squeezes tight. "I have to save Valya."

Mama's lips press into a hard, cruel line. "I'm sorry, Yulia. There is no cure."

I am tearing apart, a fission reaction spreading through my lungs. No. No. Fury is etching its flash burns across my skin. No. She's lying. She can't be right. "You designed it." Heat pours through me, into my fingertips, engulfing her. "You have to know how to undo it."

At the far end of the lab, a series of metal bolts clang open. "Go!" Larissa hisses.

"I'm sorry, Yulia. I've done what I can. Stop the summit." Mama shoves me through the doorway and, with chest-aching finality, slams the blast door closed.

CHAPTER 28

CINDY AND THE REST OF THE TEAM—of *my* team, I realize with a timid sense of pride—swarm around me as I stumble out of the T Street exit hatch. They're hurling a million questions at me. How big is Rostov's strike force? Where is Rostov? Where else do these tunnels lead? Are they still targeting the Pathway for Peace?

I answer as best as I can, but my attention is inside my head. Mama said something about the design of the virus, how it put too much strain on the genetic code. "Papa." I seize him by the wrist. "We need to go. Now. Can you drive me by Doctor Stokowski's lab?"

"Sure," he says, eyebrows knitting together. "Are you all right?"

I saw her, I think, desperate to tell him everything about Mama—her smile, her plans, her voice. Everything he wiped away. I'd started to forget it all myself. But instead I tell him, "I think I know how to cure Valya." Mama thinks there's no cure, but she's wrong—I saw it myself.

Papa presses his lips into a thin line and hastens his steps. "Then we'd best get to work."

After a hasty exchange with Cindy and Winnie, they head off to coordinate with the FBI over our findings and Papa drives me to Georgetown. Doctor Stokowski is in the middle of a lecture on uncategorized genetic disorders when I storm into the lab. A dozen faces turn toward me—bright, pale boys' faces, their noses and cheeks rosy from the April sun. I march past them, ignoring their stares, and yank open the fridge full of cultures.

"Miss Chernina," Stokowski says, face puckered. "I'll be happy to meet with you after class if you need help with your research."

"Sorry, Doctor." I cast about for the right English phrase. "Medical emergency." I snatch a cooler from the stack next to the fridge and start loading my labeled vials into the preformed slots. "I'm going to need a lot of LSD."

★ ★ ★

While Papa drives us into Arlington, toward the safe house, I perform the genetic equivalent of brain surgery with gardening shears. I scrape the lysergic acid diethylamide samples into the most promising antiviral strain, add the necessary catalysts, and load it all into a trio of capped syringes. The INFRA should suppress Mama's swollen psychic gene markers enough for the virus to strip them out without damaging the proteins around them. The samples look promising, but a thorough test would take weeks—weeks we don't have. If I'm lucky, Valya has days. There's no time to waste—I'll need to inject Valya as quickly as possible if we're going to have a chance of saving him.

Papa tries to upshift and fly past an old lady in her Bel Air, but the stoplight foils him, and he drums his fingers anxiously against the steering wheel, casting a glance my way. "You're a brave girl," he finally says. "Braver than me, to seek out your mother like that."

I shake my head, cheeks burning. "I'm just stubborn as sin."

"Do you get that from your mother?" he asks, then spreads his arms, a sheepish grin on his face. "It's certainly not from me."

We laugh, but his words hang eerily in my head, reminding me how little he must remember of her personality. Anyone who's met Mama would remember her tenacity—*my little pit bull*, Papa used to say of her. Another thing he's forgotten.

I tighten my grip around the case of syringes. Well, after I cure Valya, I hope to give him a chance to relearn it all.

Papa throws the car into park in the safe house's driveway, even though we're supposed to park down the block, especially with his flashy ride. I leap out of the passenger's seat without opening the door and ring the buzzer. The watchman has strict orders not to let anyone into the same room with Valentin, but I'm sure Papa and I can persuade him. We have to.

But it's not the watchman who answers; it's Frank Tuttelbaum, a cheerful whistle dying on his lips when he sees us.

"Yulia," he says, like it's a four-letter word. "Is there something I can help you with?"

I hold up the case of syringes. "I have the cure for Valya. Please, Mister Tuttelbaum. You have to let me see him. I promise, I can cure him. He can help us stop Rostov."

Frank quirks his mouth to one side of his face. "I'm sorry, Yulia. Val's not here right now."

My heart cracks open. I feel all my determination leaking out, drifting away from me. The one emotion I need to cling to. "Why?" I ask, but my voice sounds so fragile to me. So useless.

"We had to move him. For his own safety, of course. With Rostov's plan in motion, we just couldn't take the risk . . ." Frank pats me on the back—more to guide me back down the sidewalk than to reassure me. "Even I don't know where they're taking him. It's safer that way—what's that old chestnut your pops always says? An empty mind's a good mind?"

No. I don't understand. Valentin would be safe from Rostov right now, if only they'd let me access him. "But I can cure it. Please—you have to take me to him."

He guides me right back to the driveway, more insistently now. "You two are still barred from missions, so go home, relax, get a good night's rest, Yulia. I've got an entire network of Reds to stop. I don't have time to worry about one little boy."

Rage is like a fist around my throat, and I don't want to force it away from me. I want to feel every painful barb of it scraping me raw from the inside. But Frank is oblivious, whistling that stupid tune again as he forces me back into the passenger's seat of the Austin Healey.

"Your girl is clearly in need of a good night's sleep," Frank tells Papa, a vicious smile smeared across his lips. "I know she wouldn't be behaving so rashly if she just got some rest."

My English may still be poor, but I know how to see through the gaps in his words. I'm well versed in the shape of threats.

Papa drums his fingers on the steering wheel. I grip the sides of my seat; Papa's about to compel him. I brace myself for the nauseating static burst.

But it doesn't come.

Instead, Papa jams the shift into reverse so hard it sounds like he's about to wrench the stick off. "Wise idea. Lots to do tomorrow." The tires squeal as Papa peels out of the driveway.

"Are you joking?" I cry. "Of all the times for you to abuse your power—"

"He doesn't know where they took Valya. He wasn't lying about that. Besides." Papa's mouth is a grim slash across his face as he races through the dark suburban neighborhood. "We have bigger problems right now."

"Like what?" I ask, but then I realize where I've heard the song Frank is whistling. It's the introductory music for the KGB numbers station.

"Like the mole on the PsyOps team. Frank."

★　★　★

We try to sleep for the night, but it doesn't come easily for me. In my dreams, I grasp for fragments of Mama, jagged mirrored shards of memory, but they only slice me when I try to get too close.

Winnie, Donna, and Cindy meet me at a 24-hour diner that overlooks the Georgetown Canal. The sun is just starting to slip out of the eastern mouth of the Potomac, orange gold dripping across the water as the university crew teams row in perfect unison. Donna orders a strawberry milkshake while Cindy and Winnie grab us a booth with a great view of the city as it awakens. Their eyes are wide the whole time I explain: Rostov's plans to sow chaos at the peace summit; the way he's holding Mama hostage in the tunnels beneath the Soviet embassy. Frank, the mole within our own team, dragging Valya away to points unknown. Donna's cheeks stay sucked in as if she means to drink her shake in one terrified gulp.

"I just can't believe it's Frank," Donna says, in between sips. "But I guess it's always the ones with something to prove. Do you think he's working for them intentionally?"

"That's what I'm hoping you can find out." I shove the scrambled eggs around my plate, unsure if I can keep them down.

Cindy stares through me, no emotion on her face.

"And here I thought he was just a racist, sexist pig," Winnie says. "You're sure about this? He doesn't exactly strike me as a communist sympathizer."

"Ideology," Cindy says. "He doesn't have to sympathize with the Soviet Union—he just has to want the same thing as them, for now. In this case, that would be America's declaring war on North Vietnam. You heard him the other day. He thinks we have every reason to go to war with North Vietnam. Thinks it'll be good for us, like Korea—put another nail in the coffin of communism."

"But he's just playing into Rostov's hand," Winnie says.

I nod. "The war is a means to an end—something to keep us occupied. And then, when we're weakened, our military is elsewhere, we're vulnerable to attack—"

I don't need to finish the rest. The card Cindy lays before us, the Ten of Swords, says it all. A man lies facedown with several blades still embedded in his spine. Betrayal, destruction.

Donna chews at her straw as she stares at the card. "Heavens to Betsy, Jules. This is quite a pickle."

"This is a pickle," I agree, without being entirely sure what I'm agreeing to. "But we can stop this."

Cindy tilts her head. "What are you thinking, Yulia?"

"First, we have to stop Rostov. Frank isn't going to do anything to prevent the attack at the summit because he *wants* the war. But my mother said there's a way to control the altered scrubbers. If Rostov and Sergei can do it, then surely Papa can, too."

"So, save the world first." Donna cracks a smile. "Then what about curing Valentin?"

"That's where I'll need your special skill at—how do you put it?—'sweet talking.' You'll have to ply Frank's loyal operatives to find out where Valya's being kept. Papa read Frank's thoughts, but even he doesn't know where Valya was taken."

Donna reaches across the table and gives my hand a tentative pat. "You got it."

I don't entirely trust her, but neither have I given her a good reason to trust me. She wasn't wrong about me—I would have done anything to save Mama, even if it ran counter to the PsyOps team's plans. I offer her a weak smile back. "Thank you. Are the rest of you with us?"

Cindy nods, face solemn, while Winnie grins widely. "Wouldn't miss it."

"What about Judd?" I ask. "Tony? Will they understand why we can't trust Frank?"

"I'll have a word with them," Cindy says. "I think it's safe to count them in our plans."

"Excellent. Then Donna, you, me, and Judd will be dealing with the scrubber minions at the peace summit. We'll need all the disruption boxes you have, Cindy."

"Done." Cindy leans back from the table. "What about reaching the lab beneath the Soviet embassy and getting your family out? I worked out some details with the FBI yesterday while you were at Georgetown, but your father seemed confident he knew how to deal with Rostov in person."

"I'm afraid I can't organize any more spontaneous street festivals and demonstrations," Winnie says, "but I'll do whatever I can to help with logistics."

I shove her the rough map Mama made of the tunnel network. "Papa will be working with the FBI on storming the lab while we deal with the scrubbers at the symposium—he'll fill you in on the details."

Winnie rubs her hands together. "Can't wait."

Cindy shuffles her card deck and plucks out two more. She holds them close to her chest, but my arms are already pressed against the edge of the table; I can see them just fine. The first image makes my stomach clench: a red heart looms large in a storm-tossed sky, with three swords piercing it, each of them dripping with blood.

She catches my eye. "It's not as bad as it looks," she says. "It means you'll be too hard on yourself. The emotions will be hard to fight."

I catch sight of the last card Cindy's fingering: a skeleton atop a horse riding into town, trampling the village's ruler. Death.

"Change," Cindy says hastily. "I see change, not necessarily death. An important event brought to a close."

"Let's hope that's all it is," I reply.

CHAPTER 29

THE DOLLEY MADISON HOUSE, perched on Lafayette Square with a sideways glance toward the White House, hardly looks like a place where one should start a war. Its colonnaded porch begs for a trio of round-bellied bourgeois capitalists to smoke cigars and drink brandy while they trade tips on how best to exploit the proletariat. (So my Soviet indoctrination makes me think.) But instead of surrendering to its old money charms—the pitched roof, the gas lamps—it sets my teeth on edge.

The mansion is filled with scrubbers—dozens of them, humming and throbbing on the periphery of my thoughts like droning crickets outside my window late at night. My purse slaps heavily against my thigh; my knees buckle and my vision blurs. Donna catches me by the elbow and drags me upright.

"Careful, Jules," she murmurs. "You're not allowed to pass out just yet."

We enter the grand foyer and approach the check-in station,

where the security guard looks us over like we're a couple of circus performers. "Names?" he asks dubiously.

Donna stands up straighter. Her time to shine. "I'm not sure which last name it's listed under. I just got married. Can you check Jones for me?"

As he flips through the list of names, Donna's eyes narrow; she's looking at the list through his eyes in search of suitable names for both of us. "First name?" he asks.

"Mary. Mary Jones? When he shakes his head, she snaps her finger. "All right. Mary Griffin it is." Then she gives my hand a squeeze. *Constance Fellowes.*

"Constance Fellowes," I tell the man when he asks me, though I'm sure the real Constance would cringe to hear me pronounce it. He checks us both off the list, and we approach the velvet truncheons.

"Oh, Connie, this is great!" Donna exclaims as the guards permit us onto the grand staircase. "The senator's sure to love our report."

I force a sharp smile to my lips. "I certainly hope he appreciates the trouble we're going to."

When we reach the great hall, the scene before us looks more like a wedding reception than a peace summit—delicate clusters of flowers adorn the center of each white linen tablecloth. At the front of the room, microphones have been placed along a long table for each country's delegates; representatives from all the major news radio stations are already clustering microphones of their own around the seat reserved for the United States representative, Senator Saxton. Donna steers me toward a table in the back;

a waiter immediately deposits a plate of cream- and dill-slathered salmon before each of us.

"I wish I felt half as confident as you look," Donna grumbles. She's casting about the room, trying to sort out how we'll pull off the next part of our plan without starting an international incident of our own.

I tighten my grip on my beaded purse, holding it possessively in my lap. "We don't have the luxury of messing up."

Ready when you are, Marylou chirps inside our heads, opening up the communications link.

Good morning, my rebellious comrades. I smile in spite of myself. *Let's make some new friends.*

Through Marylou's viewing, Papa comes into focus, in the laboratory deep beneath the Soviet embassy. He's switched off the disruptor circuits like Larissa showed me, and is heading for the inner chamber where the Hound is kept. Rostov should be there with the Hound, ready to use him to amplify and beacon out his every command. Two guards rush toward Papa, but he swiftly puts their minds to sleep; they crumple to the floor.

Waiting on your order, devochka, Papa says.

I allow myself a tiny smile. Papa will stop Rostov first; then he can rescue Mama and Zhenya and Larissa. Whatever emotions hit him when he sees Mama again, at least Rostov will be handled.

The delegates file into the front of the hall; everyone leaps to their feet with triumphant applause. Unlike a Russian audience, their hands all clap out of sync, and I can't find the appropriate rhythm to join in. No one is listening to anyone else. How can they clap like this?

Then a wave of static rolls through me. This is it—the moment Rostov's been working toward. I scan the crowd for signs of the scrubbers, but it's like the world has been wrapped in gauze. I have to fight to see clearly.

A blitzkrieg of flashbulbs subdivides the scene before us. The North Vietnamese delegate screams at Saxton, accusing the US of arming South Vietnam. Saxton throwing up his hands—"Now, let's not get hasty. We're here to announce our decision."

The white noise presses in, burying me in a static snow as the scrubbers sink into Saxton's mind. The scrubbers are offering Rostov a second hand control over Saxton, unlike the complete domination he has over the scrubbers themselves, but it's more than enough for Rostov. Against a non-psychic like Saxon, one of his scrubbers would have been sufficient, but Rostov's not known for his restraint.

"The United States has decided . . ."

Now, Papa! I scream. *Now!*

He charges into the cell. The Hound—Sergei's brother, Rostov's other son—stands up with a snarl. But Papa has surprise on his side. I can't see Papa's struggle with the Hound around the white crackling noise, but I feel the shift of power over the scrubbers rocking back and forth between Papa and Rostov as the haze waxes and wanes.

Saxton stammers at the podium as the crowd murmurs around him. "We're going to . . . we've declared . . . we're not going to . . ."

The scrubbers powers are too much for him. Saxton slumps forward, forehead crashing into the table before him, as blood runs from his nose. The room sucks in its breath at once—in terror, at least, this crowd resembles the unity of thought and action that I remember from home. Rostov's minions all stand as one, including one of the Russian delegates, but no one notices them. Everyone's too busy screaming for a doctor and rushing toward Senator Saxton.

I'm sending all the minions to the bathroom to get them out of here. Hurry, girls! Papa calls.

The flashing bulbs resume, capturing the chaos and panic for the papers. Smoke and the smell of burning magnesium hang heavy in the air. The hair on my arms stands on end as if a great electrical storm is rolling through. The two opposing frequencies of Rostov and Papa chatter back and forth in my mind.

Donna and I chase the scrubbers out of the great hall, sending our glimpse of them back to Tony via Marylou, who reports back a minute later. *Great. I've IDed them all. We'll keep FBI tied up for weeks tracking them down and looking into their associates.* He laughs. *Well done.*

We're not done yet, I say.

On the other side of the powder room door, I can feel the crackle and hum of all of those powerful psychics; it brings me little comfort to know that Papa's wrestled them under his control. What if Rostov gains the upper hand? "Let's be quick," I tell Donna. She nods and tears open her purse.

With the minions subdued by Papa, it's easy to snap our makeshift disruptors—Cindy's disruptor boxes attached to dog collars—into place around their necks. It closes the circuit of the disruptor so it boxes in their power, just like Larissa showed me how to do. Once the collars are around their throats it breaks the link to Papa, and they sink down to the floor, or slump against the counter. We'll leave them here until the FBI agents move in to collect them. I wonder how much of the person they once were remains in them, in those cold stares and limp limbs and shallow, listless breaths; I force my thoughts away from imagining Valentin in this state.

Donna holds up our stack of collars that remain. "There are only eight scrubbers here."

She's right. The crowd of minions is far smaller than we expected. *Marylou? Tony? Who are we missing?*

Your mother showed us dossiers for at least twenty-five different operatives, Tony answers, via Marylou.

My heart is beating rapidfire; I scan the faces of the neutralized scrubbers in front of us. *So where are the rest?*

We've got a problem. It's Papa. The haze in his image is gone; he stands over the slumped form of the Hound, wiping a trail of blood from his nose. *Rostov isn't here.*

Then who was controlling the minions? Donna asks.

But I see the second figure now, unconscious next to the Hound.

Sergei.

He was controlling them instead of Rostov. I try to swallow, but it's as if a fist has clenched around my throat and won't let go. I knew he was getting stronger, but I hadn't realized his powers were evolving this way. *Then where's Rostov?*

Marylou sucks in her breath. *Oh, golly gee. Oh, dag nabbit all to . . .* Marylou takes a deep breath. *Look out at Lafayette Square, in front of the White House.*

Donna and I rush back into the main hallway to peer through the watery old glass. At first, I'm not sure what it is we're seeing on the square. There are the usual protestors, with placards calling for everything from repealment of Jim Crow laws to release of the Kennedy assassination files to the public to voting rights for cats. But a cluster of men in suits at the mouth of the entrance gate stands out. The guards are slumped against the guard post; the gate to the White House stands open wide.

A flock of people trudge through the gate, heads lowered, shoulders drawn. A Secret Service agent rushes toward them from the White House portcullis, but then he crumples, falling into the emerald grass. In the very center of the flock, a head above the rest, I can make out the olive-green rounded hat of a KGB commander.

Major General Anton Ivanovich Rostov.

And at his side are Mama and Valentin.

CHAPTER 30

"WAIT, YULIA. It's too dangerous." Donna grips my shoulder. "We can't overpower Rostov without your dad's help."

But he's deep beneath the Soviet embassy, almost a mile away. Distraction. *Maskirovka.* Rostov's—and the Soviet Union's—signature style. We thought the threat of war in Vietnam was meant to be a distraction for the United States. But it was a plot to distract us from *this.*

Cindy cuts in via Marylou. *Stay put, Yulia. We're sweeping the tunnels right now, but I'll try to dispatch a SWAT team to the White House, if they'll take orders from me instead of Frank. There's nothing you can do.*

You think they can stop him? With an army of scrubbers supporting him? I shake my head. *I have no choice.*

But Yulia—the Death card. Cindy's thoughts feel thin as paper. *The more you think about charging in there, the stronger it looms in my mind.*

Then I guess that's the price I'll have to pay.

I hobble down the grand staircase, Donna trailing behind me. The foyer is still crammed with reporters and diplomats, laughing nervously about Saxton's collapse, oblivious to the siege taking place at the White House next door. As soon as we run onto the patio, the air around us turns sour; it's permeated by an overwhelming sense of foreboding, like those green-tinted moments before a massive thunderstorm. Already, Rostov and his twisted herd are entering the White House, but there's still time to stop them. I just have to figure out how.

Donna twines her golden ponytail around one finger and stares right through me, like I'm one of her psychic subjects, an orange just waiting to be unpeeled. *Come on, Yulia*, Donna says, pressing the thought just to me instead of through Marylou's connection. *We can do this.*

A tiny, taunting voice—I suspect it's an echo of Misha and Masha and Frank Tuttelbaum, all rolled into one—tells me we can't. That I'll end up like the scrubbers' victims, my sanity clinging to the fast-fraying rope that is my brain, my thoughts mangled and mauled, my mind a hollowed-out husk. I remember too clearly the taste of blood down the back of my throat, the smell of it metallic and the taste salty on my upper lip. A single powerful scrubber can wipe a mind clean. What could twenty of them do to me?

Yulia. It's Papa, hunting desperately through the lab as the FBI agents rush around him. *If you can block Rostov's amplifier, you'll have a much better chance.*

But who's the amplifier? I ask.

Papa winces as he leafs through a file folder. *The Hound wasn't the only amplifier—she's an amplifier, too.* I swallow, hard, as a knot of emotions—betrayal, shock, disbelief—tangles itself tight inside my chest. *That's why I was always so much stronger with her*, Papa says.

It was never just foresight for her, though he'd made himself forget that part. In our family of three psychics, she was always our backbone, our guardian. He'd said it himself—he was always strongest with her. And she bolstered us in other ways, too. I just didn't pay close enough attention to the firebird feather right before me.

I can do this. *My mind is mine alone.* I thread my mantra through my thoughts, through my mental shield, through the rise and fall of my lungs. My mind is mine alone. My mind is mine alone.

But their minds—they will be mine.

Donna stays right at my side as I stride toward the black iron gate; I'm dimly aware of Judd moving our way from the Dolley Madison House, as well, where he'd been ready to start a fire emergency if our initial plan to stop the summit scrubbers went awry. Marylou, Cindy, Papa, and Tony hover in our thoughts, ready to help. I don't have to do this alone.

I press my hand to the forehead of the gate guard, slumped inside his command post. He stares back up at me with blood-shot eyes that won't focus. Chaotic thoughts swarm like hornets inside his head, drowning out his mind's efforts to process the world around him, to make sense of what he's seeing and hearing and feeling.

Cling to that image—there. The man's memory spits up an image of him sitting in a sunny lawn, watching his son play catch with their sheepdog. *This is you. Your memories and thoughts.* I focus on the warm emotions, the sense of peace these memories offer him. Direct him away from the negative, the fear, the pain. If I can guide him away from what the scrubber did, then maybe I can help him counteract it. *Where does this thought lead? How does it make you who you are?*

Slowly, related images coalesce around the fragment. Training the dog to heel and fetch. Teaching his son the alphabet. Grilling burgers on the back patio while his wife sets the table in her flouncy Donna Reed dress. He is, bit by bit, himself once more. The noise from Rostov's horde remains, but it's relegated to one segment of memory, rather than infecting the whole.

Donna's turn. "Those men and women. They weren't supposed to pass through here. What did they tell you? What did they show you?"

His thoughts turn over and over on her words, filtering through Rostov's lies like any other memory. "They said it's time to relieve President Johnson of his burden. Oh, God, they wanted me to—" He swallows down a sob. "It seemed like such a good idea at the time—"

"And where is President Johnson?" Donna presses. Judd jogs up to us, face flushed and red as his freckles, but keeps quiet.

"The Oval Office. He's scheduled to sign a non-aggression pact with the Viet Cong pending the outcome of the peace summit."

Donna and Judd and I glance at each other; their expressions look as sour as mine feels. "Then we'd better be on our way," Judd says.

We round the curving driveway, passing another guard, this one a soldier clutching an assault rifle to his chest as blood spills from his ears. A shiver runs down my spine as I remember

Cindy's cards, and the way her determined spin on "Death" didn't soften the interpretation much.

A KGB officer in uniform runs down the curving staircase of the grand entrance as we step inside. "Halt! It is not permitted for you—"

Then he screams as his rifle's ammunition box explodes. The conflagration spreads to his sleeve and up his arm, and he runs from us, screaming and flinging his flame-wrapped arm against the wall. The fire crackles and hisses.

"Frank said I was never good at following orders," Judd says.

We reach the top of the staircase. Psychic energy hangs heavy in the air, swampy and miserable to wade through, as if it could physically force me back down the stairs by its mere presence. There's no doubt which direction Rostov has taken them. My stomach roils like a simmering stew, and blood wells in my nose; I can't risk walking any closer with the scrubbers under Rostov's command.

Come on, Yul. We've got this, Marylou says.

Can you give me a glimpse further down the hall? Show me what we're facing?

I'll do my best.

I close my eyes and reach through my mind into Marylou's vision.

A white blur clouds our sight like a wind-whipped tundra plain. The scrubbers are phantoms looming in the mist, wisps of thought eddying around them. I push my thoughts closer, welcoming the porcupine spikes of so many scrubbers' minds. Through Marylou's viewing, I can trail my fingers along their arms, like rubbing my finger along the wrong side of a knife. Most of their minds are too far gone to salvage much, but I can wrest them away from Rostov's control. It will have to be enough.

I am Slim Pickens, riding the bomb all the way down. I am Dick Van Dyke, deftly avoiding that ottoman in my path. I am James Bond, throwing the Soviet assassin from the train. I am Cathy Gale on *The Avengers*, coolly navigating a darkened room.

My mind is mine alone.

The mist draws back. The scrubbers stand in a yellow-striped, rounded room, its high ceilings frosted in molding. So many thoughts flow together, like the thin ribbons of a river delta joining and tangling into a roaring behemoth, right at my fingertips, flowing straight into Rostov.

If we can disrupt that stream, if we can break Rostov free of Mama and her amplification—

They turn as legion to face Rostov.

Rostov is clutching an older man by the throat: President Lyndon Johnson, with his rounded nose and caterpillar brows. He howls as Rostov drills into his mind; blood trickles from his ears.

Rostov's lip curls back in a sneer. His gaunt face, like a wax statue melted and hanging off its metal wire frame, is forever seared in my memories, no matter how I've tried to forget. Even though I've been freed of his control for months, the sight of him still makes my knees buckle, as if it's written into my DNA to bend to his will and carry out his command.

The scrubbers draw tighter around Rostov. It's now or never, while they're focused on the president. I pull my vision out of Marylou's and reach into my bag. Two people to save—Valentin with the cure, and Mama with the disruptor. But I don't know if I can fight through the scrubbers long enough for even one.

"Judd?" Donna asks. "I think you know what to do."

He beams as we charge through the hallway and into the Oval Offfice.

The blizzard of scrubbing noise burns my skin like radiation and throbs deep in my marrow. It batters against my thoughts, relentless as the tide, but I neither fight it nor surrender to it. My mind is mine alone. I am the Star, I am a riverbed; these thoughts and feelings and commands rush over me and continue on their way.

Dimly, I hear the shatter and feel the spray of glass as Judd explodes the lights overhead. Mama. I'm staggering blindly through the torrent of noise. I sense the shift in the scrubbers around me, as Rostov's confidence streaming through them turns to rage. I reach into the purse still hanging at my hip.

Now that I have his attention, it'll be too much—

Give up, surrender, accept—

—I clip one of the spare disruptor collars around my own throat.

It's only a finger in the dam, only a bandage on the sucking wound, but it holds the scrubbers at bay, a frail soap bubble of silence in a room full of pins. Only a few more feet to go. Mama is slumped forward, shoulders hunched, eyes reddened and dulled, but she looks up at me as I reach for her hand. Her smile tells me all I need to know—that this is how she wanted it. That I'm making the right future shine.

Once our fingers are firmly laced together, I unclip the collar, releasing my own power while exposing myself to the maelstrom of psychic power in the room. The scrubbers' noise crashes back in like an avalanche. But we're ready, Mama's power amplifying my own. Our minds are ours alone.

Rostov and I are playing tug of war with their minds, and Mama's amplifying power is the rope—the minions jerking this way and that, their painful noise strobing against our thoughts as her power helps him, then me. I keep my grip on Mama firm to share in her power. It's my only defense against him. Even then, blood drips down my face; the emptiness calls to me, goading me on as surely as the ocean called to Valentin's mother, as the bliss of forgetting called to Papa. But Mama's power is fueling mine now, if I can just fend Rostov off—

Rostov's face turns ghoulish with a hateful sneer. "Fine. Take her. I'll do this by myself."

The air around us buckles and combusts, each molecule turned into an isotope of radiating pain. Mama's his clear target, but I'm close enough to feel the flashburn of his strength. Mama yelps as her knees buckle underneath her and she sinks to the ground.

Mama stares straight through me, her eyes marbled with blood. Red drips from her ears and slicks her lips, her chin; it pools into the hollow at her collarbone. "Mama." I reach out to cradle her head. I can undo this. I can try to straighten out her thoughts, like I did for Valentin. "Mama."

A flute's breathy melody totters through the air between us like a wounded bird weaving through the trees. Igor Stravinsky's *Firebird Suite*. The strings glissade around us, twinkling like fireflies, and a low timpani builds. "Yulia." She tightens her grip on my hand. "Stay with me." I wrap my thoughts in the music and step into Mama's world, and the entire scene of the Oval Office crystallizing around us, frozen in time.

Nothing moves around us, trapped in the moment, but I can move. Mama stands before me, not as she is now, but as she was years ago—whittled like a Siberian tiger, all sinew and sharp wit. Her smile could cut down the most pompous Party member, and her claws would protract in an instant to defend her plans. "Yulia." She glides toward me across the marble halls of Moscow State University, where her mind aparently has chosen to be, as the strings section builds with tension. "There's something I need you to do."

The square granite columns seem impossibly tall around me; maybe I'm still a little girl in her mind. "Of course. Anything."

Heavy drums quake through the halls. "Please, my darling *devochka*. Take my memories. This is your gift."

I grab a fistful of her satin skirt as the floor rolls; plaster dust pours down on us like the sand of an hourglass. "Mama, no! We just have to fight off Rostov, you and I. It's going to be okay."

"Listen to me." She kneels down and grips my chin, somehow unaffected by the building as it crumbles around us. "I can't break Rostov's psychic hold on me. If I fight back, my mind will erase itself—this is what he's done to me. But if I'm gone, Rostov will lose my power. Zhenya and Larissa will be free of him. You can stop him."

I'm shaking my head. I need an outlet for this pressure building up inside me, this overwhelming sense of terror. No. She can't do this. We need our family. I need her. Papa needs her, even if he doesn't remember it yet. "Mama, please—"

The columns collapse in a flurry of dust as Stravinsky's *Firebird* erupts.

"Your father gave up his memories to save our family. So give him mine, instead."

She closes her eyes and slumps against me. The *Firebird* melody consumes us both; her memories pour into me. Most are encoded, tangled in her and Papa's shared melodies, but a few shake loose: Mama and Papa, much younger, hiding from the SS in an alley, their arms linking together and lips seeking each other. Mama defending her dissertation. Mama giving birth to me, hand clamped around Papa's. Mama and her sister as little girls, trying to count all the stars in the sky.

And her gift—her ability to foretell the future. Rather than branch away into endless possibilities, like Larissa's, every path is converging on this single, finite point. It burns like the brightest sun, the final choice on her long journey, brilliant and sure.

"I love you," she whispers. "Tell your father I love him."

The flow of memories wanes; the symphony has drained away. Slowly, the Oval Office comes back into focus around me.

Mama's body hangs limp in my arms, but there is no music under the surface. No stream of thought. There is nothing.

Mama's mind is completely silent.

Mama. I settle her back onto the floor. No pulse. No flutter of breath. Already, the red in her eyes is blurring into cool gray. Mama.

Her memories, her emotions, amplified and swelling, wait just beneath my skin.

"Run!" Donna screams, though she might as well be on another planet for all that her words reach me. Time unfreezes around me, the world coming back into focus like the first moments of waking up: Rostov winds back into motion, Donna and Judd charge into the room, President Johnson leaps up from his desk. Blood leaks from his ears as he staggers toward a panel of curtains and activates a switch; the wall retracts behind the curtains. He slides inside and slams the panel shut behind him, moving with a haste I'd never expected from someone we'd always branded a lazy cowboy.

Something is burning—something sharp and molten and warm fills my nose. Rostov screams. He has reached for the panel to the hidden passage, but Judd sets fire to the curtains, blocking him in here with us.

But Rostov must be stopped. My mind is mine alone. I lunge toward him while he's distracted. Flames leap from the curtain toward Rostov, lapping at his uniform. I let turmoil churn inside me, then fling it at Rostov, my hand clenched to his throat, filling his head with every ounce of sorrow and pain and rage that I have to give. It pours from me like a geyser: my memories, my feelings, my entire life, all one pressure-cooked eruption of agony and noise. Rachmaninov clashing with Tchaikovsky; Dostoevsky and Marxist-Leninist doctrine and "Stars and Stripes Forever" forming a chaotic noose that draws tight around Rostov. He flails and clings to the threads, but he's caught up in the wave of pain—of his own sons' memories, of the lick of flames on his skin, of every bad thing I've had to feel living under his shadow, in Russia and here.

Every death serves a purpose, Mama said. She didn't just get her family out of the Soviet Union. She gave me the tools to stop Rostov.

Rostov's face is flushed with red and purple as he tries to repel the psychic assault. He lunges forward, as the flames gobble at his uniform—the red tabs and medals; the brass buttons; the sickle and hammer pin set inside a red star. He drops to extinguish himself on the massive round rug that bears the United States seal, and the fire goes out with a whimper. But I don't let go.

"Kill him!" Judd cries.

But death would be too good for General Rostov. I have something far better in mind. My hand is steady, so steady, as I pull another syringe from my purse and jab it into his neck.

Color rushes back into the world, blotting out the chattering white haze. The fog burns away as the air thins, as the sound dies, as the antidote courses through Rostov's veins. He hadn't been infected with Mama's serum, but the end result should be the same—the virus should devour every last traces of the genetic code that makes us psychics what we are. I breathe in, count to myself, breathe out, then force myself to press two fingers to his pulse. Slow, but stable; he's badly wounded from both the burns and psychic struggle, but he'll survive to stand trial.

What I'm more anxious for is what I don't feel.

His powers.

It's safe. The cure is safe. I release Rostov and rush toward Valentin, slumped with all the other scrubbers. Valentin's eyes are squeezed shut. Red rims his nostrils, but his nose isn't flowing like the others'. He shudders and jolts as if from a seizure, and a film of sweat sheens his forehead. He thrusts his hand forward and gropes for mine.

"*Tebya lyublu,*" he murmurs. "*Molodtsa.*"

"No. No. You can't go, Valya. Hold tight." *Please don't let it be too late*, I add silently. Mama's dead face looms ripe in my memory and a fresh pool of anguish starts to build, but I let it drip away from me as I dig out another syringe and administer the cure.

The next seconds—minutes—ache. I can barely breathe. All I can see is Valya's still eyes, and in my mind, Mama's face, so cold and empty. My antidote worked on Rostov, but what if Valya's had the serum in him for too long? What if it's already shredded up his mind and body? I reach out to brush his hair from his forehead, but I can't bear to touch him—to hear whatever psychic war is waging inside his own head.

Valentin sits up with a groan.

I fling my arms around him and hug him tight. His thoughts are right there on the surface—no shield, no subterfuge. He's trying to piece together the past several hours, but it's shattered like a mirror, refracting out of order and context. "Yulia." He buries his head into my shoulder. "Yulia."

I kiss his forehead, clammy with sweat, and swallow back my tears. "Are you okay? Please, if he hurt you—" I can hear his thoughts whirring, unguarded, merely half-formed words and ideas gone as soon as they surface. Slowly, his shield weaves back around them, but it's faint. "Valya, please, talk to me."

His lips part—and hang there. "I can't—"

His shield churns and churns, louder now. Like he's reassuring himself he can still shield his thoughts. But that steady hum of psychic energy, hungry for a target, is nowhere to be found.

"My powers. They're gone." His hands tighten into fists. "I can't—I can't hear anyone, I'm not—"

I lean back, chewing my lower lip. "I had to, Valya. It was the only way to save you."

His face softens, then, his mouth lifting with a faint smile. He runs his finger along the side of my face. "Yes. I'm safe now."

I hug him tighter, and then I feel it: how smooth his mind is, worn like a river stone, all the crackle and jaggedness erased. The mind of someone unburdened. "Are you okay?" I ask him, which is absurd, since I'm the one sobbing massive tears of sorrow and relief and joy and pain, every emotion in my repertoire spilling into and out of me.

"Of course." His eyelids sink shut. "Of course I am. I'm free."

CHAPTER 31

LARISSA IS PARDONED for espionage charges because Cindy, Papa, and I testified that she cooperated with the PsyOps team. Rostov, Sergei, Misha, and Masha, however, joined Frank Tuttelbaum in a military jail outside of Bolling Air Force Base while they awaited trial. Their cells have to be fitted with psychic disrupters so no one's thoughts can get in or out, though that isn't a problem for Rostov anymore. Tuttelbaum confesses to sharing classified information with "unauthorized foreign government personnel," which sounds so much nicer than what he was really doing—collaborating with the Soviet Union to force America into war against the Viet Cong.

Once we were able to certify that Rostov had been completely stripped of all psychic ability, we exchanged him with the Soviet Union for five of our own spies. A few weeks later, an article turned up in the Party newspaper, *Pravda*, citing the exposure and condemnation of an unnamed rogue KGB general whose defiance of the Party's wishes had been dealt with accordingly.

Larissa and I visited Sergei not long after he was locked up. He's not sad about his plight, or even his father's; he's more disappointed that the world is the way it is, and the grand ideas he wanted to purport are not so grand after all.

Now, surrounded by the bursting colors of May, we're hosting Mama's funeral—a small affair at a little graveyard along the Potomac River. Just Papa, Zhenya, Valentin, Larissa, and me, spreading her ashes to the four winds. While Larissa and Valya entertain Zhenya, Papa and I sit on the cliffs together and let the wind thread through our hair. "Are you ready?" I ask him, as the afternoon shadows start to pull and stretch.

He laces his hand in mine in return.

At first, I see only his raw, torn-edged memories of Mama, but as the music flows from me to him, wisps of images spiral away from their songs. Her face melts and swirls like a sketch artist refining it—Mama in a drab soldier's uniform, picking through a pile of rubble with a young Papa at her side as smoke rises around them and air raid sirens drone. Mama clutching a bundle to her chest as Papa and a tiny raven-haired girl peer at her. Mama's face wreathed in a field of clover as the sun splashes her and Papa in gold.

Papa's thoughts are stitching themselves back together; the frayed ends where he ripped Mama away tie themselves off, albeit imperfectly. There's a sinkhole aching in his heart where Mama should belong, but piece by piece, he can unravel her gift, and maybe someday fill most of it in.

After the FBI raided the Soviet embassy, they found twenty miles' worth of tunnels that accessed nearly every major agency in Washington. They also found five dead scrubbers and eighteen bankers' boxes full of Mama's life's research. I took the boxes to Doctor Stokowski, and he and I are going to work on them for a new research initiative when I start college at George-town in the fall.

The Soviets said nothing about the death and capture of mul-tiple Soviet spies, seizure of the Soviet embassy, and discovery of the endless tunnels, though they did announce that the Soviet Union had just acquired a lovely piece of property on the edge of the District and intended to build a newer, better embassy there instead.

Zhenya doesn't ask about Mama, but he and Papa have been nearly inseparable since Larissa brought him home. Maybe Papa never forgot that echo of Mama in Zhenya's smile.

★   ★   ★

Valentin's invited to perform at a battle of the bands at a round-domed coliseum near Union Station, where we saw the Beatles play when they first visited America. The music fills us up; the music flows out of us. Larissa, Donna, Marylou, Judd, Tony, and me—we scream and dance and sing along and sweat until my dress sticks to me like cling film. I like to imagine Mama's face in the crowd, stitched onto all the anonymous souls who know nothing of the war we've averted or the pain we've felt.

When we leave the coliseum, Papa is waiting out front for us, leaning against a transport van with Cindy and Winnie in the front seat. The smile on his face isn't so big as it usually is, but somehow, he looks happier. He feels happier.

"Trouble in Turkey, kids," Winnie says. She's ditched the Air

Force uniform, but instead of joining the Urban League, Cindy—our new PsyOps chief—hired her on at the CIA as an operations officer. Rumor has it she glared the director into submission when he initially vetoed the idea of a colored woman on the staff. She looks just as commanding in her pretty flower-print dress as she did in her Air Force uniform. "One of our diplomats has gone missing, and a courier bag full of secret documents is gone with him."

"Plane leaves in an hour," Papa says. "Zhenya's staying with the neighbors while we're gone."

"Valya, you'll be helping me at our command post," Winnie says, ticking off her fingers. "Yulia, you'll scout ahead with your dad . . ."

Valya links his hand in mine. Our melodies knit themselves together, unburdened, unhurried, pure. His lack of powers soothes him, while my power keeps me whole.

Our minds are ours alone.

AUTHOR'S NOTE

The year 1964 was a time of both victories and setbacks for America. Martin Luther King, Jr., and the countless other crusaders for equal rights, school integration, and repealment of Jim Crow laws paved the way for the Civil Rights Act. But as political unrest between the communist North Vietnamese and rebel South intensified, many Americans hoped to stamp out the spectre of communism abroad, or at least contain it, as America had attempted in the Korean peninsula in the 1950s. Sadly, it was not to be the case—by August of 1964, an incident in the Gulf of Tonkin prompted President Johnson to launch military operations in Vietnam, and the resulting American role in the war dragged on into 1973.

Since its founding in 1947, the Central Intelligence Agency has captured the imagination of Americans with its dual image of dangerous glamour and extreme secrecy. Allen Dulles's account of the CIA's creation and early days, *The Craft of Intelligence*, informed much of my representation of the CIA in this book, as did Robert Littell's *Inside the CIA*, which details the day-to-day structure and operations of the CIA now. The rubric of agent personality factors that Yulia and Valentin use to hunt for the mole are adapted from Henry Crumpton's *The Art of Intelligence: Lessons from a Life in the CIA's Clandestine Service*.

Although I fabricated the PsyOps team within the CIA and the MK INFRA experiment, both are (very loosely) modeled after real American attempts to induce psychic powers. As outrageous as it sounds, the Department of Defense's Stargate program did indeed seek to develop psychic ability and the CIA's MK ULTRA experiments actually explored espionage applications of LSD.

Less fantastical but no less damaging to the agency's credibility, however, were the projects run by people such as Frank Tuttelbaum, who tried to turn the agency into their own vehicle for egotistical political maneuvering. In the 1960s, these renegade CIA managers orchestrated political assassinations, illegal wiretapping and infiltration of American organizations and individuals, and manipulation of Latin and South American politics. In 1973, Congress created the Church Committee to investigate such government abuses and, thankfully, they dismantled many such fiefdoms. Tim Weiner's *Legacy of Ashes: The History of the CIA* touches on these programs as well as the FBI's COINTELPRO program, both of which serve as cautionary tales for government overreach today.